Deadly Beliefs
A Thriller

By
Rod Huff

Mark,
Know that you're not alone
in your battle - praying for your daily!
I hope you enjoy my story as much
as I did creating in my mind.
Hang tough - believe!
smoothly anyone when
you get home.
Rod
PHIL 4:13

xulon PRESS

Deadly Beliefs
A Thriller
by Rod Huff

Printed in the United States of America

ISBN 9781625099716

Unless otherwise indicated, Bible quotations are taken from The King James Version.

Cover Photo: iStock Photo
Cover Design: Whitney Phelps

www.xulonpress.com

To Lisa

My first encourager, my first editor, my first critic and most importantly

the love of my life for forty-one years. Thanks for believing in me!

Acknowledgements

Thanks to my Lord and Savior Jesus Christ for giving me the gift of expression and leading me through this process.

Special thanks to my family for the encouragement and help in bringing this dream to life:

Lisa - for her patience and encouragement;

Whitney - for her editing and the design of the cover;

Austin - for his encouragement, creative input and design of the logo;

Mom - for being one of the first readers and, as usual, a strong supporter.

Dylan & Meredith – for supporting me and being the best son-in-law and daughter-in-law a man could wish for.

Thanks to my agent, Tina Jacobson of The B&B Media Group, for being the first professional to give me encouragement and believe in *Deadly Beliefs*.

Thanks to Ashley for editing my manuscript and making it so much better.

Thanks to Jeff Trubey and Kyros Entertainment for marketing support and creative input—also for being a great friend.

Thanks to my Wednesday morning Bible study guys for helping me navigate life.

Special thanks for the time that Umut Ceylan and Allen Alwahab gave me during my research. They offered beneficial insight through the eyes of two Middle Easterners who converted from Islam to Christianity. Al was gracious enough to read my completed manuscript to see if I was off on any of my facts—which I was.

Thanks to Matthew Ladisa, Rick Rose and Ken Heindrichs for being my first readers, wading through a very rough manuscript—I appreciate your friendship and support.

Thanks to the many friends who passed on press items, video documentaries and other valuable information that I used in the writing of *Deadly Beliefs*.

Thanks posthumously to Michael Crichton for being my inspiration for both my writing and style. I miss learning from him and enjoying his fiction.

Character List

Al-Qaeda

Osama bin Laden – Fallen Leader

Nasi Ahsan (Hajji) – New Leader

Ayman al-Zawahiri – OBL Right-Hand Man

Dalil Ally – NA Right-Hand Man

Malcolm Shane – NNERP Expert/Project Leader

John Paterson – Assailant

Al-Qaeda – North America

Esa Mann – North American Leader and Long Island Cell Leader

Allison Tucker Mann – Wife of Esa

Taj Hatem – Antioch Cell Leader

Fadi Hares – New Antioch Cell Leader

Tamir Alam – Chicago Cell Leader

Yar Din – Juniata Cell Leader (Branch of Chicago Cell)

Mazin Bahar – Boston Cell Leader

Rafid Almasi – Los Angeles Cell Leader

US Government/Department of Homeland Security

Milton Wheeler – 45th President of the United States

Adam Ford – President's Press Secretary

Deborah Knowles – Secretary, Department of Homeland Security

Clifton Hill – Agent in Charge, Operation Peace Shield

Teddy Brewer – DHS Analyst/Middle Eastern Expert

Wayne Joseph – Detective, PA State Police (Assigned to DHS, Harrisburg)

Michael Adams – DHS Agent, Harrisburg Field Office

Nathan Baird – DHS Agent, Nashville Field Office

Craig Reeves – Undercover DHS Agent, McNichols Plant

Kyle Emerson – Aspiring Song Writer/Informant

McNichols Farm Implements – Mifflintown, Pennsylvania

Jason Lange – Managing Director

Anne Lange – Wife of Jason/Interior Designer

Henry Koontz – Plant Superintendent

Mary Koontz – Wife of Henry/Retired Teacher

Yar Din – Night-Shift Supervisor

Antioch Islamic Center Cell

Taj Hatem – Imam

Nafi Selim – Assistant Imam

Darim Fayad – Unemployed

Wazir Hoda – Intern, TN State House

Jerome Parks – McDonald's Manager

Habib Farra (formerly known as Alex Jones) – Intern Sports Radio Station

Fadi Hares – Electrical Engineer

Basel Farooq – Cab Driver

For more detailed information about the characters and other aspects of the book please visit our web site: www.deadlybeliefs.com.

PROLOGUE

May 2011

Prologue

Abbottabad, Pakistan – May 2, 2011

"Tonight, I can report to the American people and to the world that the United States has conducted an operation that killed Osama bin Laden, the leader of al Qaeda, and a terrorist who's responsible for the murder of thousands of innocent men, women, and children."

—*Barack Obama*

Nasi Ahsan didn't know what was going on, but he recognized the sounds of gunfire and percussion bombs. He was awakened slightly before the gunfire erupted outside the windows of his room, rattling in the wake of two helicopters sweeping in to change his life forever. He knew the drill as he scrambled for a secret compartment that led to a tunnel to exit bin Laden's mansion. He, al-Zawahiri, and bin Laden each had separate escape routes that terminated in the same warehouse building near the Pakistan Military Academy a few blocks away. The house, which resembled a fort, was nestled among his doctor and lawyer neighbors—neighbors who were told to look the other way by Pakistan's Inter-Services Intelligence agency.

Nasi had met bin Laden at the University of King Abdulaziz in Saudi Arabia. He was two years older than Osama, but they were fascinated with each other and became best friends—a friendship that would last decades. "The Emir," as bin Laden's friends referred to him, looked to Nasi for his spiritual direction. He was comfortable with Nasi and shared intimate concerns with him. As their relationship grew, bin Laden began bouncing ideas off him. Nasi was a great strategic thinker and planner, and they shared a common passion. Bin Laden affectionately called him "Hajji"—a name often used for people who have completed their pilgrimage to Mecca, the fifth pillar of the Islamic faith. Nasi Ahsan was not nearly as well-known as bin Laden's public right-hand man, Ayman al-Zawahiri, but in reality, he was a closer friend. Immediately before entering his tunnel, he heard footsteps nearing his bedroom doorway. His adrenaline was pumping. As he raced for his life, he prayed to Allah that the Emir had escaped safely. He knew al-Zawahiri was working in Afghanistan and wasn't at the mansion, but his concerns about bin Laden intensified as he reached the end of the tunnel, his tunic soaking wet from sweat—dusty, tired and scared. The Emir was not in the warehouse.

As they had practiced, there were handlers waiting for him to hustle him to points unknown. When he exited the tunnel, he hit a big red plunger-type button that activated the total destruction of his escape tunnel. A plume of dust followed as he reached the Pakistan Army armored vehicle. As soon as he was safely in the escape vehicle, he was told the news about his friend—the Emir was dead. He died a martyr's death, but al-Qaeda had to continue. The Emir was with Allah, but *their* mission was not complete. Witnesses saw the assailants carrying his limp body to the copter—there was no doubt that the Emir was lifeless.

As the vehicle raced toward the Afghanistan border, Nasi did what he knew best—he prayed. Operation Sky Burst was years off and much work remained. The work would be more difficult without the Emir, but Nasi had been involved every step of the way and was prepared to assume the leadership of al-Qaeda. These were big shoes but were shoes he was prepared to fill. To people outside of al-Qaeda, Nasi was a no-name, but internally, everyone recognized him as the heir apparent to the global terrorist franchise.

PART ONE

Sometime in 2015

Chapter 1

New York City – Sometime in 2015

"It is a universal truth that the loss of liberty at home is to be charged to the provisions against danger, real or pretended, from abroad."

—*James Madison*

Everything was in place. Years of planning were about to culminate in a well-executed attack on the United States. Esa was uneasy. He knew he had worked the scenario through his head and computer models countless times, but he would not and could not rest until this mission was accomplished.

The plan began after the attacks of September 11, 2001—the Manhattan Raid, as they called it. His school friend from Saudi Arabia, Khalid al-Mihdhar, was one of the muscle hijackers who crashed Flight 77 into the Pentagon. A few years older than Esa, Khalid was his role model and mentor. From those early days with Khalid and al-Qaeda, Esa had set a goal to become a part of jihad in America. He methodically worked his way into the upper levels of the organization. Now he was the top guy in the United States and had established an impenetrable cover—solid in every way.

The Department of Homeland Security was a mere shadow of itself. The once hardy governmental agency was dismantled piece by piece by the previous president and his administration. President Wheeler was trying to reassemble the system, but in the meantime, Esa and his cells operated relatively unchecked until a recent problem.

The countdown had to begin earlier than planned, and as everyone associated with the operation understood, there was no turning back. All they could do was watch the seconds tick off the countdown clock. The idea of sending four jetliners filled with fuel and innocent people into buildings shocked and devastated the bones of the country. This event would make the massacres in NYC; Washington, DC; and Pennsylvania pale in comparison.

Wait 'til they see what we have in mind for them this time, Esa thought with a slight grin.

The countdown continued as he rolled out his prayer mat for his ad-Dhuha. It was noon, and it was Friday. He had much to pray about.

PART TWO

January 2015

Chapter 2

Antioch, Tennessee – January 26, 2015

"A man's country is not a certain area of land, of mountains, rivers, and woods, but it is a principle; and patriotism is loyalty to that principle."

—George William Curtis

The group came together innocently. Excited about the prospects of a new year and prepared to grow in their understanding of their faith, the group formed to study the Quran. In an effort to grow his mosque, Taj Hatem decided that he would teach young energetic Muslims the best way to defend their beliefs and recruit new followers to their faith.

And so it started. An indiscreet flyer announced the formation of a class designed to equip people to defend themselves in discussions with non-Muslims. The flyer invited only serious participants:

ISLAMIC APOLOGETICS CLASS

Join Imam Taj after your Fajr at 7AM Monday and Wednesday mornings for an in-depth study of the Muslim faith titled "Islamic Apologetics". We are looking for serious men who wish to hold each other accountable in a meaningful way and learn the best way to defend their Islamic beliefs. The first class will meet in the main meeting room of the AIC on Monday January 26, 2015.

Taj's mosque was located in Antioch, a suburb of Nashville, Tennessee. Consequently, he was used to being treated rudely and was constantly defending his beliefs. He had studied and prayed for years to become the imam of the Antioch Islamic Center (AIC). This was not a selfish ambition for the fifty-nine-year-old Saudi immigrant; this was a desire of his heart. His years of Islamic study and teaching showed on his weathered face. He had prepared for months for this first day of class. The sun was appearing, and Taj was, as always, starting his day with the remembrance of Allah. His thoughts kept gravitating to the young men whom he was about to meet. Who were they? How many of them would show up? Where would this class lead them? What was the destiny of his apologetics study?

He rolled up his prayer mat and returned to the notes on his desk. A mixture of anxiety and excitement raced through his body. His plans were grander than the syllabus indicated. Praise Allah.

‖
db

As usual, Basel was running late—a combination of a traffic accident and not leaving enough time. It was barely light outside, but he saw a man in a suit waving for a taxi. Basel was already running late for his class, but he still stopped to ask the man where he was headed.

"I'm going to the church on the corner of Bell Road and Twenty-Third Street."

Thinking for a minute, he determined it was on his way to the Islamic Center. "Hop in."

Making small talk, he asked the man how his day had been so far.

"So far so good. I'm excited about every new day I have." The passenger seemed too happy for 6:45 a.m.

For the next several blocks, the passenger proceeded to tell him about Jesus.

His name, Basel Farooq, appeared on his license displayed on his dashboard. His dark complexion and Middle Eastern accent made it obvious that he was not from around here. This prompted many discussions and questions from curious Nashvillians and tourists. He was often stuck in traffic listening to Christians sharing their concern for his soul and explaining that, in Christianity, salvation was "free for the asking." He was comfortable with the familiar teachings in the Quran and very uncomfortable with the thought that anything as valuable as eternal life would not involve a lifelong quest of *doing* the right things. Some of his passengers were polite and respectful, but others were rather arrogant. Regardless of their approach, their comments fanned the flame deep inside of him—the flame that fueled his hatred of infidels. He had just reached his twenty-first birthday; it was time for him do something greater for the cause of Islam.

He was looking forward to sitting under Taj's tutelage. He wanted to be better prepared to answer the questions he seemed to get on a regular basis. In talking with Taj, these were the kinds of questions they would discuss in detail. They would also delve deeply into the handling of infidels—in more ways than one, ways that could possibly shock Basel.

Basel had been in the States for four years—long enough to pick up the tradition of New Year's resolutions. One of the resolutions that he'd made earlier in the month (in addition to the obligatory loss of weight) was for him to become a more devout Muslim. He desired to become a man like Taj.

Selfishly, he wanted to be able to put these Christian *do-gooders* in their place and defend the religion that was the *only* way to eternity.

Sipping on his coffee and studying the other people sitting in the meeting room, Wazir was excited about the class getting underway. As was typical for him in new situations, he was uncomfortable. Initially he was self-conscious about his chubby face and big stomach. In normal situations, he used his humor and outgoing personality to offset his self-consciousness. *Just get the class started*, he thought.

Wazir, like many people who attended the Antioch center, was born in Saudi Arabia. He came to the States for an education and landed in Nashville to study political science at Vanderbilt University. His studies came easy to him. With an IQ nearing 130, it wasn't a surprise that he could handle most academic challenges with ease, including the rigors of an education from a highly academic institution like Vanderbilt. This provided him with extra time—time that he typically devoted to socializing with his friends. He provided the lighthearted entertainment and added joy to any group that he joined. He expected this class to be the same. *But let's get this show on the road*, he thought as he was staring at the wall to avoid eye contact with the strangers. It was a little after 7:00.

At that point, Taj entered, and the room fell silent. All eyes looked to the front as he took his place behind the podium. On his way through the room, he passed out the "syllabus" for the class. Not everything he planned to accomplish with these men appeared on his handout.

"Good morning, gentlemen, and welcome to our first Islamic Apologetics class. I am extremely happy to see you and look forward to a long, fruitful, and *exciting* journey."

Chapter 3

Mifflintown, Pennsylvania – January 26, 2015

"Dream as if you'll live forever. Live as if you'll die today."

—James Dean

The alarm buzzed incessantly as Jason hit the snooze button for the fourth time. He was in that twilight state that required a few moments to realize that the alarm is sounding again. He didn't want to leave his comfy bed. Before leaving for work, he looked forward to grabbing breakfast with his wife and children. The experience was not relaxing, but it was gratifying to see his family scurrying about, cramming down their Pop-Tarts, finding books, kissing Mom and Dad, and rushing to the bus, where the ever-patient bus driver waited. Having breakfast in the Lange home felt more like a whirlwind than a family chat, but he still treasured it.

Finally, peace and quiet had descended, and Anne looked his way with a tired smile. "Do you think this process will ever get easier?" she asked as she attempted to straighten her hair.

"I keep hoping. Eventually, we'll have an empty nest with just fond memories of these mornings."

Jason often heard the older workers at the plant tell him to cherish these days, and before he knew it, his kids would be leaving home. The idea of a quiet coffee with Anne in the morning seemed appealing, but he appreciated the wisdom of their advice. It seemed like only yesterday that Ashley, his fourteen-year-old, was born, and in the blink of an eye, she was finishing her last year in middle school.

Despite no makeup and being a bit harried, Anne was still the apple of Jason's eye, and his love for her continued to grow every year of their fifteen years of marriage. She was beautiful inside and out. Anne and he were married for only a brief time when their birth control had failed. "Guess what, Mr. and Mrs. Lange? You're pregnant!" The doctor appeared to be surprised by their lack of excitement, but children were not in their plans—at least not that early in their married life. When they got the news, Jason had just completed his MBA and was only six months into his first assignment with McNichols at their corporate headquarters in Chicago. He was a rising star in the organization and had gotten the attention of many executives—bright, energetic, and eager to make a name for himself. He made the cut into a special fast-track program designed to move him quickly through the ranks. He was to learn everything he could about the world of farm equipment.

Anne had been fine with his extra hours because it was just the two of them; now there was Ashley and the added responsibility of raising a child in a crazy, mixed-up world. They were up for the challenge, and here she was—fourteen.

Jason's daydreaming was interrupted by the anchors on *Good Morning America* reporting what was anticipated in President Wheeler's State of the Union that night. The president was in the midst of trying to restore a country that was damaged by the direction of his predecessor—an inexperienced president who had *led* the country to the brink of economic, political, and social collapse in his first and only four years.

The prior administration had dodged the impeachment bullet several times with the help of a partisan Senate, but the devastation was evident. President Wheeler was rebuilding the national defense that had been nearly annihilated. The commentators reported that the president was going to announce his focus on rebuilding the Department of Homeland Security. He was placing a high priority on this initiative, as increased chatter was being detected by what remained of the US intelligence-gathering community and from allies throughout the world—true-blue allies who had withstood the years of being disappointed by broken promises, lies, and insults from the previous president.

Jason refocused on Anne as he smelled the fresh-brewed coffee that she had just placed in front of him.

"What are you thinking about, Mr. Lange?" she asked.

In a typical male response, he answered, "Nothing," as he sipped his brew.

"I could stay here all morning, babe, but I have a staff meeting at the plant and I need to prepare."

He had a lot on his mind. The economy was very slowly recovering from the Great Recession (some called it a depression) of 2009. Farmers and farm cooperatives had held off on purchasing new equipment for as long as they could. Jason's business was picking up slowly, and they were back to three shifts of forty hours per week, with an occasional Saturday overtime. Their slower deliveries were beginning to cause problems for McNichols's dealers and subdistributors. Pressure was on to speed up his deliveries while keeping costs in line and maintaining McNichols's quality.

Jason's plan of moving to rural America was for a slower-paced life. He wanted be able to enjoy his family more in the quiet surroundings of Mifflintown. Jason bundled up to face the blustery winter day in Central PA. The Pennsylvania natives complained about the temperature, but compared to the winters in Chicago, the temperatures were mild and the wind did not compare. All that said, it was still cold as he climbed into his midlife crisis, fully restored Austin

Healey 3000 to make his way to the plant. His heater never fully engaged by the time he'd made his way through the beautiful countryside to the McNichols assembly plant, ten minutes from his home.

His mind wandered as he maneuvered his agile sports car through the rolling hills. He was particularly interested in hearing how the new guys on the night shift had done. It had been six months, and besides a few veterans who had moved as a favor to Jason, the midnight to 8:00 a.m. shift consisted of new employees. McNichols was fortunate that a major competitor in a neighboring county did not make it through the five years since the recession—fortunate in that their sales force was able to pick up some of their customers and also fortunate that their skilled labor had been unemployed for almost a year. They were hungry and anxious to work. Their skills and training shortened their learning curves. They became valuable contributors to the McNichols plant in a fraction of the time of a typical new employee.

Walking into his office, he realized that he had just lost the last ten minutes of his life while his mind wandered during his short trip. He had barely unpacked his laptop when Henry, his plant superintendent, barged into his office with the crisis du jour.

Chapter 4

Mifflintown, Pennsylvania – January 26, 2015

"Nothing ever comes to one that is worth having, except as a result of hard work."

—Booker T. Washington

"We have problems on the night shift, Boss. Production isn't where it should be," Henry explained with more drama than Jason needed this early on a Monday morning. He needed a second cup of coffee and to check his dashboard report. Jason was methodical and calm in his approach to problems—he wanted data before he reacted. His demeanor bothered the locals at first, but they learned to appreciate his levelheaded approach.

"Let's go get a cup of coffee, Henry." Jason started up his computer and headed toward the door. Henry followed.

d

The night shift was an independent group of mostly twenty-somethings who didn't mind the odd hours. Jason was fortunate to have a trustworthy supervisor who had transferred from another plant through his corporate HR staff in Chicago. Jason thought that Yar Din seemed to be working out well. He was concerned at first in regard to how the dark-skinned Saudi would assimilate into the traditional Central Pennsylvania community.

Historically, Mifflintown was a predominantly white town of slightly over 1,500, with 24,000 in the entire county. It was unusual to see any non-whites in the community—until recently. A small group of Saudi Arabians now resided in the area. It had started with Yar and his wife, Raja. Now there were three families who lived in an almost commune-type environment. They rented three tenant homes on a local farm. A huge agri-business corporation now managed the farm, and the houses were converted into rentals.

The locals tended to look a bit askew at the foreigners, as they called them, but those who had contact with them were pleasantly surprised by how nice they were.

The Saudis were quite faithful to their five daily prayer times and had created a small mosque in one of the outbuildings. They also used the outbuilding for study time during which they delved deeper into the Quran.

cǐb

Jason and Henry walked toward the cafeteria. Henry realized that for Jason to fully comprehend his concerns, he needed a strong cup of black coffee.

They sat down at a corner table. Jason purposely liked to do business outside of his old-fashioned, way-too-large office in the front part of the plant. It was cavernous! The plant was built in a day when the plant manager had to have an office that reflected his position. Jason would have been happy in a fraction of the space. He wanted to be close to his employees. His door was always open, and he practiced the philosophy of managing by walking around. Often, he learned more from the people on the shop floor than he did from his insecure middle managers.

"What's up, Henry?" Jason asked as he sipped his steaming cup of java.

"The night shift is just not getting up to speed," Henry explained. This wasn't a hunch on his part, but rather, it was based on statistics that he had monitored for years. His hesitation stemmed from the fact that this was the first time in his history with the plant that they started a complete shift from scratch with nearly all new employees.

"Jason, I'm confused, quite frankly, and wanted to review the situation with you."

As was typical for Jason, he studied the numbers that Henry presented and asked for some more time to study them.

"Remember, there may be a bit of a language barrier with the new supervisor," Jason pointed out, although he hadn't sensed a problem in his dealings with Yar.

"Din was educated in the States and has lived in the US for over ten years, but this is the first time he's had to deal with Juniata County people."

With that, Jason concluded the meeting, but before getting up to leave, he asked Henry how his wife was doing. She was seriously ill, and Jason was concerned about both of them—his question was sincere.

"She's doing OK" was all Henry could muster.

"I'll study the numbers and let's get back together by the end of the week. I don't think there's anything earth-shattering that requires hasty action on our part."

Normally, Jason was spot-on with his hunches and intuition. He was a brilliant man and was able to read situations correctly, but on this one, he was off.

As he was leaving the cafeteria, he joined an impromptu discussion with several employees awaiting the fresh coffee. At McNichols, as in most factories, the

coffee machine was the congregating spot. The hot topic of the day was President Wheeler's State of the Union address scheduled for this week. As these things went, the news media already had a good idea of what he was going to say. This would be his third State of the Union since his landslide election in 2012. In the first two years of his presidency, he had already made significant steps to restore the economy. The expansion of the McNichols plant was evidence of manufacturing returning to the United States. With the antibusiness policies of the previous administration, many companies fled to avoid both taxes and excessive regulation. That was one of the first areas the president addressed. He lowered taxes on business and attracted billions of dollars into investing in American business—money that was resting on the sidelines during the previous administration.

People were optimistic about their futures for the first time in years. The people around the coffeepot were speculating what he was going to do to keep the business rally alive. Consumer confidence was high and trending higher. Consumers and businesses were spending money.

Jason gracefully extracted himself from the conversation, but before he did, he directly addressed each of the four employees by name and told them to have a good day. He not only knew all the names of the plant's 146 employees, but he also knew personal facts about nearly all of them. He was a popular manager and leader among the troops, which he worked at intentionally.

When Jason returned to his office, his assistant greeted him with a handful of phone messages and a list of people who wished to see him. He went into his office and dove into his day. The thought of Henry's concerns about the night shift was already stored in his memory bank.

ḋb

Henry sat in the cafeteria for a while longer after Jason left. He observed the rapport that Jason had with the McNichols employees and was amazed at how he could remember all of their names. It might have been due to his age, but his mind wasn't as sharp as it used to be. But the truth was, even in his younger days, he had difficulty with names.

He wondered if what he was talking to Jason about had actually sunk in. *Am I making a mountain out of a molehill?* he thought, as his granddaddy used to say. Henry had that tendency.

He knew Jason was listening. He was a great listener, and he always needed more time than Henry to digest information. He hoped that Jason, in this particular case, would move more quickly. For some reason, this slippage in production was especially disconcerting to him. What was causing it, and was there anything he could do to rectify the situation?

Chapter 5

Antioch, Tennessee – January 26, 2015

"Faith consists in believing when it is beyond the power of reason to believe."

—Voltaire

Taj was thrilled to see the turnout exceed his expectations. Previous classes had attracted the usual AIG people who showed up at the center whenever the doors were open. He expected to see those four or five diehards, but as he looked around the room, he saw several unfamiliar young faces. He thought that the subject of defending their faith would attract interest from the younger, more radical believers. He also knew that there were some informal invitations sent via text to a few. He was happy to see that they had accepted the esoteric invites.

He quickly counted as he was going through his self-introduction—there were twenty-one present.

The class appeared to be hanging on his every word, but the mood was tense. Taj was a staid, serious older man, but he wanted to do something to break the ice. After reviewing a brief personal history, he ran through his curriculum vitae. He was an extremely well-educated man, and his study of the Quran was

impressive. He explained how he had begun his undergraduate studies at the Islamic University of al-Madinah and later earned a doctorate from Georgetown University in Washington, DC.

There was a disturbance in the back of the room. Darim stumbled in the door, tripping slightly to make matters worse. All eyes immediately turned to see what the commotion was as Taj just glared disapprovingly at the young man making his dramatic entrance.

Darim's face was a bright crimson, and the stumble caused his lungee to be cocked awkwardly to one side of his face. He could feel the beads of sweat popping on his forehead and wished desperately that he had not grabbed that ten-minute mini-nap after morning prayers.

Taj continued. "As I was saying, we all need to make an extra effort to get here prior to seven a.m." His timing was perfect. Laughter erupted. This was just the thing to ease the tension in the room.

Darim apologized and bowed from the waist the entire way to the seat that his friend Basel had saved for him. Luckily, it was in the back and close to the door he had stumbled through.

He was notorious for making his friends wait. Darim was very creative, with a keen sense of style and space, but the mastery of time escaped him. What endeared him to his friends and made them tolerant of his lack of time management was his giving spirit. He was very handsome, with striking Middle Eastern dark hair and eyes. He had a heart the size of Texas and was generous to a fault. All of these attributes contributed to his friends' acceptance of his tardiness.

Taj resumed. "We are about to embark on a journey—a journey that could quite possibly change lives and the lives of others forever."

Completing his introductory remarks, Taj wanted to learn more about his students as well as have them learn more about each other. He asked each of them to stand up and introduce themselves by giving their names, their hometowns, their Islamic roots, and then something that others in the room would be surprised about—a shocking fact about their background. For the next forty-five minutes, the twenty-two young men introduced themselves to the rest of the class. Most of the class members were born and raised in the Islamic faith and of Middle Eastern linage. As they shared their stories, he sensed a real love of Muhammad and fellow Muslims, but also an underlying mistrust of Christians and Jews. The two Americans in the class both had been burned and deeply disappointed by their Christian family members and friends. They had witnessed shallowness and lukewarm attitudes. Both commented that they were fascinated by the deep commitment to the five pillars of the Islamic faith.

The most memorable monologue of the morning was Wazir, as he was extremely funny with his comments. His physical appearance was also comical. His self-abuse was endearing. His round body completely filled out every inch of his XXXL thobe. His chubby, round face finished off his "look." In the midst of his one-liners, Taj and the class saw the heart of a passionate believer who was willing to do whatever it took to defend his faith.

Taj had his students open up their Qurans. "Let us all prepare for what Allah has in store for us."

db

The lecture part of the class had not even begun before Darim started to daydream. He had been labeled as a bad boy in his hometown, outside of Kharian, Pakistan. He was so bad, in fact, that he was never adopted from the orphanage. Had he been born and raised in the States, he would have been diagnosed as having attention deficit disorder (ADD), or perhaps even ADHD, and placed on the appropriate medication. He was so hyperactive that he had great difficulty sitting still long enough to learn anything. His teachers simply passed him on to the next instructor rather than taking the time to deal with him properly. His poor performance in school was frustrating to him, but he was stuck in a perpetual cycle that eventually led to him hitting the streets of Kharian just prior to his eighteenth birthday.

"Mr. Fayad!" Taj called out, as it was obvious that Darim's mind was elsewhere.

"Sorry, sir," he replied as he took a drink of his coffee, adjusted his posture, and refocused on Taj's words. He had been asked to participate in this class through an unidentified text message. It was obvious that the person sending the text knew who he was and that he had a desire to help the cause of Islam. The mystery texter said the right things to spark his interest. He wondered how many classes he would have to sit through before he had a better picture of what his future held. He wasn't interested in classes of any kind.

ﷲ

Taj concluded his lecture by reading a few passages from the Quran.

"Please follow along as I read from God's holy word to conclude our class today." Taj reverently opened his ragged Quran—the book he had studied all his life—and turned to the selected passages:

The true believers fight for the cause of God, but the infidels fight for the devil. Fight them against the friends of Satan. (Surah 4:76)
Prophet make war on the unbelievers and the hypocrites and deal rigorously with them. Hell shall be their home: an evil fate. (Surah 9:73)

"Thank you so much for your participation this morning. I am excited about how this class will help prepare us to spread the Muslim faith throughout all of Middle Tennessee and beyond."

Taj continued. "*Assalaamu alaykum.* Peace be upon you until we gather again on Wednesday morning at seven a.m." He looked in Darim's direction. "Before you take off, please fill out the questionnaire that I handed out at the beginning of class." Taj thought the class went well—all but one of the targeted recruits had shown up.

He had to call Esa in two hours, and he needed to have a firm grasp on the facts. His report needed to be concise and to the point. The information on their questionnaires had to be studied in depth, but as for now, he focused on the invited guests. Five of the six men that he'd recruited had shown up. As he scanned the other students' information, it became apparent that there might be another one or two candidates for the cause in the class.

Chapter 6

New York City – January 26, 2015

"The day which we fear as our last is but the birthday of eternity."

—*Lucius Annaeus Seneca*

Esa studied the freshly decrypted reports from the website.

His cover was deep. As a partner in his public accounting firm and husband to a beautiful American woman, the thought of him being an international terrorist was the last thing people would think. He was a classic example of the inconspicuous businessman who would inevitably shock his unsuspecting neighbors. Then when interviewed by a TV anchor, they would say, "We never would have guessed that young Esa was capable of such evil and devastation." He and his wife were both beautiful and successful people. Esa's accounting brilliance and personality moved him quickly to the role of partner at only age thirty. He wanted to believe that he had earned this rapid ascent on his own, but in the back of his mind, he often wondered if, somehow, bin Laden had greased the wheels to make his cover more believable.

Esa Mann (formerly Mannan) was the top guy in an intricate T-cell that had operated in the United States since before the 9/11 attacks. They'd had some small assignments, but nothing that would compare to the scope of code name 911.2.0, with the nickname of Sky Burst.

The cells were scattered geographically, with no interaction between the cell leaders. Esa was at the hub of US operations for the Salafi jihad insurgency and was plugged into a very sophisticated worldwide network that used hundreds of proxy servers to bounce their internal communications around the globe. To make matters more difficult for US intelligence agencies, they inserted decoys into their net—bogus servers that were there simply to make backtracking nearly impossible. They operated in a virtual world of smoke and mirrors. In a twist of fate, the Internet was the most useful tool ever devised to aid in terrorist communications and efficiency. The facade of a backward band of unshaven terrorists moving from cave to cave was just that—a facade. Their "caves" were equipped with the most sophisticated computer-networking devices known to man, and they knew how to use their systems to the utmost degree. Their cause was the eradication of all non-Muslims who refused to convert to Islam.

Ever since bin Laden's death in 2011, the worldwide intelligence community speculated on al-Qaeda's effectiveness sans their charismatic leader. Even prior to his actual death, it had been speculated for years that bin Laden had died from the rigors of hiding and running from allied troops in the rugged mountains of Afghanistan, when, in fact, he was alive and well and living comfortably in Pakistan. After his death, the transition of leadership was quite smooth, and Ahsan effectively took control. Still operating out of a cave, he became the brains behind the whole al-Qaeda worldwide operation. Ever since bin Laden declared jihad against the United States and masterminded a successful hit on the back-bone of the country in 2001, he had been intent on killing *every* person who did not follow the teachings of Mohammed. That philosophy permeated al-Qaeda.

Esa spoke to Nasi Ahsan once per month on a satellite phone. He looked into his eyes through a video monitor. Ahsan's eyes, despite alluding to his deeply reli-gious affiliation, reflected the passion that burned deep inside of him. The jihad he advocated was not the "greater jihad" in which every Islam engaged—a war against sin. Al-Qaeda's jihad was an offensive, or "lesser jihad," that demanded death to the infidels—a war against all non-Muslims. True al-Qaeda followers understood that and rejoiced in it.

There were a few troubling reports from the Chicago cell, but other than that, the plans for Sky Burst were coming together beautifully. The infidels were going to face a slow, agonizing death. Ahsan would be proud. Islam would prosper. Infidels would die!

As he read on, he saw that the Antioch cell was getting off to a late start relative to the other cells, but that was part of the plan. The timing now was perfect, and Taj had confirmed that the cover class was scheduled to begin today. He would hear from Taj with a special report later this morning, and he was anxious to learn about the Tennessee "recruits."

♔

Two hours after the class was over, the special line rang in Taj's office. He had been reviewing the info sheets from his students and wished he'd had more time to prepare for this call.

The phone rang again, and Taj quickly grabbed the receiver. Esa was an impatient, demanding, and intimidating leader who was strictly business. There was never any small talk or anything of a personal nature. His reputation throughout al-Qaeda was renowned.

In the world of al-Qaeda operatives, working for Esa was the kiss of death for anyone who was not totally dedicated to the cause. Attempting not to let his voice tremble, Taj said, "Hello, sir. I have good news to report."

Taj tried to be calm, as he didn't want Esa to detect any weakness in his voice. Frightened, he mustered up all the strength he could.

"How are you today, Mr. Mann?" Taj asked.

He thought he heard a bit of a grunt on the other end of the phone, but there was no direct answer.

"Let's get started." Esa was anxious to hear Taj's report.

Taj knew that Esa would be most interested in finding out how many of the young men they recruited had shown up. By having conversations with integral Islamic leaders around the Nashville-Antioch area, they had identified six men whom they wanted in their "class." Then they used a very low-key combination of anonymous text messages and influential friends to get these men interested in the class.

"Sir, we had five of our six recruits show up for the class, and based on their questionnaires, all five are in."

Taj took a breath to see if Esa had any comments, but he was silent.

"Fadi Hares was our only no-show, and I will be following up with him to see where he stands. All my contacts indicated that he was excited about the class, so I'm confused as to why he didn't show." Taj felt the tension on the other end of the phone. Fortunately for him, they were not on a video call—if they had been, Esa would have seen the sweat beading on Taj's forehead.

"I am anxious to hear where Mr. Hares was. Please communicate via the web as soon as you have any information," Esa directed in a no-nonsense way. "Were there any other potential members for the cause?"

"Yes, sir. I think there is at least one more. What is your goal for the size of our group?"

"I want to keep it manageable, and we have to have people who are in our same mindset. No more than seven or eight, counting you, Imam."

Taj was encouraged to hear Esa call him by his title, and he sensed a notion of respect in his tone—perhaps only wishful thinking.

"I understand, sir. Is there anything else?"

"No. We will speak after your class on Wednesday."

Click. Esa was gone, and Taj took a deep breath, guessing that his phone report had been acceptable.

Taj had one thing on his mind. Securing Fadi Hares's participation in the group would be pleasing to Esa—an important part of the process.

"Hello, Mr. Hares. This is Imam Hatem. Could I meet you at the Istanbul Café for a cup of coffee tomorrow morning? I have something I wish to discuss with you—an opportunity that I believe you will find enticing."

Chapter 7

Mifflintown, Pennsylvania – January 28, 2015

"Experience is simply the name we give our mistakes."

—*Oscar Wilde*

A s he contemplated the night shift, Jason realized that Henry had problems in various areas every day, but he sensed that this was different. Henry had seemed more alarmed than the normal level of concern. In the back of his mind, Jason couldn't help but think that there might have been some racial motives. Henry was a good old boy, born and raised in this area by conservative Mennonite parents. The thought of having a supervisor under him who was a nonwhite might have been getting to him. *Is he being overly sensitive and actually looking for a problem?* Jason dismissed the thought, but not completely.

He decided to take off on his morning rounds. To help him recall all his employees' names, he typically followed the same route daily. Beginning on the receiving dock, he would check on key components that he knew would hurt production if they had not arrived. He had plenty of staff watching all the details, but he was always kept abreast of his team's critical issues. This also gave him something to talk about with the dock guy, Ted.

"Yes, sir. The wheels arrived this morning on schedule," Ted confirmed. He was happy that he was able to answer Mr. Lange's question immediately.

"Thanks, Ted. Stay warm back here." Jason moved on to the next department. After visiting a few other people along the assembly line, he cut his managing-by-walking-around time short, as a thought had occurred to him regarding Henry's concerns.

Jason wanted to check out a couple of pivotal metric reports. If Henry's concerns were valid, he was certain that things would show up in the numbers—this was Jason's way. He hurried back to his office, greeting a few others along the way.

Jason looked for scraps reports, excessive materials usage, overtime, and so on. Nothing appeared to be out of the ordinary; they just simply appeared to be operating slowly. Jason wondered if this would have been called to his attention if a fellow Mennonite Pennsylvanian had been the shift supervisor. He didn't want to think the worst of his loyal right-hand guy and dug deeper into the data.

⚈

The day had slipped by Henry. In his mind, manufacturing had been much easier before all these computers got involved. Every aspect of the McNichols plant was computerized, right down to the thermostats that detected when humans were in a particular area of the plant and regulated the temperature accordingly. Lights were also dimmed if no employees were around. It was truly a marvel of modern manufacturing. With computerized and robotized everything, many parts of the equipment manufactured were never touched by human hands. Henry was convinced that computers had a mind of their own, often deciding to quit at the most inopportune time. When the geeks from the IT department showed up to "fix" whatever outage they had, they never seemed to be able to

45

explain why it was broken or even what they had done to correct it—they were only able to report that it was now working.

Fortunately, Henry did not have responsibility over the information technology people. IT, along with HR, accounting, most of the office staff, and the financial analyst all reported directly to Jason. Henry wouldn't have it any other way.

He was a hands-on, get-the-job-done-with-no-computers type of guy. He remembered the good old days with fond memories. When they first opened the doors in 1976, they were not computerized. There were some accounting and production control areas that ran off the monster IBM machine that filled an entire room. The computing power of that machine could now be held in the palm of your hand. It read key-punched cards. The plant flow was monitored with handwritten cards that followed the product through the processes. People did the work, not computers or robots.

Back in the early eighties, if a piece of equipment was not assembled properly, he could talk to the employee and correct the situation. Now all he could do was call an IT tech. He felt helpless and at the mercy of a machine.

This thought brought his mind back to the night shift. He had decided that he would come in early tomorrow morning and visit with Yar and the rest of his crew. Paying a personal visit is better than studying computer data.

"I will see for myself," he said aloud.

db

Yar bounced out of bed. It was shortly after noon to the rest of the world, but to him, it was first thing in the morning. He got his typical five or six hours of sleep and had a ton of things to get done before returning to McNichols that night. Working when most people slept was an adjustment—especially when it came to his daily prayer time. He actually began his prayer day during his last break, just before the sun came up. He'd located a quiet corner of the plant, where he found solitude as he prayed. He did his afternoon, or Asr, prayers right after he woke up. Today he decided to go to the outbuilding on their property, which had become their masjid, to pray with his Saudi neighbors.

They were already deep in prayer when he arrived, so he tried to be as quiet as possible. Jabir and Jamil were there with their wives. They both had followed Yar to Juniata County and arrived about a month after Yar and Raja. Their transition from Chicago went smoothly, as Yar had found a suitable place for them to settle. Actually, "suitable" wasn't a strong enough description of their accommodations. They were perfect: three separate two-bedroom houses on a dead-end road with a large outbuilding. Each family had its privacy, while the outbuilding was a perfect common place for them to gather. It also provided a great cover for the Juniata branch of their Chicago cell.

Jabir and Jamil Khoury were completing their prayer time when they heard Yar enter the room. Jabir and Jamil were twin brothers who had moved to the States on student visas from Saudi Arabia. Being fraternal twins, they had a family resemblance, but it was easy to tell them apart. Both were graduates of Penn State's well-known school of engineering. Jabir majored in electrical and Jamil in mechanical engineering. This was not a coincidence, but rather, a part of the master plan. Jabir had nearly completed his master's degree when he received an anonymous text message requesting a meeting at a local student hangout. The sender identified himself only as a fellow Saudi.

The twins remained quite until Yar finished his noon prayers. Since all three of them worked together at McNichols, they had opportunities throughout the night when they could converse, but the serious discussions and planning took place following their noontime prayer. Their wives were all excused from this time as they set about doing their womanly responsibilities.

Yar was working on his weekly report to Tamir, his cell leader in Chicago, and wanted the three of them to collaborate. Their cell was small compared to some of the other cells working on Sky Burst, but their mission was critical to accomplishing the ultimate endgame. The weekly updates were due in the online drop box by 8:00 a.m. (EST) every Monday, but Yar never waited until the last minute to work on it. He meticulously kept track of the daily progress and used the time following noon prayers for briefings on the latest developments. Occasionally, he would invite the wives to participate. Their three wives were the procurement team of the cell, and their role was becoming increasingly more important as the real work was ready to start.

Although Yar did not understand his role completely, he did know that the purpose of their activities was to promote Islam and praise Allah. That was really all he needed to know and understand, but he often wondered what the big picture looked like. Until he needed more information, he respected Tamir and rested in that knowledge. Yar was also certain about was his distrust and hatred for Christians, or "people of the book," as they called them.

"How's your research coming along, Jabir?" Yar queried.

Al-Qaeda's vast intelligence had sought out Jabir. As a result of his focus on electromagnetism at Penn State and an association with a radical Islamic student organization, his name had popped up on al-Qaeda's radar as they built its North American team. After more background checks and their initial meeting off campus, they brought him in. When instructed to move to a rural area of Pennsylvania, Jabir pushed to have his brother become a part of the plan, as he wanted to stay close to his only living blood relative. Equally skilled in another aspect of engineering, with very similar militant sentiments, Jamil was easily accepted.

"Things are falling into place, and I'm very close to developing the bill of materials," Jabir responded.

"Do you have any concerns?" Yar pushed.

"I don't want to sound over confident, but I am not having any difficulty."

Yar moved on to Jamil.

"How about you, Jamil? How's your project shaping up?"

"I'm not in as good of shape as Jabir, because I didn't spend the last three years of my college days immersed in the subject, but I'm a capable engineer, and I am not having any difficulty with my research at this time," Jamil remarked with less confidence as his brother.

Yar had known both of these men since his secondary school days in Saudi Arabia and would trust either with his life. And that was exactly what he was doing. The plan was beginning to move forward.

Chapter 8

Antioch, Tennessee – January 27, 2015

"I believe in the religion of Islam. I believe in Allah and peace."

—*Muhammad Ali*

F adi arrived at the Istanbul Café early; receiving a call from Imam Hatem was disconcerting. What had he done to be asked to meet with the spiritual head of the center? He felt as though he were back in secondary school in Saudi Arabia, being summoned to the headmaster's office. He was faithful in his prayer life and thus wondered if something from his private life had come to the imam's attention. He obviously knew the imam but didn't think the imam would know him. So he waited for his arrival.

At the instant he was planning his introduction; the imam walked into the café and went directly to his table.

"Hello, Mr. Hares. My name is Imam Taj Hatem." Taj extended his hand.

Taken aback, Fadi shook the outstretched hand and responded, "Good afternoon, Imam Hatem. I'm pleased to meet you."

"Please, Mr. Hares, call me Taj."

"I'm Fadi, sir." He answered skeptically.

After the introduction that neither of the men really needed, Taj began to explain his Islamic Apologetics class. As Taj talked about the class and what he hoped to accomplish, Fadi recalled getting text messages inviting him to participate in the class, but the number hadn't been registered to a name, so he'd ignored them.

"I sent you a couple of text messages inviting you to participate. Several people at the center and elsewhere suggested that you would be a valuable addition to our group."

Fadi was trying to figure this whole thing out; the mystery of the text messages was solved, but the *why* was not.

"I'm honored, sir, and it sounds interesting, but I have to ask, why are you so interested in me?"

"I am convinced that it will become very clear to you once you decide to join us. Our desire is to praise Allah and expand the reach of Islam, and this class will go a long way in preparing all of us for the challenge."

After a little more prodding, Fadi finally agreed to attend the next class. Then, with the business side of the meeting out of the way, Taj and Fadi used the remainder of their time together to learn more about each other, and the nucleus of a close friendship was created.

In their brief meeting, Taj could see why Esa was anxious to have Fadi on his team. He was obviously a well-educated man with personality and skills that blended well with his. Esa had told him that he thought Hares would make a strong number two for the Antioch organization. His skills, formal education, and work experience with Dell computers were all extremely valuable as they set about their task. For a change, he was looking forward to his next conversation with Esa.

After about forty-five minutes in the café, they said good-bye.

"I'm looking forward to seeing you tomorrow morning. Class begins sharply at seven a.m."

Chapter 9

New York City – January 27, 2015

"Effective leadership is putting first things first. Effective management is discipline, carrying it out."

—*Stephen Covey*

Esa was not normally as anxious about his recruits; normally, the people he selected were honored and jumped at the opportunity. But then, he usually made the approach directly and not cryptically through another operative. He knew that Taj and Hares were meeting and that their meeting should be winding down. He hadn't directly instructed Taj to let him know how the meeting went, but he knew that Taj had sensed his anxiety.

Just as he was going back to work, his phone rang on the secure line. It was Taj. The conversation was short.

"Fadi Hares is in."

The first step in his joining the Antioch team had been completed.

"Good work, Taj!"

That was as close to a compliment as Taj would ever hear.

db

Esa was trying to get away from the office early. He and his wife, Allison, wanted to have a quiet dinner together. Their lives had been turned upside down lately, and they were feeling distant. Their relationship was such that they knew intuitively when they needed time with each other. Working in the same firm had its advantages. They ran into each other occasionally, and it was easy for them to meet for lunch. Depending upon their daily schedules, they often rode the train together as well. The disadvantage, however, was the difficulty in leaving work at the office, and frequently, their at-home conversations revolved around the happenings at Chase, Smith & Hooper.

They had made it through five years successfully by knowing when to turn off work and focus on each other. That was the plan for tonight. First, they would have a quiet dinner and then hopefully a peaceful commute home. Depending on the time, they sometimes stayed in town. They both kept an extra set of clothing in their offices for such occasions. They made a point of not bringing up the subject of work all evening.

Esa knew what they needed, but he also knew it was going to be difficult this evening. He sheltered Allison from his *other* world; she knew nothing about the things he was involved with outside of CS&H. He also knew that, for the sake of his cover, their marriage had to stay strong regardless of its true strength.

In addition to focusing their conversation on non-work-related topics, he would have to be purposeful in keeping his mind off his mission and the countless details that would have to come together.

It was 4:00 p.m. and the market had just closed slightly up for the day. He packed up his laptop and called down Allison to see if she was ready to leave.

"I'll meet you in the lobby, honey. Looking forward to tonight!"

Just hearing her voice made him smile. Her beauty was both outward and inward. He was looking forward to a nice evening as well. How had he fallen so deeply in love with this woman?

He had done everything he could to advance the cause for Monday. It was time to unwind and regroup for the sake of his "marriage."

Allison had freshened up before they left the building and looked amazingly vibrant after eight hours of work. He wasn't sure how she did it, but he was happy that she could.

Their relationship had been arranged, even though Allison was completely unaware of the setup. They'd met on a blind date orchestrated entirely by al-Qaeda operatives. From an early age, Esa was the heir apparent, destined to someday take over the leadership of al-Qaeda's North American operations. His exceptional intelligence and leadership qualities became evident to his father, who had been in bin Laden's inner circle. It wasn't just his father who'd recognized his prowess, and word traveled throughout the organization.

Strategically, he had been honed from his prepubescent days to take the position he held today. If there were ever a doubt about his destiny, it evaporated when his father was killed by a US military attack in Afghanistan in 2009. He hated the Americans more than ever, and he was determined to avenge his father's death.

"Babe, you look amazing!"

"Thanks, Esa. I love you, and I'm really looking forward to tonight," she responded with a sheepish little grin.

The original blind date with Allison was all part of the plan. Falling in love with her, on the other hand, was not. An infidel, a Christian, an American—she was a person whom he'd been raised to hate, attack, and kill. How could he have fallen in love with her?

"Where are we eating?"

Esa had found a brand-new restaurant that was getting rave reviews, and he was anxious to give it a try.

"It's called The River View, in Lower Manhattan."

"That area has always felt creepy to me since 9/11. But if you've heard good things, let's give it a try."

On the cab ride to the restaurant, Esa's mind raced through all the recent events of the project, but he had promised himself to focus on Allison this evening. Just then, Allison's voice interrupted his thoughts.

"Honey, are you with me?"

"Yes, yes. What are you in the mood for this evening?"

"I'm thinking about lamb," Allison answered quickly, as it was her usual entrée choice when they went out. She never prepared it at home since Esa didn't like it. The truth of the matter was, she rarely prepared anything at home. Cooking was one of those things that she had never really learned, and their schedules were more conducive to dining out. *Perhaps that will change when the children come along*, she thought.

Esa gazed into her eyes to help him refocus his attention. Her scent was as sweet as her beauty. How had this arranged marriage blossomed into a romance for the ages? Despite his indoctrination and brainwashing, he was in love with her—a person who was opposite everything he believed in.

It was a good thing that he'd made reservations. Evidently, many others had read about the new place as well. They were a little early, so they engaged in some chitchat while waiting to be seated.

"Mr. and Mrs. Mann, please follow me."

Esa was pleased with the table selection; they had a beautiful view of the Hudson. He showed his pleasure by slipping the maître d' a fifty-dollar bill. He liked to show his appreciation for good efforts, and he also knew that the word would spread to the waitstaff and their service would be extraordinary. After ordering a bottle of Dom Pérignon, they both sat back with a sigh.

"I love you, Allison!" Those words rolled off his tongue so easily he wondered what his fellow al-Qaeda combatants would say or do if they were to hear those words coming from his mouth.

The food was delicious, as promised, and they both agreed that they had found another favorite spot. There were thousands of restaurants, but it was always satisfying to find one that they both liked.

"How was the lamb?"

"Wonderful!"

The night slinked by, the service unhurried and relaxed. Consequently, they decided to stay the night in the city, and on their way back to their hotel, the taxi drove past the World Trade Center memorial, built at the spot of the tragic attack—tragic from Allison's point of view, but a triumph as far as Esa was concerned. What a dichotomy there was in the backseat of that taxi, and Allison didn't even realize it existed.

She thought she knew her husband of five years, but the truth was, she knew very little. Esa had been able to keep her totally isolated from his work with the North American ops. A combination of bogus business trips, partial days away from the CS&H offices, and various other diversions permitted him to move the operation along without his wife's knowledge. His brilliance combined with some work behind the scenes kept him current with his partner responsibilities, so he was also able to snow his peers and bosses.

His whole setup was perfect in every way. The deep cover and his executive role allowed him to control the flow of money in and out of the United States, then to and from other al-Qaeda cells and operations. He established legitimate-looking shell companies to move the money around with ease. The front for these bogus companies was thorough, complete with annual reports, boards of directors, and professional websites.

Esa Mann was the ideal operative.

A black Suburban followed discreetly behind the taxi. The silhouettes of two men—their eyes covered by dark glasses despite the fact that it was nighttime in NYC—could scarcely be seen through the dark tint of the windows.

Chapter 10

Mifflintown, Pennsylvania, and Washington, DC – January 28, 2015

"I have no ambition to govern men; it is a painful and thankless office."

—*Thomas Jefferson*

J ason felt comforted pulling into his driveway. The light glistened off the snowy front yard, making the thought of a warm fire in the den even more inviting. His kids were teens, so they didn't run and jump into his arms as they had—that was no longer "cool"—but he could tell that they were happy to see him nonetheless.

He had purposefully left his schedule open for this evening, as tonight was the president's State of the Union address. Ashley had mentioned to him that she was required to watch it for her civics class, so they'd made an informal date to do so together. He realized that part of her interest was in anticipation of getting his help with her assignment. He didn't care about her motives; he was just thankful for the time with her. Jason realized that the reason God had created the teenage years was to help ease the separation pains as children left the nest. He was hoping that his kids would be different.

Anne had spaghetti cooking, and the aroma hit him as soon as he walked through the door. He loved her cooking—her Italian ancestors would have been proud of her culinary skills. His timing was perfect, as Anne hustled them all to the dinner table. The Lange family had somewhat of a ritual during the evening meal. It was something that Jason had started when the children first entered school. Each night, he would hold up one finger—the signal for Ashley and Hunter to share one thing that they had learned in school that day.

"One thing," Jason said, looking in Hunter's direction.

"I learned that Millicent Dunbar is a creep."

"Come on, get serious. We don't want an update on your social life."

"I learned about synonyms, antonyms, and homonyms."

"Would you like to be a bit more specific?"

And so it went around the table. Ashley talked about the importance of tonight's speech from President Wheeler and how critical such speeches were for the president's approval ratings. The president was finishing up his second year in office. His approval ratings had actually increased since he'd taken office, and Ashley was beginning to realize that, as the leader of the free world, the president of the United States had to be a natural leader—a person of conviction who makes decisions regardless of his or her popularity. The Langes decided that it would be a good idea to watch the speech as a family and discuss it afterward. They would also watch the Democratic response.

Adam Ford, President Wheeler's press secretary, labored over the president's speech with the speechwriter, making those all-important final edits. At this stage in the game, they were discussing inflection and the best delivery approach. Adam had been on staff during the president's candidacy and gained more confidence as the months and years went on. He was well respected among his peers and other staffers. He was dedicated to the cause.

"I expect this comment to bring everyone in the audience to their feet, so we need to build in a pause for the teleprompter." Wheeler's use of a prompter was simply a safety net, as he seldom used it. He studied his material meticulously. Finishing up, Adam grabbed his notes and headed for the Oval Office for his last-minute briefing with President Wheeler.

dᵢb

The network evening news reporters buzzed with anticipation. Bits and pieces of the speech were always leaked to the press beforehand, yet everyone knew, even without the spoilers, that the hot topics would be the economy, homeland security, and health care.

These areas were the focus of the Wheeler administration's first two years—all three had been in shambles when he'd taken office. Within weeks of his inauguration in 2013, he signed for massive tax cuts, which immediately started to turn the economy. The "tax and spend" philosophy of the previous president had proven only to make the unemployment higher and the recession deeper.

Wheeler was a breath of fresh air, as companies began to expand. In turn, this expansion created new jobs in numbers not thought possible in the years prior. Just as in the years following the Great Depression, happy days were here again.

Homeland security was not as hot of an issue. Islamic terrorists—and specifically, al-Qaeda—had been relatively quiet in America. There were a few sloppy attempts at attacks four or five years ago, but nothing significant. Their lack of activity had lulled the American people into lowering their guard. The death of bin Laden added to that complacency. Nevertheless, Wheeler still thought the public wanted to be reassured that the defense posture of the nation was secure.

He had some sweeping initiatives to introduce this evening, and the Lange family would be listening.

Their enemy would also be listening.

Wheeler had jumped onto the political scene quickly and without warning. He became the white knight of the Republican Party and was the natural leader that the country yearned for. Not from Washington, but from Wall Street. A Wharton MBA in finance, he had made millions as a principal of a major Wall Street investment brokerage. Early in the presidential primaries, Wheeler became tired of how Washington was killing American business and decided that he would put his career on hold and make a run for it. He held a wide appeal and was able to capture the interest of the people.

Faux pas after faux pas from his predecessor had both sides of the aisle ready for a change. He carried the country by 63.4 percent of the popular vote, which was the largest landslide ever. The American public had spoken, and Wheeler's marching orders were clear: "Mr. President, change what has happened over the previous four years." And that was what he was working on. It was refreshing to hear a president who was positive about the United States and confident that the capitalist system was alive and well. Popular opinion was rallying around him in unprecedented ways.

Adam Ford walked with President Wheeler to the West Wing portico, where the motorcade waited to rush him off to Capitol Hill. Adam was very conscientious about his assignment.

"Break a leg, Mr. President." Adam declined an offer to ride with the president and closed his door for him. He then returned to his office before heading to Congress—he had to e-mail a copy of the final speech to his boss.

The president's speech lasted just under an hour, with the Democratic response adding another twenty-five minutes. Ashley was diligently taking notes as she carefully listened to every word, while her brother had dozed off about fifteen minutes into the speech.

His address hit on every hot button, and as far as Jason was concerned, he was right on. His pro-business policies were sure to have US manufacturers trend positively.

There was some mention of education, Social Security, welfare reform, and health benefits for the uninsurable, but nothing noteworthy.

The discussion of the intelligence community focused on how successful the administration had been in thwarting the world terrorists, keeping them at bay.

Jason helped Ashley sort through an hour and a half of the political discussions, and she went off to her room to complete her civics assignment. Anne woke up Hunter enough to usher him off to his bathroom to prepare for bed.

Anne and Jason crashed on the den sofa for a little time with each other. Jason had had a long day, and he had a lot on his mind, but now was not the time to muddle through all of that.

"How was your day, Annie?"

"The usual—laundry, straightening up, and waiting for my phone to ring with a new client."

Jason chuckled. He knew that very few people in the area would think to use Anne's interior design expertise—actually, none.

"How was your day at the plant?"

Jason hesitated, then answered, "It was fine, just fine."

They briefly discussed President Wheeler's speech and decided to veg out with an obscure movie on HBO. Both were asleep before they figured out what the film was about.

Chapter 11

Mifflintown, Pennsylvania – January 29, 2015

"If you pick the right people and give them the opportunity to spread their wings—and put compensation as a carrier behind it—you almost don't have to manage them."

—Jack Welch

It was pitch-black outside on a cold and windy morning. Henry was normally an early riser—he accomplished much before taking off for the plant. With Mary's illness came added responsibilities at home. He loved her so much, and it pained him to see her suffering through the chemo. If there were any way, he would simply take on her pain and her cancer. She was a trooper and insisted that he continue working, so Henry used work to take his mind off the inevitable.

Normally, he made planned visits and had meetings set up with the shift supervisors, so they expected him. They would also follow a planned meeting agenda. But this early morning's visit was different. He wanted to drop in on Yar unannounced to see if he could stumble upon anything out of the ordinary.

He made sure that Mary had everything she needed and was off into the cold night, just a few minutes past 5:00 a.m.

db

Yar was getting ready to take his last break of the day. He always attempted to take this last break with Jamil and Jabir. They had managed to find an isolated area in the warehouse to have their morning prayer. They discreetly slipped off to their meeting place, while the other guys rushed to the lunchroom. Spreading their prayer mats down on the hard concrete floor, and with the help of the compass built into their mats, they faced in the direction of Mecca, the birthplace of Muhammad.

The three of them used their last break of the day to pay tribute to Allah with the first prayer of the day. It was a bit odd to them at first to have their morning prayers as their workday was winding down, but many aspects of their new assignment were different.

They were trained experts and adapted accordingly.

db

Henry parked in his reserved spot near the front office. The older he got, the more he appreciated this perk. Not for the status, but for the convenience of a shorter walk to the front door—especially in the dead of winter.

He dropped off his briefcase in his office and went to the lunchroom to greet the guys on their break. His plan was to grab Yar and do a quick walk-through, but he was nowhere to be found.

He inquired with a few familiar faces, but none of them knew where Yar was, either. He learned that "they" (meaning the Arabs, as they were derogatorily referred to) seldom came to the lunchroom on this break. His suspicion growing, he left the room and started his walk-through without his supervisor.

In an assembly line operation, when one took a break, everyone took a break. The line couldn't move without all the stations manned. Henry walked the line, finding everything in order, but still no Yar and his countrymen. He decided to check the warehouse, and as he was about to turn and head back to the line, he heard some mumbles coming from a back corner. He followed his ears, and there, in a far back corner, he found the three Saudis, prostrate on their mats. He quietly and respectfully backed away; he wasn't quite sure what he was seeing. They were the first Muslims whom he had ever known, and he really didn't know them well.

Henry returned to Yar's office adjacent to the line to wait for him. He checked his watch but knew that, out of necessity, their break had to coincide with the rest of the line.

Yar was startled when he opened his door and realized there was someone sitting there waiting for him.

"Mr. Koontz, what a surprise to see you. I didn't get any notice that you would be visiting."

"Hello, Yar. Come in. I couldn't sleep and decided to come in to get a jump on my day. I didn't mean to startle you. I'm sorry!"

Not realizing that Henry had observed their morning prayers, Yar proceeded. "How's your wife, sir? I'm sorry to hear of her affliction."

"Thanks for asking. She's not good, but she has an amazing attitude, and if anyone's going to beat Stage IV, she will."

Henry was a very direct person, so as the pleasant exchange concluded, he got straight to the point, the real reason he'd stopped by.

"I've been looking at your numbers, and truthfully, I thought that your numbers would be higher than they are at this stage of your ramp-up. Are you having any particular problems that I could help you with?"

Yar was noticeably uneasy. "No, sir, but let's take a walk around."

The two of them went on a complete tour of the line. Henry was impressed that Yar greeted every one of his men by his name, and they seemed to have accepted the outsider. Henry continued to be confused by the corporate involvement in the selection of a supervisor for *his* night shift.

Everything appeared to be in order, and nothing jumped out at him that could explain Yar's disappointing numbers.

"Yar"—Henry held out his hand to shake Yar's—"my door is always open, and if there is anything I can do to help you, I'd be happy to."

Yar returned the handshake. "Thanks, Mr. Koontz. You will not be disappointed in me. I am a good worker, and I will deliver."

Indeed, he would.

PART THREE

February 2015

Chapter 12

Antioch, Tennessee – February 2, 2015

"Aim at heaven and you will get earth thrown in. Aim at earth and you get neither."

—C. S. Lewis

At the conclusion of each class, the "inner circle" developed a habit of going out for coffee at the Istanbul Café. The owner of the café was supportive of their cause and arranged for them to be seated in a private room, isolated from other patrons. After nearly every class, Taj, Basel Farooq, Darim Fayad, Wazir Hoda, Fadi Hares, Jerome Parks, and Habib Farra, the second American in the class (who had changed his name from Alex Jones following his conversion to Muslim), met to discuss the class and other topics of interest. It had become routine, but it was something that each of them looked forward to. They lined up to order their drinks.

Wazir was first in line almost every time. In addition to his drink, he usually ordered a Middle Eastern pastry. One look at him and it was easy to tell that he ate too much of the wrong kind of food.

"May I help you?" the exotic-looking Middle Eastern girl asked.

"Yes, I'd like a small coffee in a large cup with two pumps hazelnut, two pumps vanilla, two pumps caramel, two Equals, and four Sweet'N Lows, filled to the top with cream, with extra cream on the side, double cupped, with no sleeve, a stir stick, and a stopper put in the top, at one hundred and eighty degrees Fahrenheit."

They were getting used to his overly precise drink orders but still loved to make fun of him—Wazir was an easy target. His jovial, fun-loving spirit took some tension out of their classes and following meetings. Today they focused on all the artificial sweeteners.

Fadi laughingly remarked, "Wow, it's a good thing that you keep the calories down by using Sweet'N Low!"

Wazir took it in stride and slipped off to the side while he waited for his order.

Within earshot of Wazir, Taj said, "I'll have a large half white mocha, half café vanilla iced coffee, easy on the ice, with two shots poured over the top with whipped cream and caramel drizzle." When the laughter had subsided, he said, "Just make that a large regular coffee."

It was clear that Wazir was in for it today.

They all grabbed their drinks and moved to the private room at the back of the Istanbul. Wazir was last to arrive for obvious reasons. His late entry brought a new round of harassment and jabs.

When everyone had settled around the large table, Taj began to conduct the post-meeting. Each team member had received instructions over the past month for various aspects of what he had to deliver.

The cell had evolved quite naturally. Starting with twenty-two members, the class quickly dwindled to fifteen. Of the fifteen, based on Taj's research and information, nine were there for the stated purpose of the class—to learn more about their faith so they could defend it and win people over to become followers of Mohammed, i.e., convert people peacefully through dialogue.

The six guys who were asked to become part of Taj's inner circle had different views on converting the nonbelievers. The class was a front and a reason for them to gather and have their post-meetings. They were all serious Muslims and were taking in the teachings of Taj, but in general, they were too impatient to convert people by conversations—they wanted to hurry the process along. Their tasks were very specific and represented only part of the overall North American assignment. Esa shared with Taj only what he needed to know, and Taj did not pass on everything to his inner circle. Communication was tightly controlled.

A few of the guys who were researching specific aspects of their assignment were given access to the secure network as well as one-way communication through the esoteric website. The post-meeting actually had begun with deeper review and discussion of what was taught in the morning class. Taj would then pull each of the guys aside for updates on where they were on their piece of the project. These conferences did not have anything to do with the apologetics class.

After every meeting, Taj got more excited about what was unfolding. This was what he'd been waiting for his whole life. He couldn't believe that he was involved in such an earth-changing movement. He couldn't believe that the plan was coming together and the AIC was a key component. Taj always preferred to talk with Fadi last for a couple of reasons. First, he felt like Fadi was the sharpest of the bunch, and consequently, Taj shared a little more deeply with him. He also used him as a sounding board for ideas. His reaction to certain issues was a barometer to help him determine if it was wise to mention to Esa. Fadi was the eldest of his group, but even at twenty-eight, Taj was still twice his age.

Fadi's background in electrical engineering was critical for what the Antioch cell had to deliver. His biggest strength—his intelligence—might also prove to be a drawback as they proceeded. Fadi was a questioner.

"Taj, I need you to level with me. Where are all these discussions and our assignments leading?" Fadi was direct.

Being purposefully vague, Taj responded, "What do you mean, Fadi?"

"I don't think I can be any clearer. I want to know who we are connected with and what the endgame is."

"I can only tell you what you need to know, when you need to know it. Fadi, you need to be patient."

Fadi sensed frustration building within Taj and knew it was time to stop his questioning. Being patient wasn't his normal disposition, but he respected the wise imam.

db

After the post-meeting, they all went their separate ways, with most heading off to work. Basel Farooq was the youngest of the group and had been in the States the shortest period of time. He was uneducated, but had gotten into the country with counterfeit papers from Pakistan through an al-Qaeda connection. He left Pakistan in a hurry, as the al-Qaeda underground had picked up on the fact that US counterintelligence agents were ready to pull him in for questioning. Just that fast, he was secreted away with a new identity. His passion for the cause made him a natural to be plugged into the cell network in the United States. Years ago, Basel's radical views had alienated his family. He was obnoxious and wanted his family to share his feelings about infidels. They didn't, so when he received word of his precarious position, he didn't think twice about leaving Pakistan. He was funded, but to maintain his cover, he drove a taxi and delivered pizzas whenever he could borrow one of his friend's vehicles.

He left the Istanbul in his taxi and headed for the airport to start his day. In the queue, waiting to be called for a pickup, he laughed and joked with his fellow cabbies. Several were from his native country and spoke Urdu. This eased his homesickness. Even though he had been alienated from his, family he still missed them. These brief conversations were a touch of home to him in this strange land.

Finally, he reached the front of the queue and received a nod from the coordinator to leave for the terminal. Basel had calculated that the fares and tips were better from the airport than running around Nashville, even when figuring in his wait time in the holding lot.

Basel jumped out, opened his trunk, and assisted the passenger with his luggage, welcoming him into his taxi.

"Where to?"

"The Radisson at the Music City Center, please."

"Yes, sir. Straight away."

"What brings you to Music City?"

The gray-haired gentleman in a slightly wrinkled dark suit replied, "I'm here for the Christian products convention."

Immediately, Basel tightened up. *Is this going to be one of those rides?* "Welcome, sir. I hope you enjoy your stay."

"Thank you. Where are you from?"

"Pakistan originally."

Basel anticipated that the questioning was going to pick up, and he noticed that I-40 traffic was much heavier than he'd anticipated. There must have been an accident. *Great*, he thought.

"What brought you to the States?"

I'm here to kill everyone who doesn't agree to convert to Islam, he thought.

"I came for a better way of life. Hopefully, I will make enough money to bring the rest of my family to your beautiful land."

This approach always netted him better tips and avoided the inevitable questioning that he knew was to come, something along the lines of, *Do you know where you will be spending eternity?*

Though not quite as direct, his passenger next asked, "Do you practice Islam?"

"Yes, sir, I do." This was where it usually got dicey. "I attend the Antioch Islamic Center, just outside of town."

"Interesting. I've studied your religion a bit."

OK, here we go, Basel thought. He was certain that Mr. Christian Products Guy was about to launch in on all the reasons why Islam was off the mark. Basel was stuck—stuck in his taxi, stuck in traffic.

For the next forty-five minutes of what was normally a twenty-minute drive, the Christian zealot quoted scripture and attempted to convince Basel that the religion he'd loved and studied all of his twenty years was wrong and he was going to hell.

This guy and his fellow Christians were the reason that he so adamantly wanted to kill them all.

Finally, he reached the convention center hotel and got a dollar tip on his thirty-nine-dollar fare. The passenger's generosity was less than impressive.

Chapter 13

Fairfield, Connecticut – February 2, 2015

"We can't plan life. All we can do is be available for it."

—*Lauryn Hill*

Anasty nor'easter had settled into the area, and their little town was getting buried by an inch of snow an hour. Predictions called for six to seven inches on top of the eight that were already on the ground.

The snow came so quickly and with such ferocity that it virtually crippled the city. Trains in and out of New York were stopped. The removal equipment was trying to make headway, but the snow was falling too rapidly.

Monday mornings were difficult for Esa to get started under normal weather conditions. The snowstorm made it easy for him to decide to work from home. As it was, he might not have had a choice.

He and Allison decided to have a leisurely breakfast while they watched the beautiful landscape out their rear window. The snow, combined with the sunrise, created a picturesque setting, one that generated a feeling of serenity and peace.

"This may be Allah's way of forcing us to spend some time together," Esa teased.

Allison laughed and ignored Esa's comment about Allah. For the most part, she tried to keep their conflicting religious backgrounds at check and separate. They never discussed their beliefs. They never spoke of God or Allah. She was raised in a Christian home in the suburbs of Chicago. Her parents were what most would call fundamentalists. They believed that the Bible was the inerrant word of God. Allison strayed from those teachings while she was at Northwestern. Her first exposure to the real world was more than she could handle. Though she had never returned to her faith, there were still some elements that popped up in her psyche from time to time. Years of Sunday school and private Christian school had made an indelible mark.

Her parents were disappointed in her, and she knew it, but they still had a rich, loving relationship. Her parents believed that a couple should not be unequally yoked, according to the Bible. In other words, Christians should marry Christians. Having different religions would inevitably drive a wedge into their relationship. All of these thoughts raced through Allison's mind at Esa's simple mention of Allah.

Since religion was not important to either of them, she discounted her parents' warnings. She knew where she stood with her Maker and thought she knew where Esa did as well. The thought of what religion they would raise their children had never entered her mind, since they had never thought of having children. Like religion, the topic of children was the elephant in the room. The discussion had come up briefly while they were dating, but they quickly moved on when they couldn't agree. Esa was only interested in his career, his ambitions and his other goals. Children did not fit into his plans at present, but Allison loved children and, quite naturally, thought that someday she would be a mom. Like religion, they shelved their disagreement on a family, to be dealt with later. She loved Esa so much that she was blinded.

The snowstorm continued, with no letup in sight. Esa battled the weather to grab a bundle of wood from under their deck and got a fire blazing in their fireplace. They took their coffees from the kitchen and cuddled in front of the beautiful view. Their love was strong, and they felt close. Perhaps her parents were wrong in their beliefs, she thought as she rested in the comfort of her husband's arms. Or perhaps they were very right.

Esa was comfortable as well. The only light in the room came from outside and the glow from the fireplace. Allison looked beautiful. Her natural beauty was more radiant than ever. It was hard to believe that she had jumped out of bed and looked the way she did—no makeup necessary.

He knew he had some things he had to do today, but he figured the world would be slowed by the weather. Before leaving the comfort of the moment and hitting the computer, he basked in the solitude.

They both must have dozed off, as the grandfather clock in the room struck 9:00. Where had the morning gone? Off they went to their home office, husband and wife taking their positions behind their respective half of the huge antique partners' desk that filled the middle of the room.

The market had opened, so there were a few trades that Esa needed to make. Allison did not hold as key a position in the firm, so after checking her e-mail and reporting that she was stranded, she returned to the den and grabbed the book she had been reading. Everything was nearly perfect, but even after her two-hour nap this morning, she was extremely tired. Chase, Smith & Hooper would easily survive a day without Allison Mann, and she was planning on enjoying the moment.

d‌b

Outside the Manns' gated community in Fairfield, Connecticut, on the two-lane road that eventually led to I-95, a black Suburban was buried in snow in the parking lot of a rustic group of cabins. Inside one of the cabins, two men waited patiently for the front to pass. In the meantime, no one was going anywhere in this part of the world.

Chapter 14

Mifflintown, Pennsylvania – February 2, 2015

"All the people like us are We, and everyone else is They."

—Rudyard Kipling

Mifflintown was on the edge of the devastating snowstorm that was blanketing the East Coast. They were fortunate, with just a dusting, while Harrisburg, just sixty miles away, was crippled.

The guys had finished their night shift, and as they typically did, after a few hours of sleep, they met in their makeshift mosque for noon prayers. Yar, the twins, and all of their wives finished up their daily ritual and began to discuss their plans for the day.

The weather was the hot topic of the day, and they all seemed to be a bit disappointed that the storm had missed them. Having grown up in Saudi Arabia, even the dusting they received was fascinating, but they yearned for more. They checked the Weather Channel, and it appeared that a dusting was all that they were going to get. The guys convened to discuss the project, and the girls decided that they would go into town to pick up some groceries.

Mifflintown was a quaint Pennsylvania town that was not large enough for the giant megastores. Consequently, their downtown shopping area was alive and well, complete with the usual small grocery store, hardware store, Jewish jeweler, and miscellaneous small gift shops. The stores wrapped around a typical town square, with a monument, flag, and other artifacts. Established to commemorate the participation of the Juniata militia in the Battle of Gettysburg, the town square in Mifflintown was nearly one hundred years old. They lost fifteen brave men that day—a devastating blow to a group of thirty-two. The monument also featured a couple of disabled Civil War–era cannons, which stood as a tribute to the brave men who had given their lives for the cause of freeing slaves and restoring the United States.

They had each visited the shopping district before, but never as a group. The sight of three exotic-looking Middle Eastern women with their faces covered was out of the ordinary for the town. The conservative attire worn by Amish people from the surrounding area was common, but burkas were not.

"I feel like all eyes are on us," Raja Din commented to the twins' wives.

Raja and Yar had been married for three years. She was a subservient wife and knew nothing different. Her exposure to the freedom that American women experienced did not seem to impact her. She was content in her role, as spelled out in the Quran.

As they stocked up on the essentials at the grocery store, they were still hoping that the storm would shut down the plant so that the three couples could be snowed in together.

Jamil's wife, Nyla, commented, "I feel so out of place. Perhaps we should dress in black and drive to town in a horse-drawn carriage. Maybe then we wouldn't be so *different*."

Farah laughed. "I guess we just have to be patient."

Jabir and his wife, Farah, were the newlyweds of the group. They had gotten married in Chicago about six months earlier, in a traditional Arabic ceremony with all the Muslim customs. The bride and groom wore exotic garb studded with precious metals and jewels. The appearance and music of the event resembled that of a Western wedding, with one glaring exception—men and women were segregated. Jabir's twin brother was his best man and the only representative of his family present. Both Yar and Raja had also been in attendance; thus, the three couples often reminisced about the wedding weekend.

"That's a good point," Raja continued. "We are living in an alien world, but we all know why we're here."

The girls stopped by a small coffee shop with a view of Main Street and Monument Square. None of the girls spoke of it, but they all understood the irony of the Juniata militia monument and the Juniata cell in which they were involved—both groups were so dedicated to their cause that they were willing to give their lives.

For confidentiality reasons, the girls spoke in their native Arabic. They felt safe in that none of the locals had a clue what they were saying, but it added to the mystery and apprehension of their neighbors. They were able to freely discuss the operation, or at least what they knew about the operation. Theirs was a small piece of the puzzle, but they were thankful to their husbands to trust them enough to play even a small role.

They finished their coffees amid the locals' continued stares.

ḋb

Unbeknownst to the Din and Khoury women, there were other strangers in town that day. They were able to blend in with the Pennsylvanians, but then, they were only from Harrisburg. Their unmarked black sedan was parked inconspicuously in a garage down the street. They were following up on an anonymous lead. Their office usually didn't devote any time to a lead if the person was not willing to disclose his or her identity, but their phone interrogation of the gentleman had given them the impression that he was a credible informant. Their office chief decided that it was worth the investment of a few man-hours. And so there they were, observing.

Chapter 15

Antioch, Tennessee – February 4, 2015

"The ink of the scholar is more sacred than the blood of the martyr."

—Muhammad

Taj had been curious about Esa's interest in Fadi from the start. What was it about this young man that had caused Esa to make sure that he was a part of Taj's team? Taj knew that he couldn't come right out and ask him, and he realized that it was really none of his business, but nevertheless, his curiosity was getting to him.

While making some last-minute preparations for his class, Taj decided to run a quick Internet search on Fadi prior to leaving for the AIC assembly room. He went to Google and typed in "Fadi Hares" to see what would come up. Perhaps there would be a clue. He only had about ten minutes before class started, so this exercise had to be brief. The number of hits the name had returned surprised him; there were over four pages of exact matches before the results shifted to a portion of his name, similar names, or other spellings. At the top of the search results were the typical LinkedIn, FamilyFocus, Facebook, Bebo, MyLife, Friendster, etc. pages, but they soon got into the meaty mentions of Fadi. There was a lot of material to peruse, but he needed to get to class before the 7:00 a.m.

start time. He minimized all the open windows on his computer screen, grabbed his Quran and accompanying notes, and ran.

As he greeted the class and began his lecture, there was one thing, and one thing only, on his mind. He needed to focus on the class, however; his Fadi research would have to wait.

☪

Basel's fare from the airport to the convention center was still fresh in his mind. The Christian had come at him boldly and armed with what was obviously a somewhat rehearsed speech. He had his points nailed down and was direct in his approach. Basel had not been in the United States long—less than six months—and although this wasn't his first exposure to a zealot, this one was by far the most intense. He felt totally unprepared. Of course, he had never experienced anything like this in Pakistan and had very little knowledge about Christian beliefs. He was raised to see them only as his enemy.

He had heard of Jesus through the mentions of him in his holy book. According to the Quran, Jesus was a messenger of God who delivered God's message to the people of Israel. Basel had learned as a young lad in Quran lessons on Sunday mornings that the crucifixion story was make-believe. Jesus did not really die; Judas replaced him on the cross. He couldn't have died for the sins of man, as his passenger had implied, since Basel knew that it wasn't him on the cross. His resurrection was not real, and although Jesus was a wonderful person, he was just that—a person and not God, as Christians wished to believe.

Basel knew this well; he'd had it drummed into him all his life. But his passenger had been so passionate that it caused Basel a brief moment of hesitation. He had never questioned this fact before, but what if Jesus *was* the true God and savior of all mankind and Muslims were wrong? He was surprised that his mind had even taken him to that thought—a thought that would stay buried deep inside his psyche. But the experience had given him the courage to share his encounter with Taj and his classmates.

Taj always gave his students time at the beginning of class to bring up anything they wished regarding the information they had studied. Basel hesitated for a moment, then sheepishly raised his hand.

"Yes, Basel? What is it?"

"After our coffee at the Istanbul, I went straight to the airport to begin my workday." Basel proceeded to give a blow-by-blow description of the events of that day. He did not, however, get into the thoughts the experience had conjured up in his mind.

Taj decided to use this opportunity to critique his experience and instruct him on how to handle a similar situation in the future.

"Basel, it *will* come up again, and this is the *purpose* of this class."

"Thank you, sir, but I felt totally inadequate and like this particular infidel had defeated me."

"By the likes of your description, I, too, believe he did. But as long as you remain firm in your convictions to take care of the five pillars of Islam daily, you will win in the end." Taj was unusually warm in his delivery of this message, since he was sensing Basel's stress. "We will be victorious in the end! Trust me when I tell you that Christians are not normally as well prepared and bold as your passenger that day. They are weak and mild mannered and do not wish to make anyone feel uncomfortable. They are much more likely to sway from their beliefs and convictions than we are."

With that, Taj, using Basel's experience, broke into a discussion of how best to approach this type of confrontation.

To get the rest of the class involved, Taj had developed some scenarios for role-playing, and in pairs, the group acted out the various roles, performing their scenarios in front of the class. One of the most interesting exchanges of the morning involved Darim portraying a Muslim employee and Wazir as his

Christian boss. Wazir's character was a fundamentalist who, despite company policies, was always trying to get his young employee to visit his church some Sunday morning. Darim and Wazir got into their roles—perhaps too much.

"I just don't understand why y'all won't visit my church," Wazir said in the best Southern accent he could muster." Why don't you come this Sunday? We can have lunch afterward. My wife, Rosie, will fix us some fried chicken."

Darim, trying to hold in his laughter, responded with anger. "When will you ever understand that I'm not interested in your Jesus and I am already worshipping the only true God, Allah?"

Wazir egged him on some more, until Taj interrupted and asked the class to comment on what was happening.

"What are your thoughts on how Mr. Fayad played the role of a Muslim with a pestering boss?" Taj threw the question out to the class.

Several hands went up. Fadi, who was sitting in the front, caught Taj's attention first.

"Yes, Mr. Hares? What do you think?"

"I think Darim's reaction was quite natural given his and most of our upbringings and backgrounds, but we really need to learn to subdue those natural instincts that have been passed from generation to generation. Our hatred for one another dates back to Isaac and Ishmael," Fadi continued, "and to this day, those feelings are close to the surface for all of us. To be taken seriously in this alien land, we cannot be as vocal as we could be in a land where Islam dominates."

Fadi concluded with a very logical and, in Taj's opinion, correct way of handling this situation should it ever occur. His advice centered on the fact that if they were to win over the infidels and convert them to Islam peacefully, they first had to create relationships. "Our Quran is clear on this subject. We must first try to convert the infidels. If that fails, then we handle them differently."

Part of his dissertation was for the benefit of the class members who were not part of the inner circle. The inner circle knew that their mission had already escalated to jihad.

☾

Basel felt better following the class and was encouraged by what Taj had to say, but he was still frightened by those feelings that he'd buried in his soul. He decided that to better argue with the Christian passengers of the future, he would do some clandestine research on his own and pray that Allah protected him and prepared him to defend his faith against Christians and Jews alike.

☾

After class, Taj told the inner circle that he was going to be running a bit late to the Istanbul today.

"Go ahead, get your coffees, and I will be there as soon as I can. I have something I have to do, so I'll be there in about thirty minutes."

What he didn't tell the inner circle was that he was anxious to get back to his computer to read about young Mr. Hares.

The second article that he pulled up was from an online campus newspaper of Vanderbilt University—an interview with Fadi Hares, president of the Vanderbilt Muslim Students Association (MSA). The article sang the praises of a young, dynamic Saudi Arabian who had taken the MSA at Vandy from ten students to one of the largest student religious groups on campus, at over two hundred members. Vanderbilt was the most vibrant branch in their whole MSA system in the United States or Canada. This was the first of many articles of his involvement in this radical organization. He became president his sophomore year and held the position through his graduate work. As Taj read more, it was obvious that Fadi had participated in many national meetings of the group and helped to formulate their campus strategies throughout North American.

It all made sense now. Fadi Hares was an all-star and had associated with Islamic student leaders all around the country. His performance in class today dovetailed precisely with what he was reading—a smooth, articulate, intelligent man.

He looked at the clock on his computer and realized that it had been forty minutes since class ended. He needed to get to the Istanbul; the boys would be waiting.

Chapter 16

New York City – February 4, 2015

"Each nation feels superior to other nations. That breeds patriotism—and wars."

—Dale Carnegie

E sa had some issues that needed to be addressed with Taj on his weekly call, scheduled for 3:00 p.m. (EST) every Wednesday. Mainly, Esa had some concerns about things that were going on in the Antioch cell. Just as he'd started to run through them in his mind, the phone rang at the preappointed time, and the caller ID verified that it was Taj Hatem.

"Good afternoon, Taj."

"Hello, sir. How are you today?" Taj was always tense, but as the call progressed, he usually settled down. Today's call would be different.

Getting straight to the point, he said, "I was wondering, Taj, why were you investigating Fadi Hares online?"

This question sent Taj's head spinning. "Uh, uh. . .What do you mean, sir?"

"You know what I mean. Why were you researching one of your guys?"

Trying to bluff his way out of the situation, Taj came up with an explanation. "He is such a standout in my class, handling all of his assignments with ease, I was curious about his background."

"What did you uncover—anything interesting?"

Taj wanted to blurt out, *If you know what I was investigating, I'm sure you know what I found out*, but didn't. "I was not surprised to learn that he was a leader in the MSA and that there were many positive things written about Mr. Hares."

Taj knew that Esa was a powerful, well-connected man, but this disclosure from him had thrown Taj for a loop. If Esa knew this, he had to have access to everything on Taj's computer. He could tell where Taj went online and how he used his time. The imam, being a man of God, did not go places on the web that a man in his position shouldn't go, but nevertheless, he felt totally violated. His privacy had been breached, and he was offended—not only by the intrusion, but also by Esa's apparent lack of trust in him. If he did trust Esa, why would he be looking over his shoulder?

Building up all the courage he could muster, Taj asked, "Why, sir, did you feel compelled to track my movements on the Internet?"

"This is standard procedure. I have all my cell leaders monitored very carefully. We cannot risk mistakes, and I report to someone high in the organization. I can't trust anyone. I have to have safeguards in place. It's brave of you to ask the question, but frankly, I'll do whatever it takes to accomplish our mission. I could care less if I offend you in the meantime."

Taj took it all in and began, "But—"

Esa interrupted him. "But *nothing*. I do what I do, and I'm going to continue to do it. Toughen up, Imam! The truth of the matter is," Esa continued, "you are dropping behind schedule with your assignments. I hope you will show me significant progress today."

Taj's stomach was a mess; he was ready to vomit. *What have I gotten myself into?* he thought. Attempting to defend himself, he said, "Sir, we got a late start, and I've been attempting to catch up since we got the cell organized."

"No excuses, Imam. I can only have results. Now, let's get on with your report."

Taj proceeded to report on their progress, and Esa kept pushing him. Taj's meetings with Esa had gotten progressively tenser. Taj wanted to be a strong contributor to Esa's mission, but he had very little understanding of what it was and where they were headed. He was following blindly, thinking that he would know what he needed to know when he needed to know it. Being browbeaten at every step of his report was difficult for him to take. He was a knowledgeable holy man who had studied his faith his whole life. He had never been trained, and he was beginning to question whether he had what it took to lead a cell for Esa Mann. His doubts were growing, and his confidence was dwindling.

"We'll talk next week," Esa ended the meeting abruptly.

Taj was not even given the opportunity to say good-bye.

Click. . .dial tone.

⛁

Esa was upset with things in Tennessee.

He called Allison. "Ali, can you meet me in the cafeteria for a cup of coffee?"

"Sure. What's up?"

"I just need to get away from my office."

Esa had arrived at the cafeteria first and already had Allison's favorite coffee waiting on the table for her. He knew her well. As she walked into the room, she looked uncharacteristically tired. Knowing that it was probably a bad question to ask, he asked it anyway.

"Honey, are you OK? You look very tired."

"I have been feeling exhausted."

"You need to see Dr. Henderson," Esa directed.

She must have been feeling badly, because she didn't put up her usual resistance. "I'll call when I get back to my office. What's up with you?" she asked.

"It was another bad day on the market."

"I'm sorry. Have you been getting beat up?"

"I sure have."

Despite continuous improvement in the stock market since President Wheeler had taken office, people were selling to secure their profits. Though this was typical market activity, it was still a good cover for his stressed appearance, but he knew that it wasn't the real reason. Even as he talked to Allison to get his mind off Tennessee, his mind wandered. What was he going to have to do? Was it time to make a change of leadership?

Allison knew, as women do, that she had lost his focus. She didn't get angry; it was probably best that she got back to work. She grabbed what was left of her coffee, and as she got up to drag herself back to her office, she hugged Esa and was reminded by how she felt to call Dr. Henderson for an appointment.

db

After their late-afternoon coffee - how she looked and how he felt - he needed to hire a car to take them home. Allison was thrilled with the idea; she didn't want to think of fighting for space on the train.

They climbed into the back of the black town car, and the next thing either of them heard was, "Mr. and Mrs. Mann, you're home."

Sleeping the entire way home, they were oblivious to being followed.

The light from the moon was reflecting off the snow that their housekeeper had shoveled off the walkway. It was a full moon, which transformed the night into daylight. They were happy to be home.

As they walked—or rather, staggered—up their front walk, Allison mentioned that she had been able to get in to see Dr. Henderson first thing Friday morning.

"Good. I'm anxious to hear why you're feeling so bad." Esa then said, "I don't know about you, but I'm going straight to bed. I think I may have caught whatever it is you have."

Chapter 17

Mifflintown, Pennsylvania – February 4, 2015

"Love takes up where knowledge leaves off."

—*St. Thomas Aquinas*

It was late afternoon and already beginning to get dark. Jason was unwinding at his desk after a hectic day in which he'd faced one problem after another. He was ready to join his family.

He loved the concept of just-in-time inventory, but any disruption in the supply chain wreaked havoc with an assembly plant. The massive snowstorm had missed the Mifflintown facility, but they were not spared from the repercussions. Many of their suppliers to the north and east were shut down. Being dependent on daily deliveries to keep everything flowing smoothly had McNichols constantly living on the edge. The economics of not keeping a backup inventory was profitable when everything flowed. It was hard to appreciate the additional profits on days like today, when Jason was pressured to keep the line moving.

The day had flown by, but he felt like he had accomplished very little. He could stay there and work late into the night, but he had made a commitment to himself years ago to place his work third on his list of priorities, behind God and his family. That value system had served him well.

He was anxious to see Ashley this evening, as he and Anne had decided to have a special evening to honor her. She had just learned that she was asked to join the National Junior Honor Society at Juniata County Middle School. She was thrilled, as she prided herself in academics. Ashley was also a talented field hockey player and enjoyed the sport, but she really excelled academically. She valued this recognition even more than the fact that she had been voted captain of her team.

Anne was preparing Ashley's favorite meal, which would be served on the red You Are Special plate. The plate was a regular part of the Lange family traditions and was greatly heralded. Along with the special recognition went the relief of after-dinner chores for that evening. Hunter thought that perk was much cooler than a silly red plate, but tonight was his sister's night.

Jason was tying up a few loose ends when an e-mail from Henry caught his eye. His wife, Mary, had taken a turn for the worse, and hospice was being called in to care for her. He informed Jason that he would be late getting into the plant the following morning, as he had several things to deal with. Jason had always admired Henry and his dedication. He was old school, from a generation that often put their jobs ahead of their families. He fired off a quick reply and told his dear friend not to think about work and that he and his family would be praying for them. He shut down his computer and took off for the parking lot.

dᵢb

Henry and Mary had just returned from her monthly oncology appointment with Dr. Sherman. The news was not what they had been praying for; they were in a state of shock. She had been feeling better recently and had hopes of beating her disease. She knew it was Stage IV, but she also knew that her God was a powerful God, and she was resting in that faith. As they sat numbly in their den, the conversation with Mary's doctor seemed like it had been years ago instead of an hour. Her doctor's words ricocheted in her mind: *Mary, I'm afraid it's worse than I anticipated. The cancer has metastasized and has shown up in other regions of your body. It's time for you and Henry to prepare. I'm afraid it's only a matter of days.*

As those words sunk into their conscience, tears welled in both of their eyes. They had been madly in love since high school and were preparing to celebrate their fortieth anniversary in a month. Now that celebration might not happen.

The doctor suggested it was time for hospice and introduced them to a representative before they left the office. Her words brought them some comfort—but they only comprehended every other word.

Later, after a silent ride home, Henry and Mary sat staring at each other. They knew that this moment was beyond words. Henry moved to sit next to her on the sofa. Suddenly, the worn carpet that they both had been intent on having replaced wasn't noticeable. They hugged and cried in each other's arms. Henry had tried desperately to be strong for her, but he had just been told that his best friend and the love of his life was about to die—soon. Henry knew that she would be cancer-free in heaven, but he didn't want to think about life without her.

Henry knew that he needed to call the girls and let them know about this news, but he simply wasn't able to face the thought of that now. They were simply holding on to each other. It would be only a short period of time before they wouldn't be able to do this.

Tears continued to flow freely—the sobbing had slowed, but their red eyes and wet cheeks evidenced their emotions.

The circumstances of Mary's condition occupied Jason's mind during the short ride home. He'd thought she was doing better and may even lick it. He was looking forward to celebrating Ashley's great accomplishment, but this news had put the evening in perspective. Life was fleeting, and he needed to cherish every moment they had with one another.

Anne could see by the expression on Jason's face when he walked through the door that there was something seriously wrong.

"Hi, honey. What's the matter?"

"Sorry, I just received some horrible news on my way out of the plant."

Anne, thinking it was something work related, said, "Please put the plant behind you for this evening—it's Ashley's night."

The stress etched in his face indicated to her that it was more serious than she had initially suspected.

"It's Mary. She took a turn for the worse, and they're calling in hospice."

Mary had been Anne's adopted mother ever since they moved to Pennsylvania. Tears welled in Anne's eyes, and Jason enveloped her in his arms. Anne wanted to call Mary, but she knew intuitively that Henry and Mary just needed time with each other.

Dinner was nearly ready, complete with the red plate for Ashley, but first, Jason decided to call Ashley and Hunter into their den to break the news to them. The kids could tell by the look on their parents' faces and the redness in their mother's eyes that something big had happened.

"What's wrong?" Ashley was scared.

"It's Aunt Mary. . ." Anne started but got choked up and couldn't continue.

"Aunt Mary's cancer has gotten much worse, and she will probably pass away soon," Jason finished Anne's sentence.

Ashley broke down in tears, and although he tried very hard not to, Hunter also succumbed to the thought of Aunt Mary not being around. What would it be like without her? Henry and Mary were the kids' babysitters of choice when Anne and Jason had to leave town for overnight trips. They always greatly enjoyed their time with the Koontzes.

95

Jason thought that the best thing they could do right now was to pray for Mary and Henry. He led the family in a special prayer asking God to spare Mary and give both her and Henry peace in these frightful days.

Ashley suggested that it might not be a good night to celebrate anything. "This makes my National Honor Society thing seem totally insignificant."

Ashley and Hunter's compassion for others was one of the many things that made Jason so proud of his children. He was incredibly grateful to Anne for the time that she had invested in both of them. He knew that she was a talented person who could have easily climbed any corporate ladder, but instead, she had decided to devote her boundless energy and resources to their children. This was one of those moments that reassured both of them that Anne's decision to give up her career and stay home to raise their children was the best decision she'd ever made.

"No, sweetie. You know that Aunt Mary would not want her condition to impact your celebration," Jason said purposely, trying to change the mood of the evening. He knew that what he'd said was true; Mary was one of the most selfless people he knew.

A subdued Lange family moved to the dining room for Ashley's dinner.

⚕

When Henry had gotten his wits about him and they both had settled down a bit, he called their pastor. He had been with them every step of the way through Mary's battle. He needed to hear about Mary's appointment today.

Pastor Bryant picked up his cell phone on the first ring; he knew it was Henry and could tell immediately by his tone that it wasn't good.

"Hey, Mike. This is Henry. Could you come over to the house this evening?"

Chapter 18

Antioch, Tennessee – February 4, 2015

"Defeat is not the worst of failures. Not to have tried is the true failure."

—*George Edward Woodberry*

T aj decided to communicate with the inner circle in a method they would respond to the fastest. He sent a mass text message: *We are having a mandatory meeting this afternoon at 4:00 p.m. at the Istanbul. There is an urgent matter that we need to deal with immediately. Attendance is required!*

When the guys saw Taj's image show up on their phones, they knew something was up. Taj was old school and didn't normally text; it was always e-mail or a phone call.

Wazir was having lunch with Darim when their phones signaled almost simultaneously that they had received a text message. As nearly all of their age group did, both men instinctively reached for their phones.

"It's from Taj?" Wazir said with a smile.

"Mine too. This is strange," Darim said, glancing at Wazir with a slight grin. I wonder what's going on."

They finished up their lunch while speculating what could have prompted Taj to call an unscheduled meeting.

"I'll see you later," Wazir said as he shook Darim's hand, working on his Western mannerisms.

"Later!" Darim replied as he made his way to his car.

They started arriving at the Istanbul around ten minutes to 4:00.

Taj had been there for over a half hour going through his speech. He sensed that Esa was near the end of his rope. He knew he needed to do something—either step down or give it one last shot. He chose the latter. He was a proud man and had never failed in his life. He had passion for the cause but had never really led a project team. He had, however, led hundreds of classes, prayer sessions, and other religious activities associated with this and other mosques. He was an accomplished holy man.

Cutting straight to the reason for the meeting, Taj began without any of the usual barbs at Wazir's expense. Taj's normal low-key voice was absent. "Gentlemen, we have a serious problem! We are not accomplishing our tasks on the schedule that I expected, and we are in serious jeopardy of spoiling the entire plan."

There was a noticeable awkwardness in the room as the guys tried to not make eye contact with Taj.

Taj continued. "I want answers, and I want them now. By first thing tomorrow morning, I want a complete report from each of you regarding where you are with your assignment, including any problems that you are having, any help you might need, and when you anticipate completion. The entire project is resting on our shoulders, and I've been embarrassed for the very last time. I need answers, and I need them now!" he reiterated, again with a raised voice. Taj was surprising even himself.

Deep down, Taj doubted his ability to pull off the assignment, and he knew that Esa was ready to turn command over to Fadi. This inner struggle was intense, but this was his last attempt. He would give the guys until tomorrow morning, then see how they reacted to his browbeating. It was uncharacteristic of him, and it didn't fit nicely into his demeanor as a holy man, but he knew that the end justified the means. Other than being the leader, Taj was having difficulty seeing how he would fit into the group as a team member. He had no skills that Esa needed, and he knew everything about the Antioch cell. He might be too big of a risk to Esa and the operation. The result could be his death as a martyr. The concept of going to the land of milk and honey with his seventy-two virgins was something that he had contemplated since getting involved with Esa, but it had always been off in the distant future. He loved his life in Antioch, but this could be the end.

"Before I let you go, is there anything that we need to discuss as a group?"

Darim raised his hand sheepishly. "Yes, sir. The three of us who have been researching and procuring the materials keep running into dead ends."

Taj had assigned the less educated members to tasks that required Internet research. "We 'find-it' guys need more guidance. The information we are getting from the techs isn't sufficient. We need clearer specifications."

With Darim's boldness, Jerome piped in, "I agree. We are very much behind on our deadlines, and the three of us just can't get it goin' in the right direction."

Rather than getting defensive, Fadi spoke up, representing all three members of the technical group. "Thanks for calling this to our attention. We will be more purposeful in our instructions to you. It doesn't help the cause if we're not moving toward our goal."

Taj thanked Fadi, and with no other comments from anyone else, he dismissed the group with one final direction, which probably need not be said. "Use the encrypted e-mail system, and have your reports to me no later than nine tomorrow morning. Good day, gentlemen."

As his lack of self-confidence grew, Taj was impressed with the way Fadi had handled the flare-up among the group. He could see the leadership ability brimming in Fadi. It was going to be a long night as he awaited the reports from his team—a long night of internal struggles as he worried about his future.

Chapter 19

New York City – February 6, 2015

"Lead, follow, or get out of the way."

—*Thomas Paine*

T he reports arrived prior to his 9:00 a.m. deadline, and as Taj read them, he was shaken. He had anticipated the worst based on his recent meeting, but it was even worse. The techs were blaming the researchers, and the researchers were blaming the techs. The techs needed materials to start the building, and the researchers claimed they were not given clear direction on the techs' needs. They were frozen in place, and nothing had progressed in the past week. He had not learned how to deal with such leadership issues at the Islamic University of al-Madinah. They taught him about the Quran and some interpersonal/coun-seling skills, but project management was not part of his formal education.

He was, however, a man of honor and knew that he was in over his head. For the sake of the cause, he needed to step down and let Fadi take over. In doing so, he had to throw himself at the mercy of Esa—if Esa knew how to be merciful.

cĭb

Esa was in his Manhattan office and picked up the phone on the first ring. His caller ID had identified Taj, and he was anxious to hear of his cell's progress—or lack thereof.

"Hello, Imam Hatem."

Taj got straight to the point. "Mr. Mann, my team is failing at our assigned tasks, and it is time for me to step down."

"I have seen this day coming for the last couple of weeks. What is your recommendation for Antioch cell?" Esa asked, already knowing the answer.

"The choice is obvious; Fadi Hares is by far the best man for the job."

"I agree, but what will your role be?"

That question stumped him; he had not anticipated Esa asking for his input. He stuttered at first. "I-I want to be a part of your plan. I will serve in any way I can."

"What way would that be?"

Taj felt that he had to shoot straight with Esa. "I know how to be a holy man. Please allow me to be the spiritual leader of our cell."

Esa realized that if Taj suddenly left the mosque, it would be very suspicious and the cover of the apologetics class would be in jeopardy, but he needed some time to think through Taj's role in the cell with Fadi as the new leader.

"I will sleep on it and get back to you tomorrow."

Taj knew that it would be another long night, as Esa held Taj's future in his hands. He rolled out his prayer mat in his office and proceeded to praise Allah and ask for his blessings.

db

As soon as Esa hung up with Taj, he called Fadi.

"Fadi, the old man has stepped down, and as we have discussed from the start, I want you to take control of the cell. I expect immediate results, and I am demanding that you get the group back on track very quickly."

"Yes, sir," Fadi responded with confidence.

"I will get the group together tomorrow and let them know of my expectations."

Upon hanging up with Esa, Fadi called Taj. "Please call a meeting at the Istanbul tomorrow morning for seven a.m."

"Fadi, it's Saturday."

It's statements like that that has led Esa to make this change, Fadi thought but didn't verbalize. "We can delay no longer, and we have to get back on schedule immediately."

Taj was embarrassed by Fadi's comment, but he was right. "I'll send a message. Do you want me to be there?"

"Yes, you need to deliver the message of our change. I've talked with Esa about your future role in the cell, and we'll talk with you tomorrow after our group meeting."

c̈b

Esa was thinking about what to do with the imam when his thoughts were interrupted by his cell phone ringing. It was Allison. For a moment, he had forgotten about her doctor's appointment this morning.

"Hello, honey. Have you seen the doctor?"

Sounding a bit sheepish, she responded, "Yes, I did."

"Well, what did he say?" Esa's impatience was obvious and probably worsened by what was going on in Tennessee.

"Are you sitting down?"

Raising his voice slightly, Esa asked, "What do you have?"

"I'm pregnant!" she replied with joy in her voice.

Esa was stunned. It hadn't been in his plan to develop true feelings for Allison, and certainly, a child was the last thing he needed. He had no idea what his fate would be after the project was over, but he knew that the danger was great. He was prepared to die for Allah.

"Esa?"

"Sorry, honey. I'm shocked. It never crossed my mind. We weren't planning for a child. What in the world happened?"

Allison chuckled, trying to lighten the moment a bit. "Babe, if you don't know, I think it's maybe a bit too late for me to explain it to you."

"I'm not joking, and this is not a joke!"

"I thought you would be as happy as I am."

Allison was right that, under normal circumstances, it was natural for a couple in love to have children. What Allison didn't know was that her relationship with Esa would not qualify as a normal relationship. It was anything but.

PART FOUR

March 2015

Chapter 20

Mifflintown, Pennsylvania – March 16, 2015

"Some people are so afraid to die that they never begin to live."

—*Henry Van Dyke*

The gray, cold winter was hanging tough in Central Pennsylvania. Punxsutawney Phil had seen his shadow on February 2. In Pennsylvania folklore, this meant six more weeks of winter. Well, the six weeks were up, but an end to winter wasn't in sight. Phil had been wrong again! Today was going to be particularly difficult. Henry would be back at work—his first day since Mary died. She had faded fast and slipped away before their eyes. Jason tried to convince Henry to take some time off with one of his daughters' families, but Henry was convinced that the best thing for his grieving would be returning to McNichols. So here it was, a little more than a week after her funeral, and he was coming back to work.

Jason left a message for Henry to come by his office around noon for lunch. He had worked a day here and there during Mary's final days, but he'd been distracted. Henry still had his doubts about the night shift, and Jason was becoming a believer as well.

Jason tried not to be prejudiced toward the Middle Easterners, but being honest with himself, he was. His prejudice went back to 2001, when radical Muslim terrorists attacked the United States. Jason was only twenty-four at the time, but he remembered it as if it were yesterday. He remembered the patriotic reaction to the attacks in the months that followed. He also remembered how those patriotic feelings waned as people forgot. He remembered the insult to the city of New York when permission was given for an Islamic mosque to be built at Ground Zero. The audacity of the Muslims was an irritant to the entire country. All of this was accomplished under the guise of political correctness. The details of their religion and their holy book were soft sold, and all the positive statements of the Quran were emphasized. Writings of the *angry* Muhammad after he was exiled from Mecca and the subsequent discussions about jihad were glossed over and/or attributed to a small group of extremists. Muhammad transcribed the Quran by himself—every word, thought, and concept from one mortal man. The angel Gabriel delivered the words from Allah. Consequently, Muhammad's moods could be detected in the text.

Jason had embraced Henry's skepticism and was following the numbers of the night shift carefully; there *was* reason for concern. Based on his suspicions, Jason decided on a plan. He had a college fraternity buddy, Wayne Joseph, from the Chicago Institute of Technology who had also settled in Pennsylvania. With his degree in criminology, he had joined the detective branch of the Pennsylvania State Police out of college and worked his way up through the ranks to department chief. Jason knew few details of what his friend did, but he did know that he was on temporary assignment with the Department of Homeland Security in Harrisburg, dealing with counterintelligence activities throughout the state. Wayne and Jason were close friends during their college days and had grown even closer since Jason moved to Pennsylvania. Wayne also knew Anne from their days at CIT. Wayne's job was stressful, and he tried to make the fifty-mile trip to the country to spend time with the Lange family as often as he could.

Wayne wouldn't and couldn't talk much about what he was working on, but Jason could tell that it was daunting. Jason decided to give Wayne a call to see if there was anything happening in the area that could be tied to Henry's—and now, his—suspicions of the Middle Easterners. Jason punched his speed dial for Wayne's cell phone.

"Hey, JL!" Wayne answered, using Jason's college nickname.

"How's it going, buddy?"

"Same old stuff." No time for small talk. "What do I owe the honor of a call from a top McNichols executive?"

"I have something that is out of left field. Do you have a few minutes?"

"Sure. I have a meeting to get to in an hour, but I'm open until then. What's up?"

Jason proceeded to unfold the happenings of the past couple of months and how his plant manager had brought his concerns about the night shift to his attention.

"I downplayed Henry's concerns and wrote them off to his old-fashioned ways and inborn prejudice of people who are different. Henry went through some tough times, and as I took over for him in his absence, my concerns grew as well."

Jason went into details about the strange way that corporate had sent Yar Din to head up the night shift and how it was the first time corporate had gotten involved at that level in the organization.

"Henry noticed his production numbers were off, so I began to track their productivity as well."

Wayne listened intently, asking Jason to repeat certain details, which led Jason to believe that Wayne was taking notes. Wayne was extremely interested in the fact that Mr. Din had brought in the Khoury twins and dug deeper into the situation by posing some pointed questions.

They concluded their conversation after about forty-five minutes.

"Mifflintown is under the jurisdiction of another detective. I will get with him, and one of us will get back to you after we see if any of this has hit our radar. Thanks for the call, JL. It was good to hear from you. I need to get up there for a visit; I miss Anne and the kids."

"Absolutely. I look forward to hearing from you."

Jason's curiosity about Yar Din and company was heightened by Wayne's reaction to his concerns. He could read his friend well; they had been through much. From pledging their fraternity, to a trip through Europe after college, to a relationship that had grown stronger as they matured, his intuition told him that Wayne knew more than he was letting on. He was anxious to hear back from him.

db

It was nearly time for Jason's lunch with Henry. Jason was concerned about his plant manager and dear friend. Henry and Mary were like surrogate parents to him and Anne, and grandparents to Ashley and Hunter. His family missed Mary, but he couldn't imagine the pain that Henry must have been feeling with the separation from his wife of nearly forty years. He had no agenda for their lunch other than making sure Henry knew that he was there for him—whatever he needed.

Henry stuck his head in Jason's office door, "Hey, Boss. Hungry?"

"Sure am. Come in here." Jason extended his hand but decided that a hug was more appropriate.

The two men embraced, both of them choking back tears.

"What are you hungry for, Henry?"

"I haven't been eating much lately, but my stomach is growling and I feel like I could eat something. Why don't you decide?"

They walked toward the parking lot, deciding to go to the country club. It was a special time for both of them.

Jason was impressed with the strength that Henry had demonstrated throughout the viewing and memorial service. Henry had no doubt where Mary was at this time. His faith told him that she was in a new body and in the presence of their Lord and Savior. Henry and Mary had embarked on their spiritual journey together from the moment they started dating. Their quest for truth had brought them to the Christian faith, and they had based their lives on the Bible. They were fundamentalists, filled with the Holy Spirit and exuded the joy that all Christians should. Their daughters naturally followed in their parents' footsteps and were both devout believers. Now, with the help of their husbands, they were passing the legacy of their parents' beliefs to their children.

"Jason, I miss her intensely, but if I had an opportunity to bring her back to me, I would not it. Her pain had gotten so severe in the later days that her face was contorted, but she still mustered up a smile for me every time I entered the living room, where her bed was set up. I long for the day when I'll be with her again, but I know that she would want me to move on with my life and patiently wait until I get called home."

Jason sat quietly and let his friend talk. Nothing was said about the night shift—or McNichols, for that matter. Jason was learning from Henry how a Godly man handles loss. Jason had always known that the Lord would never give them more than they could handle. The man sitting across the lunch table from him was living proof that God was true to His word.

They took an extra-long lunch break and headed back to work after two hours of conversation and reminiscing about their beloved Mary. It was a respite that both men needed.

cb

After his lunch with Henry, Jason's Monday continued to drag on. He forced himself to start on some quarterly reports that were due right after the month-end closing. Between his emotional lunch with Henry and his earlier conversation with Wayne, Jason was distracted and needed a break. Writing had always been a diversion for him, so he threw himself into the narrative that had to accompany his report to Chicago. His tried and true writing diversion wasn't working today; his mind kept wandering.

His cell phone vibrated, and Wayne's image came up on the screen. He picked up immediately.

"Hey, buddy. I didn't expect to hear from you so quickly. Do you have any information for me?"

"Yes, I do, but here's the deal. What I'm about to share with you cannot be shared with anyone, even Anne," Wayne said. Knowing he could trust his friend with sensitive information, Wayne continued. "We don't know much about the three Saudis who are working on your night shift, but they have shown up on Homeland's watch list. We received an anonymous tip and have done some surveillance. They do not appear to be extremely dangerous, but they have been connected with some surly characters that are part of al-Qaeda. We have not made a direct relationship between those men and al-Qaeda, but I think it's worth a trip to Mifflintown for me and one of my compadres soon."

"Wow!" Jason's level of concern had just elevated. "I would love to see you. How soon do you think you'll be coming?"

"Would tonight work for you?"

"Sure. What time do you think you will get to the plant?"

"Under the circumstances, I think it would be better if you drove a bit south and met us at the Starbucks in Thompsontown off Exit Twenty-Eight. You'll understand more when we get together, and I apologize for taking you from your family on a weeknight like this, but it's necessary."

Looking at his watch, Jason saw that it was 3:45 p.m. "What time would you like to meet?"

"We're getting ready to pull out of our motor pool right now, and we'll be able to get there in just under an hour, so let's meet at five. Will that work for you?"

"Ah, sure. I'll be there."

Wayne hung up, and Jason's head was spinning. Nervousness consumed him. He called Anne to let her know that Wayne was in the area and that he was meeting him for coffee.

"Where did that come from?" Anne asked, surprised by his announcement.

Jason never lied to his wife and made a point of being truthful at all cost with her and everyone he dealt with.

"He's on an assignment with another detective, and they will be in Thompsontown."

"OK. Tell him I said hello, and tell him to come back and spend a weekend with us soon. The kids miss their uncle Wayne."

"I will, honey. I love you! I won't be late, as he has to drive back to Harrisburg this evening."

With that, Jason packed up his laptop and decided he would set up shop at the Starbucks while he waited for the detectives to show up.

Chapter 21

Fairfield, Connecticut – March 16, 2015

"Every child comes with the message that God is not yet discouraged of man."

—Rabindranath Tagoreme

E sa was conflicted by his feelings. Cold-blooded jihadists did not have room in their lives to love a woman—it was simply a distraction. Allison was meant to be a part of his cover, but somewhere in the course of their four years of marriage, he'd let his guard down. At first, he was simply acting out his role of husband to her. Her beauty and her charm were too much for him to stay uncommitted, and he unintentionally fell in love with her.

It had been slightly over a month since she called him with the news of her doctor's visit and the fact that she was carrying his baby. He remembered how shocked he was. They had been using birth control. How could she possibly be pregnant?

He knew that his mission in the United States was very dangerous, and there was a high probability that he would die as a martyr, or at the very least, be arrested. In the past, he was uncommitted to Allison. Consequently, the thought of leaving her alone was not a concern, because he had no feelings for her. She was simply one of the infidels. Now his heart swelled and beat faster at the sight of her.

When Allison and he got together the night she'd found out the news, their conversation was tense. He remembered it clearly.

"Is there a possibility that Dr. Henderson could have made a mistake?"

Allison was taken aback and hurt by such a question and the fact that he did not seem to be excited about her pregnancy. "No. Why do you ask? Are you hoping it's not true?"

This was the first of many awkward discussions that often turned into arguments. The biggest of which had taken place about two weeks ago, when Esa brought up the prospect of having the baby aborted. This prompted a bitter argument, which ended in them sleeping in separate rooms.

Their religious differences once again came up. Allison's Christian upbringing had instilled in her that a fetus was a human being from conception, and she felt strongly about that. She was reminded of a dear friend in high school who had made a mistake with her steady boyfriend. Her lapse in discipline had led to a pregnancy. While other friends had tried to convince her to abort the baby, Allison's friend stood her ground, and that "mistake" had just turned ten years old. Her friend eventually married the father, and they all lived happily ever after. Allison had often thought back on that situation, and although she had not been practicing her religion on a regular basis, there were still aspects of her faith that resonated with her. Abortion was one of those principles.

She believed in her heart that the baby growing inside of her was a human soul and a gift from God. Esa had been raised to believe that the soul was placed in the fetus after 120 days, so to him, the possibility of abortion still existed. It was no big deal; it was a matter of convenience.

Realizing that the clock was ticking on the 120 days, he decided he was going to attempt one more discussion, at the risk of spending another night in their guest room.

"Allison, we need to talk about your condition."

"My condition! Esa, there is a baby growing inside of me. It's not a condition!"

He was off to a bad start.

"Calm down, honey. Let's discuss this rationally. How would this baby impact our careers? We are busy on our way up through the organization at Chase, Smith & Hooper."

Those words added fuel to her fire.

"Please don't tell me to calm down! I'm more interested and more excited about being a mother than worrying about how a baby will impact my career path, or yours."

"Sorry, but I'm not excited about being a dad. I'm a partner, and my responsibilities are increasing as my client roster grows. I want to be a great dad but don't feel like I have the time that he or she will demand of me."

"Abortion is out of the question. I am not going to kill my baby!"

"But it doesn't have a soul yet."

Allison did a double take. "What?"

Esa proceeded to explain to her the teachings of Mohammed and his interpretation. There was a wide range of disparity on the first 120 days prior to God giving a soul to the baby.

Allison understood his stand a bit better, but it didn't change her position. She realized, of course, that he'd had a role in the conception of the child, but it was growing inside of her body, and she was not going to waver on her stance.

Esa was stuck. Evil thoughts ran through his mind. His love for her gave him great concern about ordering any type of foul play, although he knew it was a phone call away.

He had a couple of months before reaching the 120 days, so he had time to try to convince Allison, but he knew that she was headstrong. He backed off on the discussion for tonight; it was too cold to think about sleeping alone.

Esa went to hug Allison, who felt rigid in his embrace. "Let's talk about this later," Esa whispered in her ear.

He felt some of the tension leave her as they continued to hug.

"Honey, I'm going to my office. I have some phone calls to make, and I'll be in bed soon. I love you."

"I love you, too."

db

Esa made three quick calls—to the Boston, Chicago, and Los Angeles cells. Competent operatives who had played behind-the-scenes roles in the 9/11 attack ran each of these cells. He had no problems with any of them, and his conversations were more informational. He wanted to keep them in the loop, the materials were nearly ready to be distributed.

In the back of his mind, Esa was beginning to prepare for his monthly satellite videoconference with Hajji. He had good things to report on all the teams' progress, especially now that he had a new leader in Tennessee. Ahsan was an excellent people reader, which was why he demanded a monthly face-to-face meeting with all of his remote commanders. Esa was fearful that he would pick up on the personal turmoil that Allison and he were embroiled in. If he knew, Esa would be *terminated* immediately.

Chapter 22

Antioch, Tennessee – March 16, 2015

"Being a Christian is more than just an instantaneous conversion—it is a daily process whereby you grow to be more and more like Christ."

—Billy Graham

Basel's encounter with the Christian in his cab continued to bother him. He was a firm believer in Islam, but he had always been curious about Christ. He was curious and feeling guilty about it. Shortly after his encounter with the Christian zealot, he recalled having difficulty getting his cab started in the parking lot of his apartment complex. Frustrated, he hadn't known where to turn when a jovial young man in his twenties approached him.

"Can I help you somehow?"

That was Basel's first introduction to Kyle Emerson, a clean-cut, all-American guy with blond hair. Basel had seen him around the complex but had never spoken to him before, although he had always noticed his smile.

"I can't get my car started, and I have to get on the road."

Holding out his hand to shake, Kyle introduced himself. "Hi, I'm Kyle Emerson. I live right there in three-oh-two."

"Basel Farooq. It's nice to meet you."

Kyle wasn't a mechanic, but he knew enough about cars to do some trouble-shooting. From listening as Basel tried to start his cab, it was obvious to him that the battery was dead.

"I have some jumper cables in my car. Let me pull it up and give you a jump."

All the time he was helping him, Kyle was very pleasant. Basel had found Tennesseans to be very friendly in general, but there was something special about Kyle.

His car started immediately.

"Unless you left your lights on last night, you should go get your battery tested. How long have you lived here, Basel?"

"I've been in the US for slightly less than six months. I moved here from Pakistan in search of a better life."

"That's cool. Do you have family here?" Kyle was full of questions.

"No, I'm all by myself. I live in apartment one twenty with a couple of friends I met at the mosque."

Kyle's interest was piqued. "Would you be interested in having coffee some-time? I've been curious to learn about your religion."

Basel responded skeptically. "Sure. What is your phone number?"

They exchanged numbers, and Basel was sure that would be the end of it. Nashvillians are known for their hospitality, but lacking a bit in their follow-through. Being nice was culturally relevant in the South, but Basel sensed that this guy might be different. He seemed to have a genuine interest in Muslims.

Basel's instincts had been correct, and less than a week later, Kyle reached out to him for coffee. They'd met a couple of weeks ago and got more acquainted. Kyle was Basel's first American "friend," and through their first meeting, he learned that Kyle was a very serious Christ follower. He didn't bring up the subject of the obnoxious Christian for fear of offending him. As the seeds that the zealot had planted continued to roll around Basel's head, he sensed that Kyle would be a good person to ask about Christ and his teachings.

"Kyle, I would like to get together for another coffee as soon as you can."

"Sure. Is there anything wrong?"

"No, nothing is wrong. I just want to get to know you better."

Basel wasn't completely truthful, as he really wanted to learn more about Christ and Christians.

"I'm off today and could meet you later this afternoon, if you wish."

"Thank you, Kyle. I would appreciate that. There's a small coffee shop near the corner of Nolensville and Old Hickory—let's meet there. Would four p.m. work?"

"See you there, Basel."

Basel got off at 2:00 and thought he would do some more online reading about Christianity. He had research to do for the "project," but he could squeeze some other reading in, as he was slightly ahead of the techs.

Basel arrived at the coffee shop at about the same time that Kyle did.

"Hey, man. What's sup?" Kyle held out his hand.

"Good to see you. Thanks for meeting with me, Kyle," Basel said, taking Kyle's outstretched hand.

"No problem. Can I buy you a cup of coffee?"

"No, Kyle. I asked you here. What do you want?"

They grabbed their coffees and found a table in the corner.

Kyle was curious what this meeting was about, since there seemed to be a sense of urgency with Basel. To get the conversation started, Kyle asked, "Is it OK for me to call you Bass?"

"Sorry, but with all due respect, in the Islamic tradition, nicknames are frowned upon, so if it's all the same to you, I would prefer Basel."

"Absolutely. Basel it is. What's on your mind?"

Basel walked Kyle through his experience with the Christian zealot in early February.

"I need to apologize, but some of us Christians are so on fire for our Lord that we burn people around us."

Basel chuckled, appreciating the analogy. "That's not why I brought it up; I'm not looking for an apology."

He went on to explain how the man had made an impression on him and that he had been doing a bit of research online. His only inkling of Christ and Christianity had been what he'd learned from his parents and various imams over the years. "I have been taught all my life that the Christian beliefs are blasphemous. How can there be three Gods? There is only one God, Allah."

Basel explained how the concept of an eternity *free* for the asking, with no works attached to it, was outside his scope of understanding. He wanted to meet with a true Christian who might help him understand what it was all about.

Kyle viewed this invitation from Basel as a huge opportunity, and just as Basel was curious about Christianity, he too had many questions about the Muslim beliefs.

And so it started—a very unusual friendship between two men in their early twenties from vastly different upbringings, countries, and cultures.

Basel explained to Kyle that their meetings would have to remain low-key and somewhat secretive, as his friends from the mosque would not understand. Indeed, he didn't understand completely himself.

Chapter 23

Thompsontown, Pennsylvania – March 16, 2015

"A man's growth is seen in the successive choirs of his friends."

—*Ralph Waldo Emerson*

As Jason pulled off Route 322 and into the Starbucks parking lot where Wayne and he were to meet, his earpiece notified him that he had a call coming in, and the soothing female voice told him that Wayne Joseph calling and to please hold.

"Hey, Wayne. Are you near?"

"Yep. We're about three miles away, according to this government-issued navigational system. So we'll see you in about five minutes."

"OK. Drive carefully."

Walking into a Starbucks in the middle of Pennsylvania was just about the same as walking into a Starbucks nearly anywhere in the world. The decor, the noises, the scents, and with the exception of some local flavor, the people were all the same. Jason never really liked Starbucks for business meetings because of the noise, but under the circumstances, it was a good choice. He couldn't hear himself think let alone the people at the next table.

It was a small store, but Jason spotted an empty table in the back corner and grabbed it. He sat down and surveyed the place to make sure that he didn't see anyone he knew. Gathered around several tables were students from a local community college obviously prepping for a test, their notes strewn around them and the floor next to their backpacks; at another table was a "local" sipping on some kind of expensive coffee drink and pounding on the keys of his tablet; and ensconced in a pair of armchairs were a couple of friendly ladies catching up with each another—all typical for a Starbucks crowd at this time in the afternoon.

Wayne arrived in a little less than the five minutes he'd projected. Whoever was driving must have been standing on the gas pedal most of the way. Jason had brought in his laptop to check his e-mail, but he was still busy checking out the customers when Wayne approached him.

"JL, it's good to see you. This is Mike Adams."

"It's nice to meet you. Thanks for coming up on such short notice."

"Our pleasure. How about some coffee?"

The three of them went to the counter and ordered their drinks. Jason had a thing about the Starbucks sizes. He refused to order a small coffee by the Starbucks nomenclature of "tall."

It never failed that the hip, young person at the cash register would repeat his order back to him: "That will be a *tall* Pike Place coffee, correct?"

He wanted to respond, *No that will be a small regular coffee!* But that response always stayed in his mind. "Yes, please."

The other two placed their orders, and the three of them returned to their table. Wayne's sidekick, Mike, was what the Department of Homeland Security called an LESO, or law enforcement security officer.

"Where are you from originally, Mike?" Jason asked to break the ice a bit.

"Originally, I'm from Gulf Shores, Alabama, but after graduating from Penn State, I loved the area so much that I decided to stay here."

"Interesting. What did your parents think about you settling in the Northeast?" Jason wasn't prying; he was curious about how a boy from the Deep South had ended up in this part of the country.

"Actually, the draw to Penn State was their football tradition and the success of their program. I'm a huge football fan, and in Alabama, you're either a Bama or an Auburn fan, and I was always the weird duck, loving the Nittany Lions."

After some catching up by the two college friends, they got into the reason for the meeting.

Jason segued into the discussion. "Truthfully, I was a bit taken aback by the response that my inquiry generated this morning."

Wayne took the lead. "Jason, what I'm about to share with you cannot be discussed with anyone, as I told you, not even Anne. Do you understand that?" he asked, looking directly into Jason's eyes.

Jason, realizing that he had seen this side of Wayne only a few times during their lives, responded seriously and quickly, "Of course."

"Yar Din has been on our watch list since he arrived in the States in his late teens. He has a rough background, and we have intelligence that he fought with al-Qaeda in the mountains of Pakistan just prior to getting a student visa into the States."

"Sorry, but how could a suspected terrorist get a student visa?" Jason was shocked.

"I know, it's embarrassing, but it's another example of how our law enforcement and intelligence databases don't talk with each other." Wayne got into all the details of Din's connection to a cell group in Chicago and how Homeland Security was digging deeply and quickly into that cell's infiltration of McNichols's headquarters and now their Mifflintown facility.

"Jason, your suspicions about the night shift's activities and your confusion about why corporate got involved with hiring a plant supervisor are valid. We have nothing on the Khoury twins or any of their spouses, but we are tracking them down and may know more soon. Your call this morning was a huge break-through in a web that we have been trying to unravel for some time. And here it is, right in our own backyard. We have been watching all three families for several weeks now based on the Chicago connection."

Wayne explained that it was difficult to send undercover agents to a town the size of Mifflintown, where everyone knew each other. The good thing was that the Saudis didn't know strangers from lifelong Mifflintown residents, so the perps wouldn't suspect the DHS people.

"We've watched them and listened to them through listening devices we planted throughout their compound, but they are very experienced. Their communication has been encrypted, and their verbal communication always takes place with ambient noise to mask their conversations. These are not your normal run-of-the-mill suicide bombers or terrorists; they are more sophisticated and appear to be part of a bigger project."

Jason sat silently while Wayne and Mike shared some more facts about the case, but they stopped short of telling him everything they knew about al-Qaeda operations in the United States. The details of that were reserved for people with the proper security clearances, but besides the clearances, Wayne would not want Jason and his family involved in a situation that could put them in jeopardy. Learning any more than he now knew could be extremely dangerous.

"Thanks, friend, for taking the initiative and calling us today. Our counter-parts in Chicago were extremely interested in this discovery and almost jumped on one of their planes to join this meeting. Mike and I have something that we would like you to consider. We would like to send someone into your plant undercover. He would be a highly trained agent from our Counter Terrorist Unit."

"He would be a Muslim, and we already have the perfect person in mind for the job," Mike added.

Wayne asked, "Would a person or two being hired cause suspicion on Din's part, or would it be perceived as natural?"

"Our business is picking up, so it would be considered normal to scale up our night shift. The thing that may be tricky is the part about him being Muslim. The three couples are probably the only Islamic people within at least a thirty-five-mile radius of us."

"Let us think through that. We may want to go a different direction regarding their religious affiliation, but we need to move quickly and have the person be accepted by the group. In the meantime, you will want to have your plant manager back off. If he keeps digging, he may spook them, and they'll run for cover."

"I'm not sure how I'll handle that one. Henry is a stubborn old Pennsylvania Dutchman. He's convinced something is going on."

"For his sake and safety, get him refocused. We cannot afford to have anyone get in our way on this. You just have to trust me on that."

With that, Wayne and Mike stood, shook hands, and headed back to Harrisburg as quickly as they had arrived.

Jason wished that he could talk with someone about this, but he knew keeping it bottled up was his only option. His pulse raced.

It was 5:45 p.m. He would call Anne when he got closer to let her know he'd be home soon. Jason was looking forward to seeing his family—tonight more than usual. Had their decision to escape from the hustle and bustle of the corporate job and city life to the quiet town of Mifflintown been a good one?

Chapter 24

Al-Qaeda Headquarters, Afghanistan – March 17, 2015

"The difference between ourselves and the west is that they love life, but we love death."

—Osama bin Laden

I t was a typical cold, miserable day in the mountains of the Afghanistan-Pakistan border, but one would never know it from inside the compound. Super bright halide lights hung from the ceiling, and flat-screen monitors filled the wall adjacent to the huge conference table. This shocking amount of technology defined the juxtaposition between the two worlds—the world of the rugged, mountainous region with a cave-like entrance and that of the bright, modern al-Qaeda headquarters.

By dressing in rags and camouflage and using poor-quality video footage with a rugged backdrop, Nasi Ahsan, or "Hajji," as his closest colleagues knew him, was portrayed as a rugged mountain man. He carried on the image of the fabricated persona that bin Laden had created. There was much uncertainty following bin Laden's death, with people speculating that al-Zawahiri would be his successor. Ahsan's low profile in al-Qaeda added to the mystery of who was leading the terrorist organization, again providing an intentional distraction for the intelligence community desperately trying to decipher post–bin Laden al-Qaeda.

In regard to physical well-being, Ahsan, unlike bin Laden, was the picture of health and monitored by the top medical staff in the Arab world—nearly all of them trained in the best med schools in the United States. Hajji was also a fitness fanatic who worked out as faithfully as he prayed, in a fitness facility adjacent to his office at the back of the compound.

Countless Middle Eastern men scurried about, dressed in neatly pressed khaki military-style uniforms, with the hum of computer processors providing the background noise to discussions throughout the huge hall. Their desks were neatly aligned, but there were no divisions or cubicles; all activity was conducted out in the open, and a sense of urgency permeated the space.

Deep into the compound, after passing through several fingerprint- and iris-recognition systems, was the inner sanctum. Very few of the hundreds of al-Qaeda operatives in the compound had ever came close to this part of the complex, where Hajji controlled his worldwide empire. His office was equipped with every modern convenience known to man. From his massive custom-built mahogany desk, he could control everything within the vicinity, as well as cameras in buildings around the world. With the push of a button, he could jump from viewing the office of his European head to his Asian head to Esa's office in New York City. No less than two dozen LED flat panels filled the horizon in front of his desk, with the front-and-center screens dedicated to CNN, FOX, BBC, Sky News, al Jazeera and other world news agencies—his informal intelligence-collecting agencies.

His life was very structured—again, a contradiction to the madman jihadist who seemed to act on whims. He had regularly scheduled satellite communication with his operatives in every civilized part of the world. These meetings, which started like clockwork and followed a tight agenda, were scheduled for the same date and time every month. Though there was a method in place for any of

Hajji's territory chiefs to contact him, this extremely rare form of communication was reserved only for matters of the utmost importance.

Ahsan's second-in-command, Dalil Ally, served as his chief of staff and gate-keeper. Nothing happened in Ahsan's life without first going through Ally. Work was progressing worldwide that would catapult al-Qaeda into a position of world power, with Hajji in control. A fully synchronized attack on the world's electronics was not something that just happened. At his headquarters, the project had been under development for over ten years—before the dust had even settled at the World Trade Center.

Hajji hated all infidels and had his entire life. The plan that he was pulling together would advance Islam to the dominate world religion, and although not all infidels would die as a direct result of the attack, the resulting chaos and confusion would have nearly all of them dead within months. In his prayer time, he praised Allah and asked for his guidance to pull off the mission successfully. He smiled as he daydreamed of watching the news releases from his compound on that eventful day. His thoughts were interrupted as Ally entered his office.

"Imam, it is thirty minutes until your meeting with North America."

"Yes, thank you, Dalil. I just finished my prayer time. Can you get me Esa's most recent report?"

He graciously backed out of the room and returned with a huge folder. Dalil had already reviewed the reports carefully and then prepared the three things that he suggested Hajji address with young Esa. "Young Esa" was how he would forever be referred to by Hajji, for he remembered the days of his youth when he'd first met Esa as an energetic kid who accompanied his father on safe, routine missions. Through his father's relationship with Ahsan, bin Laden, and Khalid al-Mihdhar (one of the hijackers on 9/11), Esa had joined al-Qaeda in his early teens and subsequently impressed his leaders. His father and friends had paved the way, but he earned his place in al-Qaeda through his mission perfor-mance. There were other operatives Hajji had considered for the leadership of this pivotal country, but his gut told him that Esa Mann was the best pick for the assignment. Many people close to Hajji, including Ally, thought he had lost his mind. Yet Esa continued to prove Hajji right and the distracters wrong. North America was on track to deliver on the designated date.

As Hajji read through Ally's notes, he noticed that the center screen, the largest in the array, had brought up a shot of Esa Mann behind the desk of his office within Chase, Smith & Hooper. Esa could not see him, but he could see Esa clearly. Esa was also preparing for the call. At the exact time, Hajji pushed the button that brought him up live on Esa's monitor.

"Good afternoon, Esa. It's good to see you."

"Likewise, sir. It's always a pleasure."

"How is your wife?"

Esa avoided any physical reaction to this question. It wasn't unusual for him to ask about his wife, but under the circumstances, it made Esa pause briefly.

"She's fine, thanks," Esa responded, wondering if Hajji knew about the pregnancy. Ahsan's tentacles extended deep into his operations.

"Let's get straight to the agenda, Esa. I know you are a busy man."

Hearing that from the leader of al-Qaeda also gave Esa pause, as he viewed himself as a small, yet critical, cog in the massive machine prepared to change the world forever.

As expected, Hajji got straight to the Tennessee operation, and Esa brought him up to speed on the transition from Imam Taj to Fadi Hares.

"I see the change took place. Has everyone accepted their new roles?"

"Yes, Taj has been very gracious and has been supporting Fadi in the change of roles."

"What are your plans for Taj?"

The question went straight to the heart of the matter about Taj. "I plan to use him in a researching role, and I have asked him to be the spiritual leader of the Antioch cell."

"I see" came a very noncommittal answer from Hajji.

Esa prayed to Allah that the discussion would move on, as he didn't want to be forced to handle Taj differently.

They had gone through the thirty-minute agenda without any problems, and Esa began to breathe easier. He knew there was always one final question, however, that Hajji would ask prior to terminating the call.

"What do you plan to do for the cause of Allah and our mission today?"

Knowing it was coming every month, Esa always gave much thought to his response.

"I will live my life and give my life, if necessary, to honor Allah. I will spend a minimum of two hours nightly on my prayer mat, asking God for guidance and direction with the project and wisdom to lead my men to honor Allah. *Alhamdulillah!*" (All praise is due to Allah!)

Ahsan repeated the Arabic phrase, and Esa's screen went black.

Hajji sat back in his chair and watched Esa for several more minutes after disconnecting his feed to him. He didn't want to be overly concerned, as he had the highest respect and trust for Esa, but he had seemed a bit uneasy at times during this month's call.

Chapter 25

Antioch, Tennessee – March 17, 2015

"Faithful are the wounds of a friend, but the kisses of an enemy are deceitful."

—*Proverbs 27:6 KJV*

Taj concluded another Apologetics class. The classes continued without skipping a beat, and with the exception of the inner circle, no one realized that Taj had experienced any change in his private life. Despite his personal situation, he maintained an exceptional attitude for his class, his regular duties at the mosque, and his work with the inner circle. Taj was simply keeping his head low, but he was a wounded man.

"Thanks for your attention today, gentlemen. For next Monday's class, we will begin our study of the Fifth Article of Faith—the belief in the Day of Judgment. That would be chapter eight in our textbook, and answer the questions at the end of the chapter. We will probably spend several lessons on this topic since it is an important one for all of us. It needs be ingrained in our spirit deeply. We must live our lives with the Day of Judgment in sight. Have a great weekend, everyone!"

As usual, the inner circle hung back as Fadi reminded them to meet with him at the Istanbul.

ℳ

The guys grabbed their drinks and snacks and went to what was becoming known among them as "their room." Fadi seemed to be in a particularly good mood. He was mostly upbeat and somewhat pleasant, but today he was almost bubbly. They were curious as Fadi began the meeting.

"I had a particularly positive meeting with Esa yesterday afternoon, and he wanted to pass on to each of you that he is very pleased with our progress."

This was a test for Taj. In all of his dealings with Esa, there had never been a positive word, only the opposite. He felt as though the eyes of the other guys were focused on him; whether they really were, he didn't know. What Taj knew was that Fadi had taken over and was delivering.

"I also have another great thing to share with you. Thanks to Jerome, we have found a small warehouse facility for us to meet as we begin assembly."

Jerome had grown up in the projects with only his mother and an older brother to raise him. It was a miracle that he'd survived. He had lost several friends in senseless gang-related shootings. He looked up to his brother, and his brother had steered away from gang involvement. He knew what it had done to him, and he didn't want his little brother to live a life of fear. Jerome's brother had a connection to the chop shop that his gang used to break down stolen cars, and there was a space for rent a few doors down, tucked away in a dangerous neighborhood—perfect for what they needed to do.

"We will not be able to come and go as a group. In fact, I don't want any more than two of us ever to arrive together. Esa deposited more cash into my account, so if I owe any of you money, please see me with your receipts. We will continue our informal meetings here at the café, but I will be putting together a schedule of the times that each of you will need to be at our new building. Please write down this address and memorize it. As soon as you memorize it, destroy the piece of paper. The address is 7654 South Twentieth Street. The work schedule will begin on Monday. Until then, gather the components or supplies that you have purchased, and bring them with you to your first assigned work time. I am placing Taj in charge of the inventory, so, Taj, be thinking of the best way to keep track of everything. The project is going to pick up steam now, so everyone needs to be dedicated to the cause. Imam Taj, could you please pray over us as we go our separate ways?"

The last couple of minutes of the meeting changed Taj's demeanor drastically. Fadi had assigned him an important job and asked him to pray. Both were small, but to Taj, it showed that Fadi wanted to keep him involved. Looking at the positives, if Fadi was going to utilize him and keep him plugged in, his life would be a lot less stressful.

Fadi didn't share with the group about his conversation with Esa on another topic. They had actually spent the majority of their time discussing Taj and what kind of liability he was to the operation. They couldn't have gotten the cell off the ground without his cover, but he'd failed miserably as the leader. Fadi's focus on assigning duties to Taj was a diversion. Esa had put a plan in motion to eliminate Taj from the picture—permanently.

Chapter 26

Mifflintown, Pennsylvania – March 16, 2015

"In the face of an obstacle which is impossible to overcome, stubbornness is stupid."

—Simone de Beauvoir

J ason was so engulfed in thought following his meeting with Wayne and Mike that he couldn't remember driving the ten miles home from Thompsontown. Wayne's words had resonated with Jason and been bouncing around his subconscious since he'd heard them:

Yar Din has been on our watch list since he arrived in the States in his late teens. He has a rough background, and we have intelligence that he fought with al-Qaeda in the mountains of Pakistan just prior to getting a student visa into the States.

Jason could not believe that he had someone under the roof of his plant who was a dangerous, international criminal. In his mind, the DHS should have hauled all three Saudis off to jail, but he knew that everyone, including terrorists, was innocent until proven guilty in the United States. Thank God he had acted on his and Henry's suspicions and at least gotten the process underway.

As he exited Route 322, he came back to reality and remembered that he wanted to call Anne to let her know he would be home soon.

Anne picked up on the first ring. "Hi, honey. Are you on your way home?"

"Yes, I'll be home in about five minutes. What's for dinner?"

Ignoring his question, she asked, "Did you meet up with Wayne?"

"Yes, he was on his way back to Harrisburg and wanted to know if I could join him for a cup of coffee." Jason was stretching the truth slightly, but everything he'd said was now true. Wayne *was* on his way back to Harrisburg. What he'd failed to mention was that Wayne had driven the forty-five miles to Thompsontown just to brief him on a terrorist who was employed by McNichols in Mifflintown.

"That was a surprise, wasn't it?"

"Yes, it was."

"What's new with him?"

"Same old Wayne, enjoying life and his new assignment."

"Where did you meet him?" Anne was more curious than inquisitive, as they trusted each other without question.

"We met at a coffee shop." Jason was hoping that she would just drop this line of questioning so he wasn't put in a situation that would jeopardize his integrity. Fortunately, she did. "I'm pulling into the driveway. I'll see you in a few."

"Love you!"

He hung up the phone and pulled into the garage. It was exceptionally cold for mid-March, but his home, as usual, looked warm and inviting. There was still snow on the ground. *When will spring arrive?* he thought. After today, he needed the comfort of his family. He tried to compose himself before walking into the mudroom. Anne and he could read each other like the morning paper, and this evening would be a test of his acting ability. As he walked in, Ashley, who was coming down the hall, ran up to him and gave him a big welcome hug.

"Hi, Daddy!"

Ashley was at the age where she was conflicted between being Daddy's little girl and a *mature* teenager. Around the house, she would cuddle up next to him on the sofa for a movie, but outside of the house, with her friends, he was lucky to get a wave.

"Hey, peanut. How was school?"

"It was OK. How was work?"

"It was good. Uncle Henry came back to work yesterday, so that relieves me from a lot of pressure."

"How's he doing?"

"He's a proud man and he's wearing a brave face, but I know that he's hurting."

The two of them walked into the kitchen. He never did get an answer from Anne earlier about what she was preparing for dinner, but he could smell the distinctive smell of Anne's meatloaf. It was her mother's recipe and a favorite of the Lange family.

"Where's Hunter?"

"He's working on his homework."

"Great!" Jason was impressed.

Hunter heard Jason walking down the hall. "Hi, Dad."

"Hey, bud." They bumped fists, then shoulders—a manly greeting.

"Dinner's ready," Anne announced.

They gathered around the kitchen table and asked the Lord to bless their food and their conversations. In his mind, in a private payer, Jason asked the Lord for protection from the "cancer" that had apparently been growing in his factory. Jason successfully made it through dinner and the rest of the evening without Anne being too inquisitive about his meeting with Wayne.

After dinner, he excused himself and told the family that he wasn't feeling well. The pit of his stomach ached, and he knew exactly why. He wanted to collect his thoughts and formulate a game plan as to how he would keep Henry from going after Yar Din and company. He also needed to spend some time praying and reading the Bible. His prayer would ask God to protect him, his family, and all the people in Mifflintown. He had no idea what Din was up to, but based on his background, he knew that it could be devastating. In his study, he opened up his laptop, and while it was booting up, he reached for his favorite Bible. It never failed that when he didn't know where to turn, he would randomly open his Bible to see what the Lord may have to say to him. And today this exercise did not disappoint. Opening to the middle, he happened upon Proverbs, and several verses down from where he started to read was the following verse:

Trust in the Lord with all thine heart; and lean not unto thine own under-standing. In all thy ways acknowledge Him, and He shall direct thy paths. (Proverbs 3:5–6 KJV)

This was a familiar verse to him and exactly what he needed to hear. He prayed and thanked the Lord for the reassurance that He was in control of the situation.

He opened up a new document, and for lack of a better idea, he called the document "Henry Focus – March 2015" and proceeded to outline his plan for keeping Henry out of the way of Homeland Security. Henry needed to back off. He didn't realize what he was dealing with, and Jason could not tell him.

Chapter 27

New York City, and Atlanta, Georgia – March 17, 2015

"Every unpunished murder takes away something from the security of every man's life."

—*Daniel Webster*

Esa hung up the phone with Fadi after deciding on Taj's future. He went on his computer to an encrypted file in a folder that required a password. Even the password was changed every ten seconds, which required Esa to utilize a special key code that he stored in the safe. In addition, his computer was equipped with facial and DNA recognition software. No one was accessing this file without the proper clearance. The file contained the names of al-Qaeda operatives throughout North America. It was a highly valued list since most people on it were American al-Qaeda sympathizers. Being American gave them certain freedoms that were not available to the Middle Eastern operatives.

Within this list, nearly every trade and skill imaginable could be found. It was a sophisticated database that could be sorted in any way possible. Esa was comfortable with the database, as he utilized it many times a week. Ahsan controlled access to it, and Esa was the *only* person in North American to have that access. Similar databases existed for other parts of the world, but Esa could only view his territory. If obtained, the list's value to intelligence agencies was unimaginable.

Knowing exactly what he was looking for, Esa went straight to the list of assailants, with a secondary sort for southeastern United States. After he'd entered his parameters, a list of twenty-three names popped up within nano-seconds of his touching the enter key. He had actually worked with a couple of the guys out of Atlanta, but he wanted to view the entire area to see if there was someone perfectly suited for this job. Esa never wished to tell his people how to conduct their business, but he did have some ideas about how this would have to go down, considering Taj's status at the mosque and his notoriety around the Nashville Middle Eastern community.

The information on each person was very impressive, including a compre-hensive curriculum vitae—a career summary of all the people who had been terminated or seriously injured, complete with links to online news articles that described the crimes in detail. In some cases, there were statistics straight from police files. To pare down the list slightly, he added the word *poison*, as he needed Taj's murder to be subtle.

Nothing popped up in Nashville, but there was a familiar name of a person whom he had worked with in Atlanta. His list of hits featured some very public figures, and in checking the news reports, most were listed as heart attacks or some other natural cause of death. The actual contact information for each individual was not available to Esa; Nasi Ahsan approved and coordinated all contact. His request to Hajji included a brief explanation as to why he needed the services performed.

At the bottom of the e-mail granting permission to Esa was a short note:

Good choice. Good luck, Nasi.

He was ready to set the process in motion.

"Good afternoon, Mr. Paterson. My name is Esa Mann, and I have something to talk with you about."

Esa had no idea if John Paterson was his real name or not. He really didn't care to know much about him except that his expertise was in eliminating people *before* their time, making it look like it *was* their time. Having Hajji agree that he was a good choice was all the reassurance he needed.

"Hello, Mr. Mann." Paterson knew immediately who he was, and from the start of their conversation, a degree of professional courtesy and respect was evident in both men.

"Is it a good time for us to talk?"

"Certainly. How can I be of service to you?"

"I have some business that needs to be conducted in Nashville. Would you be interested in helping us out?"

"Absolutely. I love that city and welcome any reason to visit. Will I have anyone in the Nashville area to assist me in getting inside information?"

"Yes, I will have you contact our local cell leader, and I'll inform him that you will be calling."

Paterson was a bit surprised by Esa's description of what needed to be done. This would be the first holy man whom he had ever eliminated, which gave him pause—but only for a moment. The more Esa talked, the more Paterson understood how dangerous the imam could be to the cause. Paterson knew nothing about the project that Esa and Hajji were working on, but he understood human liabilities, and he understood that they needed to be taken care of accordingly.

"This assignment is important to us, and we will compensate you appropriately."

"Obviously, I need to know exactly what that *appropriate* figure is before I give you my decision." Paterson spoke boldly, but he knew he really didn't have a choice with this assignment if he wanted to stay in good graces with al-Qaeda.

"It will be two hundred and fifty thousand dollars US now and two hundred and fifty thousand when I read the imam's obituary."

"OK, that will work. What is your timeline?"

"I understand that these types of *eliminations* take some time, but I need you to start the process immediately, and I need to read that obituary no later than the end of this month."

Acting as if that were going to be a challenge, but really wanting Esa to think he'd gotten a bargain, Paterson replied, "I will do the best that I can, sir, but there could be extenuating circumstances that would be beyond my control."

"Make it happen."

With those words, the two men simply hung up, with no good-byes or other pleasantries.

Paterson got off the phone and got started immediately. He had his own database in his home computer. He was a well-educated man who had decided to drop out of medical school after his first year of residency. Something in his mind had snapped, and he ended up in a psychiatric ward of an Atlanta hospital. After that, he had never been the same and had no desire to return to med school. Needing cash, he started to hang out with the wrong crowd, searching for something significant in his life. In his mind, *his* god had failed him, and he was looking for a different one. He went from church to church, synagogue to synagogue, temple to temple, and eventually, mosque to mosque. It wasn't until he'd found a mosque in northern Atlanta that he felt a connection to a religion that made sense. Still holding on to the anger about what *his* old god had done to him, he set forth on a life of crime. His newfound Islamic religion allowed him to perform these deeds for the sake of Allah.

Esa hadn't given him much background on the imam. All he knew was that he appeared to be in fairly good health and had just turned sixty in February. His phone alerted him that a text message had just arrived from Esa with Fadi Hares's phone number. Not wasting any time, Paterson made the call.

"Mr. Hares, this is Mr. Paterson." Paterson proceeded to ask Fadi a ton of questions about the imam. He took notes and actually recorded the conversation so he could refer to it later if necessary.

During the conversation, he learned that the imam had just lost over twenty pounds but had a goal to lose about ten more.

"Interesting. How is he doing it?" Paterson asked.

"Really just by watching what he eats." Thinking a little longer, Fadi continued. "He has also sworn off soft drinks and now drinks only water—and a ton of it."

"Tap water?"

"No. Bottled water. He keeps an ample supply in a small refrigerator in his office. I've watched him down three sixteen-ounce bottles in an hour-long meeting."

The call with Fadi ended in the same abrupt manner as his call with Esa had. This gave him an idea. He knew he needed to poison his mark, and the resulting death would need to appear as if he'd succumbed to a heart attack. The bottled water was going to be his key. He simply had to break into his office and inject the poison into his supply of water. The dosage had to be such that if he offered a visitor a drink, it wouldn't be discernible. It had to be a drug that would build up in his system and eventually stop his heart. And all of this had to be completed in approximately two weeks. He had to pick his poison, as it were, since there were several options available. Back to his computer he went.

Criminal investigations had gotten much more sophisticated in the last decade, so new heart attack-emulating drugs that were undetectable post-mortem had to be developed by the underworld. Fortunately, there was no reason for anyone to suspect foul play in this case. After all, who and/or why would anyone kill a holy man?

Chapter 28

Antioch, Tennessee – March 18, 2015

"True friends stab you in the front."

—*Oscar Wilde*

Kyle waited patiently for Basel, who was ten minutes late. They were meeting at an upscale coffee shop within a bookstore in the Green Hills area of Nashville. They needed to get away from Antioch for fear that someone from the inner circle would see the two friends meeting. Basel sold the concept of meeting away from the area by telling Kyle that most of his fares were from this part of town, and it was easier for him to break away for a cup of coffee.

Kyle spotted Basel rushing in, and waved. Basel saw him and was pleased that the table was tucked away in the back of the shop—more protection from an unwanted observer.

"Kyle, I'm so sorry. I picked up one too many fares before I headed over here, and the last fare took me downtown."

"No problem. I bought something for you while I was waiting." Kyle pulled out a bookstore bag and handed it to Basel.

"What's this? Why did you do this?"

"I think it will shed some light on our discussions of my beliefs."

Basel pulled out a Bible. "Thank you very much, but I would not want any of my friends to see this in my apartment."

"I can keep it for you, but I encourage you to begin your reading in the first four chapters of the New Testament, as those books lay out the life of Jesus Christ, and you will learn much more about him than you did in the Quran. Speaking of your holy book, I also bought a copy of it and a history book on the life of Muhammad for myself."

Basel smiled appreciatively. "Thank you very much for the Bible and for taking an interest in my beliefs."

They exchanged some pleasantries and asked each other how things were going in their lives. With the exception of an occasional language barrier, which mostly stemmed from American slang that Kyle used, they got along nicely. Kyle was interested in learning more about Islam, but not for the reason of converting. He felt as though he needed to be better versed in their customs, since over the past four or five years, it had become the fastest-growing religion in the United States.

The evils of the attack on the World Trade Center towers were a distant memory, and with the exception of some botched attempts of terrorism in the latter part of the last decade, al-Qaeda had been quiet. The tolerance of Americans to people of all nationalities made the acceptance of Islam common-place. This was taken to an extreme in some conservative minds, especially as the whole country now recognized every October as Islamic Heritage Month. This celebration did not sit well with many, but 2015 would be the second year of honoring the contributions made by Muslims to the American society. The prejudices that had existed following the attacks of September 11th were mostly gone and forgotten. This new acceptance of Muslims made it possible for these two young men to become friends without being looked upon suspiciously by anyone.

Kyle accepted Basel as a friend, but he did not agree with the fundamentals of the Islamic faith. In his heart, he knew that Basel would not have eternal life with the beliefs he had now, and he wanted to present *the* truth to his new friend.

Over coffee in Green Hills, they shared more about each other. Kyle was surprised to learn that Basel had been separated from his family due to his radical thinking. He didn't view Basel as a radical. He was concerned but knew that God had brought the two of them together for a reason. The fact that the relationship had been initiated by Basel told Kyle that he was striving to learn more about Christianity. Whether or not he admitted it, this information put him on guard with his new friend.

Kyle told Basel about his interest in music and how his parents were not excited about the direction his life had taken, yet they were still supportive.

"You are fortunate, my man. My parents were not open to my way of thinking and now act as if I don't exist."

Kyle then asked Basel a very direct question. "What is it about my beliefs that you struggle with the most?"

"From my early childhood in Quran school, they taught me about Jesus, but I have developed some questions about a few things about your beliefs."

"Such as?" Kyle pushed.

"Such as what you call the Trinity. There is only one God, Allah, and saying that there are three gods is blasphemous."

Great, Kyle thought, *I had to ask him and push for his questions, and of course, he picks one of the most complex items of faith that even most strong Christians cannot completely understand.*

"Basel, this is confusing for us as well, but the best way I can describe it to you is that there is one God who exists in three persons—the Father, the Son, and the Holy Spirit, all in one Godhead."

Kyle could tell by the look on Basel's face that he was still confused.

"Look, buddy, that is a postgraduate question, and we're still in elementary school. Let's do this: I'll read some of the Quran and the life of Muhammad while you dig into the first four books of the Bible's New Testament, and let's plan to get together a week from now right here at four p.m. Does that work for you?"

"That will work."

They finished up their drinks and went their separate ways. Basel was actually looking forward to reading the Bible that Kyle had given him. He decided to keep it with him and buried it deep in his knapsack. He wanted to form his own opinions or confirm what he had been taught as a young boy. His head was swimming with thoughts and questions. Was this the right thing for him to be doing?

⟨b⟩

Once he saw that the al-Qaeda money had hit his Cayman Islands numbered account, John Paterson wasted no time starting his project. It was easier for him to drive to Nashville, so he jumped in an indiscreet sedan and took off for the Music City. He had thought of a few more questions for Fadi after their initial conversation. In order for him to calculate how much poison to insert into each water bottle, he needed some more facts. He called Fadi once he'd gotten outside the Atlanta city limits.

"Mr. Hares, I need one more bit of information on the imam."

"Yes, sir. What is it?"

"I need to know approximately how much he weighs and how tall he is."

"I actually know exactly how much he weighs; he's been so proud of his weight loss that he's been telling everyone. He was one hundred and ninety pounds before he lost his twenty pounds, so he weighs one seventy and is approximately five feet, ten inches."

"Perfect, thanks."

As he drove, he started to do the calculations in his head. He knew what dosage of Levonitriantin it would take to kill a man of Taj's height and weight. This drug, with the nickname "Levo-nite," was only used in the Islamic terrorist world, and the police were not wise to it yet since it had been used so rarely— this would be the first time in the States. It had actually been developed in the laboratories at al-Qaeda's headquarter, and in the few instances that it had been used, it worked perfectly. Using his med school chemistry, he figured that Taj would need to drink eight bottles in a weeklong period, or less, and he would die with what appeared to be a heart attack within hours after consuming his eighth bottle.

⚭

As was Paterson's custom, he checked into a fleabag motel in a seedy part of Nashville and unloaded his tattered duffle bag containing a few changes of underwear, the Levo-nite, an industrial-style syringe, his break-in kit, and his toiletries. It was a bit past dinnertime, but he wasn't thinking about eating. He lay down on top of the disgusting comforter and turned on what had to be one of the last tube televisions in the country. The last thing he remembered before falling asleep was a news anchor reporting on an apartment fire.

A couple of hours later, he woke up shortly after 11:00 p.m. It was time for him to visit the mosque. Taking the address that Fadi had provided, he grabbed his duffle bag and took off.

He didn't anticipate any problems breaking into the Antioch Islamic Center or the imam's office, but he was prepared to short-circuit any burglar-detection devises just in case.

After a short drive, he carefully pulled into the parking lot of an adjacent building and observed the mosque. It was totally dark, with the exception of some safety lights in the hallways. He found a side door that was covered in shadows and partially hidden by some large overgrown shrubbery, then opened it quicker than most people could have done with a key. He had learned from Fadi generally where the imam's office was located. The halls were well marked with directions, and he found it easily.

He took a moment to look around Taj's office; he was often curious about the people he eliminated. Not from an emotional standpoint, but more as a morbid curiosity. The refrigerator was in the corner as promised, and fortunately, the imam's assistant must have recently restocked it, as it was full. Loading his syringe, he carefully inserted one-eighth of a lethal dose in about two dozen bottles. The overage would account for the imam's visitors, and unless they drank eight sixteen-ounce bottles in one week, they would not experience any discomfort or illness.

This was much easier than he had thought it would be. He made sure not to leave behind any sign of his visit, packed up his tattered bag, jumped in his sedan, and was on his way back to Atlanta.

"Esa, this is Paterson. The trap has been set, and now we'll see how thirsty the imam is."

Chapter 29

Al-Qaeda Headquarters, Afghanistan – March 20, 2015

"Every American man is an enemy to us."

—*Osama bin Laden*

As usual, the headquarters compound was buzzing. The project was coming together. The entire headquarters staff quickly took on Hajji's mood. When he was happy, everyone breathed a sigh of relief, and when he wasn't, everyone was on edge. The stakes were high when working this closely to one of the most powerful men in the world. There was no second chance, as many had learned.

Back in his office, he was performing his daily routine of checking in on his division heads around the world. Sitting behind his desk, the huge three-dimensional images made him think he was actually sitting across their desks from them as they diligently worked on the project. The only problem was that the people on the other end of the broadband satellite links didn't know he was watching. Hajji liked it that way. There wasn't even the slightest hint of guilt in his body about killing innocent infidels, so the thought of eavesdropping on his trusted staff didn't register as unusual. He was a voyeur, but a voyeur with a mission.

Things couldn't have been going any better, especially in America—his biggest enemy. Hajji had purposefully planned several failed missions to add fuel to the fire that al-Qaeda without bin Laden was no longer a threat. Unsuccessful attempts at bringing down an airplane, botched destruction of a subway train, bombing Times Square, bombs on freight airplanes, bombs found in children's hospitals, the highway infrastructure, et al were all well-orchestrated failures. The operatives who had been selected were pulled from the same database that had yielded Paterson for Antioch, but these men came from a different cross section of the data. These men were low IQ, highly passionate supporters who would do anything that Hajji asked. They were not mentally equipped to pull off the missions. It was all part of his plan. These failed terrorists made al-Qaeda look bad and America lower its guard. Hajji smiled as he sat back after his esoteric video tour around the world. All of his guys were busy doing what they were supposed to be doing—working diligently on the project.

Ally interrupted his pleasant reflection by knocking and coming into his office area.

"Sir, Mr. Mann is on the phone and needs a few minutes of your time."

"Do you know what he wants?"

"All that he would tell me was that it pertains to a money issue."

Money issue was the key that allowed Ahsan's chiefs to pass through Ally to Hajji easily and quickly, as he tightly controlled all monetary transactions. Allah provided the funds for al-Qaeda. The majority of it had originally come from the vast resources of bin Laden's family's wealth, but now money flowed from Muslim countries and supporters of jihad around the world. By far the largest supporter of what he was doing came from the Middle Eastern oil riches, and the majority of that came from Saudi Arabia. Their funds were nearly inexhaustible, thanks to the world appetite for oil and gasoline. Ironic, he thought, that he was now going to use American and European dollars to bring them all down. Money had never been an issue for him.

"Hello, Mr. Mann. How are you today?"

"Fine, sir. The trap has been laid to terminate our relationship with Imam Hatem, and I have paid him the first half of the money."

"Very good. Was it the same amount that we had agreed on the other day?"

"Yes, sir. But that sum has taken me below the mark at which it was time to request more funds." Esa continued before Hajji could respond. "I am at a place in the project where large sums of money are going to be dispersed. I am on the budget we agreed to, and the timing is in alignment, but I didn't anticipate the five hundred K to sever our relationship with Imam Hatem."

"I will authorize a movement of five million dollars immediately through the normal investment channels of Chase, Smith & Hopper. Look for it in your project account first thing in the morning."

"Thank you, sir." *If only real-world transactions could be that easy*, Esa thought as he hung up.

He had no idea how large the coffers of al-Qaeda were, but he did know what his piece of this project was costing—and that was only the North American piece. The funding appeared to be bottomless, but he never spent any time thinking about monetary matters, and Hajji liked it that way. He wanted his guys solely focused on completing the project on time. If they were on budget, it was a nice plus, but he didn't want them to cut corners just to stay on target.

Esa was set. The five million dollars would take him through the end of March. He had dinner plans with Allison in the city this evening, and he was looking forward to relaxing. But he also knew they needed to talk about her condition, and he wasn't looking forward to that discussion.

Chapter 30

Mifflintown, Pennsylvania – March 20, 2015

"Avoiding danger is no safer in the long run than outright exposure. The fearful are caught as often as the bold."

—Helen Keller

J ason, as he sometimes did with difficult issues, put off his discussion with Henry. He justified his procrastination by thinking that Henry was busy just getting caught up with his work. He combined that rationale with the fact that Henry hadn't mentioned anything about the night shift since he'd returned. No matter how he rationalized it, Jason knew that he had to have Henry back off on his scrutiny of the Saudis. Based on what he had learned from Wayne on Monday, if Henry kept digging, he could run the risk of tipping them off and spoiling the entire investigation.

He buzzed Henry and asked him to step into his office, and he was there in moments.

"What's up, Boss?"

"Have a seat. I wanted to see how the week has gone for you. How are you doing?"

In his typical Dutchman stoicism, Henry replied, "Everything is going well, but you know it's difficult going home to an empty house."

"Are you sure you don't want to get away for a little while—visit one of the girls or simply head off to the shore?" Jason tried this approach to simply remove him from the scene, but he really didn't expect it to work.

"No, Jason. I really think it's best for me to throw myself into work. That way I don't have to think about how much I miss her."

"I hear you, but I also think your daughter and her kids could use the same therapy."

"I have too many things going on."

"You know we're starting up another line on the day shifts, and I still have that issue with the night shift. I may have to make some changes around here. I've been visiting and monitoring the night shift guys while you were out, and I honestly think that they turned it around."

"Well, Boss, I haven't had much time to dig this week, but from the numbers I've been seeing, they are still low."

"Yes, they are, but they are improving. I want you to focus on the new line out there. Marketing is chomping at the bit to launch this tractor, and Chicago is holding them back until we're ready to deliver."

"I hear you, Jason, but I feel like I'd be shirking my duty by letting those guys skate by with the numbers I'm seeing."

Jason was not surprised by Henry's reasoning and stubbornness, but he had to lay down the law. "Henry, I will take full responsibility for the night shift, and I need you to help me out with the MFI 237 and work out all the kinks in the line. We need to get those tractors rolling immediately. The pressure from Chicago is getting to me. I really need your undivided attention and focus—I need a personal favor."

Henry was obviously disappointed as well as a bit confused. He knew that he could handle both projects. "Whatever you say."

Trying to quickly change the subject after that agreement, Jason asked, "Do you have anything planned for the weekend, Henry?"

"Yes, sir. There are chores building up around the house." He looked down as he said that, as a pang of remorse coursed through his body.

It was 2:12 p.m. and Henry would normally work for several more hours, but Jason told him to take off.

"I have a few more things to get off my desk, and then I will. Thanks."

Jason didn't feel good about this directive, and he felt terrible asking Henry about his weekend plans. *That was pretty stupid, Jason*, he thought to himself. Of course he wouldn't have weekend plans, and this weekend would be the first one in an empty house. Last weekend, his girls were still with him.

"Let me know if you need any help with anything, Henry."

The two men shook hands, and Jason went back to his desk with an empty feeling in his stomach.

db

Jason needed to talk with Wayne since he hadn't heard from him since their Thompsontown meeting.

"Wayne, it's JL. How's it going?" The small talk seemed ridiculous, so he cut right to the reason for the call. "I thought I would hear from you sooner. What is going on?"

"Sorry, Jason."

Jason was taken aback; he couldn't remember the last time that Wayne had called him by his given name.

Wayne was very serious. "Let me call you back on a secure line." Within minutes, he called back. "Your Saudi shift supervisor is much more dangerous than I first thought. I was going to call you this evening. Before I continue, I need to remind you of the need for confidentiality and the fact that you cannot discuss this information with any one."

"You got it. Go on."

"Jason, he is a ruthless killer that should have never gotten into the country in the first place, and his two sidekicks, although less experienced, have been trained at the al-Qaeda training center in Afghanistan. The reason I didn't call was that the bosses in DC wanted to arrest them immediately. They are frightened about the collateral damage that could affect the people of your plant and community."

Wayne allowed that to sink in with Jason while he figured out the best way to approach the rest of the information.

"As I told you on Monday, we have learned that they are connected to another cell group in Chicago, but we have reason to believe they are involved with several more similar covert operations around the country. From the information that we collected in the States, combined with intelligence that we're picking up around the world, it appears that they are planning something big."

"I thought that al-Qaeda was a has-been terrorist organization?"

"So did we. We have heard responses similar to yours throughout our organization, but there are some of us rethinking that. The CIA is on the case and working through their network in Afghanistan. They have called in their best clandestine officers in the vicinity of or with a focus on Middle Eastern operations."

Wayne was unable to get into all the details—he wasn't even aware of all the details—but he wanted Jason to understand the scope of what his night shift was a part of.

"Jason, we need to put someone in your facility, and we need to do it immediately. We have taken your advice on a Middle Easterner and understand your concerns, but a white guy would have difficulty slipping into involvement with Din and the Khourys. Our man will be black, with an American name. He will work under the guise of a recent convert to their religion. We know that there aren't many blacks in your area as well, so he will be commuting from Lewistown. We have him picked out, and he will be coming by the plant on Monday to apply for a job, so you will need to release HR to add a couple of people on the night shift this afternoon. We obviously need your cooperation, but I hesitate to put you in such a dangerous position. If you prefer, I can drop all of this, and we can haul the thugs off to jail and attempt to break them."

"No. I am concerned for my family's safety, as well as the staff at the plant, but I want to see their entire plan spoiled and not just the piece here. I'll do whatever you want."

"JL, there is something else you need to know."

"There is at least one and possibly more people very high in the McNichols organization in Chicago who are involved with this. You cannot trust anyone!"

Chapter 31

New York City – March 20, 2015

"Every man dies. Not every man really lives."

—*William Wallace*

E sa had forgotten to make reservations at their favorite restaurant, so he and Allison waited. The maître d' greeted him by name, and Esa slipped him a fifty-dollar bill, but judging from the size of the crowd, they would still have a wait.

"Yes, sir, Mr. Mann. Welcome to Chez Rive. I will get you a table as soon as I can."

"Thank you, Oscar. We appreciate it."

Allison and he moved into the bar and found two stools and a round table with a view of the busy street outside. New York was a fascinating city by anyone's standards, but to Esa, who had grown up in a remote village in Saudi Arabia, the city was a marvel. He could sit for hours and just observe the pedestrians hurrying to and from who knew where. So with a view of the street, he could be content for a while. They ordered drinks, but Esa, knowing the work he had left to do, and Allison, thinking of her baby, both ordered Diet Cokes.

"How was your day, babe?" Allison asked.

"It was good, but I didn't get everything finished. I need to return to the office for a few hours after dinner. I'll arrange for a car to take you home, and I may spend the night in the city. You're welcome to join me, if you like."

"No, I have some things I have to tend to at home." Allison took care of their personal finances. They had a personal financial manager who actually processed the checks, etc., but she needed to review their bills and get them ready for him. He always stopped by the third weekend of the month. "What has you so busy?"

"I just received a huge amount of money that's flowing into one of my client's accounts, and he's given me orders on how he wants it invested. I need to have the trade orders ready to go first thing Monday morning, and I don't want to work all weekend. He's the type of person who will be calling me about an hour after the market opens to verify that I did it."

"What a pain."

"He is a pain, but he's worth billions, so I'll put up with his idiosyncrasies."

Truth was not a major issue with Esa. He had no qualms about lying to Allison—or to anyone, for that matter. Character and integrity were not part of his al-Qaeda position profile; in fact, he lived in a world of lies.

After about twenty minutes of small talk, Oscar came for them.

"Right this way, Mr. and Mrs. Mann. I have your favorite table for you."

They had eaten at this restaurant so often that they could have ordered for each other; they were predictable creatures of habit when it came to Chez Rive. The food was wonderful, as always, and after dinner, the chef stopped by their table to thank them for coming in.

He and Allison's dinner conversation was light. Esa had not brought up her pregnancy. He knew where that topic would lead, and it wasn't necessary to push it at this point.

As they finished up their coffees, Oscar returned to the table.

"Mr. Mann, your car has arrived, and it's waiting for you outside."

"We better get going, Allison."

He felt a pang of love as he watched her get up from the table and walk outside. It was true what he'd heard about the glow of a pregnant woman. Allison was more beautiful than ever. When they got to the car, they hugged, and Esa headed back to his office. Allison was asleep before they crossed the bridge.

ِِclb

Besides the cleaning crew, he was alone in his twenty-third-floor corner office. His office was larger than any house he had ever lived in growing up. The amenities and equipment were beyond his imagination. He didn't take any of it for granted but was willing to give it all up *insha Allah* (if God wills). He also realized that, for him, his only guaranteed path to paradise was to give his life in battle for Allah. He longed for the day when he could die a martyr.

An e-mail notification on his computer broke his chain of thought. It was the message that the money he had discussed with Hajji just this morning had already hit his project account. That was the first thing he worked on. He divided the funds out to the five cells based on what he knew their needs to be for the next couple of weeks. Each cell had its own numbered Cayman account. He knew that Allison was going home to prepare their bills for their finance guy to pick up tomorrow and smiled at the irony. Allison had taken on that chore because she was fearful that Esa would be careless; she perceived him to be a spendthrift and worried that he would squander away their money if she let him. As she was reviewing their three hundred–dollar electric bill, he was dealing with numbers that contained four or five more zeros after them.

Completing the allocation quickly, he moved to the next priority on his list for tonight—a conversation with his Chicago cell leader, Tamir Alam. Knowing he would be in his office, Esa called Tamir's secure satellite line.

"Tamir, how are you?"

"Fine and you?"

Tamir was his top cell leader and held a critical spot in the organization. His senior-level executive position at McNichols Farm Implements had been quite strategic in their planning for the project. Wall Street did not have a clue that the majority of McNichols was part of a chain of holding companies in the United States that were actually owned by wealthy Middle Eastern al-Qaeda supporters. In fact, al-Qaeda controlled twelve of the fourteen seats on the board of directors. McNichols's profit was one of many that fed Hajji's mighty machine.

Esa delighted in his talks with Tamir, as he was the most educated and intelligent person on his staff. In addition, he was consistently well prepared. Esa also looked forward to their discussions on current political and economic matters that could possibly impact their lives and their project. Esa viewed Tamir more as a peer than a subordinate, but he maintained a respectable boss-subordinate relationship.

Things were progressing smoothly in his area. The anti-Islamic sentiment that festered in the early part of this decade had subsided as the idea of "freedom of religion" offset the conservatives' concerns about radical jihadists. Islam was widely accepted as a mainstream religion, and the death of bin Laden combined with the silence from al-Qaeda only added to the acceptance level by Americans. There were still some conservative talk show hosts who were trying to ring the bell of freedom and be modern-day Paul Reveres, but people wanted harmony and were tired of all the bickering between the three political parties.

After they had discussed all the items on his list, Esa wanted to ask Tamir's opinion on something.

"Did you hear what Glenn Beck had to say on his radio show today?"

"I didn't hear it, but I read about it."

"What do you think?"

"It was a bit unsettling to hear him talk about Hajji. Nearly everyone else has written him off as being totally ineffective, while Beck is still sounding the alarm."

"Is it anything we should be concerned about affecting our project?"

"I don't think so, as Beck has been labeled a radical religious person, and the tone of this country is that extremely religious people get labeled as being a bit *off*. We need to watch the polls and may want to commission some research of our own. I'll read up on it over the week, monitor the reaction and we can talk early next week, if that's OK with you, Esa?"

"That sounds good."

Ending his call on a more personal note, Esa asked, "Any hint of spring up there in the Windy City yet?"

"Spring is a long way off for us, but at least the lake is starting to thaw."

"That makes me cold just thinking about it. Tamir, thanks for all your efforts on behalf of Allah. Hajji and I both deeply appreciate your contributions to the project. We will be celebrating in paradise someday, my brother. Enjoy your weekend, and we'll talk next week."

"Peace be upon you."

"And you as well. Good night."

d̈b

On the twenty-third floor of a building directly across Forty-Second Street from Chase, Smith & Hooper, in an office with a direct visual into Esa's office, was a man with a highly technical listening device, monitoring the conversation that Esa and Tamir had just ended. Likewise, another agent was positioned in an office building adjacent to the McNichols headquarters on West Ninety-Eighth Place with a similar listening devise, picking up the Chicago side of the conversation.

Both were reviewing their recordings and already sending the information off to several different analysts who would break down the conversation to decipher any piece of the elaborate puzzle that they could.

The Department of Homeland Security was getting a glimpse of the big picture, and they didn't like what they were seeing.

Chapter 32

Antioch, Tennessee – March 23, 2015

"A thing is not necessarily true because a man dies for it."

—*Oscar Wilde*

I t was nearly 7:00 a.m. and all the class members were rushing to their seats. They knew that if they were late, they ran the risk of Taj embarrassing them in front of the whole class. Taj was not at the front of the classroom; he was nowhere to be seen. Instead of Taj, young Imam Selim stood in his place, visibly shaken.

"Gentlemen, please take your seats." His eyes were swollen as if he had been struggling with allergies, but his condition was not a result of early spring ragweed. "Gentlemen, I need to have your attention."

They all settled down and became immediately quiet. They all knew who Nafi Selim was; he had actually sat in on many of the classes this year. He was serving an internship/apprenticeship under Taj Hatem. Officially the assistant imam, he had been at the AIC for over five years, and it was often speculated that he would eventually take over the AIC when Taj retired—that was, of course, if another mosque somewhere didn't grab him before that day came. When Nafi went to bed on Sunday evening, he had no idea that the day for him to step up as the imam would come so soon.

He received a call around 5:00 a.m. from Taj's assistant. The medical examiner estimated that Taj had passed away sometime in the early morning hours. Taj had dialed 911, but passed away before the paramedics arrived.

"Gentlemen, I'm afraid I have some terrible news. Our dear Taj died this morning."

An audible gasp spread through the meeting room as the words that Nafi had uttered sunk in. This couldn't be—he had been the picture of health and had just lost all that weight. They were confused.

"The preliminary indication from the medical examiner's office is that it appears to have been a heart attack. I do not have any details about his funeral, but we know that it will be within the next twenty-four hours."

Tears welled up in Nafi's eyes, as well as those of many class members—especially the inner circle.

Fadi managed to muster up a few fake tears.

Nafi continued. "Class will be canceled today and Wednesday. Some of you may be called to assist in the funeral. I will take over the class a week from today, and we will pick up exactly where we were to be today."

"Go in peace."

The class respectfully left the mosque.

Instinctively, the inner circle went straight to the Istanbul.

db

"Mr. Mann, this is John Paterson."

"Hello, Mr. Paterson. What can I do for you?"

"I wanted to let you know that Imam Hatem has passed on of an apparent heart attack."

"Thank you, Mr. Paterson. I appreciate the call. The balance of your funds will be deposited shortly."

Esa was surprised that he had heard the news from Paterson before Fadi could call him. He wasn't sure how Paterson had been notified so quickly, but he was just happy that the risk of Taj was off his shoulders. He drafted an e-mail to the Hajji and logged into his project account to transfer Paterson's funds. Telling the truth was not a part of Esa's character, but living up to his commitments was. There was honor among thieves.

About twenty minutes later, the guys walked into the Istanbul, where the staff of the café had heard the news. News traveled fast throughout the close Middle Eastern community in Nashville. Taj was well known and loved by all—well, nearly all.

They assembled and Fadi took charge.

"Guys, Taj would want us to complete the project. I think we need to dedicate what we are going to accomplish to Taj. Of course, we are doing it for the honor and glory of Allah, but we also need to dedicate our actions to Imam Hatem."

Heads nodded all around the group, but nobody wanted to focus on anything but their loss.

"Fadi, can we just take some time to remember Taj?" asked Darim.

"I think we all need to do that privately."

Fadi could see quickly that he wasn't going to accomplish much for a few days. In discussing Taj's fate with Esa, he had anticipated that this would happen, so the two of them added three days to the schedule for the Antioch cell. Nevertheless, he wanted to try to keep them on track without the grace period that Esa had granted.

His phone buzzing an announcement of a text message interrupted Fadi. Nafi notified him and the other class members that the funeral for Taj would be tomorrow afternoon at 1:00 p.m. at the center. He went on to ask that anyone who could help should report to the mosque at 10:00 a.m. He made the announcement for anyone who may not have been personally notified. Fadi was frustrated and realized that nothing was going to get done in the next twenty-four hours.

"Guys, I'll see you tomorrow morning. Please plan for us to reconvene here tomorrow after the funeral.

Fadi returned to his apartment and decided to put together a complete schedule for the inner circle to start logging extra hours at the warehouse. It was time to get the components lined up.

He wished to honor Allah, but more than that, he wanted to be honored in the eyes of Esa and his bosses. He couldn't state that out loud to anyone, but deep in his heart, that was his desire. Ever since Fadi joined the cell, Taj Hatem had been in his way, and now he was gone.

His computer had started up, and he opened his project task lists, along with each cell member's availability. He was excited and was beginning to see light at the end of the tunnel. His mourning for Taj was behind him.

Chapter 33

Mifflintown, Pennsylvania – March 23, 2015

"Some of the bravest and the best men of all the world, certainly in law enforcement, have made their contributions while they were undercover."

—*Thomas Foran*

J ason had just finished his morning walk-around when his assistant, Beth, handed him his list of calls.

"Any of these important?" He laughed.

Smiling, she replied, "Looks like the same old stuff. There are a few new ones, so just maybe. . ."

Jason laughed at the irony of her comeback and wish that he didn't know what was going on either. There wasn't a call from Wayne but he did see that Mike Adams, his partner, had called. He went to his desk and immediately returned Adams's call.

"Mike, Jason Lange here. What do you have for me?"

"We have the agent ready to be embedded into your night shift. He's in his mid-thirties, but looks like he's under thirty. He has worked undercover assignments before, and he's batting a thousand in connecting with the people he's been assigned to infiltrate. He's been with our Counter Intelligence Unit for just over six years, and everyone at CTU raves about him."

"What's his name?" Jason was trying to get the basics down. He felt like this thing was moving too fast, and in his mind, he was able to slow it down by capturing details. He was the consummate detail person, and undercover counterterrorism was going to be no exception to the way he operated.

"Sorry. Of course. His name is Craig Reeves—that's the only name you'll know for him. He's African American, and get this, his *hobby* has been studying world religions."

It was as if God had his hand in this operation—that was Jason's hope.

"He will be living in an apartment in Lewistown that DHS has leased for a number of years, as they have been tracking drug trafficking throughout the area. It's indistinct, in an apartment complex of over a hundred units, so his movements will not be noticed."

"That sounds good. When will he be starting?"

"You need to coordinate with your personnel people, because we want him to start tonight."

"That will take some hustling. After his shift tomorrow morning, he will go through orientation in our human resources department."

"So this all sounds like it will work without causing suspicion?"

"Yes, it has fallen into place quite naturally. In fact, as luck—or more likely, as God—would have it, we had a resignation from one of our night shift people last week, and it's an unskilled job that Mr. Reeves could easily be trained to handle."

In the back of Jason's mind, the only hurdle he would have to address was Henry's opinion on this new hire.

"I only hope that Henry doesn't push back on this candidate. I will be setting him up as a recommendation from a highly respected friend of mine. I don't anticipate a problem, but he's still sensitive about me telling him to take the pressure off Yar Din and company.

"Mike, please let Mr. Reeves know that he will have two interviews before me, and I will e-mail you the reference information from an old college friend so that he can include it on his application. It's not a local reference, so he'll just have to fabricate a story regarding his relationship with this person."

"Will your HR person be calling to check references?"

"No, when I personally vouch for someone, they forego that step."

It was close to 3:30 p.m. when Jason's assistant notified him that there was an applicant waiting to be interviewed.

Not wanting to seem overanxious, he said, "Give me a couple of minutes, Beth, and then bring him in."

Minutes later, she appeared in his doorway. "Jason, this is Craig Reeves."

"Hello, Craig. I've heard good things about you from Ken Madden. Please come in and have a seat." Jason gestured to an informal seating area in the corner of his office.

"Thanks, Beth. Please close the door on your way out." It was quite normal for Jason to close the door for interviews, unless the applicant was female. The conversation he was about to have with Craig Reeves had to be confidential.

Jason grabbed his notepad, as one of the listening skills he had developed was to take copious notes during any and all conversations, but he would not be documenting this meeting in any way. His notes would not have any relationship to this initial conversation with a CTU agent.

"Is it OK that I call you Craig?"

"I want to be referred to in whatever way you refer to your employees."

"OK, then Craig it will be. Craig, I came to this sleepy town to take on the management of this factory to get away from the stress of corporate life, and now I find myself in the middle of a terrorist op. I'm not happy about it and I'm frightened. I assume that you will be communicating with Wayne or Mike, and I don't really need to be in the mix. In fact, I would prefer that I don't know that much about the operation. I don't lie and I'm a terrible actor."

"Mr. Lange, we concur completely."

"I'll let HR give you the details of your job, your security badge, and what time to report tonight. Craig, I'll be praying for you and for all of us."

Chapter 34

Antioch, Tennessee – March 24, 2015

"There's nothing certain in man's life except this: that he must lose it."

—*Aeschylus*

According to Islamic tradition, funerals were to be held as soon as possible after a person's death. Since Taj was the leader of his mosque, it was a bit more complicated; he was usually the driving force to get things done. Nafi had officiated at several funerals, but Taj and his assistant had been the ones helping the family with all the arrangements. Things had been chaotic since the news of Taj's heart attack. Taj's assistant had sent out a mass e-mail to all the members, and there were appropriate tributes to the imam posted on the AIC website. His obituary was already present on local news websites, and word spread quickly through the community.

People immediately began placing pictures, flowers, and miscellaneous tributes along the steps of the mosque. The community loved Taj, and the AIC staff members had to keep adjusting the makeshift memorials to maintain access to the mosque.

A guest book was located right outside the entrance courtyard where the service was going to be held. The funeral home staff had placed it there to obtain a record of the people who came to pay their respects to the imam. Hundreds were showing up, and the line caused by mourners stopping to sign the book stretched alongside the mosque and halfway around the block. It shouldn't have been a surprise to anyone, but there were several local pastors, priests, and even a rabbi in the crowd. It was an ecumenical tribute to a highly respected and cherished man. The funeral service was scheduled to begin in fifteen minutes, but it was doubtful that the crowd would be through the line and jammed into the courtyard in that short a period of time.

Imam Taj Muhammad Hatem rested in a finely polished coffin at the front of the courtyard. Inside, under the closed cover of the coffin, he lay on his side, with his eyes pointing toward Mecca. In the Islamic faith, he would have been washed immediately and simply wrapped in clean white linens. Since Muslims adjusted their rituals slightly to conform to the country in which they resided, a wooden coffin could be used. Everybody stood for Muslim funerals. Under the circumstances, it afforded a larger crowd to participate.

Nafi surveyed the crowd as he waited at the front. This would prove to be by far the largest funeral he had ever attended, let alone officiated. He was nervous but had confidence that Allah would watch over him. Per his request, Taj's students volunteered to help with the service. Taj did not have any family in the area, but he did have his last wishes formalized in a will. In that document, there were several people from the mosque identified to be pallbearers and six men whom he had recommended to speak in the short service. He asked that no more than three be selected from his list. Nafi was diligent in keeping within Taj's guidelines.

Nafi was honored to see his name on the list, and he knew that he wanted to speak his personal thoughts in addition to the formalities of the service that he would lead. In his conversations with Taj, Nafi knew that the apologetics class had held a special place in his heart, and three of the six names were students from that class. Surveying the list and trying to think through who would be best equipped to handle the eulogy, he called Fadi Hares, as he was well-spoken and highly educated. He knew he would do a fine job preparing and presenting to the group. He was pleased when Fadi had agreed.

It was ten minutes past when the service was scheduled to begin, and there were still people waiting outside, so Nafi started the service by reading from the Quran.

"Welcome, everyone. We are here this afternoon to honor the life and good deeds of Imam Taj M. Hatem, born on February 26, 1955, and died in the early morning hours of March 23, 2015. Allow me to begin by reading from the Quran, Surah 35 Al-Ra'd: 'The parable of the Garden which the righteous are promised! Beneath it flow rivers. Perpetual is the fruits thereof and the shade therein. Such is the End of the Righteous; and the end of the unbelievers is the Fire.'"

Following the reading, Nafi proceeded to honor the man who had taken him under his wing, teaching him what it meant to be an imam. He was an incredible example of a caring, soft-spoken man of Allah.

Nafi's words were touching, and there was some sobbing evident throughout the courtyard, though their faith forbade excessive wailing or screaming.

Nafi continued. "We will miss the imam, but we have to remember that Allah is the one who gives life and takes it away, at a time appointed by him. It is not for us to question his wisdom. As the Prophet Muhammad has told us, there are three ways to benefit a person after he dies: charity during life which continues to help others, knowledge from which people continue to benefit, and a righteous child who prays for him. No one in this courtyard would question that Imam Taj Hatem will continue to benefit in death from all three of these opportunities. In the imam's last wishes, he named several people whom he wished to say something at the time of his death. You will now hear from two of them."

Fadi had prepared a glowing tribute to this holy man. He was not at all nervous, but thankful that he didn't have to go first. It gave him more time to run through his notes in his head. The dark side of him wanted to get up and tell the imam's people that he was a terrorist who couldn't hold up his end of the bargain and that he was killed for his ineptitude. But instead, he would give a flowery description of a man who was teaching him how to be a better Muslim. Fadi would dig deep in his memory bank to his high school drama classes and would stoically wipe a few timely tears from his eyes. As the other speaker stepped back into the crowd, Fadi turned toward the mass of people.

"Imam Taj Hatem made my beliefs in Allah come alive and was a role model for me to emulate as a holy man. Over the last several months, he became a friend. He was a listening ear that allowed me to be honest. I respected him tremendously. His wisdom on matters of the Quran was above reproach."

Fadi heaped praises on the man that he had assassinated. No one, including the inner circle, could guess that foul play had been involved with his death, and certainly, no one ever would have guessed that Fadi Hares had been the instigator.

Nafi dismissed the group and invited the men in attendance to attend the graveside ceremony. The crowd slowly and reverently left the courtyard. Sadness was in the air, and the gray, cloudy, chilly March afternoon only added to tone of the day.

Most of the men fell into the procession to the cemetery. The long line of cars that followed the hearse was yet another tribute to the popularity of the imam. The pallbearers carefully moved the coffin into place at the gravesite as men gathered around.

The ceremony was brief, with Nafi reading Surah 20:55 from the Quran: "we created you from it, and return you into it, and from it we will raise you a second time."

After the reading, everyone present grabbed a handful of dirt and threw it on top of the coffin as it was lowered into the ground. Taj was in his final resting place, until the Angel Israfil blew the horn that marked the start of the Day of Judgment. On that day, Allah would resurrect all of mankind who had ever lived on Earth, to judge them by their deeds and assign to them paradise or the hellfire.

Tears fell as all men filed past the gaping hole, depositing their dirt onto the coffin. As Basel turned to head toward his taxi, he was shocked to see his new friend Kyle waiting by the car.

PART FIVE

April 2015

Chapter 35

Al-Qaeda Headquarters, Afghanistan – April 2, 2015

"A terrorist is someone who has a bomb, but doesn't have an air force."

—*William Blum*

Nasi Ahsan was explaining his plan to his lieutenants today. It was time. The project overview was kept secret in the territories and their cells; they each had a piece, but the pieces were shrouded in mystery. The time was right for Hajji to disclose his plan to a wider circle. He debated this decision with himself and his closest staff, but his opinion was the only one that mattered. He made *all* the decisions and expected his people to fall in line. Those who didn't disappeared.

He would not share intricate details on the timing, but he knew that he was nearing the point in the schedule when things would move fast. He would continue to share only a forty-five-day window of the schedule, but after today, his territory leaders would know the scope of the attack.

The tech support people had been performing tests in preparation for the meeting. Technical difficulties were unacceptable, so all connections were checked and rechecked. Technical issues for IT people in corporations could lead to lost jobs; technical issues with Hajji could lead to lost lives. Their system was advanced, with technology that wasn't on the market, some of which had been built from the ground up in their laboratory.

Another group of support people readied the amenities of the room, including Hajji's favorite snacks. Each of the five 3-D flat panels was labeled with an electronic signature of the city and territory that would appear on that screen. No names were used in these meetings, so from left to right across the bottom of the screens read the following: *Tokyo/Asia, London/EU, New York City/ NA, Moscow/Eastern Europe*, and *Cape Town/Africa*. The leaders of these territories—each of whom represented thousands of al-Qaeda operatives—would eventually fill the screens.

Hajji always liked to have the North American territory head directly across from his position, which was at the center of the huge conference table. North America was his biggest enemy, his biggest target, and would be his biggest prize. To Ahsan's right would be Dalil Ally, who would diligently log the events and any action points. His notes would be automatically transformed into electronic tasks. He then assigned each to the appropriate person and assured that they get completed on time.

To his left would be a new face to the conference calls. Assisting and, in fact, handling most of the presentation today would be the brains behind the operation, Malcolm Shane. Shane was the world-renowned scientist who had forged the path in research on electromagnetic pulse technology. He was the first to discover that an electromagnetic pulse could be generated in a way other than a nuclear blast. Malcolm grew up in London and converted to Islam after going through a bitter divorce and custody battle in which he lost nearly everything, including visitation with his children. Bin Laden had been following his research from afar, and when he joined a local mosque in London, Osama made the call himself. Shane thought someone was pulling a prank on him when the caller identified himself as bin Laden, but realizing that it really was the leader of al-

Qaeda, he was honored. The assignment was just what he needed to get his mind off his personal situation.

Shane was a workaholic, and it had cost him dearly. When Hajji approached him to join his battle against the infidels and earn a place with Allah in paradise, he jumped at the chance. His work and his discoveries were all that he had left in this life.

After accepting the position, he left London and made his way through several rendezvous with al-Qaeda members, who ushered him in a very roundabout way to the headquarters. Like any visitor to the headquarters, he was amazed as he entered through the cave-like entrance into a world of modern marvels. Several major advancements had been made since his arrival in Afghanistan. The difference now was that his findings were not being published for the scientific community; the advancements were only known within the organization and would only be used for the operation.

With all the various time zones represented, it was impossible not to have some territories inconvenienced; no matter what time they started. Consequently, Hajji started the meetings when he was at his best—midmorning. At precisely 11:00 a.m. Afghanistan time, all the screens came alive, and all players were in place. No one was *ever* late for these meetings. Hajji had a great view, as did all the participants. The participant's thirty-two-inch flat-screen monitors were also three-dimensional, with the screens subdivided into six equal parts. The program would then automatically enlarge the section of the screen showing the person speaking, while minimizing the other five views. As Hajji began the meeting, he was front and center on everyone's monitors.

"Good morning or"—Hajji chuckled—"evening, afternoon, wherever you are." He seldom used humor, but it immediately lightened the tone of the meeting.

All the territories responded with their greetings.

"Gentlemen, we are making steady headway toward our goal, and you have all been working diligently though I have kept you in the dark. I'm sure that you all understand the reason behind the secrecy, and as I begin to roll out the plan, it will become even clearer. Today I am going to open the curtain slightly so that you will get a better understanding of what we have all been laboring over. You will still not know everything—for instance, the exact date of the operation will continue to be a secret. I have the utmost respect for each of you, and we must continue to be diligent. I do not have to tell you that I will not rest until we completely dominate the world and Islam is the only religion. All infidels must convert or die, and this project will speed the process along exponentially. To assist me in introducing the means to our end will be a new face to you, but he has been in our organization for nearly five years."

The camera spanned to show Hajji and Malcolm.

"Dr. Shane is *the* authority on our weapon of choice for the project. He is actually attributed with the discovery of the weapon, and he has been perfecting it for over fifteen years since his initial invention. His credentials are as impressive as his discoveries. Dr. Shane holds a PhD in physics and electrical engineering from MIT. He has been published in every respected scientific journal that you could name or imagine—until he joined us in 2010. Since then, all the advancements that he has made are ours and ours alone. Gentlemen, please join me in welcoming Dr. Malcolm Shane to our team and our meeting today."

The three-dimensional images showed all the territory chiefs applauding, and with the help of total surround sound, it seemed as if everyone were in the same room. The camera zoomed in to the full face of Dr. Shane, who was now front and center on each man's monitor.

"Thank you all. *Alhamdulillah!*"

"*Alhamdulillah!*" The response came in unison from everyone, including the other two participants in the headquarters conference room.

"I will attempt to make this presentation as basic as I can. I have read each of your dossiers, so I will gear our discussion accordingly, but I wish it to be informal. Please feel free to ask questions as you have them."

With that, the men saw a digital presentation titled "NNEMP 101" (non-nuclear electromagnetic pulse) pop up in the corner of the same frame that Dr. Shane occupied on their monitors.

"The weapon of choice for our project is one that was somewhat of an accident—a by-product of another weapon."

Dr. Shane's images on his digital presentation were very interesting. While he was talking through this dry subject, vintage video clips, sound bites, and other graphically pleasing images kept the territory chiefs interested.

"The effects of an electromagnetic pulse, or EMP, were first discovered during the very early days of nuclear bomb testing in the early 1950s. The scientists noticed that some of their instruments would fail. As the testing intensified, the results of EMP were more noticeable."

Dr. Shane brought the group up-to-date on the origins of the weapon and how he had pioneered the concept of EMP without the use of nuclear weapons.

"In those early days, the electronic equipment was much more rugged, so the results of EMP were quickly repaired. As our world has become more and more electronic and computerized, the results of EMP are more far-reaching and damaging."

He rattled off example after example of how reliant we are on electronics and how strategically located EMP devices could effectively shut down the entire infrastructure of a region.

"Think about your own worlds and how dependent you are on electronics. An obvious example for all of us would be our computer networks and our dependence on data and research through the Internet. Your computer hard drives would be toasted, your computers ruined, data gone, electronic communication impossible. But, gentlemen, that is only the tip of the iceberg. Transportation would grind to a halt, our autos would not start, airplanes would drop from the skies at the time of the attack, and complete energy grids would crash. In a matter of seconds, our world would devolve back to the late 1800s.

"Our plans call for the development and use of NNEMP, or non-nuclear electromagnetic pulse devices. These weapons, when launched in a coordinated effort around the world simultaneously, will cause the infidels' economies to completely collapse. Your territories and your cell organizations have been strategically located to accomplish a high percentage of corruption. The beauty of our plan is that the United States and the other major world powers have written off the threat of an EMP attack to be inconsequential, since the range of a device would do very limited regional damage. As a result of their findings, their guards are down."

Hajji interrupted the presentation to add how his intelligence had reported the lack of a plan to defend against an EMP attack worldwide.

Dr. Shane continued. "This sounds boastful, but since I have dropped off the radar and went undercover with Hajji, the whole discussion of EMP in the scientific world has lessened, and I am more convinced than ever that what we have planned will turn the world upside down. There will be casualties—some immediate and others in time. Our mosques and our agents' equipment, vehicles, and computers will be guarded from the EMP blasts. We will be able to take over vast areas and give the infidels a chance to convert—perhaps one last chance. What you and your teams have been working on is the gathering of all the materials necessary for us to deliver light missile payloads at high enough altitudes to deliver mortal blows to our enemies. Each of your various cells has been working on different aspects of the weapons, and in the very near future, these components will be repositioned to allow for assembly to begin."

For the remaining thirty minutes of the meeting, Dalil Ally went over the logistics of how the materials were going to be delivered. The way the plan was laid out, each territory had the same number of cells operating within it. Each cell was identified with the territory initials and the number of the cell. The master plan showed each individual cell and its accompanying responsibilities. Ally flashed the master grid for the operation up on the digital presentation screen. If squinting, it appeared to be a giant spider's web—and indeed, a deadly spider's web.

"The movement of materials will begin three weeks from today. All materials will be in place at every cell by the end of May. We will be moving carefully and precisely to avoid detection. We will keep under the radar, and we *will* be successful. Praise Allah!"

"Praise Allah!" reverberated through the 9.1 surround speakers.

A slide appeared on the screen that listed three works by Dr. Shane on the topic of NNEMP.

Ally continued. "I encourage you to download these books and read more on the subject. You need not be an expert, but you do need to have some general knowledge."

Hajji concluded the conference with a serious threat to keep everything completely confidential.

"Remember, gentlemen, nothing gets shared with anyone. You know the consequences of disobeying my directives. Go in peace. *Alhamdulillah!*"

"*Alhamdulillah!*" radiated from the speakers as the screens simultaneously went black.

Chapter 36

New York City – April 2, 2015

"The best thing to hold onto in life is each other."

—*Audrey Hepburn*

With his adrenaline pumping, Esa signed off the conference call. He knew the project was big, but the description of how it was coming together was thrilling. It was early evening in New York, and he'd had a rough day, but listening to the al-Qaeda leaders gave him new energy. The scope of the project was much bigger than he had thought, and the importance of North America to Hajji was evident. He was feeling the pressure.

Signs of spring were beginning to appear in the city and in Connecticut. Spring marked new life. His mind bounced from subject to subject as thoughts of the child within Allison flashed into his mind, then were replaced by thoughts of Allison and his unexplained feelings for her. He had been in love before, but he wasn't supposed to be in love with her.

Meanwhile, Allison was waiting in her office for a call from Esa, as she had planned to go home with him this evening. Train or car, she really didn't care about the mode of transportation; she just wanted to spend time with him. Allison thought that his conference call was only supposed to last an hour, but she knew how those things went. She had just dug into another stack of papers on her desk when her phone rang.

Recognizing the extension number on the screen, she answered, "Hello, babe. Is your meeting over?"

"Yes, it just finished."

Allison detected something in his voice. "Is there anything wrong?"

"No," he answered quickly. "No, everything is going great, and the project that we met about is very exciting. Client confidentiality prohibits me from getting into the details, but I will as soon as I am able to." A lie—he would never be able to tell her anything about the project.

The thought of what would happen to Allison had never crossed his mind. Their relationship was a convenience, not a romance. But now those concerns were beginning to surface as his love for her grew daily.

Her question brought him back to consciousness.

"Are you ready to leave, or do you need some more time?"

"I need a few minutes. I'll swing by your office when I'm ready. It won't be long."

"Great, see you then."

Esa had suggested they take a car home, and the idea sounded great to her. Resting in a peaceful backseat in the arms of her love was what she needed. After he ordered the car, he sat back in his desk chair and gazed out over the Manhattan skyline. It was beautiful, but he wasn't thinking about its beauty. What would it look like dark with planes hitting the ground all around the island? What would it look like with millions of people stuck in cars that no longer worked, all of them trying to call their loved ones on cell phones that were worthless? Chaos would not even begin to describe the scene. *The nonbelievers deserve it*, he thought, and a smile crept to his face—an evil smile.

A black Suburban with two agents inside was parked in the garage of Esa's building. After picking up intel by using their electronic long-range listening devices, they had decided to step up their surveillance. Over the past several weeks, they had successfully implanted wireless listening devises in and around Esa's office. Today was the break that they had been waiting for. The reception wasn't excellent, but the words they captured would give the analysts in Langley hours of work, and in today's call, they got the first glimpse of what it was they were dealing with and that it was going to happen relatively soon. Their intercepts were encrypted and spotty, based on the filters that were on Esa's computer.

The driver of the Suburban started the engine, as he realized that Esa and Allison were headed down to the street to catch their ride. They followed the limo at a discreet distance and continued their surveillance as best they could in the city. Reception improved as they moved away from the concrete jungle.

db

As they snuggled in the backseat, Esa thought they needed to discuss the baby. In his religion, it was getting close to the time that the fetus would gain its soul and make abortion a violation of his beliefs.

"Honey, what are we going to do about this baby?"

Allison tensed immediately, and Esa felt it. The softness of her shoulder under his arm turned rock hard.

"What do you mean, what are we going to do about *this baby*?" she asked indignantly.

"Allison, I want to have the baby aborted."

"That is out of the question."

As in their prior conversations about the baby, the end result was always the same—a big argument followed by silence—and tonight was no exception. The conversation was going nowhere.

Understanding how Hajji would receive the news of a pregnancy, Esa realized that he might have to take matters into his own hands.

The black Suburban took its parking place in the cottages near the entrance to Esa and Allison's gated community. Inside their cottage, they resumed their regular nightly positions, taking turns with the headsets and recordings. The bugs inside the Manns' home worked better than the ones in the city.

Chapter 37

Mifflintown, Pennsylvania – April 3, 2015

"I'm a great believer in luck, and I find the harder I work, the more I have of it."

—*Thomas Jefferson*

C raig had just returned to his apartment and picked up his secure satphone to call Harrisburg. His first two weeks at McNichols had gone smoothly, and as he had expected, he was able to handle his job duties without any problems. Yar Din appeared to be pleased with his progress.

"Hello, Wayne."

Wayne was expecting his call. Mike Adams was also listening on the speakerphone in his office to get the update from McNichols.

"How's it going, Craig?"

"Things are well."

"So you are able to hold down that janitor's job?" Wayne joked.

Ignoring the wise guy comment, Craig continued. "I have had casual conversations with most of the other night shift employees and even took a break with Jamil Khoury. I was reading my Quran in the lunchroom when he asked if he could join me. He asked me if I was a 'true believer.'"

190

Craig, understanding the jargon of the religion, had said yes, but went on to explain in detail that he was a recent convert. This break-time conversation had set the stage to get closer within the operation. He reported that the Khourys worked in the maintenance department and that this gave them great flexibility to roam around the plant. In addition to their flexibility, it gave them access to large metal-cutting equipment that was used to manufacture replacement parts for the plant's equipment. They had a vast amount of raw steel at their disposal, and both had been trained in programming computer numerical control machines. These machines, known as CNC machines, are designed to cut perfect parts from instructions generated by computer-aided design, or CAD, files.

"Access to these machines could give them the ability to generate components for outside jobs quite easily under management's nose."

Wayne and Mike made eye contact while Craig continued to give them the lay of the land from the inside.

"My job allows me the ability to roam as well. The maintenance/machine shop is part of my normal runs, so I'm going through there two or three times daily."

Most of this information had already been picked up from their conversations with Jason. The Khourys' only supervision was Yar Din, which made for a very convenient setup.

"Now that they think I'm Muslim, I have started to join them for the last break of the day—their morning prayer time in the warehouse—and I feel like I have earned their trust. I have started to use some radical rhetoric, and I expect that, in the very near future, they will be recruiting me to their cause."

"Great job, Craig!" both Mike and Wayne said simultaneously.

Wayne went on to say, "Keep us posted, and be careful. Talk to you later. Thanks, Craig."

Wayne and Mike hung up and immediately began adding this information to the huge digital screen that filled one whole wall of their conference area.

They had figured that the McNichols connection would be providing hardware of some kind for the al-Qaeda plan—that was not a surprise. What puzzled them was the fact that there were only three of them in the plant. The automation and speed of the CNC equipment could explain the need for so few people, but they remained curious.

Homeland Security was intimately familiar with how the al-Qaeda cell system worked. Wayne doubted that McNichols-Mifflintown would supply all of the hardware, but they were beginning to better understand the project.

What they hadn't shared with Craig was the beefed-up surveillance of the Din compound. They had sent a team of two more people into the area to see what they could uncover with the use of their best technology. Within Homeland Security, great strides had been made in sharing information within DHS and with the other intelligence agencies, but there were still some holes in the system. In fact, Wayne was not sharing everything he had on the plant with the entire grid, partly out of selfishness and partly out of fear of something going wrong. He had dragged one of his closest friends into the process, and he was going to be extra cautious of calling undue attention to Mifflintown, Pennsylvania.

He had heard in a project briefing that there were suspected cells operating in Boston, Los Angeles, Nashville, and Chicago, all working on the same project. Communications had been tracked connecting all of these cells through what appeared to be the hub in New York, but this information was sketchy and high level. All the details remained in offices like his, and each agent had his or her own ideas how to best solve the riddle. Consequently, there were missing pieces and gaps in the intelligence.

db

It was Friday night and Wayne needed a weekend, but as he looked at the digital wall clock, his e-mail folder, and the mess on his desk, he knew the possibility of that was slim. It was late and he was tired, so he decided to pack up his laptop, grab a few folders to take home, and leave. On his way to his apartment, he would call Jason to fill him on what he had learned.

It was a cool early-spring evening, and he was excited to finally see some life return to the barren Pennsylvania landscape. Spring was his favorite season, but he wasn't sure what this spring would bring.

Jason picked up on the first ring, and Wayne knew why. Jason was anxious and alone; Wayne was the only person whom he could share his concerns with.

"What's happening?" Jason asked immediately, and it wasn't in the form of a hello. He really wanted to know what was going on.

Wayne went into *nearly* all the details that Craig had covered.

"Things are going well, and we're actually a bit ahead of schedule."

"Have you learned anything about McNichols headquarters? Have any names surfaced?"

"Sorry, Jason, if there has been any, they have not been passed on to my office as of yet. It's probably best you don't know."

"I understand," Jason replied, then added, "You should know that, yesterday, Din asked for permission to work his maintenance guys, including Craig, overtime this weekend."

"Interesting. That's actually very good news. Jason, try to have a good weekend."

db

Huddled in the bushes two hundred yards away from Yar Din's compound, three DHS electronic surveillance specialists monitored activity. Each was tuned into a different home, eavesdropping on the Saudis.

Yar had walked out his front door, and shortly after that, the Khoury twins exited as well. All three were headed for the outbuilding/mosque. One of the twins jumped into the driver's seat of his pickup truck and backed it up to the double doors. The other two were already hauling items from the building, and judging by how slowly they were moving, they were very heavy. They took turns, and after loading a couple dozen pieces of whatever it was into the truck, they threw a large tarp over the truck bed and tied it down securely.

The agents dropped their headsets and began taking pictures. The Saudis' every move was being documented with three heat-sensitive cameras through the highest-quality telephoto lens. While two of them took pictures, the third agent pulled out a sophisticated piece of equipment that could perform a complete chemical analysis from a remote location. He targeted the long, heavy bars, and a green light along with a small, barely audible beep registered when the bars had been identified. He then checked several more loads to confirm that all of the bars were the same and discovered that indeed they were. He was astonished, however, to see *palladium* show up on the digital readout of the detector. Millions of dollars' worth of metal had just been loaded into the back of a beat-up old Toyota pickup truck.

The three men returned to their homes and prepared to leave for work. It was Saturday, but since the managing director had given his approval, Yar was bringing his maintenance crew in to work overtime hours on the machines. No production would be going on—only maintenance.

Before the Saudis had reentered their homes, the digital images were in route to Harrisburg.

One of the agents followed the truck to McNichols, where he observed and documented the bars being unloaded from the truck. Din served as lookout, while the Khourys did all the manual labor.

The puzzle pieces were taking shape.

Chapter 38

Antioch, Tennessee – April 6, 2015

"Discontent is the first necessity of progress."

—*Thomas A. Edison*

Nafi attempted to pick up where Taj had left off, but it was difficult. Today was the third class since the break for Taj's death. He was feeling a bit more comfortable, but he was still uneasy.

Attendance had dropped off, but the inner circle still showed up for every class. Publicly, they supported Nafi, but privately, they expressed how much they missed Taj. The word around the AIC confirmed that there was some doubt in people's minds if he was ready for this transition. In the original plan, Nafi was to sit under Taj for at least four more years; he needed that time with Hatem, he needed further mentoring and teaching, but there would be no more of either.

At the Istanbul following class, there was more discussion of the void Taj's loss had created. Everyone was involved with the discussion—everyone but Fadi, who was uncharacteristically quiet.

Fadi had heard enough. It seemed to him that the imam's image inflated more and more as time went on. In Fadi's mind, Taj was deadweight and wasn't contributing anything to *his* group; his cell was much stronger as a result of Taj's death.

"Let's get down to some business. As I've told you before, Taj would want us to continue."

Fadi suggested—with a straight face and with all the sincerity he could muster—that they work diligently to accomplish tasks in Taj's honor.

"I have our work schedule. My boss passed on some information to me about our schedule and gave me permission to share it. All of the components need to be completed and distributed throughout the country by the end of May. We are currently on schedule to accomplish that, but to put it in perspective for all of you, we are only one-third if the way finished."

Fadi had the schedule planned out precisely, with a customized sheet for each guy—only two of them were permitted to arrive or leave at the same time.

"Guys, I need to emphasize what a dangerous neighborhood it is, so be careful, and if you own a weapon, carry it. I know many of you have been accumulating materials, so bring them to the warehouse. I want everything in our possession as fast as possible. We need to get a handle on our inventory."

"Sir, do you want us to bring everything we have immediately?" Wazir asked.

"Were you just listening? Yes, within reason and within the physical limits of the materials." Fadi acted a bit disturbed by the interruption, then continued. "I have asked Jerome to fill the slot left by Taj in tracking and logging our inventory."

Fadi had selected Jerome Parks for three reasons: first of all, being African American, he would be able to come and go to the warehouse with the least amount of attention; secondly, the warehouse was very convenient to where he lived with his mother on the south side of Nashville; and lastly, being a manager at McDonald's gave him the ability to control his work schedule and the number of hours he had to work, all of which would be beneficial down the home stretch.

"Gentlemen, I'm sure I do not have to remind you of the importance of what we are going to accomplish. My boss was very excited after his last meeting with Ahsan. I don't know any of the details but they are beginning to unfold the project. He pledged to let us know as soon he can, and until then, he appreciated what we are doing and promised me that we will not be disappointed. A very high level of paradise awaits us."

Those words reverberated in Basel's head. He'd been taught his entire life that dying as a martyr in a fight against the infidels would be rewarded by a place in paradise—a high place filled with virgins—but as he'd been reading the Bible and having his discussions with Kyle, a shadow of doubt had entered his thinking. What if Muhammad was not a prophet of Allah? What if his promises in the Quran were bogus? Basel contemplated being damned to hell for his participation in the operation. Working for the death of innocent people was not as appealing as it had been prior to his ride from the airport with the Christian zealot. His doubts about Islam were growing as fast as his fascination with the man named Jesus.

"As soon as my boss gives me the information and the ability to share it with you, I promise I will. That's all I have for you right now. Please review the schedules and let me know immediately if there are any problems. You will have one opportunity to have me adjust your days. After that, you are expected to be present or find a substitute from the team to work for you. I will not be a nursemaid. Go in peace. *Alhamdulillah!*"

"*Alhamdulillah!*"

Chapter 39

Washington, DC – April 7, 2015

"Government is not reason; it is not eloquent; it is force. Like fire, it is a dangerous servant and a fearful master."

—*George Washington*

In a huge war room of the Homeland Security headquarters, there was an electronic board similar to but much larger than the one in the Harrisburg field office. It was early morning and a skeleton crew was working; the budget cuts had limited staff in all but absolutely essential areas, the majority of which was assigned to the nine-to-five shifts. This war room was solely dedicated to Peace Shield, the code name of an operation that DHS had been monitoring for nearly a year. And finally, the picture was beginning to come into focus.

Cliff Hill leaned back in one of the conference room chairs, with his hands clasped behind his head. He found that the early morning hours were the best time for him to think, as he could survey the board without distractions. This was his baby; he was the agent in charge (AIC) of the whole operation.

Cliff had been in DHS since its creation in 2002 and had worked his way up through the ranks. He now reported directly to the secretary of DHS. She had the utmost confidence in him and his direct reports, which she had demonstrated in naming him the AIC of the most significant perceived threat to the United States since 9/11.

Cliff studied the board, hoping that something would jump out at him. As new intelligence surfaced, he was given dotted-line oversight of the reporting field staffs. This gave him more resources, but with the reduced budgets, everyone feared for their jobs. Tied closely to this was the fact that every agent wanted to show his or her value to the department. This protectionism tended to interfere with the free flow of information. Critical things were passed on, but sometimes all the details were not. Agents felt if they could solve the puzzle, they would be the "star," giving them job security. Unfortunately, this jeopardized national security. Knowing this, Cliff had his morning war room ritual.

He was a top-notch analyst in his own right. Prior to joining DHS, he worked with the CIA at Langley, where he concentrated on Pakistan and Afghanistan, but more specifically, on al-Qaeda and the Taliban organizations. He observed bin Laden's rise to power by pushing the Russians out of Afghanistan. In bin Laden's mind, Allah was blessing his jihad. As Cliff watched the second jet slam into the World Trade Center, he knew immediately that bin Laden was behind the attack and shared that insight with his boss at that instant. As a result, he earned the immediate respect of his chief and others watching the Middle East.

As he studied, he tried to fill in the gaps of Peace Shield. It was becoming obvious that the hub of the cell was New York. He knew that his New York field office had recorded conversations of the person who appeared to be the top guy. They had also pinpointed al-Qaeda operatives in Chicago, Boston, and Los Angeles who were heavily involved. Recently, something had popped up on the radar out of Central Pennsylvania—ironically, in the heart of the peace-loving Amish country. The Harrisburg field office had something going on at a tractor factory.

Concerned that he may not be getting one hundred percent of the information, Cliff decided to visit Harrisburg. He had hired Wayne Joseph and trained him when he first joined DHS, and as a result, they had a great, almost father-son relationship. There was mutual respect between them, but he still wanted to take a firsthand look. He opened his tablet and sent an electronic note to his office coordinator to arrange for a car; he wanted to be on the road by 9:00 a.m. He would call Wayne on the way to let him know he was coming.

His thoughts returned to the board. *Am I missing something?*

Chapter 40

New York City – April 7, 2015

"Abortion is the ultimate violence."

—Robert Casey

Esa was getting nowhere with his discussions about aborting their baby. It had become such a hot topic that the mere mention of it turned Allison's face red. He was stuck. He was certain Hajji would remove him from his position; a baby would be viewed as treason to the cause. Early in the pregnancy, he thought an abortion would eliminate the problem, but he hadn't anticipated Allison's reaction. The *cause* came above everything in his life, and Allah's plan must be completed. Esa knew that he had to take the termination of her pregnancy into his own hands.

His thoughts were often clearer when he saw them written down in black and white, so he pulled an old-fashioned yellow legal pad from his desk drawer and began to scribble some options:

Baby needs to be eliminated.
Allison refuses abortion.
What would Nasi Ahsan say about a baby?

Use drugs that would terminate pregnancy?
Arrange an accident?
Allison is interfering with Sky Burst.
Does Allison need be eliminated?
My feelings for her are confusing.
What would Ahsan say about my love for Allison?
Allison needs to be eliminated.

His assistant walked into his office to remind him of a meeting, so he quickly turned the pad upside down and welcomed his 9:00 a.m. appointment. He went through the motions of the meeting and was very cordial, but his mind was on the legal pad lying face down on his desk.

As soon as the gentleman left, he quickly returned to his desk and buzzed his assistant to tell her that he did not want to be disturbed before lunchtime. He looked at his notes. His love and dedication to Allah came first, as he knew the eternal rewards were much greater than the pleasure that he was experiencing from Allison in this world. He loved her and his love had grown, but he knew what he had to do.

His mind was made up as he reached for his encrypted cell phone.

"Mr. Paterson, this is Esa Mann. I have another project for you."

"Mr. Mann, I didn't expect to hear from you so soon, but it's a pleasure to talk with you again. What's up?"

"I think this might be a bit difficult for you to understand."

"Well, sir, I've been in this business a very long time. I'm almost fifty, and I started while I was still in high school. I don't think anything could shock me at this point. After all, the last time we spoke, you gave me a holy man to kill. Who is it that you want offed this time?"

"I need my wife eliminated."

Paterson was silent for a few seconds. "I don't need to know any details, and I will do whatever you want me to do, provided that the price is right."

"There's one more thing, Mr. Paterson. She's pregnant."

Paterson was a hardened murderer, and he had been hired to eliminate spouses in the past, but since hooking up with al-Qaeda, he thought that he had gotten past the domestic violence stage and moved into worldwide terrorism.

"I'll leave the technique up to you, and I would rather not know the timing, but I need to get it completed quickly. What will this cost me since it's coming out of my pocket instead of my project budget? I need you to cut me a break."

Paterson really didn't care which bucket of money it was coming from—a hit job was a hit job.

"I will give you a deal. I won't charge for the baby, and I charge less for women." Paterson possessed little regard for women since he had converted to Islam when he was twenty-two. "It will be a hundred and twenty-five thousand dollars now and one twenty-five when the job is done."

"Do it."

"Are there any special instructions like I had when I did the imam?"

"No. Just get it done quickly."

The phone clicked. Esa leaned back in his chair and recanted what had just transpired. He generated the wire transfer to move the first half of the fee to Paterson's numbered account.

To get his mind off his situation, he opened up the report from Rafid Almasi, his Los Angeles cell leader. He suddenly realized that he was shaking. *Allah, help me!*

ḋb

Within minutes after Esa's call, he received the electronic notice that the money had been deposited into his account, and so he went to work.

Compared to his last job with Esa, this was going to be a cakewalk. There were many accidents that could take the life of a young mother-to-be; he just needed to decide which way to go. Getting Esa's home address off the al-Qaeda database, he entered it into the computer to get the lay of the land. He could tell by the images that the road leading into their gated community was steep, with many sharp curves.

Like Taj, there could be no suspicion of foul play. Esa hadn't said that, but it went without saying in the terrorist world.

He knew that she worked at Esa's firm, so he figured they commuted together. Perhaps this needed to be a weekend job where an auto accident could happen during a shopping trip? The staged robbery route was another possibility, but there was sure to be an intense investigation.

He noticed that their house sat about fifty feet up from the surface of the street. There was no ice around anymore, but a fall and subsequent head injury could easily happen.

One thing he knew for sure was that he needed to get to New York, so in his tattered duffle bag, he packed only his essentials and a change of clothing. He didn't know how long it would take. If he needed any tools, he had connections on Long Island that would help him out. He went online and booked his flight.

Just another day en route to paradise. He rolled out his prayer mat for his noon prayers prior to heading off to Hartsfield International. It was a beautiful spring morning, and he was off to eliminate another obstacle for Esa.

Chapter 41

Harrisburg, Pennsylvania – April 7, 2015

"America will never seek a permission slip to defend the security of our people."

—*George W. Bush*

Cliff decided at the last minute to bring one of his analysts with him to Harrisburg. On his way back to his office from the war room, he stopped by the cubicle of his ace Arabic specialist.

"Hey, Teddy. Did you enjoy your day off yesterday?"

"Yes, sir. It was a beautiful day, and I got caught up on a million little annoying errands that I needed to do. What do I owe the pleasure of this visit from the AIC?" Teddy asked with a smirk.

Teddy was the young buck on Cliff's team and your typical super intelligent nerd. His IQ was literally off the charts, and since he was in elementary school, he'd had an incredible fascination with the Arab world. Before he was a teenager, he was fluent in Arabic and studied the Quran in its native translation. According to most Muslims, it was the only way to study their holy book; any translation distorted the words. He read Arabic history books and studied the culture from their point of view. He had two master's degrees from Princeton: one in computer science and the other in Arabic studies—the perfect combination for Cliff's Peace Shield team. Teddy had actually shown up on the FBI's watch list as a result of his interest is Islam. He was recorded visiting Arabic websites, ordering Arabic books, and so on. When the FBI investigated, they realized what an asset he would be and hired him right out of graduate school at the ripe old age of nineteen. He worked at the FBI for a few years before he was transferred to the heart of the country's efforts against terrorism. When Peace Shield was organized, Teddy Brewer's name came up as a key player, and Cliff recruited him heavily. If the truth be known, Teddy had no choice.

"I'm going to visit Wayne Joseph and his guys in Harrisburg and would like to take you with me."

Most Washington bureaucrats jumped at any chance to get away from their cubicles, but Teddy was different; he viewed it as a distraction from his mission.

"Do you really need me, Boss? I'm really on to something that is starting to get my attention in Boston, and I could really use the time to focus on that."

"Teddy, I need your attention on this thing in Central PA. Your knowledge of the entire picture will help me see if there's something the field guys are missing."

"OK. When are we leaving?"

"Grab your computer, and I'll meet you in the motor pool."

Within minutes of their conversation, they were sitting in the back of a fully equipped bulletproof black Suburban headed north on the Beltway. Teddy was able to work on the built-in desks that pulled up around the comfortable captain's chairs. The truck was outfitted with Internet access that exceeded the speed and reliability of most personal and commercial service providers. They had a direct feed from the DHS satellite with virtually no distortion or interference from other users.

Cliff called Wayne to give him notice. "Wayne, Teddy and I are en route to your office, and we'll be there shortly."

"Do you want us to prepare anything for your visit?"

Harrisburg, Pennsylvania – April 7, 2015

"No. Just clear your war room and we'll meet in there. We want to be briefed on Peace Shield, and I'm anxious to hear how your undercover guy is doing in that plant."

"You got it, Boss. We'll see you shortly."

Cliff and Teddy were focused in their own worlds as the driver exceeded the posted speed limits by twenty to twenty-five miles per hour the whole way. Their vehicle gave local authorities a designation, which in layman's terms meant: *Don't even think about pulling us over. We are on official government business.* They made what would normally be a two-hour-plus trip in less than an hour and a half.

db

Wayne contacted Mike via the intercom.

"Mike, we're going to have a visitor. Grab your stuff and meet me in the war room."

"I'll be there."

Mike and Wayne got their thoughts together. It wasn't unusual for Cliff to drop in unannounced. It was standard protocol and part of the side effects of working on extremely sensitive government information. As an agent, they always needed to be prepared. Knowing that Cliff would be focused on new information, Mike and Wayne pulled up all the most recent activity from McNichols front and center on their digital wall.

Wayne clarified, "We'll hit this new stuff immediately."

db

The receptionist buzzed directly through to Wayne's phone on his belt.

"Agent Hill is here."

"Send him right in."

Wayne excused everyone but Mike from the war room.

After the welcoming formalities were over, they sat down and focused on the board. Teddy had been here on several other occasions and spoke to Mike on almost a daily basis. Likewise, Wayne and Cliff worked closely together, so they dug in.

Wayne began. "We had a weekly debrief Friday evening with Craig Reeves, our guy on the inside."

Wayne disclosed the movement of materials that had taken place from the Din compound to the McNichols plant. On the board were the indication of the palladium that had been transported and the overtime authorization for the past weekend.

Teddy was fascinated with the metal. "Did you say palladium?"

"Yes, that's what our remote spectral analyzer identified it to be."

"That is a very interesting component." Something clicked for Teddy. "Wayne, if we hadn't come here today, exactly when were you217 going to share this info with me?"

"Cliff, we just got the info late Friday night, and my team was digesting it yesterday."

"But this is big. I would have liked to know about it Friday night or Saturday."

"Cliff, I realize that there is no room for this type of thinking in this business, but I have a personal involvement in this operation."

Cliff shook his head. He had forgotten for a moment how this lead in Mifflintown had originated. "Wayne, I think you are putting your friend, his family, and his plant at greater jeopardy by not keeping us informed."

"I'm scared, sir. I don't want any innocent people to get hurt."

"That is what we are *all* about!"

Teddy was bored by this conversation and wanted to dig into the palladium information. "Excuse me, guys, but can we get back to Peace Shield? How much palladium did they move into the plant, and did your instruments pick up any more material at their compound?"

"We estimated about fifteen hundred pounds, and all the scans of their buildings and houses did not turn up any more palladium."

"So we have it all at the plant—unless, of course, they have more on order. They must have been stockpiling it over time, as that big of a purchase would have drastically impacted the trading price."

"What are you thinking, Teddy?" Mike asked.

Teddy explained that it was a very rare metal with very limited uses, and as such, this information would be invaluable in helping him figure out what al-Qaeda was up to. "The value of that load sitting in McNichols is in excess of twenty million dollars." Teddy calculated in his head.

The four men stared at each other as they simultaneously reached the same conclusion. The dollar value of that material in the hands of three low-level operatives meant that the overall scope of their plan was unimaginable.

They wrapped up their meeting by passing on how successful Craig Reeves had been in his undercover job.

Wayne explained, "Yar Din has recruited him to be a part of their cell."

"Excellent!"

As they said their good-byes, Cliff pulled Wayne aside and told him that he understood his situation. "Trust me, son, I will do everything in my power to protect Mr. Lange and his family. I suspect that these guys will very quietly complete the component of whatever device they are working on, totally under the radar, with no plans to injure the people of Mifflintown—for now."

"Thanks, Cliff. I appreciate your understanding. But God help us all if we can't stop whatever it is that they are up to."

"We are going to stop it. We have no choice."

Chapter 42

Al-Qaeda Headquarters, Afghanistan – April 8, 2015

"I'm fighting so I can die a martyr and go to heaven to meet God. Our fight now is against the Americans."

—Osama bin Laden

Nasi leaned back in his overstuffed chair and surveyed the world via his TV monitors. He was thankful to Allah for so many things and was convinced that Allah's desire for him was to be successful in what could be his last great accomplishment.

He almost couldn't help but smile. He and Dalil Ally were an ominous pair. Ahsan was bold in his beliefs and a natural leader, which combined nicely with Ally's organizational skills. They were unstoppable.

With all the modern conveniences of technology at his disposal, Ahsan was still a bit old-fashioned. He didn't have a computer, tablet, or even a satellite cell phone for his personal use. His people, mostly Ally, provided everything he needed. He even asked Ally to keep a loose-leaf binder updated on Sky Burst so he could readily check the progress of all five territories. This notebook was a private nuance between Ally and him, since he didn't want anyone else to know that he relied on such an ancient method of tracking his sophisticated operation.

Looking at his book, he realized that tomorrow was when all the intricate sets of drawings, computer files, and other details would be disseminated around the world. The system was such that each of the five world territories contained five cells. The subdivision of work was equally divided throughout the five cells, and every world territory had the skill level to accomplish its mission. So as Ally planned the disbursement of information, an army of twenty-five couriers was ready to be dispatched to hand-deliver all the vital information around the world. It was a masterful, well-organized plan.

When the couriers arrived, each cell would have a very clear picture of its piece in the puzzle, but they still wouldn't know or understand how it fit within al-Qaeda's overall plan.

Malcolm Shane had labored over the intricate detail that went into each device. The devices were tested successfully in the laboratory, and then scaled-down versions were detonated in the mountains surrounding their headquarters. In all cases, they disabled any electronic equipment within the vicinity. Following these successful scale-model tests, Dr. Shane simply had to calculate the full-size dimensions and break them down into easy-to-complete tasks. He led this process, but a team of accomplished scientists did the work. They checked and double-checked each other's work to make sure that there wouldn't be problems in the field. They had to make the process so straightforward that even totally unsophisticated cell members could follow them. The instructions were provided in English as well as meticulously translated in the native tongue of each cell member. Photographs, where appropriate, accompanied the step-by-step plans.

Ally would hear from each courier following the successful delivery of the plans. Each was to text a code back to him, which could only be accomplished with missing numbers provided by the twenty-five cell leaders. This fail-safe method made sure that the plans were delivered, and delivered to the correct person. Every detail had been considered.

Hajji called for Ally and Dr. Shane to join him in his office, where he greeted them both with a big smile.

"Gentlemen, today marks a big milestone in our battle against the infidels, and I wanted to get together with you to *toast* the occasion."

His gesture was tongue-in-cheek since toasting was not a custom in the Middle East; in fact, the Quran forbid the use of alcohol in any form. But in a mockery of Western customs and to celebrate the milestone, Hajji poured three tall glasses of mint iced tea.

Holding his glass up and toward the other two, he said, "Here's to the completion of a major milestone."

The three laughed as they clinked glasses.

Dr. Shane couldn't help himself. "Cheers!"

Chapter 43

Mifflintown, Pennsylvania – April 9, 2015

"Be courteous to all, but intimate with few, and let those few be well tried before you give them your confidence."

—George Washington

An elegantly-dressed gentleman knocked on Yar's door shortly after 1:00 p.m. Yar had alerted Raja that a package would be arriving, but she had pictured a UPS-type delivery guy making the drop-off.

"Good afternoon, madam. I have a delivery for Mr. Din. May I see him?"

Knowing that the package was direct from Hajji, she invited the distinguished-looking man into her living room while she woke up Yar.

Yar had never really fallen into a deep sleep.

Rubbing his eyes, he greeted the courier. "Hello, sir. I'm Yar Din."

"I need your signature on this receipt," the courier said, handing his tablet computer to Yar. He then presented Yar with an impressive leather briefcase, which appeared totally natural in the hands of the executive, but completely out of place in the stubble-faced Saudi's possession.

As the briefcase was given to him, Yar provided the courier with the code that he needed to report back to Ally.

"There is an e-mail in your secure inbox that contains the combination to open it. Everything in the case will be self-explanatory. Have a good rest of the day, and may Allah richly bless you and your endeavors."

He was gone as quickly as he had come.

Yar asked Raja to gather the Khoury twins and their wives and meet him in the outbuilding. He went to his e-mail.

db

Yar placed the case on the table as everyone huddled around. He entered the combination and instantaneously heard the mechanism move and the latches snap open. It was suspenseful, as they all realized that they would finally know more about their mission.

Inside the case were detailed plans drawn and notated in English and their native Arabic. It also included a flash drive labeled "CNC Programming" that would handle the program for the powerful cutting machines at McNichols. They could quickly see the shapes of their pieces, but they were still not able to figure out what it was they were doing.

They now knew that they were making components of something and that they needed to be completed by the end of May.

They immediately scanned the drawings and instructions, made two physical copies, and stored them in safes in two of their homes. They also made copies of the files on the flash drive. These instructions were all in the case, and they followed them meticulously.

Perhaps the piece of the instruction case that got them most excited was the personal note signed by Hajji himself. He thanked them for their dedication and support of al-Qaeda's efforts in the jihad.

db

Henry stopped by Jason's office on his way back from lunch.

"Hey, Jason. Can we talk for a moment?"

"Sure, Henry. Come on in and have a seat. What can I do for you?"

"Jason, I respect you and have followed your instructions in regard to the night shift, and as you said it would, production numbers have improved."

"I feel like there is a 'but' coming." Jason smiled.

"Yes, there is."

Henry pleaded his case and wanted to dig back into the production issues he felt were not where they should have been.

"I really need to visit with Mr. Din. After all, he does still report to me, doesn't he? He sent me a note yesterday asking why I wasn't coming by to meet with him anymore."

Jason had been hoping that this wouldn't pop up again, but he wasn't surprised that it had. He was actually surprised that Henry hadn't pushed back sooner.

"Go ahead and meet with him, but don't come down on him for his numbers, as I am working on that situation."

Henry walked away feeling like he had just been patted on the head by his father and told to go outside and play. He was upset but tried not to show it.

Jason, however, sensed his frustration.

d̈b

As soon as Henry had left, Jason called Wayne.

"Wayne, it's JL."

"What's going on? Is there a problem?" Wayne asked quickly.

"Well, yes, there is."

215

Jason related the conversation that he'd had with Henry, explaining how Henry had obediently followed his commands but was feeling uneasy about the situation, as now even Din was wondering why he hadn't been around.

"Wayne, I need to ask you to trust me on this. There is not a more reliable, more trustworthy person in the world than Henry Koontz, and I want your permission to let him in on what we have going on here. I owe it to him, and I think it best for all of us."

"Jason, it's dangerous for him to know more than he does now."

"I think it's more dangerous for us if he doesn't."

"Bring him in, but tell him that it's a matter of national security and he can't tell a soul—not even his wife."

"His wife passed away several weeks ago, and he lives by himself. If I tell him not to breathe a word of it to anyone, he'll take the secret to his grave."

"JL, I've been putting you through a lot. I would prefer that you're the only one who knows what's going on, but I'll yield to your judgment."

db

Jason buzzed his assistant. "Please ask Henry to step back in here."

Chapter 44

Antioch, Tennessee – April 9, 2015

"God's angels often protect his servants from potential enemies."

—*Billy Graham*

From the day that Kyle had shown up at Taj's funeral to comfort him, Basel knew that he had a special friend who legitimately cared about him. When they got together last Monday, they had decided that it would best if they picked a day and time when they would meet weekly. Thursday seemed to work for both of them.

Kyle and Basel showed up at the bookstore at nearly the same time, grabbed their drinks, and found a secluded table. There was no formal agenda, and they just dived into whatever questions each had about the other's faith.

Basel began their discussion. "The thing that confuses me about your Bible is that very few Christians read it in the original language, and then, on top of that, there are countless variations in translations."

Kyle chuckled, as he appreciated how they could openly tell each other their honest feelings. "You're right about that. It is difficult to find a translation that works best for each individual, and very few of us are fluent in Greek or Hebrew. There are huge debates within my faith regarding the validity of the various translations, and some Christians argue that the King James Version is the *only* legitimate translation that was authorized by the king in the early 1600s. The other translations that came after that were to make the Bible easier for people to read and understand," Kyle concluded, wanting to move on to another topic. The translation issue was a difficult one for Muslims to comprehend; they believed that the Quran should only be read in the original Arabic. Kyle asked, "Do you have such a thing as Quran studies where you break down the words of the Quran to see what Allah is trying to tell you?"

"No. The words of Allah are the words of Allah, and any study of those words would be an admission of doubt. We accept the words of the Quran as a direct revelation from Allah—no questions asked."

Kyle could see that he had jumped out of the frying pan and into the fire. *Next topic*, he thought as he went over his notes. "Can we switch to a discussion of Muhammad?"

Basel smiled. "Yes, but be careful."

"Muhammad had some questionable things in his life. How does that sit with you? Shouldn't a prophet be a near-perfect reflection of a holy man?" Kyle immediately wanted to take back his words.

"Muhammad is the vessel through which Allah delivered his word to us. Any discussion of Allah's vessel is blasphemous. Sorry, my friend, but our discussion is not going well today. Let's finish our coffees and plan to get together next week."

They finished up their time with some small talk about each other's job (or in Kyle's case, job search), family, and friends. No hurt feelings or sensitive topics—they had had enough for one day.

As Kyle drove back to his apartment, he called his friend from church, Al, who had converted from Islam, to talk about today's session. He felt awkward, and he didn't want to ruin the relationship he had built with Basel. His friend confirmed what he had learned the hard way. The sanctity and validity of the Quran was held near and dear to Muslims. Muslims perceived their holy book as the revelation of God, and questioning the Quran would be like Christians questioning Christ.

"I hope Basel shows up next week," he said out loud to himself.

Fadi had been alerted that his instruction kit would be delivered sometime after noon and that he should remain at his apartment. There was a loud knock on the door, and as Fadi viewed his visitor through the peephole, he saw a dignified middle-aged man in a dark suit and tie who stood imposingly with his head silhouetted by the dazzling sunshine. Fadi opened the door and invited the man into his foyer.

"Mr. Hares, I have your instructions here for you."

"Thank you, sir."

"Please sign here." The courier handed Fadi his tablet computer and a stylus to sign his name. "Everything will be very clear." With that, he presented Fadi with a very expensive-looking briefcase. "You will have an e-mail with the combination to open the case in your secure inbox."

After Fadi had provided the courier with the code he needed to report back to Afghanistan, he left.

"Have a good day, Mr. Hares, and may Allah bless you in your mission."

With the e-mail in hand, Fadi opened the case in the quiet of his bedroom. The plans were all there, along with the bilingual instructions.

From his discussions with Esa, he knew that he needed to complete the instructions found in the case by the end of May, but he didn't have any more details now. He could tell that his cell was going to be doing some programming and electronics work on whatever it was they were doing.

Fadi had arranged to have all the guys meet at the warehouse on their staggered shifts. This case would give them clear direction for the next forty-five days. His confidence also grew stronger after experienced the precision in which his instructions had been delivered. It was obvious to him that al-Qaeda was in control of the mission, Operation Sky Burst, and that every detail had been thought through meticulously. There was nothing left to chance. He was in good hands, and the infidels would never forget what it was they were working on.

ḋb

"O you who believe! When the call is made for prayer on Friday, then hasten to the remembrance of God and leave off business; that is better for you, if you know."

With these words from Quran 62:10 in mind, Nafi readied himself for the biggest service of the week at the AIC. He had been preparing and practicing his khutbah (sermon) all week and planned to continue his rehearsal right up until his delivery, just before Jumu'ah. Attendance was mandatory for all male members of the mosque, and women were also permitted to attend. He knew there would be hundreds of people there—hundreds of people comparing him to his mentor, Taj Hatem. Following the Jumu'ah, he was also responsible for leading a communal prayer.

In the folklore of their faith, a companion of Muhammad reported, "When it is Friday, the angels stand at every door of the mosque and record the people in order of arrival, and when the Imam sits on the pulpit for delivering the khutba they fold up their sheets and listen to the mention of Allah, the speech." If the pressure from the members were not enough, Nafi also had to please the angels at the doors to the mosque.

Chapter 45

Fairfield, Connecticut – April 9, 2015

"The resolution to avoid an evil is seldom framed till the evil is so far advanced as to make avoidance impossible."

—*Thomas Hardy*

Paterson arrived at LaGuardia with duffle bag in hand, rented a car, and was off to Fairfield. He had been thinking about this job ever since Esa had hired him. He wasn't concerned; Allison Mann didn't compare to the enemies of al-Qaeda whom he normally handled. Not knowing what he was going to do and not wanting to involve Esa, he kept everything to himself, stored neatly in the evil corner of his mind reserved for thinking about murder.

He checked into an old-fashioned cabin-style motel at the base of the hill near the Manns' gated community. As soon as he had thrown his bag in the closet, he took off on foot, under the cover of the early spring night. Only a sliver of the moon in a cloudy sky fractured the pitch-black darkness. His dark jacket and black stocking cap made him almost invisible when he got away from the fancy streetlights of their neighborhood. The Manns' enormous house was situated on top of a hill. There were four garages, but Esa had told him that Allison's car always stayed outside. It angered Esa, as the sun was doing a number on her convertible top, but it was one of those battles that he wasn't going to win, so the six-figure Porsche was taking a beating from the weather.

Allison and Esa had not arrived from the city yet, but their staff was busy throughout the house. Paterson just observed. He noticed steps from the house that led down to where her car was parked. A trip wire could be easily camouflaged but could possibly catch the maid, maintenance guy, or even Esa by mistake, and even if it did catch Allison's ankles, it might break an arm instead of a skull.

He continued to observe. Their automatic gates opened, and a black town car pulled into their drive. A gated house in a gated community seemed a bit superfluous to him, but what did he know? He was just a hired killer.

Esa and Allison exited the car and walked arm in arm through the back door. Watching them, one never would have guessed that one of them wanted the other dead.

Esa, besides telling Paterson which car she drove, had also told him that she only drove it on the weekend, but her weekend drive was a ritual she hardly ever missed.

Paterson needed to tell Esa not to use her car; he had decided on his plan. He huddled in a dark corner of the property and waited until the outdoor lighting system turned off and the occupants of the house had apparently settled down.

Grabbing his tool kit from his jacket pocket, he crawled under her car and disconnected the car's break lines in the front-left wheel. He calculated that, the way the car was tilted, all the brake fluid would be drained by Saturday. She would have enough fluid and pressure to stop her as she pulled out of her driveway, but after that, it would be a free fall down the hilly road. She might make the first hairpin turn, but not the second. He doubted that she would survive the accident, but for added insurance, he tapped into the car's computer and disabled all the air bags so the front and side panels would not activate.

He hiked back to his cabin home away from home and settled into the warm bed and thick comforter. He was exhausted from his hiking and day of travel. He knew he would sleep well tonight. He never noticed the black Suburban that was parked in the back of the lot near cabin No. 10.

After their dinner, Allison and Esa went their separate ways: Esa to his home office to continue working and Allison to the couch to crash and watch some foolish reality show on TV. She was experiencing the exhaustion that came during the first trimester of pregnancy.

Esa went straight to his secure e-mail, where he learned that all twenty-five of the couriers had been successful today. The details had been intricately planned; even the number of countries and then the number of cells within each one was significant to Hajji. Five was an important number for Muslims in that there were Five Core Beliefs and the Five Pillars of Islam. It wasn't an accident that Hajji had selected *five* countries and that each country had *five* cells. Hajji followed the example set by bin Laden, who was also a proponent of symbolism, even down to the selection of the date 9/11 for the Manhattan Raid.

On September 11, 1697, the Ottomans (Muslim Turks) suffered defeat in the Battle of Zenta in which Prince Eugene of Savoy and his troops killed twenty thousand Ottomans, seized the Ottoman treasury (with its artillery and provisions), and captured ten of the sultan's wives. After the battle, the treaty of Karlowitz was signed, ceding Croatia, Hungary, Transylvania, and Slavonia to Austria. It was a dark day in the history of the religion—one that bin Laden wanted to etch into the minds of all Americans, one he wanted to avenge.

There were other theories regarding why September 11th had been selected, but Esa had heard it directly from the source, in a private conversation he'd had with Osama while working for him in Afghanistan.

Although tried, Esa couldn't stop thinking about the fate that lay ahead for Allison. He knew the cause had to come first in his life, but he also knew that he was going to miss his wife—his arrangement that had turned into a love affair.

Chapter 46

Washington, DC – April 9, 2015

"It is possible to provide security against other ills, but as far as death is concerned, we men live in a city without walls."

—*Epicurus*

Teddy had slept very little in the past two days. He started working on his palladium theories on the ride home from Harrisburg, and his findings were alarming. As he had speculated, there weren't very many uses for the rare metal. He ran some calculations and concluded that the purchase of that much palladium would have dramatically impacted the commodities price. That being the case, and since there were no obvious spikes in the price of the metal, Teddy hypothesized that it had been purchased over a period of time and perhaps at several different locations. He gathered his thoughts, grabbed his notes, and rushed into Agent Hill's office, not stopping to be announced by his assistant, who guarded her boss carefully. She saw only a blur as Teddy hurried past.

"Agent Hill, I have something big," Teddy said, ignoring Hill's assistant, who was trying to head him off at the pass.

"I'm so sorry, sir. Teddy, please come with me, and I'll set you up an appointment."

The agent spoke up, knowing what Teddy was working on. "No, Janet, it's OK. I'll meet with Mr. Brewer right now, and please close my door on your way out."

The frustration was obvious in her face as she turned and grabbed the door.

"What is going on, Teddy?"

"I've been researching this high volume of palladium since we returned from our meeting on Tuesday, and what I'm finding is not good."

db

President Wheeler's secretary of the Department of Homeland Security sat at her desk going over the public appearances that she was scheduled to make in the next couple of months. Deborah Knowles was only the fourth secretary in department's brief history.

With terrorist activities on the wane, her job had evolved into more or less a PR position for the Wheeler administration, representing the US government at anything from state funerals to commencement addresses and reviewing state immigration policies and procedures. None of which was what she had expected when she left the Senate for the cabinet post, but she was enjoying it nonetheless. She loved the people of South Carolina, but she didn't miss their complaints and issues.

Her assistant buzzed her. "Madam Secretary, Agent Hill and Mr. Brewer have requested an immediate meeting with you."

Removing the travel brochures from her desk, she responded, "Please send them in."

She knew that Hill was working on one of the few "hot" operations that were going on under her watch, so she was anxious to hear why they had requested an urgent meeting.

"Excuse us for the unplanned meeting, but we have something important that you need to be briefed on immediately."

Hill and Brewer tag-teamed what had transpired in the last two days since their weekly Monday-morning staff meeting. Her eyes got wide, and her pulse quickened.

Brewer dived directly into the details. "Madam, the only explanation that I could come up with what would utilize this amount of the precious metal detected in Mifflintown is for use in electromagnetic pulse weapons."

She could feel perspiration forming on her forehead and palms. She had been briefed on EMP devices when she was a member of the Senate Committee on Armed Services. Her subcommittee, Emerging Threats and Capabilities, had heard from worldwide EMP experts. She knew of the devastating effects that the use of these devices on US shores could mean, but in those same hearings, she also remembered learning that the threat of a broad-reaching attack was almost nil.

"Palladium is ideal for use in nonnuclear devises as a result of its paramagnetic properties."

He proceeded to get deep into highly technical details, which were way over the secretary and Hill's heads.

Agent Hill interrupted. "Teddy, let's stick to the high-level facts."

Madam Secretary took the break in the presentation to ask a question from her limited knowledge base on EMP devices. "I thought that the consensus opinion was that they presented a relatively low threat to our national security?"

"Yes, Secretary Knowles, that has been the widespread consensus, but the volumes that we are talking about here appear to be a real threat."

Agent Hill spoke up. "The amount of palladium could indicate that they are planning a massive attack on our country."

"The discovery of this amount of palladium in suspected terrorists' hands could mean a nationwide nonnuclear electromagnetic pulse, or NNEMP, attack

227

that could render our defenses, not to mention our electronic infrastructure, useless," Brewer added.

Noticeably shaken and looking at Agent Hill, she asked, "What do you suggest?"

"Madame Secretary, we have to issue a security advisory."

She knew he was right, but the country had been operating at a Blue Level, or "guarded" condition, for so long that the thought of rising to a higher level was a new experience for her and this administration.

"What level do you think—Orange?"

"No, Red Level. We need to alert everyone about the severe risk of a terrorist attack. We need all citizens and agencies to be on the lookout for suspicious behavior. Red will raise everyone's consciousness and allow you and President Wheeler flexibility to handle the crisis without congressional approvals."

Knowing that the threat level had only reached "severe" once in the history of the advisory system, she was reluctant to go there based on the information of the palladium, but she realized from other briefings and meetings that there was a lot of chatter throughout the al-Qaeda organization and a clearer picture of what their plans were was formulating.

She picked up her direct line to President Wheeler. "Sir, this is Deborah. We have a situation that requires your immediate attention."

db

The trio was whisked from DHS headquarters to the side entrance of the White House and rushed to an emergency meeting of the president's Joint Chiefs of Staff. Upon hearing Secretary Knowles's briefing, the president agreed that the nation had to be placed on guard and that he needed to make the announcement personally. Press Secretary Ford also agreed, and they excused themselves to go work on the bullet points to be covered. Ford had been getting bits and pieces of intelligence from the President's Daily Brief (PDB), and now it was beginning to make more sense. When he was finished with the president, he quietly slipped off to send the information to his boss. This was not good news.

db

Approximately two hours later, Secretary Knowles sat in the front row of the press briefing room as President Wheeler walked in and took the podium behind the usual assortment of network microphones. The video cameras remained idle as the journalists stood to show their respect to the president. They all thought that this was going to be a typical noneventful press briefing from the president's press secretary and were surprised to see President Wheeler appear. There wasn't time to notify their networks, so they broke out their recorders and tablet computers, while the more astute networks broke into their afternoon programming.

"Ladies and gentlemen, I have grave news to deliver this afternoon."

With that preamble and subsequent explanation of the escalation in Homeland Security's terrorist threat level to Red, the press core was visibly shaken and frantically sending out electronic notes from the meeting. Twitter erupted around the world. As was typical with threat level changes, the details were sketchy at best.

The intent was not to scare the public. This level of threat immediately set in motion countless protocols throughout the government and military. As a result, there were more unanswered questions than not. The president declined to answer any questions, and he left as quickly as he had arrived.

Chapter 47

Mifflintown, Pennsylvania – April 9, 2015

"We must build dikes of courage to hold back the flood of fear."

—*Martin Luther King, Jr.*

Anne was parked in front of the TV in their kitchen when Jason arrived home. The thunderclouds were rolling in over the Seven Mountains, and the skies looked ominous. In Jason's mind, he thought it was a fitting depiction of the pending storm facing his country. Anne was watching CNN and their constant coverage of President Wheeler's surprise escalation of the threat level from Blue to Red, skipping Yellow and *Orange*. The move from near the bottom to the top had taken the media and the American population off guard, but not Jason.

"Jason, I'm frightened."

"Calm down. It's just a precautionary measure," he said, knowing that if Anne knew what he did about McNichols's night shift, she would be beside herself.

"But this is only the second time since the system was established that they indicated a *severe* threat. The kids came home from school in a panic. All the kids at school are saying that this is the end of the world."

"Where are they?"

"Watching the coverage on TV in the den—even MTV is covering it."

"We probably need to take their minds off of it at the dinner table."

"Jason, help *me* get my mind off of it. I'm scared."

Jason went into the den and, after greeting Ashley and Hunter, sat down with them to watch how the young hipsters of MTV were covering the crisis.

"Dad, we're scared," Hunter said.

"We'll talk at dinner, but you know that God is in control."

"We know that, but we have our lives ahead of us, and if we get attacked, our lives could be over," Ashley added.

"Ashley, Mifflintown would not be high on the list of targets that terrorists would go after, would it?" Jason smiled.

That comment brought a chuckle from Ashley and Hunter as Anne called them to dinner.

Everyone was in a somber mood, and as Jason tried to do his usual "tell me one thing you learned in school today," they both just looked at him.

"OK, let's skip the normal stuff, and let's discuss this terrorist threat thing."

To give their discussion some historical context, he decided to share a story that his father, their pap, had passed on to him from the early sixties.

"Your pap was about your age when there was another serious threat to our country. It was discovered that there were missiles in Cuba armed and pointed at strategic targets throughout the US. Just as you have experienced today, his school was buzzing about how the world was going to end right then in 1962, and of course, it didn't."

The kids insisted that that wasn't a real threat, but Jason pushed back.

"Ask your pap if they thought it was a real threat."

"What's the point of your story, Dad?" Hunter asked with a bit of a wise guy tone, which Jason swiftly corrected.

"I want you each to remember this day and where you were when the announcement was made and who you were with. It is a historic day, and one that you will want to share with your kids and grandkids someday."

As he was calming down his family, Jason's mind wandered to the plant and Yar Din.

"What do you say about having a family game night tonight?"

Without much enthusiasm, they began to argue about which game to play.

cᵈb

Yar, the Khoury twins, and Craig took their first break of the shift together, as was their custom. They didn't discuss it, but the escalation of the terrorist threat was high on their radar.

"There's nothing we can do, but our jobs and our instructions are clear. Why on earth would they suspect our little cell in the middle of Pennsylvania?" Yar asked, echoing Jason's rationale to calm his family.

Craig was so fast that the jobs he had to accomplish were already finished. Yar wanted him to begin moving the palladium into position near the CNC machines so that the Khourys could begin making the parts as inconspicuously as possible. Yar had cleared an area that was out of eyesight of the employees. The programs that had come in the briefcase that afternoon were already loaded into the machine's computer.

From this point forward, any time the machines did not have McNichols work, they would be spewing out the parts for their *purposes*. As the opportunity had presented itself, Yar decided that Craig would take the parts and hide them behind the container where he dumped the trash.

Prior to asking Craig Reeves to join his group, Yar thoroughly vetted him through all his sources, including his comrades at the top of McNichols. Everything that Craig had indicated to the three of them came back confirmed. There were no red flags, and he was now one of *them*. The DHS experts were pros at creating covers.

The parts had to be perfect, and defects were noted and discarded. Yar did not realize the value of the palladium, so he instructed Craig to dispose of those pieces and bury them in the trash containers. Besides, he had no real budget constraints. Craig planned to smuggle some defective parts out of the plant and get them to DHS as soon as he could.

As he pocketed one of the defective parts, he didn't realize that Jamil Khoury was standing at the other end of the machine.

Chapter 48

Harrisburg, Pennsylvania – April 10, 2015

"Never was anything great achieved without danger."

—*Niccolo Machiavelli*

It was Friday afternoon when Agent Adams rushed into Wayne's office with disheartening news.

"Wayne, we have an issue at McNichols."

"What's going on? Did you hear from Craig?"

"No, I had an urgent call from our guys surveilling the Din compound. It appears that Jamil Khoury saw Craig slip a piece of scrap metal into his pocket. There apparently was a major discussion following their noon prayer time."

"Have we contacted Agent Reeves yet?"

"No, I wanted to bring it to your attention so we could discuss our next steps. We have our weekly call with him shortly. Judging from our Arabic interpreter, we are not terminal at this point. Reeves still has a degree of creditability with them, and Yar Din seems to be downplaying it."

Wayne quizzed, "Are we placing Reeves in danger by not aborting?"

"I know it's a bit early, but let's get Reeves on the phone. We need to have him give his report before we get into this intelligence."

They apologized for calling a couple of hours early, but they told Reeves that they had something they needed to discuss with him immediately.

"Are you ready to report on your week?" Wayne asked.

"Yes, sir. Let's get started."

Reeves had already informed both of them in his nightly recap about the detailed instructions being delivered yesterday. What he had to add was that he'd actually gotten to see the briefcase and the specifics of the plans for their parts.

"The plans were laid out in intricate detail, complete with the programming to cut the parts on their CNC machines. It was quite impressive, but judging from their pieces of the device, there must be several other cells working on other components."

Bin Laden and now Ahsan had each done masterful jobs in franchising the organization and replicating the operation with the use of cells.

He went on to report that their parts were already being manufactured as time on the machine permitted and that he expected hundreds of component parts to be made tomorrow while the rest of the plant was closed. The machines were so automated that they could do their maintenance assignments throughout the plant while their parts were being cut. If something did go wrong, the machine simply stopped, and a huge red light started flashing. When that happened, some parts needed to be scrapped.

"I've been able to grab some of those discarded parts since they were not concerned about salvaging the metal. I thought that the Washington analysts would love to get their hands on a few parts—scrap or not."

Wayne Joseph spoke up. "Craig, I'm afraid that that is the reason we called you earlier than scheduled. It appears from our agents monitoring their compound that Jamil observed you pocketing at least one of those pieces."

Feeling embarrassed, the only thing he could think of to say was, "Oh no!"

"The good news is, it appears that you have won over Yar, and he was defending your honor among the boys."

"How do you think I should handle it?"

Craig, Mike, and Wayne kicked around different ideas, but the consensus was that he needed to be super vigilant and confirm Din's conclusion of what Jamil had witnessed. This was going to test his nerves and his ability as an undercover agent.

"Craig, I need not remind you that these guys are willing to die for their cause, and they have brought you into their band of thieves. Let's write this one off to experience, but one more slip up and I'm pulling you out, and you know how critical you are to helping us connect the dots."

"Boss, I am so sorry, and believe me, I will not make another mistake like this, and if I do, I totally understand what you have to do."

Then Craig added, "I only have one more thing to include in my report for this week. The superintendent, Henry Koontz, is coming in Monday morning to meet with Din. I saw a note on Din's office pad."

"Thanks, Craig," Wayne responded. "We had to bring Mr. Koontz in on our operation, so he's aware of your involvement and we knew about this meeting."

Chapter 49

Fairfield, Connecticut – April 11, 2015

"Always have a plan, and believe in it. Nothing happens by accident."

—*Chuck Knox*

Esa woke up in the middle of the night in a cold sweat; he wanted to stop what he had set in motion. He called Paterson, but it went to his voice mail.

"Mr. Paterson, please call me immediately. I've changed my mind about Allison. You can keep the first half of the money, but I don't want you to proceed."

By dawn, he had not heard back from Paterson and called him again. Again, it went to voice mail. Again, he left a frantic message. "I'm pulling the plug. You can keep the money. I don't want Allison killed. Call me on this number immediately!"

ďb

Allison looked forward to her weekly drives in her Porsche. She could easily have one of their employees handle her errands, but her drives were therapeutic. She enjoyed putting her sports car through its paces. The cleaners, snacks at the grocery store, coffee with a friend, and the like were all small, insignificant things that she really enjoyed. She was disappointed when she saw that it had been raining through the night; she would have to watch her speed on the slick roads.

She kissed Esa on her way out the back door and went down the steps to her car. She didn't see the puddle of brake fluid, as it blended in with the rain puddles. Her car roared to a start—a sound that she appreciated more than the usual female. She had a deep appreciation of cars, which she had inherited from her father.

The rear end of her car fishtailed slightly as she took off from their driveway, confirming her sense that the roads would be slick.

db

As Esa watched her taillights disappear around the corner, his phone rang.

"Mr. Mann, this is John Paterson. What can I do for you?"

"I've told you—I've changed my mind about Allison."

"Did she leave for her weekend chores?"

"Yes, she just pulled out."

"Mr. Mann, it's too late, but even if it weren't, I'm afraid I couldn't do anything about your wishes. Hajji ordered this hit. He was happy to hear that you had also ordered it, but Allison's elimination was out of your hands."

Esa's knees weakened as he hit the floor of the mudroom, visions of Allison's brake lights in his mind. What had he done? He sobbed and slipped off to his office to isolate himself from his staff.

db

Coming down their hill, Allison hit the brakes to slow her Carrera, but the brake pedal didn't feel right to her. She knew her car well and the pedal felt mushy—the only way she could describe the feeling. Her car was gaining momentum and speed. She barely made it around the second curve en route to town; the pedal had gone straight to the floorboard. Panic set in. *What in the world?* she thought as she approached yet another curve. This time, though, she didn't make it. Her car broke through a small wooded guardrail, and she screamed as her expensive piece of machinery went airborne. She blacked out on impact at the bottom of a forty-foot embankment.

db

The Fairfield police didn't have much to keep them busy. The most common crime in their community was speeding. Their police-to-citizen ratio was very high—evidence of their wealthy tax base. Criminals knew that Fairfield was no place to try to pull anything off, so the police cars cruised and set up speed traps. The criminals visited less affluent communities that were easier marks.

Most, if not all, of the influential people in town lived in or around the Manns' neighborhood, so their road was heavily patrolled.

Two police cars were parked outside the town's bagel shop as the officers decided on their routes for their morning rounds. One took the hill, while the other headed down Main Street; there weren't many options in Fairfield.

As his car made its way up the hill, Officer Murphy noticed the broken decorative guardrail. His mind immediately went to vandalism by local teenagers, but he turned on his blue lights and pulled off to the side of the road to see if they had carelessly left any clues behind. This was as close to crime detection as he would come to today—or so he thought.

He spotted a black sports car deep in the bottom of the ravine, its wheels spinning and steam pouring from under the hood.

db

Within moments of his discovery, an emergency call went out, and in a few more minutes, the road to the Manns' neighborhood was completely blocked by emergency vehicles, their blue-and-red flashing lights illuminating the dreary morning.

Paterson heard the sirens from his bed in the cabins. He suspected that he knew the reason for the commotion—at least he hoped he knew. He had decided to stay put in Fairfield, waiting for this morning. He didn't have any other pressing engagements, so he wanted to make sure his plan had worked.

Paterson turned up the volume on his police scanner and heard the commotion firsthand on the radio waves: "There is a late-model sports car over the side of Hillside Drive, and the driver is in the car—unconscious."

It sounded like at least the first part of his plan had worked.

He jumped out of bed and took a hike up the hill to get a bird's-eye view of the situation. When he arrived at the scene, he was one of the many Fairfielders who had been attracted to the site of the accident. On a nearby policeman's walkie-talkie, he heard emergency personnel calling for the Jaws of Life to be brought down to the car.

Bad news—she's still alive, the cold-blooded hit man thought.

Esa picked up the phone in his kitchen. He had dreaded the call and intuitively knew whom it was from before checking the caller ID, which read, "CITY OF FAIRFIELD CT 203-555-1899."

"Hello, this is Esa Mann," he said in a questioning manner.

The somber voice on the other end of the line sounded like a middle-aged female. "Mr. Mann, I'm afraid I have some bad news for you. Your wife has been in an automobile accident near your home, and a patrolman is on his way to escort you to the scene."

db

Paterson watched as carefully as he could from the other side of the police barriers as they cut Allison from her mangled car. He couldn't see much blood, but she was definitely out cold. The paramedics, ready to go if she was still alive, stood next to the firefighters manning the cutting device.

As the paramedics jumped into action, it was obvious to Paterson that he hadn't satisfied his contract—yet. Applying CPR and checking her blood pressure, they gave a thumbs-up to their fellow emergency workers watching from the road. Allison was carefully hoisted to the road and loaded into an awaiting ambulance.

Lights and sirens blazing, they rushed her to the Fairfield Regional Medical Center located a few miles away.

db

The emergency vehicles were performing their cleanup around the scene as the patrolman chauffeured Esa. He had informed Esa when he picked him up that his wife was alive and had already been taken to the hospital.

"We will go straight there, sir."

It was clear that Esa had been crying—this was not an act.

The officers on the scene lowered the barriers to make way for Esa, who was anxiously looking out the rear window of the squad car. It was quite surreal, as he could see the tow truck pulling her car up the side of the hill. It was in dreadful condition, and he wondered how she had ever survived. Esa was conflicted. He wanted her to live, but knowing Hajji was controlling Paterson, it would only be a matter of time until she was dead, even if she did survive.

Having radioed ahead, hospital orderlies met Esa at the door of the emergency room. He was ushered into a private waiting room and was told that

Allison had been taken directly to surgery. She was alive, but her blood pressure was extremely low, and she was not breathing on her own. A doctor met them in the waiting room.

"Mr. Mann, your wife is in extremely critical condition. We are doing everything we can for her, but she is bleeding internally, and we suspect that there may be head trauma."

Esa was in shock.

"Can we call your pastor or any family members for you?"

The reality of their different spiritual upbringings set in, as well as the fact that neither of them was really following a formal religious path.

"No, thanks. I have my cell phone, and I'll call some people whenever we know more."

"Mr. Mann, I was thinking about support for you."

db

Allison had been in surgery for over three hours when Esa's phone vibrated. The incoming call was an encrypted line that he recognized even though he had received very few calls from the number.

"Good morning, sir."

Nasi Ahsan greeted him. "Hello, this is Ahsan. I have been in contact with Mr. Paterson, and I understand that your wife has experienced an accident."

Now *he* was in a state of shock. "Yes, sir. I'm at the hospital now."

"I know." Not knowing about his earlier conversation with Paterson, he continued. "I just wanted to reassure you that you have made the right call, and it has restored my confidence in you. For you see, Esa, I was aware of your baby."

Chapter 50

Antioch, Tennessee – April 11, 2015

"For where God built a church, there the Devil would also build a chapel."

—Martin Luther

F adi's decision to put Jerome in charge of the warehouse operations turned out to be brilliant. He and Fadi spent countless hours working on the proper layout and division of labor; then they converted their run-down, dirty building into an efficient assembly plant. Their preparations continued for almost three weeks, in which time the boys adhered to Fadi's work schedule. In every trip, they delivered the materials they had procured, and Jerome used bits and pieces of shelving, tables, and whatever else he could lay his hands on to apply organization to the chaos of the old warehouse.

Fadi was excited about how his team had rallied around his leadership after Taj's "untimely" death, and he knew Esa was pleased. He had formed a close relationship with Jerome and had a deep appreciation for his work ethic. Jerome's mother had done a fantastic job of raising him and preparing him for the world; her evangelical Christian beliefs were passed on to him in the form of strong faith in a higher being. In his youth, he was a radical born-again Christian, so it was natural for him to fall into that same mold with his friends at the Antioch mosque. He was now a radical Islamic terrorist.

Jerome's father had never been part of his life, and being the oldest of four half brothers and sisters, Jerome took on the role of father to his siblings from an early age. This responsibility had prepared him for this assignment. Jerome and Fadi had invested far more hours than the rest of the team, but they knew the boys would be diligent now that their marching orders had been issued.

The two of them kicked back for a short break.

"Jerome, what are you thinking?"

"I've been thinking that I'm nearing the point of no return, and truthfully, I'm concerned about how my family will be impacted by what we are working on."

"I understand. It will be up to you and your relationships with them to have them follow our teachings. Jerome, they will spend eternity in hell if they continue to be 'people of the book.' What we are doing will get their attention, and you can be there for them—you will be their *savior.*"

"You don't know my momma."

Fadi smiled. He understood how strong the convictions of a single mother could be. Cutting straight to the point, he asked, "Are you having second thoughts about what we are doing?"

"No, sir. But while I'm looking around this building, it is becoming more real to me. I have many friends who are infidels."

"So do I, Jerome, but they are lost forever if we aren't able to convert them."

"We better get back to work. Most all of the guys are scheduled to be here sometime today and tomorrow. Weekends will offer us the most focused hours, so we need to be ready for them."

Just as Jerome had finished his sentence, Habib and Wazir came in the door together, ready for their shift.

db

Basel had about an hour before he was scheduled to be at the warehouse, so he was picking up some random fares to earn some extra cash. Secretly, his desire and drive for money was so he could return to school, but outwardly, it was simply part of his cover. Nevertheless, he was diligent and took every opportunity he had to drive his taxi.

His phone rang.

"Basel, it's Kyle. Spur of the moment thing—but would you be interested in going to the movies tonight?"

Basel was happy to hear from his friend, but he had never really caught on to the American custom of attending movies. He really had no desire to see things jumping out at him from huge screens; in fact, the motion often made him dizzy and somewhat nauseated. Regardless of his sentiment, he appreciated Kyle's invitation. His schedule at the warehouse would have him working from late afternoon into the night, so he would have to pass. "Sorry, my friend, but I have to work."

Kyle continued. "I was thinking about something. I would be interested in attending one of your Friday noon prayer services—I think you call it *salah*—and I'd like you to come to church with me some Sunday. What do you think?"

This offer distressed Basel. He was curious and was enjoying his time in discussion with Kyle, but he wasn't sure if he was ready for such a public display of their friendship. He wasn't as concerned about visiting Kyle's church as he was with having Kyle attend the AIC on a Friday.

"I would be interested, but I can't do it tomorrow." Fadi had scheduled him for the morning shift this Sunday. "Perhaps we could do it next Sunday, but let me check out when it would be good for you to visit my mosque."

"We just celebrated our most holy day of the year, Easter, last week, so attendance generally falls off."

This confused Basel since the weekly *salah* was mandatory for all Muslim males to attend; he didn't understand why there would be a decline in attendance following their holy day.

"You understand the importance of Easter to us, as it marks the celebration of Christ's resurrection from the grave following his crucifixion? It's the basis of our faith."

"Yes, I do. But you understand that the Quran has a different depiction of the events of that day?"

"Yes, I do. I picked up on that. So if I don't see you before, I'll see you next Thursday, and I promise that I won't offend you."

Basel dropped his fare at their destination and realized that it was time for him to head off to the warehouse. Christianity was a confusing thing to him, as he saw their symbol around the necks of scantily dressed young women on billboards and what little TV he watched. How did this activity relate to their religion? He had many unanswered questions, but the most confusing thing to him was the concept of how this Jesus was also God was also the Holy Spirit and how, to be accepted by him, a person simply needed to admit that he or she was a sinner. Fascinating but confusing.

Chapter 51

Fairfield, Connecticut – April 11, 2015

"I remember my mother's prayers and they have always followed me. They have clung to me all my life."

—Abraham Lincoln

Esa was still recovering from his Ahsan call when a large silhouette appeared in the doorway of the family waiting room. He could not make out the man's features, as the bright lights from the hallway created a hallo around his head. Allison had been in surgery for over six hours, with no word as to her progress, so he suspected that the imposing figure was one of her doctors. As the unknown visitor walked farther into the room, however, Esa recognized Paterson.

"Good afternoon, Mr. Mann. Sorry to hear of your wife's accident. I wanted to stop by to see if there was anything I could do to help."

The double meaning of his comments did not go unnoticed by Esa, who was shocked by the nerve of Paterson.

"Mr. Paterson, thanks for coming."

"I'm here just in case you need me," he nearly whispered with a slight grin.

One of the doctors entered the room with a very serious look on his face.

"Mr. Mann, I've been in surgery with your wife, and we did everything we could to save the baby, but unfortunately, he didn't make it."

Esa was relieved that the baby was gone, but he couldn't reveal his true sentiment. A tear developed in the corner of his eye as he lowered his head. Paterson, going along with the act, put his arm around Esa in a man hug.

"How is Allison?" Esa asked, sounding as if he was holding back from sobbing.

"She has very serious injuries, and there's a team of doctors still working on her. One of them will be here to talk with you as soon as they know anything. As for right now, if you're a praying man, she needs God's help."

Esa called Allison's parents as soon as he had gotten to the hospital that morning. Her brother lived in Boston but was temporarily out of the country. Esa called him as well. He knew it was the proper thing to do. Her parents rushed straight to O'Hare and caught the first available flight to New York. Her brother was attempting to get back to the States from China—a challenge.

After several hours, Allison's parents entered the waiting room. More tears—her mother and father were both emotional wrecks. When Esa told them of the baby being dead, there was audible sobbing; they had not told her parents that she was pregnant.

"We wanted to be certain that everything was normal and progressing along before we told anyone. I'm sorry."

Her parents understood but immediately wanted to know how the accident had happened. Esa blamed it on the slick roads. Seeing the conditions of the roads on the way to Fairfield from LaGuardia, the "slick roads" explanation made sense to them—at least for now.

"Mr. and Mrs. Tucker, I'd like you to meet a friend of mine, John Paterson."

In what may have been the most awkward moment of his life, he witnessed his in-laws greeting the man who had been hired to kill their daughter.

Another hour passed, with the four of them engaged in small talk, before another doctor visited.

"I'm Dr. Hartman, and I have been the chief surgeon with Allison today. She is in recovery. We have stopped the internal bleeding, and now it's a matter of waiting."

Mrs. Tucker wanted to know more, and the questions flowed for the next ten minutes, until the doctor was conveniently paged.

"Excuse me, I have an emergency. I'll be back in a few hours to check in with you. In the meantime, our staff is here to serve you."

"When can we see her?"

"It will be a while."

The Tuckers were not hungry, but they all went down to the cafeteria to waste some time. Paterson had a full meal.

$$\mathrm{d}\!\mathrm{b}$$

Later that evening, the family was asked to come into a secluded conference room, where several doctors were waiting for them. A pastor from a local church who volunteered at the hospital for moments such as these was standing in the back corner.

The doctor who appeared to be the senior staff member spoke up. "Mr. Mann, Mr. and Mrs. Tucker, we have done everything we could for Allison. All of our testing indicates that she is being kept alive by machines. Mr. Mann has indicated to us that Allison has a living will, and it is her wish not to be kept alive with artificial means."

Mrs. Tucker lowered her head and cried with Mr. Tucker, and Esa hugged her, and they comforted each other. Esa had a huge lump in his stomach. He was going to miss her, but he knew that what he'd done was with Allah's blessings.

"It is OK for you to see her and say your good-byes, but I must warn you that she is badly injured. After that, we will ask you to leave as we prepare her and disconnect the machine. You will be able to come back in for her final moments. We are very sorry."

Chapter 52

Al-Qaeda Headquarters, Afghanistan – April 11, 2015

"America is a great power possessed of tremendous military might and a wide-ranging economy, but all this is built on an unstable foundation which can be targeted, with special attention to its obvious weak spots. If America is hit in one hundredth of these weak spots, God willing, it will stumble, wither away and relinquish world leadership."

—Osama bin Laden

It was hard to differentiate between a weekend day and a weekday at al-Qaeda headquarters. People worked around the clock, seven days a week. Ahsan never took any time off. His family had been decimated by the Americans, and there was little reason to go anywhere. It was not safe for him to leave the lair. Once the Americans had figured out that he was in control, there was a high price tag on his head. His hatred for all infidels had grown more intense each year, but his hatred of the American infidels was more severe than any other. From his childhood, he was taught to hate Jews and Christians. He was taught that they were born from apes and pigs and that it was OK to kill them. He had never considered infidels to be human. The radical Muslim propaganda machine perpetuated the teaching that he heard from radical imams. All of this formed the person he'd become. He was raised to hate.

Having just run through his clandestine virtual tour of his five territory chiefs, he found all but one working diligently in their offices. The only one not working on Sky Burst was Esa Mann—for obvious reasons. He knew that they had just pulled his wife off life support and were waiting for her to take her last breath. Esa had contracted—or so Esa thought—and coordinated the effort, which restored Ahsan's confidence in his leader of North America. Not wanting to disrupt his revenue stream from Esa, Paterson decided not to inform Ahsan of the conversation he'd had with Esa that morning.

Ahsan thought through the past week. Much had been accomplished, but there was a major problem other than Esa's love interest that concerned him about America. The president of the United States had raised the terrorist threat level to severe, and the whole intelligence/military community had been placed on high alert. *Why?* he wondered. What could have signaled such a measure from the people in Homeland Security? Ahsan was under the impression from Esa that everything was going smoothly, but was it?

I have everything under control, I'm not scared, but I am curious, he thought to himself. *It may be time to accelerate the operation.*

He had a special date determined—a date that he had not shared with anyone, even Dalil. It was a personal and meaningful date to him and most Muslims, but he doubted that he could wait that long. Malcolm would be back on Monday, after a couple of days off, and they needed to figure out how quickly they could complete their planned attack. He made a note in his mission binder to have Dalil arrange a meeting for the three of them.

Chapter 53

Mifflintown, Pennsylvania – April 11, 2015

"The best way to find out if you can trust somebody is to trust them."

—*Ernest Hemingway*

T he plant was dark as Yar's crew entered; they were the only people working this weekend. There were maintenance flags throughout the assembly line that had to be handled. Typically, they knocked out their tasks quickly, and then they could all, including Yar, focus on making as many parts as they could—parts for an unknown weapon that was destined to earn them a spot in the highest level of eternity.

After hearing the report from the surveillance crew, Craig knew he would have to put on a masterful acting job. He was nervous, but he couldn't give any of the Saudis reason to suspect him. He had won their trust, but he knew that trust was fragile, and in his case, losing their trust could, and most likely would, mean losing his life.

If the surveillance team had to rush the plant to rescue him, the entire Peace Shield operation could be destroyed without uncovering the al-Qaeda network. Sure, he thought, at least three terrorists and their families would go down, but all their affiliations would not be discovered, and DHS would take a huge step backward. There was a lot riding on his acting. Those drama classes that he'd taken as easy electives would be put to the test. In his mind, the mantra *I am a terrorist, I am a terrorist, I am a terrorist* helped him set his mind to the task at hand—ultimate method acting with extremely high stakes.

They all hit the entrance door at the same time.

"*Marhaba.*" They all nodded along with the informal Arabic hello.

Craig greeted them. "*Assalamo Alaikum.*" (May peace be upon you, and may Allah's blessings be with you.)

As they walked into the factory, Yar made his way to the electric panel. The click of the circuit breakers echoed throughout the plant as the buzz of the energy-efficient fluorescent bulbs grew in intensity. The lights flickered on, and it became daylight in McNichols-Mifflintown.

"OK, gentlemen, let's knock out this work and get busy with for the glory of Allah."

"For the glory of Allah!" the twins and Craig responded in unison.

Yar gave out assignments to the twins, and Craig knew what he had to do. They went their separate ways.

Yar retreated to his office, where he noticed a note reminding him of Henry Koontz's visit on Monday morning. Yar wondered why he was nosing around; he hadn't heard from him for a couple of weeks. *I guess it was because his wife died,* he thought. *Perhaps he's getting back into the swing of things.* He remembered that, during his last visit, he'd made him nervous with questions. Yar let his mind wander. *I hope it's nothing, or Mr. Koontz may be joining his wife in eternal damnation sooner than later. We can't afford to have an old codger stirring up interest in what we have going on here.*

They had a perfect situation, and he planned to keep it that way.

Yar didn't know, however, that the US government was aware of his every move and was monitoring every conversation in the plant and at his compound. The only things not intercepted were the thoughts in his head.

Putting thoughts of Mr. Koontz aside, he pulled out his handwritten tally sheets to see how they were doing with their production. At the rate he was able to produce during their workday, he calculated he would be able to hit his target date easily. Today would be bonus production, and he was confident that they would get better as they proceeded. Things were looking good at McNichols.

The issue that Jamil had called to his attention about Craig weighed heavy on his mind. He needed to watch him carefully, but his gut told him he was OK. Back home at their compound with their wives, as they kicked around what had happened, one of the guys made a joke pertaining to the Westerners' notion of women's intuition.

"Perhaps we should have our wives interrogate him and see what their opinions are," Jabir had said jokingly.

At the time, it had been a joke, but as they discussed it more, they decided that it would be a good idea to have Craig visit their compound. Women's intuition or not, the more people to observe and judge him, the better. Yar was convinced that everything was fine, but there was much at stake.

db

As the day progressed, Craig was feeling more comfortable, and he was acting to the best of his ability. The four of them worked together closely as the huge CNC machines continued to spit out parts from the palladium raw material. There was less need to be covert on Saturdays, so they had their boxes for the various parts spread out on the floor adjacent to the machines. Counts were updated as Yar transcribed their production numbers to his ledger.

It was quitting time, but Craig, wishing to get back into their good graces, had an idea.

"Mr. Din, I'd like to make a suggestion."

"Certainly, Craig. What is it?"

"I think the twins and I should punch out so our quitting time is as Mr. Koontz expects it to be, but we should continue to work off the clock. The machines are running smoothly, and I think we should knock out as many parts as we can."

Looking toward the twins, Yar asked, "What do you guys think?"

"Let's do it!"

"Great idea, Craig. To the glory of Allah!" Yar liked his spirit.

Again, in unison, they shouted, "To the glory of Allah!"

They continued to pound out parts until it was time for their noon prayers.

"I think it's time to call it a day," Yar suggested. Not waiting for an answer, he continued. "Let's wrap it up. We had a great day!"

As they began to shut down the machines, Yar pulled Craig aside. "Can I speak to you for a second?"

Shivers coursed through Craig's body as moisture surfaced under his arms. "Absolutely. What's up?"

"The boys and I would like to invite you to our homes for a traditional Saudi Arabian meal early Sunday evening. Are you interested?"

Greatly relieved, he smiled and graciously accepted. "I appreciate the invitation, and I look forward to meeting your wives!"

Yar thought, *They are looking forward to meeting you as well. . .*

Chapter 54

Fairfield, Connecticut – April 12, 2015

"No one can confidently say that he will still be living tomorrow."

—*Euripides*

The harsh reality of what had happened the day before overwhelmed Esa as he awoke. Allison was dead. All his life, he had been raised in a radical Muslim home. His father was notorious in the world of terrorism, and Esa placed him on a pedestal. His goal was to be just like his father—for the sake of Allah and his position in paradise. Of course, he didn't have his father's world stage, but soon the world would know his name. Allison had simply been a part of his plan, but his feelings for her had grown despite his radical upbringing. He knew it was OK to kill the "people of the book," so the thought of having Allison and the baby killed for the sake of Sky Burst seemed quite natural to him. But why was he having feelings of remorse? He was certain that bin Laden hadn't felt any remorse after the Manhattan Raid when thousands of infidels died. *Why do I have this feeling for one death and a fetus that wasn't even awarded a soul yet?* he thought.

Her mother and father stayed in the guesthouse, and her brother would be arriving shortly, finally able to get back from China. The main house was mostly empty, but he heard some of his staff stirring downstairs, and he knew the smell of breakfast would soon be wafting into his bedroom. He was not hungry. He was not looking forward to seeing her brother, for he too had won a spot inside his hardened heart. Esa wasn't having difficulty in "acting" sorrowful; he was filled with grief—a confusing grief.

He decided to get out of bed to see if a shower would help him feel better and, in some strange metaphor, wash away his hurt.

Esa had just finished dressing when he heard the doorbell ring. He knew it was Chad, Allison's brother. He heard his maid greet him as he started down the stairs. Prior to going downstairs, he had buzzed Mr. and Mrs. Tucker on the intercom to invite them to the main house to greet Chad and attempt to eat some breakfast.

Tears welled in Chad's eyes as he spotted Esa. "Brother, I'm so sorry."

They had often referred to each other as "brother," but it was particularly touching as Esa hugged Chad.

"I'm so sorry, too. I'm going to miss her!" As soon as he'd said that, Esa heard Chad's parents coming in the back of the house.

More hugs, more tears, and more pronounced sobbing commenced from all three Tuckers. Esa joined in.

"I wish I could have been here for you," Chad got out between cries.

Esa stepped quietly out of the picture to let the family have some time together. He heard her father mention, "We will be together in heaven," with all three of them agreeing.

The thought struck Esa that he wouldn't be in heaven or paradise with Allison—in fact, none of the Tuckers would. The sobering thought sent him deeper in despair.

While the family was comforting one another, Esa slipped off to his office to wire Mr. Paterson's final payment into his numbered Cayman Islands account.

db

"Mr. Mann, breakfast is served."

Esa went back into the den to invite the Tuckers in for breakfast. They had regained their composure, at least for now, and the three started to reminisce about Allison and Chad's childhood in Wheaton, Illinois. Laughter was interspersed with tears as they forced some nourishment into their bodies. Chad hadn't eaten since somewhere over the West Coast, and the airplane food didn't cut it for a man his size, so he gobbled down a couple of pancakes, eggs, and steak. The other three played with their food more than consumed it.

They all knew that they needed to start talking about the final arrangements and had decided last night that it would be best for the funeral to be held in Chicago. Nearly all of their friends and family were within the vicinity of the city, and many of Allison's friends had stayed in the Chicagoland region. One of Mr. Tucker's best friends was a funeral director, so they contacted him. He had already started working on the arrangements and told them that he would come to see them as soon as they returned. Everything would be taken care of, including the transport of Allison's body.

The dates for the memorial service and visitations were set, but there were hundreds of minute details that their family friend was already thinking of. The four of them were scheduled to fly into Chicago first thing in the morning, so Mr. Tucker suggested that today needed to be a day of quiet reflection and prayer. Esa shook his head; prayer was an integral part of his life every day. Today would be no different.

Chapter 55

Washington, DC – April 12, 2015

"I know not with what weapons World War III will be fought, but World War IV will be fought with sticks and stones."

—*Albert Einstein*

Teddy had lost himself in the Peace Shield project since his trip to Harrisburg—nothing else captured his interest. It was early Sunday afternoon, but he didn't really know what day or time it was. He noticed that there weren't as many people running around the headquarters building; it must have been a weekend. He buried himself in his cubicle nearly twenty-four/seven, offset with an occasional walk to the war room; he liked to see his work on the giant screens. In his intricate mind, the bigger display allowed him a bigger view, and things became clearer.

He had studied the Middle Eastern situation for over ten years and had developed an incredible understanding of their thinking. Working in the intelligence business had garnered him an impressive résumé of contributions leading to the disruption of hundreds of terrorist threats around the world. He was instrumental in leading the analysis of the information gleaned from the Guantanamo Bay detainees—information that led to the death of bin Laden. He was working out of Homeland Security's offices, but his top secret security clearance included several Sensitive Compartmental Information (SCI) authorizations that gave him access to intelligence networks around the world. Ever since the discovery of palladium in Central PA, he had been pounding the databases of the British MI6, the newly amalgamated EUIA of the European Union countries (except England), Russia's SVR, Japan's Naicho, and Africa's NIA looking for clues to see if what he observed in the United States was global.

In recent years, DHS had acquired the role of being the hub of the intelligence community, with all activities funneled through and analyzed by their agents. President Wheeler made this change early in his presidency when he repositioned the United States as the dominant world leader. Consequently, international intelligence agencies around the world looked to DHS for leadership.

Teddy studied the digital board. The precious metal palladium had been identified in larger-than-normal volumes in five random territories around the world. But the more he studied the huge board, the more it became clear to him that perhaps they weren't as random as he'd first thought. His analysis that morning studied the similarities. All five stashes of the metal were located at factories that manufactured large, durable goods, and they had been spotted as a result of the surveillance of at least one person at each location with ties to radical Islam. As he contemplated those points, he realized that each of the five regions of the world represented areas where the Muslim religion held a minority position; there were no Muslim countries in the mix.

One by one, he dug into the intelligence reports from the other countries, and the pattern started to develop—a pattern that he was familiar with. He was unraveling the typical T-cell system that was a trademark of al-Qaeda. With this information, it was clear that what al-Qaeda was building in the United States was being replicated possibly four more times. This frightened him, but in Teddy's mind, it made the process a bit easier. If, as he suspected, there were various T-cells, he and the other analysts could make some assumptions that would hold true in each other's countries. The organization of al-Qaeda in its prime was masterful. Perhaps, despite common beliefs, they were still effective and were planning something larger than ever. Teddy, in a weird sort of way, was excited about what he was uncovering, but then the thought struck him. *What if we don't thwart their attacks?*

He sent Cliff Hill a text message and suggested that they meet as soon as he could get into the city.

dib

When Teddy's text buzzed, Cliff had just finished the twelfth hole. It was one of the first beautiful days of spring and the first opportunity he'd had in months to hit the links, but his respect for Teddy was such that he headed back to the clubhouse immediately. Teddy was not frivolous and always seemed one step ahead of him and the Secretary. He could count on one hand the number of times that he had found a flaw in his reasoning or analysis. He left the beauty of his Virginian country club and headed into the city.

About an hour later, he found Teddy in the war room.

"What do you have for me, Mr. Brewer?"

Teddy noticed that Cliff was obviously fresh off the course and apologized. "Sorry to be calling you in on a Sunday, but I think I'm on to something that makes our discovery of last week seem small."

Smiling with tongue in cheek, Cliff said, "This better be big."

"Sir, I think whatever al-Qaeda is planning here in the States, they're replicating in three or, more likely, four other countries around the world."

With that introduction to get his attention, Teddy walked Cliff through the intelligence gathered from his colleagues. He started in the United States and laid out the way he foresaw their plan coming together. The decryption of intercepted electronic communications combined with intercepted voice communications from LA, Chicago, Boston, Central Pennsylvania, and the center of the cell in New York led Teddy to believe that he had identified the five spokes of the US cell.

"The only thing that doesn't make sense to me is that I have not been able to identify where the electronics and computer circuitry is being built. I have all the hardware necessary to build a number of NNEMP devices, but I haven't been able to pin down the computer, or electronic brains, for these devices—the component responsible for their detonation."

This had been puzzling Teddy since first putting his theory together on Friday, and then it came to him in the middle of that night.

"Boss, Pennsylvania was such a random location for cell activity that I began to question their position in the big plan."

"But, Teddy, there is no doubt about their activities since that was the break that opened up the whole can of worms. Is there?"

"You're correct, but my theory is that they are simply a branch of the Chicago cell, under the direction of Tamir Alam. It is *that* link that positioned the Saudis at the McNichols plant to begin with. Alam is a senior executive with McNichols."

Again, Cliff smiled, this time pleased with Teddy's acumen. "If that is accurate—and it sounds very credible—that means we're missing a cell completely in the US. We have a renegade cell out there that is providing the electronic guts for our bombs."

"Exactly, and we need to find it quickly."

"Do you have any guesses as to where it could be?"

"No, not really, but if we look purely at demographics, the Houston and Dallas areas are missing. Houston is the fourth largest city in the US."

"I'll have Secretary Knowles put the word out on her hotline to the intelligence community to focus on the missing cell."

Teddy furthered his discussion on the international front. "Continuing with the 'five' theme, our counterparts in other free world countries have discovered chatter and, more importantly, palladium stashes in four other territories."

Teddy directed Cliff's attention to the digital wall.

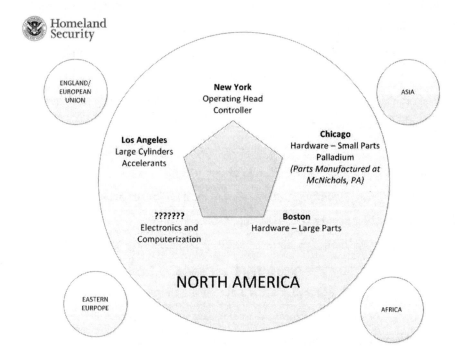

With his digital pointer, he walked Cliff through the five points of activity that he had assembled and confirmed with collaboration of other intelligence analysts, both domestically and abroad. As he moved through the presentation, Cliff became more and more impressed with the amount of work that had gone into Teddy's theories. They were well-founded and very believable—especially when he began to click on the other countries and was able to demonstrate similar patterns to the States.

Teddy had a small touch screen that replicated and controlled what was on the wall. With the use of color-coding, it was easy for him to demonstrate how the information had been consolidated and coordinated with his analyst friends around the world. He touched and dragged Asia over top of North America, and the missing links were obvious. The same five cells were spread throughout Asian territory. The pattern replicated itself when each of the other three schematics was dragged over the previous one. Each country had missing links, but the confirmation that al-Qaeda was up to something beyond imagination became evident quickly.

"Where do we go from here?" Cliff asked Teddy, knowing that Teddy would have developed a game plan before calling him off the golf course.

Chapter 56

Mifflintown, Pennsylvania – April 12, 2015

"All great change in America begins at the dinner table."

—Ronald Reagan

C raig had mixed feelings about his dinner invitation to the Din house. On one hand, he was glad that they had invited him, as it indicated acceptance into the group, but on the other hand, he needed to be on guard and act naturally, knowing that they were all aware of the incident in the plant on Friday.

He arrived at the farm complex a few minutes early. The sun was getting ready to set, so everything had a yellow-orange cast to it. It was a beautiful day. As soon as he left the main road and hit the gravel drive to the tenant homes, he detected the scent of his dinner. He had never really developed a taste for their cooking but was prepared to appreciate the cuisine.

He exited the car and walked up to the front door, and the aroma became even more intense. He had decided to wear a nice pair of dress slacks and one of his best shirts. He assumed that they would be in their traditional garb, and when Yar opened the door to greet him, he saw that he was correct.

"Welcome to my home, my brother."

Prepared but still surprised, Yar took Craig's hand and pulled him in close, air-kissing him twice—first to his right cheek and then to his left. Both twins repeated the greeting. The ladies lined up dutifully behind their husbands, and each man introduced Craig to his wife. One thing was striking. They each had beautiful eyes, which was all he could see through their burkas.

The men moved into the living room, while the women went straight to the kitchen. Much of what Craig was witnessing in respect to their wives was partially an act, as all three women had been Americanized, but tonight they would play the role of traditional Saudi wives.

A pitcher of lemonade was waiting for them on a tray, along with four glasses filled with ice cubes.

"The lemonade has been made in the traditional Middle Eastern manor," Yar said as he offered Craig a glass.

"Thanks very much. What makes it different?"

"It contains orange blossom water and some finely chopped mint."

Taking his first sip, Craig exclaimed, "This is very tasty, thanks!"

They sat down and talked briefly about what a good day they'd had in production on Saturday. As Craig was looking around the room, he noted the presence of typical Middle Eastern art, but in one corner of the room near what appeared to be a desk was a picture of a "Whiteout" at Penn State's Beaver Stadium. In the weeks that they had worked together, the topic of Penn State had never come up; in fact, Craig suddenly realized that he had learned very little about any of their personal lives outside of their religious convictions.

"Did you go to Penn State, or are you just a fan?" Being a fan though not having attended the university was commonplace in that part of the state; everyone loved Penn State football, especially as the scandal that had hit their program in 2012 was fading. The program was returning to it's pre-scandal years.

"Yes. In fact, that's where I met the twins. We were active in the Islamic center on campus. All three of us and Nyla, Jamil's wife, met there. We were very active in the movement."

Raja Din came to the entrance of the room and announced that dinner was ready. "Please come to our table. We have prepared our favorite dish—chicken kabassah."

As they got up to enter the dining room, Craig wondered how the women were going to eat without lowering their burkas. Then, turning the corner, it became clear—there were only four place settings. After the women served the men, they went into the kitchen and ate privately behind a closed door. Periodically, the women entered the room to see if anything was needed. Craig felt self-conscious. It seemed to him as if they were paying particularly close attention to him. Little did Craig know how right he was in his suspicions. Behind the door, the women huddled together and listened carefully to the conversation—especially Craig.

db

Henry was alone on Sunday evening. He was now alone for nearly every evening, but Sundays had always been a special time for Mary and him, as they made a point of spending time together then. Mostly, it meant that Henry would relinquish control of the remote to Mary, and she would get to watch her silly reality shows that were of no interest to him. He laughed to himself as he sat there watching one of Mary's favorites; she had gotten him hooked on the show.

One of the reasons he valued Sunday evenings so much, besides the time he had with Mary, was it gave him a chance to prepare to return to work. He loved his job, but he also loved weekends. Sunday evening was a transitional period, his buffer between relaxation and the day-to-day grind. This workweek would begin with a visit to the night shift. Normally, Henry wouldn't think twice about this type of appointment, but normally, he wasn't meeting with a terrorist. There was no pressure since his visit was more formality than meaningful, but he couldn't act too differently than he had in the past. He ran through the list of items he had sent himself Friday—a list of the things he wished to review on Monday.

This was going to be an interesting meeting.

Craig thanked his hosts and their wives and left to get ready for work. As evidence of the Americanization of their wives, the men helped with the cleanup before assembling in the living room to discuss the evening.

Meanwhile, the DHS operatives had their electronic ears focused on the conversations from their hideout in the woods.

Another indication of their Westernization was the fact that they spoke English nearly as much as they did Arabic.

Yar began. "You all have heard our discussion regarding Craig and what Jamil observed. We wanted to get all of us to focus on Mr. Reeves and poll our collective opinions. I can't understate the importance of our evaluation. If we believe that he's detrimental to our cause, he needs to be eliminated immediately. He knows too much. Let's start with the women."

At first, the women just stared at one another, and finally, Raja took the lead. "I think he's sincere. As we listened through the door, I carefully followed your conversations, and he seemed to be genuine, especially when talking about Allah and our project. I sensed excitement and anticipation in his voice."

Farah Khoury's body language demonstrated that she concurred with Raja. "I agree. He seemed to be quite comfortable within your home and with all of us. I did not detect any uneasiness, as I would expect if he were not one of us."

Nyla cleared her throat to prepare to speak. She was the only female member of the group to have graduated from college and the boldest of the three. She was not afraid to speak her mind, even if it differed from the men. "I don't have anything concrete to base this feeling on, but I just sensed that there was something about him that didn't feel right."

Somewhat cutting her off, Yar suggested, "Let's hear from the twins, and then we'll have a group discussion."

"I'm the one who started this thing by catching him putting the piece of metal in his pocket, and I've spent much time observing his actions and replaying them in my mind. I think he's one of us, and we should go about our business and put this behind us. It will be counterproductive to our cause if not."

Jabir agreed, so Yar opened the discussion to focus on the one dissenting opinion.

"Perhaps I've misread him. You brought him to your home to hear from our feminine 'intuition,' and I'm giving it to you. Time will tell, and I'm willing to concede with the consensus, but I think you guys still need to stay on your guard. Watch for any more abnormalities," Nyla warned.

After some more small talk, the women retired to their homes, while the men prepared to leave for McNichols.

The two men in the woods looked at each other, smiled, and gave the thumbs-up signal before calling Agent Joseph and Reeves, who were both anxious to hear if he had passed the test. He had won over everyone except for Jamil's wife.

The uneasiness in Nyla grew in intensity as she tried to slip off into sleep.

Something is not right about Mr. Reeves, she thought.

Chapter 57

Al-Qaeda Headquarters, Afghanistan – April 13, 2015

"The operations are under preparation and you will see them in your houses as soon as they are complete."

—*Nasi Ahsan*

L ike clockwork, Ally and Malcolm filed in and joined Hajji at his smaller conference table in the corner of his office. He was spoiled by the effectiveness of his right-hand man; a scribbled note in his notebook was all it took for Ally to handle any command.

"Good morning, gentlemen, and welcome back, Malcolm. I trust you had an enjoyable weekend."

"I did, sir, and thank you for making the arrangements."

"I'm anxious to get started with our discussion this morning. I'm sure by now that you have heard that Wheeler placed the US on a red alert, suspecting an imminent terrorist threat to his country. None of us have gone public lately with video messages intentionally, so their intelligence network must have picked up on something. Esa swears he has no problems in North America, but I'm certain he does and just doesn't know it."

Ally added, "Most of the world has followed their lead, so we may have problems in other parts of the world as well."

"That's correct. - we have not yet discussed the date of Sky Burst, which was intentional, as I didn't want anyone to know—not even you two. I can tell you now that my original plan needs to be accelerated. My original plan was to have Sky Burst coincide with our New Year on October fourteenth. What greater remembrance of our Prophet Muhammad's migration from Mecca to Medina than to set off a catastrophic event that would put infidels in their places and in their graves?"

Ally and Malcolm nodded their approval and understanding as to the reason for accelerating the plan.

"What I need from the two of you is help in determining how quickly we can execute. The reports that I'm getting from my field commanders indicate that they are all on schedule or ahead of schedule to begin the transfer of components by the end of May. We need them ready by the end of April. My first question is, is that possible?"

Both men immediately turned to their tablet computers, then realized that they needed more time to examine all the facts.

Ally spoke first, "Imam, may we have a couple of hours?"

"Yes, but before you leave, here is my second question. What is the absolute quickest date that we can launch Sky Burst? I have an alternative date that would be fitting, but I want to see what you two come back with first."

"Yes, sir. Can we reconvene at eleven thirty a.m.?" Ally asked.

"Certainly. *Alhamdulillah!*"

Both answered, "*Alhamdulillah!*" as they exited the room.

Hajji was confident that they would come back with a workable plan. His only question was, would their date be fast enough?

The morning had flown by, especially for Ally and Malcolm as they labored over the master schedule. The complexity of Sky Burst was intense, but their model of replication and division of responsibilities allowed them to look at the big picture in one territory and duplicate it in the others. Since North America was their most significant target, they started their analysis of how a change in the schedule would impact the United States.

They reassembled in Hajji's office.

Anxiously, he asked, "What did you determine?"

"It will require added stress to everyone's lives, and we're certain that Allah will need to intervene in some circumstances, but we believe the best we can do is June. We could hit June first, but the later it is in the month, the less stressful it will be to our system and the more likely we can pull it off flawlessly," Ally said, presenting the ten thousand–foot view.

Hajji smiled. "Wonderful. We have told everyone to be ready to distribute their components by the end of May. What does this do to that date?"

Malcolm Shane chimed in. "We need to be underway two weeks earlier."

"We have an amazing system and dedicated martyrs lined up and ready to support us for the sake of Allah and our cause. Just as the Manhattan Raid marked the beginning of jihad in America, Sky Burst will mark the conclusion, our victory over the infidels, and the end of jihad in America. The date must be meaningful to al-Qaeda and our radical Muslim followers."

The previous president, in what was the ultimate in olive branches extended to Muslims in the United States, created the first annual Islamic Heritage Month. June was selected since it wasn't encumbered with any other monthly recognition. In a bit of twisted irony, Wheeler's predecessor made the announcement at a ceremony marking the tenth anniversary of the 9/11 attacks. In another bit of irony, it was the last major impact he made on the American society prior to his defeat in 2012.

"What better way for us to acknowledge Islamic Heritage Month than to launch our Sky Burst attack during that month? Additionally, fasting begins for Ramadan on June eighteenth. Gentlemen, we have our date. Let's make it happen."

As they left, Hajji thought back with fond memories of the days leading up to the Manhattan Raid. Al-Zawahiri was there with bin Laden, the mastermind. He remembered how the Magnificent 19 had trained and prepared for that devastating blow to the US economy. (The pilots of the group were trained in US flight schools.) He thought, *With the exception of one of the targets, it went off without a hitch, and in the biggest of the attacks, thousands of infidels were sent to hell in Lower Manhattan.* Sky Burst would be the killing blow in a battle that had started back in the eleventh century with the Crusades of the Christians.

"Finally, victory will belong to Allah! *Alhamdulillah!*" he said aloud as it echoed in his lair.

Chapter 58

Mifflintown, Pennsylvania – April 12, 2015

"The threat of terrorism is not stronger than the will of the American people."

—*Chaka Fattah*

I t was probably bad timing on Henry's part to schedule a meeting with the night shift on the same day that he was reviewing budgets with Jason and the plant controller. Budgets were not his "thing," so it was going to be a long day, made longer by the early start.

There was a heavy fog that made the road blend into the sky. Fortunately, Henry had driven that road hundreds of times and knew it well. He dropped his jacket off in his office and headed for the plant just as the end-of-break buzzer sounded.

Yar, the Khoury twins, and Reeves were returning to the plant from their prayer corner. It was a déjà vu experience, as his mind raced back to his first encounter with the Muslims. Memories of his first suspicions were renewed as a cold chill swept down his spine. He fought a shiver. His factory had become an extension of al-Qaeda, and there wasn't anything he could do about it but remain quiet and do his job. He was frustrated, but he understood.

"Good morning, gentlemen," Henry greeted the group.

Yar and Henry went into Yar's office.

"Mr. Din, how has it been going? Sorry I haven't been around for a while."

"Mr. Koontz, no need to apologize. I am so sorry for your loss. How have you been doing?"

"Well, to be honest, it's very lonely without Mary. We were married for nearly forty years. The comforting thing is knowing that she is now with our Heavenly Father and is not in pain any longer."

Yar smiled, but he was thinking about how wrong the old man was. *She is spending an eternity in hell*, he thought, but instead, he said, "I can't imagine what you are going through."

"Thanks for your concern, but let's get to business. Do you have any problems with your staff or process that I need to know about?"

Playing the role of loyal employee and supporting the extra hours he needed, Yar replied, "We have been having an inordinate amount of equipment downtime. My maintenance team has to work every weekend to keep up with the repairs."

Knowing the real reason for the extra maintenance time, Henry decided to harass him a bit. "Yes, I've been noticing the excessive overtime, and I've been thinking about having some of my day shift maintenance guys work overtime to give you a hand."

Perhaps too quickly, Yar said, "That won't be necessary. We have it under control."

Henry enjoyed the curveball that he had just thrown the terrorist. "OK, but let me know if you need some help." Then he added, "Are all your employees working out OK? I haven't seen any changes coming through, so I assume all the new hires are cutting the mustard."

"Yes, sir. HR has done a great job filling my open positions quickly with good people."

As they went through the rest of Henry's agenda, Henry became more comfortable. Ironically, so did Yar.

db

Jason had only two more days to prepare for his budget meeting in Chicago. He'd had the numbers together for over a week, and his presentation was being polished and fine-tuned. He had one final meeting scheduled with the two guys who had helped him develop his plan—Henry and Bud Levinson. Bud was his plant controller, with over thirty years of accounting experience at McNichols. Jason was blessed with an incredible mind for numbers and a steel-trap memory. His move from corporate to Mifflintown drastically reduced the amount of numbers he had to recall. He went from keeping up with the entire corporation's numbers to a single plant. Jason was confident about his meeting in Chicago but still wanted the review time.

The three of them met in his office. He started by running through his OptiPresent slides with them.

"Please scrutinize the slides carefully for typos or points that don't make sense."

He ran through forty slides and took notes on the comments from Henry and Bud. Bud received a call from their banker that he had been waiting for, so he excused himself for a few minutes.

When he left, Jason turned to Henry and quietly asked, "How did it go in your night shift meeting this morning?"

"It was weird meeting with him now that I have been informed and know what they're up to."

"Did anything strange happen?"

"No, I purposely rattled his chain a bit about the overtime because I think he would expect that from me."

Bud reentered the room, and they got back to their meeting.

"What do you two think will be the areas of focus? Please fire some questions at me as if you're one of the big muckity-mucks."

Bud took the ball and ran with it. "I think they will be most interested in the MFI 237 since it's the new addition to our plant in the past year."

"Good point, and that's where I've been focusing."

For the rest of the meeting, both men role-played and grilled Jason on all aspects of his budget and performance over the past year. His numbers looked great, and he had reduced the standard cost by over 10 percent compared to his current budget. Besides his comfort level with his budget, he had great relationships with all the executives of McNichols; after all, he had been one of them just over a year ago.

They continued to review the numbers until they broke for lunch. He had promised Anne that he would go to lunch with her since he was going to be leaving for Chicago. They met at the coffee shop on Monument Square. The weather had broken, so they were able to eat alfresco.

Jason got a table and waited for Anne. In the other corner of the patio, he spotted the wives of the night shift Saudis. *I would love to hear what they're saying*, he thought.

Chapter 59

Chicago, Illinois – April 15, 2015

"For the most ambitious young people, the corporate ladder is obsolete."

—*Paul Graham*

ason arrived in Chicago the night before his meeting. He hated traveling and being away from his family, so he'd taken the last-possible flight. When he was a corporate officer, he had looked forward to the meetings, but this would be different. He had to defend his budget rather than simply fire questions at nervous managers. The redeeming value of his trip to Chicago was his stay at the Ritz-Carlton. Their impeccable service made being separated from his family a bit more tolerable.

Henry, Bud, and he had spent many hours over the past month working on their budget. For the past week, he had worked on his presentation. The entire executive team would be in the meeting, and they would be focused on him. He practiced incessantly, but his butterflies kept interfering with his enjoyment of the Ritz's amazing breakfast. He was confident but nervous.

He arrived at McNichols headquarters an hour early. The meeting would not start until 10:00 a.m. since the executive in charge, Tamir Alam, McNichols's senior vice president of administration and human resources had an earlier meeting with his financial advisor from New York City.

Jason went straight to one of the visitor offices adjacent to the boardroom. *I'll run through it one more time to be safe.* He had delivered it to the mirror in his room no fewer than fifteen times the night before, plus a couple more this morning.

db

Esa was staying with Allison's parents in Wheaton. The funeral had gone as well as could be expected. No matter how coldhearted one was, it was always difficult to see parents mourn the loss of a child. He handled the funeral with an appropriate amount of grief and found that it didn't require acting; he missed her and he was going to continue to miss her, so he had to focus on his mission and his responsibilities to keep his mind off of her.

Before leaving for the airport, he had arranged to have a face-to-face meeting with his Chicago cell leader, Tamir Alam. Alam had a busy week scheduled, but of course, he set aside time for Esa.

Esa arrived promptly at 9:00 a.m. as scheduled.

"Good morning, Mr. Alam."

"Good morning, sir. I am sorry to hear about your wife. How are you and her parents doing?"

"I'm having a hard time, and you can imagine how her parents are handling it—not well. Let's get straight to our business at hand. Hajji is very concerned that the reason for the president heightening the security threat level is connected to Sky Burst, and I am having one-on-one meetings to look each of my guys in the eyes to see if Hajji's concerns are valid. Do you have any reason to suspect that your cover has been compromised?"

Alam was very confident with his reply. "When I heard the White House announcement, I became quite paranoid and interrogated all my men. Mr. Mann, I believe them and have great confidence in them. I do not have a problem in my cell."

"So far, I've gotten the same response from everyone. I just hope and trust in Allah that we are not compromised."

For the next forty-five minutes, they got into details about the operation, and Esa felt reassured. Then Alam's executive assistant came into the room to remind him that his budget meeting would begin in ten minutes. As they exited past his assistant, they made up some conversation about rebalancing his portfolio and making the trades as requested.

Esa grabbed his carry-on bag and walked down the hall toward the elevator. Jason was walking in the opposite direction to the boardroom. As the two men passed in the hall, they nodded and smiled at each other. Esa was smiling for a different reason. Esa had just heard from Alam that his team in PA was far ahead of schedule, and their boss didn't have a clue. Jason connected his laptop to the projector and prayed silently that his presentation would go well.

ↄb

He was running through his slides and talking points one more time silently as his boss walked in. He was the first to arrive. David Lawhon was perhaps one of the last great Horatio Alger stories in American business. He started as a shift worker in McNichols Farm Implements's very first factory, which was in Pennsylvania, but in a different city, Scranton. He literally worked his way through the ranks to the level of chief operating officer in charge of all operations for the company internationally—with just an eighth grade education. Jason always enjoyed his time with Dave; the two of them had made the transition from peers to boss and subordinate painlessly. Their relationship was built on mutual respect and convictions of faith.

"Hello, Jason. How goes the battle in Amish country?"

Smiling, Jason replied, "Just wonderful, but those buggies can cause some interesting traffic problems."

"How are Anne and the kids?" Dave always started their conversations by getting caught up on his family.

"Growing like mad—the kids, that is. Anne is still adjusting a bit to the rural life, but she seems to be enjoying the peace."

Jason knew that Dave had not been brought in on the night shift situation, and it pained him that he couldn't tell him.

"Are you all set?"

"Yes, sir. I would feel more comfortable with my guys by my side, but I'm feeling good."

"I ran through your presentation yesterday, and it looks good. You present the facts well, and you know I have your back."

"Thanks, Dave. Yes, I know."

The rest of the execs were making their way into the room, and there were cordial greetings all around. In addition to Dave, the entire executive committee was assembled: chairman, CEO, CFO, CIO, CMO, and the one responsible for the meeting, the senior vice president of administration and human resources, Tamir Alam. Each of them had at least one key guy from the area attending with them. Everyone grabbed their beverage of choice and settled in to listen to McNichols-Mifflintown's budget presentation for the 2015–2016 fiscal year.

d̈b

Jason stared out at a roomful of important-looking people ready to scrutinize his work and his presentation. As he stepped up to the podium, he visualized himself back in his room at the Ritz. Knowing that the person who had planted the terrorists in his factory was in his audience, he cleared his throat and began. He could tall as he surveyed his audience that he had their undivided attention. It flowed well just as it had in the mirror of the Ritz.

He concluded his plan and distributed a handout. His presentation was flawless—both electronically and oratorically.

Three-dimensional OptiPresent presentations were somewhat commonplace, but Jason's customized transitions between slides were new for this group. He had wowed them. The numbers were accurate and presented very logically.

"I thank you for your attention and I would like to open it up for questions."

All their heads were buried in the handout, and Jason knew that everyone, with the exception of Dave, was looking for errors.

There were several basic cost questions from the CFO that Jason was able to handle easily. Then the chairman raised his hand, and Jason recognized him immediately.

"Yes, sir?"

"You covered the money aspects and the human capital aspects of our new tractor, but have there been any operational problems in getting the MFI 237 off the ground?"

Jason, of course, didn't catch it, but Alam looked up immediately as the question was asked. He was carefully watching for Jason's reaction.

Taken aback, Jason said, "There were a few productivity problems, as most of the people were new to the company and our operation, but my plant superintendent, Henry Koontz, ironed them out swiftly. Since then, it has gone quite well."

It hurt Jason to lie, but he knew that al-Qaeda was represented in the meeting, and he was simply acting on the best interest of his factory and community.

Jason continued, "For a brand-new product line, I have been quite pleased."

The chairman added, "Jason, we have, too, and I want to commend you on a job well done."

The meeting lasted through lunch, and Alam concluded the meeting by telling Jason to expect their feedback by Friday. The room cleared quicker than it had filled.

Dave stayed behind. "Are you staying in town tonight?"

"No, I need to get back. Ashley has a regional field hockey playoff game tomorrow afternoon, and I have a ton of work to do tonight so I can get there."

"You have your priorities right, son. I plan on visiting the plant within the next month, and we'll be able to spend more time together then."

"We'll be looking forward to it."

"Jason, you did an excellent job today. You made me look good, and I appreciate your efforts."

Chapter 60

Antioch, Tennessee – April 16, 2015

"Humor is mankind's greatest blessing."

—*Mark Twain*

J erome sent a message from his tablet computer to Fadi, giving him the latest count on their components and, within seconds, received a response commending him. Fadi was excited about their progress and that his cell had really bonded. Everyone was showing up early for their scheduled times and staying late.

Fadi arrived at the warehouse seconds after he had sent his reply to Jerome.

"That was quick," Jerome said.

"I was in the neighborhood and wanted to see if I could give you a hand."

"Certainly, grab an empty workstation."

Fadi added to his electronic message. "It's great to see everyone being so conscientious for the cause."

Jerome smiled to the point of laughing. "Do you want to know what the real attraction is?"

"You mean it's not serving Allah and working for our cause?" Fadi asked with a little sarcasm.

"Of course, but in addition to that, Wazir is their entertainment. The guys are working extra hours just so they can get their daily dose of our own stand-up comedian. He's due here any minute, so you'll be able to see for yourself."

No sooner had he mentioned Wazir's pending arrival than he walked into the building. Scattered applause was heard around the warehouse. Holding his hands up like a prizefighter, he took his place and began working. He was more reserved with Fadi there, but in a few minutes, his jokes and comments started to fly. Unfortunately for his coworkers, that wasn't all that was flying, as they heard strange noises coming from his lower body.

"Oh, excuse me," Wazir apologized. "I have a serious gas problem today."

The guys were laughing—until the aroma hit them.

"Oh no! Wazir! What the heck have you been eating?"

Wazir went into a lengthy explanation of the fiber bars that he was eating as a part of his plan to lose some weight. They were full of fiber, with antioxidants added. He wasn't sure if it was the fiber or the antioxidants, but he figured out that one of those components was causing great eruptions in his unsettled stomach.

"The good news is that I lost over twenty pounds—only one hundred and fifteen left," he said boastfully.

He apologized again, but the apology had barely left his mouth when something else left another part of his body. With that, several of the guys grabbed his workstation and dragged it away from the rest of them. Darim found an old box fan in one of the abandoned offices, plugged it in, and aimed it in Wazir's direction—away from the rest of the group.

"Wazir, you'll have to speak up so we can hear your banter from over there, above the fan noise and the other noises that are coming from your direction, but we want to be entertained." Darim grinned.

"OK, boys, no problem!" With that, he proceeded to break into his monologue, similar to the late-night talk show hosts, but without the filters from the broadcast regulators. Political correctness was also ignored, as most of his jokes were at the expense of Jews and Christians.

Jerome looked at Fadi. "Do you see what I mean?"

Laughing, Fadi found a workstation and followed the instructions that Jerome had prepared for each position and started working.

Now that Basel had gotten to know Kyle better, he was offended by many of Wazir's off-color jokes. In the prior month, he had learned more about Christian beliefs than he had his entire life. He also realized that much of what he had learned about Christians and Jews as a child in Pakistan was fabricated and apparently untrue. He was learning, to his surprise and amazement, that it was a religion of love.

d͡b

It was Thursday and Kyle was looking forward to his weekly meeting with Basel. Kyle had learned much about Islam and had come to appreciate the fact that the Muslim religion was getting a bad rap from the press. In his mind, they should always differentiate between Muslims and radical Muslims. In his research, they all couldn't be lumped together. The radicals represented a very small percentage of the 1.5 billion Muslims in the world. Kyle found it fortunate that the al-Qaeda organization appeared to be inept and that Islam appeared to be becoming a more acceptable way to worship God. But the more he read, the more questions he had for his new friend Basel. He had been at the bookstore for a couple of hours digging for answers.

"Hey, Basel."

"Hello, Kyle. What have you been up to?"

"Same old stuff—hangin' and trying to write some music."

"You'll be teaching me about Islam before we're finished."

"I know you explained the reason for this before, but I don't think I'll ever understand your holy book and the way it jumps around with one disjointed thought to another."

"That's because it was recorded straight from Muhammad, word for word—"

"I know, I know," Kyle interrupted, "but it is still hard for me to follow."

Basel, wanting to change the subject, asked, "Can I buy you something to drink, Kyle?"

Ignoring Basel's offer, Kyle continued. "Have you given any more thought to visiting my church with me?"

"Yes, and I would like to go this Sunday if that still works for you."

"Absolutely. I'll stop by your apartment around ten thirty, and we'll ride together. Plan on lunch afterward, because I'm sure it will generate some questions."

Chapter 61

Antioch, Tennessee – April 19, 2015

"Church attendance is as vital to a disciple as a transfusion of rich, healthy blood is to a sick man."

—*Dwight L. Moody*

Basel had not spent much time in the south side suburbs of Nashville; nearly everyone in that part of town had their own cars and no need for taxis. He was amazed at the size of the homes, and when Kyle pulled into the parking lot of his church, Basel's mouth nearly fell open. It was larger than the largest mosque he had ever seen—even in his native Pakistan. The buildings and the parking lot went on forever, and men with bright-orange sweatshirts smiled, waved, and directed cars.

"My goodness, man, look at the size of this place!"

Kyle had been raised in this town and grown up in this church, but he could understand what Basel was saying. It was huge.

"How many people come here?" Basel asked with his eyes extra wide.

"Usually somewhere between six and seven thousand each Sunday."

"And attendance is not a requirement for your people to earn salvation?"

"No, that's right. We believe that Christ paid the price for us on the cross—once and for all."

That was a difficult thing for Basel to comprehend. The Antioch Islamic Center was filled every Friday afternoon, but he knew why—it was mandatory. The prayers of his people were one of the Five Pillars required to earn salvation.

"On Easter, a couple of Sundays ago, there were over ten thousand people who came to worship here."

"Wow!"

Today was a picture-perfect spring morning. The sky was a vivid sapphire blue, and the eighty-foot white steeple glistened in the sun. Kyle took all of this for granted, yet he couldn't help but notice the clarity of the sky. All around the campus, trees were beginning to come alive after their dormant winter. Kyle prayed silently for Basel—that his first experience in a Christian church would be a good one.

It was unusual for Basel to see so many cars in traffic without taxis peppered into the mix. They parked where they were directed to by the orange-shirted guys and walked toward the steeple, falling into the parade of Bible-carrying Christians.

People were coming, and people were going; back-to-back services shuffled the crowds in and out all morning. The 11:00 service was the last one for the day. Kyle liked it since it was more hip and filled with people he knew. His age group gravitated to the later service so they could sleep longer on Sunday morning. It was ten minutes until worship started, and the sanctuary was nearly filled. There were ushers asking people to move to the center of their aisle, plus a lot of socializing and commotion. Basel's only point of comparison was his services at the mosque, where people entered reverently and stood side by side. There were no pews, and everyone faced toward Mecca and the imam—no noise, no talking, and no music.

Just as they had gotten settled in their seats, the two huge high-definition three-dimensional screens on either side of the stage came to life, running a video featuring all the weekly announcements of the church. With the lights dimmed, the professionally edited presentation with music and special effects caught the attention of the people; it was particularly intriguing to Basel.

"Is this the way your service starts every week?"

"Yes, it gets everyone's attention and lets the people know that it's time to stop talking."

Then Basel noticed another strange thing—from both sides of the stage, men and women dressed in expensive-looking navy-blue gowns filled the platform.

"Who are they?"

Kyle was enjoying Basel's reaction to everything, as he understood how overwhelming this would all be to a person seeing it for the first time. "They are the choir, and you will hear them singing in a moment."

As soon as he had said that, the orchestra started up, and lights illuminated the entire front of the church as they broke into a rousing chorus. The words to the songs were on the screens; everyone stood, as if on cue, and began singing along with the choir. It was very upbeat American-style music, and as he read the words, Basel realized that they were praising this Jesus he was learning so much about. Some people's hands were raised, and everyone seemed to be smiling and singing loudly. The singing went on for a couple more songs, until the man in the front motioned for the people to sit down, and as they did, everyone focused on the choir, who then sang a song without the rest of the congregation joining in. It was another upbeat, joyous song in praise of Jesus, and the people in the choir all appeared to have smiles on their faces. Basel watched the people around him and noticed that they were all tapping their feet, nodding their heads, and a few had their hands raised to the ceiling.

Leaning over to Kyle, Basel said, "I should have brought a notebook to write down all of my questions."

Kyle picked up a pen from the back of the pew and pulled a page out of the journal that he carried with him everywhere. "There you go, man. Write away."

Basel was writing down question after question as he took it all in. Kyle had looked ahead in the order of worship, curious to see what Pastor Jack would be speaking on today, and was a bit nervous. Of all the Sundays to bring Basel to visit, he had to bring him on a day when the verse was John 14:6:

Jesus saith unto him, "I am the way and the truth and the life: no one cometh unto the Father but by."

The sermon was going to be a bit awkward since that topic was probably the most controversial aspect of the Christian faith, and as such, the verse had varying degrees of acceptance by different denominations. But it was what Kyle believed, and he knew from which position Pastor Jack would be speaking. *Interesting discussion to follow*, Kyle thought.

db

As Kyle had suspected, the sermon was a straightforward message of the need for Christ to enter heaven. He glanced over at Basel's sheet of paper; it was filled with notes, and more were being added as the pastor preached.

What the pastor was saying wasn't new to Basel; he had heard it from Kyle, read about it in various books, and even read it in the Bible. But there was something different about hearing it in this setting. It gave Basel a different perspective, and one point that the pastor made really made him stop and think: "If you were in a burning building with your friend, about to burn to death, and you knew which door he could go through to escape the fire, wouldn't you want to tell him which door it was?"

Basel knew that the pastor was talking to the Christians, encouraging them to be bolder with their friends, but it really helped him understand what was driving his conversations with Kyle. He truly wanted to show Basel which door to enter.

Could it be that the door I've been going through all my life is leading me to a life of torment and eternal fire? Basel thought and wrote a note, realizing that the sheet Kyle had given him was nearly full on both sides.

db

As the service came to a close, the pastor welcomed anyone who wanted to talk with him to see him after the service. He would be hanging out in a room off the foyer. Then the guy who had led the singing at the start of the service came to the front and led them in one more song.

Basel gathered his notes and his composure as he and Kyle headed to the back of the church.

"How about eating right here? We have a café at the other end of the building, and we can talk more there," Kyle suggested.

As they walked out of the sanctuary and toward the café, it seemed to Basel that Kyle knew everyone in the entire church. Basel was impressed with how friendly and cordial all the people were.

"I am obviously different looking than the people here, but they are all so friendly to me."

"May I introduce you to Pastor Jack?" Kyle asked.

Fascinated but scared, Basel declined. "Not today."

db

After what seemed like hundreds of introductions, the two of them finally got to the café, where they ordered a couple of sandwiches and took a table in the corner, out of the way. Kyle didn't want any interruptions, as he knew that Basel was filled with questions and observations.

"Your people seem to be filled with love, and everyone has been so nice to me. I have to tell you that I'm a bit overwhelmed."

"They're nice people. The love you see and have experienced comes from their relationship with Jesus."

"All my life, I've been taught to hate your people—your people who have been born by monkeys and pigs. My head is spinning, as I'm seeing people acting completely different than I was taught," Basel said with tears forming in the corners of his eyes.

Their conversation went on for over two hours.

Basel was scheduled to work that afternoon and evening—work that was targeted at killing the infidels who he had just encountered and many, many more.

"Kyle, thank you for bringing me, but I have a commitment that I can't be late for. I really need to be going."

Chapter 62

Mifflintown, Pennsylvania – April 22, 2015

"What separates the winners from the losers is how a person reacts to each new twist of fate."

—*Donald Trump*

R aja and the Khoury wives were returning from their weekly trip to the Belleville farmers' market. The market was filled with Amish people, but their burkas presented another form of a unique lifestyle. The local Amish referred to everyone outside of their sect as "English," but the dark-skinned ladies with their faces covered were not your typical English. They just stared and looked away as soon as one of the Saudis made eye contact.

The ladies had been going to the market ever since discovering it. Selection at the market was limited at this time of the year, though. There were some early berries showing up, and they had homemade candies, housewares, and sweets year-round. They never talked with the Amish. They grabbed lunch at the market cafeteria and kept to themselves. The Amish and the Muslims were curious of each other.

They decided to head back to Mifflintown a different way; they liked to explore the beautiful mountains and were in no real hurry to get home. Their part of the project was complete, so they were just providing moral support for the men, who would just be waking up from their "night."

As they neared the compound, Farah noticed something out of the corner of her eye. "There's a car parked over there near our houses," she said, pointing to the plain black sedan parked off the road. The progressive Amish drove black cars, but this one looked different; it had several antennae scattered around the rear deck.

"Maybe it's always parked there. This isn't the way we normally come home," Raja added.

Just as she had said that, they all noticed two men carrying cases walking deep into the woods.

Her voice quickened. "What are they doing?"

Their hearts raced as they rushed back to the compound. Trying to act nonchalant and resisting the desire to run to the comfort of their husbands, they retrieved the packages out of their trunk and carried them to their homes.

"After you unload your purchases, come back to my house." Raja said with nervousness in her voice.

The guys were deep in conversation and hardly noticed that their wives had returned. Yar looked up from his conversation to see an odd look on his wife's face. Just as he was about to say something, the Khoury wives entered, also with the same strange, frightened look.

Yar asked all three of them, "What in the world happened at the market today?"

Raja spoke up. "It wasn't at the market." Her voice was noticeably shaking, which added to the anticipation.

Yar was becoming anxious. "Tell us what happened," he said in a loud voice that demanded a quick answer.

Motioning for the men to go outside, Raja said, "We saw a black car parked by the road on the other side of our property."

"Is that it?"

"No, we saw two men carrying cases headed toward our houses in the woods to the south of us."

Instantly, the men's faces mimicked the same look of concern.

Yar wondered what was in those cases, but he knew it couldn't be good. The fact that strange men in a black car were walking toward his compound spelled trouble for his operation. Looking to the twins, Yar whispered, "Go get your Tasers and your handguns, and get back here as quickly as you can."

The women huddled together; they were scared.

Yar went to the hidden panel in his living room that stored their high-tech gear. The door slid into the wall and exposed an array of flashing lights and LED displays. He remembered Tamir having him record random, innocuous conversations that he and the Khourys had had early on in the process.

"You may need a diversion someday," he had directed Yar.

Praise Allah that he had, as he thought about how they needed to get to the men with the cases.

Within minutes, they were reassembled in the Din living room. Meanwhile Yar had been whispering to the women to get a more precise location for their visitors.

Yar motioned for the guys to go into the soundproof room as he started the playback of the recording in the living room. They strategized their approach and agreed that once they left the room, they would only use sign language and signals. They held the element of surprise, but they had no idea what kind of resistance the two strangers would offer.

They hugged their wives and left through the windows on the side of the house opposite from where their "watchers" were set up. The women were stoic, but tears streamed down their cheeks. Yar went in one direction, with Jamil and Jabir going in the opposite. They circled deep into the woods.

297

Yar was the first to spot them. Their camouflaged clothing made them almost indistinguishable. There were two of them with headsets on connected to what appeared to be electronic listening devices. The twins arrived momentarily and made eye contact with Yar. They had prearranged a hand count of 1-2-3 before grabbing them. The headsets and the diversionary recording made sneaking up on them relatively easy, but all three men's hearts were about to beat out of their chests. Yar raised his fingers with the countdown, and before the DHS agents knew what had hit them, they were unconscious from the Taser hits.

The three men bumped fists and hugged. Jamil headed back to the compound to get their McNichols MFI 765g four-wheel-drive gator and a trailer to cart the two large men back to the compound. The women, watching expectantly from behind the drapes, saw Jamil return and rushed out. He assured them that all had gone well.

By the time Jamil returned with the four-wheeler, the two men, still unconscious, had been bound with wrist and ankle straps. Yar and Jabir put them in the trailer.

Back in the outbuilding, Raja, still visibly shaken, asked, "What do we do now?" Then it hit her. "Remember how Nyla's intuition registered a concern about Mr. Reeves?"

They all nodded, trying to figure out what this had to do with their two uninvited guests.

"We need to have these guys eliminated, so let's invite Mr. Reeves to the party and have him do the honors. That will clearly show us if he's one of us."

Yar was shocked that such a dreadful thought had come from his beautiful wife, but he was impressed, and they all nodded in approval. They decided to call Craig and ask him to come over after sundown. In the meantime, Yar suggested that they take a quick count of the parts. They all knew that they would have to pull up stakes and run for cover. There was going to be collateral damage.

Two—and if Nyla's intuition was correct, three—infidels were about to begin their lives in hell.

Yar called Craig Reeves.

"Hello, Craig. We need to meet with you this evening. Can you come by the compound around six p.m.?"

Yar wasn't familiar with DHS protocol, but he suspected that the unconscious agents wouldn't be expected to check in with their bosses in the middle of the afternoon, so they had some time before all hell broke loose. They had no time for wasted steps, however. Yar pulled up his parts inventory report on his computer. They were about a week short of completing their assignment.

His hope was that they would be able to get the unused bars of palladium as well as all their parts, instructions, and discs containing their programs out of the McNichols plant prior to DHS showing up. They would have to get in and out of the plant and then take off for cover, as far away from Mifflintown as they could get. According to their contingency plan, the three families would separate and run in different directions. Adrenaline was pumping in all six of them; they didn't have time to think about what all this meant. Their lives had been turned upside down in one afternoon. They were about to scatter from their beautiful Pennsylvania valley for destinations unknown.

ᴄb

Craig arrived just before 6:00. The nervousness and sweaty feelings had returned. It was a repeat of his visit of the other evening, but he didn't know the reason for this invitation. He didn't think it was anything serious, however, since he hadn't heard anything from the people in Harrisburg. But he was wrong—possibly dead wrong.

Raja directed him to the outbuilding. He knocked and walked in without waiting for a response.

"What's up, Boss?"

He was led to a room in the back, where their prisoners were slumped on the floor, still drowsy from the Taser attack. Seeing the two agents in the camouflage jumpsuits startled Craig.

"Where did you find these guys?" was all he could think to say.

Yar did all the talking. "We found them in the woods with listening devices pointed at our houses."

Afraid of what the answer would be, Craig asked, "What are *we* going to do with them?" acting as if he were still a part of their "we."

The following words registered like a blow to his gut.

"*We* need to eliminate them."

Chapter 63

New York City – April 22, 2015

"Terrorism is escalating to the point that Americans soon may have to choose between civil liberties and more intrusive means of protection."

—*William S. Cohen*

E sa returned to New York after a hectic week that included the funeral of his wife. He took advantage of the bereavement leave that Chase, Smith & Hopper offered him. But of course, he didn't take time off from his al-Qaeda duties. In the past week, he had visited each of his cell leaders for face-to-face meetings. He needed a diversion from the recent events. He also wanted to be reassured personally that his cells were on schedule. Prior to his visit with Mazir Bahar, his Boston cell leader, he spent two days at a remote cabin on a lake in Maine—totally alone. There were no electronics to distract him, not even TV or radio. He simply fought through his feelings about Allison; he missed her company and dreaded returning to Fairfield. To put off the inevitable, he went straight to his office from LaGuardia.

Everyone had left for the day by the time he arrived, so he went to his e-mail—nothing out of the ordinary. He grabbed his tablet from his briefcase to digest and review all of his meetings. The briefest meeting of the trip was in

301

Chicago with Tamir. He was by far the busiest leader on his team, but he was also the best. He was a pillar in the community and well respected throughout corporate America—the perfect operative. When he looked Esa in the eye and said everything was under control, Esa was convinced that it was.

In reviewing his notes, Esa recalled that Rafid, his LA leader, was confident that they could hit the May date with no difficulty. They had a few difficulties but nothing serious. The two of them ate at Esa's favorite restaurant and spent almost the entire next day getting caught up, followed by a visit to the LA operating facility buried in an industrial park in the sprawling suburb of Santa Clarita. There was so much business activity in that part of California that ten people gathering in a warehouse flew under the radar. The fact that three-quarters of their team were radical, white American Muslims made their cover even better. Southern California had always been a hotbed of radical beliefs, so recruiting for Rafid was easy. The radical movement had infiltrated a couple of mosques, and the imams in those mosques were all part of his network and plan. American radicals were prime candidates.

His next stop was with Fadi Hares in Nashville, and again, he was pleased with their progress. Just as he was digging into his Nashville notes, his secure cell phone buzzed. *Who could be calling me at eleven o'clock at night?* Caller ID identified the caller—it was Tamir.

"This is Esa. What's going on?"

"We have a serious problem and I needed to notify you immediately, but I don't have all the details yet."

"Tell me!" He was short of patience these days.

"Our cover has been compromised at McNichols-Mifflintown. Mr. Din and his guys have captured two men with listening devices in the woods near their houses."

"Did they initiate the scramble protocol?"

"No, not yet. They have not dealt with the threat at hand, and the four of them need to get to the plant to try to salvage the parts and materials before they leave town. In fact, I didn't talk to Din; he had his wife phone me to give me the alert."

"This is horrible news! Tamir, you said four of them. I thought we only had three guys in the Pennsylvania operations. Was I wrong?"

"They recruited a young American Muslim who started working with them a few weeks ago."

Surprised, Esa asked, "Did you vet him properly?"

"Absolutely. He checked out and has been a valuable part of the team there."

"I needed to know about him prior to the plan collapsing. Do they have time to salvage anything, or should they get out of there now?"

"We suspect they have a little time, as the two guys were taken totally by surprise and didn't have time to notify anyone. Exactly how much time we have, we don't know."

ḋb

Esa's question about Craig Reeves prompted Tamir to pull up the research and the vetting that Yar had sent him to assure himself that he was clean. Their cover was blown. *How in the world did they find us in the middle of rural Pennsylvania?* Everything in his file appeared to be solid. As he was thinking about Craig, Tamir realized that if the US government wanted to create a good cover, they could, and perhaps they had. Al-Qaeda did it daily.

"Yar, I need a complete status report as soon as you have everything under control!" Tamir was frustrated by getting Yar's voice mail but realized that he didn't have time to answer and needed to deal with the situation at hand.

Chapter 64

Mifflintown, Pennsylvania – April 22, 2015

"Death, after all, is the common expectation from birth. Neither heroes nor cowards can escape it."

—*Ellis Peters*

C haos in Mifflintown—just hours ago, everything was going well, or at least they thought it was. In reality, they had been compromised.

The captured contractors were still woozy from the Tasers. Each man had two burn marks on the back of his neck. In the commotion, the Saudis were not careful about injuring their two enemies. They were going to end their lives, and the Tasers were simply a way for them to buy time and orchestrate their demise in a more orderly manner. They freed their legs so they could attempt to walk, but for the two men, who appeared drunk, putting one foot in front of the other was challenging.

Jamil grabbed a couple of shovels and picks as the group headed back into the woods, now darkened by the moonless night. The contractors were soaking wet from nerves. It was a cool spring evening; the sweat was not from temperature. Their only hope was that Reeves would somehow be able to rescue them, but at this point, he was playing the terrorist role.

They reached a spot in the woods where they were between the highway and the compound, with no signs of civilization in either direction.

"Give them the shovels," Yar sounded irritated as the frightened men started to move dirt—digging their own graves.

Digging too slowly for them, Jamil kicked one in the back. "Get busy! We don't have all night."

His comment brought some snickers from the other three. Thoughts raced through Craig's mind: *What could I do? How can I save my coworkers? How can I save myself?*

The holes weren't six feet, but they were deep enough. They all knew that it would be no time at all before the bodies were recovered, but they would be long gone—scattered.

"That's enough digging." Yar shouted.

The words resonated in Craig's head. He wanted to save the men, but national security and Project Peace Shield were all of their first priorities, including the contractors in the hole. Employees of Homeland Security knew when they were hired that they might be called upon to give the ultimate sacrifice, but their sentiments about death were different than their Saudi captors.

Heart beating, adrenaline pumping, Craig Reeves grabbed a pick lying next to the makeshift graves as quietly as he could, but his movement caught the corner of Jamil's eye.

"What are you doing, Craig?" he yelled, and the other two turned toward him immediately.

Blood splashed as Craig drove the pick into Jamil's back. Jamil instantly fell to his knees and then face down in the pile of dirt. The two contractors were attempting to make a run for it when guns started firing. Flashes, gun smoke, and all-out commotion erupted as Craig tried to wrestle the gun from Yar's hand.

Both of his coworkers lay dead in pools of blood. Seeing that, he decided to make a run for it to notify Harrisburg and the local authorities to stop Jabir and Yar.

Jabir took off after Craig, while Yar made certain that the contractors were dead. More gunfire and Craig felt a burning sensation in his left bicep. Not bothering to throw any dirt over the agents, Yar ran toward the compound to get Raja and his vehicle. He had to clear out the plant and follow their protocol—their protocol written for times such as this.

The girls had heard the gunshots— Nyla was correct. In a strange twist of irony, Nyla's intuition about Craig was correct, and he was responsible for her husband's death.

Yar grabbed Raja and Nyla and told them to get in the car immediately. Part of their contingency plan included three vehicles parked at designated places in the woods near the compound. Pulling up next to them, Raja knew exactly what to do. Nyla was in shock, Raja was near panic, but they jumped into the hidden car as Yar raced toward the plant. Yar hoped that he wouldn't get stopped for speeding. Making it to the plant in only minutes, he was early for the shift change and tried to maintain his composure as he hurried to the warehouse and their parts.

Craig had escaped Jabir, albeit with a glancing bullet wound. Jabir had to return to the compound to get his wife on the road. They too went to the extra cars, where they made the switch and headed up US 322 North—headed for a predetermined location that was programmed into the car's GPS system.

Craig was out of breath, his clothing filled with blood, briars, and dirt. He had made it to the highway, but there were no cars. He had to take cover and hide from the only car that passed him; it was Jabir and Farah making their escape. He started to run toward town, but it was miles away. He reached for his cell phone, only to find an empty holster. Feeling ridiculous, he remembered charging it in his car charger.

Realizing that Jabir was gone and figuring that Yar had also made a run for it, he went back down the driveway to the compound. His car was there, but all four tires were slashed, and his cell phone was gone.

Chapter 65

Washington, DC – April 22, 2015

"When written in Chinese, the word 'crisis' is composed of two characters. One represents danger and the other represents opportunity."

—*John F. Kennedy*

Teddy Brewer was burning the midnight oil—his normal hours. Since he was a mere child, he needed far less sleep than his friends. If he did get sleep, he would generally start his day between 3:00 and 4:00 in the morning. He tried to sleep later, but once his eyes first opened, it was impossible for him to slow down his mind enough to fall back to sleep. He was single and lived alone; consequently, his lifestyle was acceptable. This morning, his day started at 3:30 a.m. He grabbed a cup of coffee and headed off to his office in the city. He looked fresh, and one would never guess he was operating on so few hours of sleep—a bottle of energy drink on his commute helped.

His intense schedule worked well, as he was able to compare notes with the other intelligence units around the world. He worked long enough that his schedule was sure to correspond with any time zone. He had been positioned as the head of this operation even though, technically, he was under the project manager, Agent Hill. After almost a week of diligent focus, he still had not been able to crack the puzzle of where the "electronics and brains" were coming from; all of the other components were aligned to cells.

He had just returned to his cubicle after walking around the facility; he found that he occasionally needed a cobweb-clearing walkabout to reboot his brain. Opening up everything fresh, he began the grind once again, looking for a clue or a tip that would open up the door enough that his megabrain could walk through and figure out the puzzle. Just as he was beginning to dig in, the light on his phone began flashing. The red color of the light told him it was serious.

"This is Teddy Brewer. How can I help you?"

The urgency was apparent when he heard the panicked voice of Wayne Joseph. "Teddy, I called into your direct line since I knew you would be there, so please report what I'm about to disclose to you to Cliff ASAP. For obvious reasons, I need to proceed quickly. Craig Reeves is on the phone here with us, and I'll let him explain what's going down in Mifflintown."

Craig explained the disastrous outcome of the surveillance team at the Din compound. None of the bloody details were spared.

Craig continued. "Teddy, I've mobilized the local authorities here in Mifflintown to get to the plant, but it took me over forty-five minutes to get to a telephone. I'm at a convenience store several miles down the road from their compound."

Teddy let the conversation proceed without asking questions. He had to slow down his brain in these situations as he patiently waited, taking in all the details but wishing that Craig would speed up.

"My guess is that at least one of the two survivors of the cell is going to try to salvage the parts from the plant."

Wayne, anxious, stepped into the conversation. "Teddy, we need you to broadcast the word throughout the company regarding what's come down here. This is obviously not part of Ahsan's plan, so we all need to be diligent to see how the other cells react to this curveball. It has broken much more quickly than we would have liked."

Craig added, "We also need you to send photos and descriptions of Yar Din, Jabir Khoury, and their wives out to every available outlet within a two hundred–mile radius of Mifflintown. Include Jamil's wife, for we suspect she's with them."

Teddy asked to be kept informed, moment by moment.

Craig answered, "Absolutely, and as soon as the local police pick me up here, I'll call you with a new cell phone number. Teddy, one more thing, see if you can ping my old cell phone. It may give us a lead on where they're headed."

Teddy did as he was directed and immediately refocused his attention from the electronics cell to the Mifflintown group. Every law enforcement and DHS contractor in the entire northeast region received his emergency broadcast. Now he needed to try to figure out where they would go and what they would do. The ping on Craig's cell phone did not work, as Teddy had surmised. He was certain that Craig's phone was at the bottom of a creek or had reached some other terminal fate. Teddy put a call out to Cliff; after all, the urgent work had been completed.

"I'll be in the office as soon as I can."

Cliff was on the Beltway in a matter of minutes.

Chapter 66

Mifflintown, Pennsylvania – April 22, 2015

"When it comes to the pinch, human beings are heroic."

—*George Orwell*

After dropping Raja and Nyla off at their escape car, Yar raced to the factory. Parking in his assigned spot, he jumped out and ran for the entrance. Once he hit the entrance, he had to slow to a fast walk; he was early for his shift. He didn't know where Craig had gone. A clock in his brain was ticking.

He walked past the mid-shift supervisor and headed back to the maintenance shop.

"What are you doing here so early? Trying to get points with Henry?"

Smiling with his tongue firmly planted in his cheek, Yar responded, "Exactly. I need all the points I can get right now."

He carried two heavy-duty duffels and grabbed another one in his office. He went straight for their hidden parts bins. Filling two and a half bags, he had all the parts and hurried out through an exit in the rear of the shop, where Raja was waiting in the extra car. After throwing them in the trunk, he ran back into the plant.

"Where are you going?" Raja protested. "We need to get out of here!"

Without answering, he ran to the CNC machines to grab the discs and clear their instructions from the machine's computer. He knew his time was evaporating, the palladium was forfeited—that could be replaced.

The mid-shift supervisor tracked down Yar.

"Yar, I need to talk with you. We had a problem on line 3A this evening that you need to know about."

Sticking the discs and plans into his jacket pocket, Yar said, "I'll be back in a minute. I left something in my car."

It had been nearly a half hour since he dashed out of the compound. Everything was happening so quickly he didn't have time to realize that he had lost a good friend. His life was changed forever, but he kept his sights set on their ultimate goal. This was all for the sake of Allah. There was no need to worry about Jamil, as he would be rewarded with the highest level of eternity possible.

Yar jumped into the driver's seat. They knew the drill, as they had practiced the escape protocol numerous times, but always hoped they would never have to execute it. Raja had the GPS already turned on, and its voice was calling out instructions in Arabic. They didn't know where they were headed; they just knew it was away from Mifflintown.

There was urgency about them as they left the McNichols parking lot, but they had to maintain decorum. As they turned left, heading toward Mifflintown, it appeared that every Mifflintown Police Department, Pennsylvania State Police, County Sheriff's Office, and unmarked vehicle was descending on the plant. Yar had the two girls lie down on their seats as he nonchalantly drove past his frantic pursuers.

He had Raja reach into the glove compartment for the cell phone that had been placed there just for this occasion. Following the escape protocol, he pulled up a number stored in the phone's contact list labeled "Fire" and pushed send. The phone rang and immediately went dead. At the other end, a firestorm erupted throughout the Din compound. The fire burned quickly, and all of the buildings were leveled within minutes.

ꝺb

A cop pulled into the convenience store shortly after Craig had hung up with Teddy and Wayne. They handed him a cell with which he promptly called Teddy.

"This is my new cell number. I'm on my way to the plant."

Craig was impatient. He was certain that Yar, Jabir or both had headed to the plant to destroy any traces of the parts they were manufacturing, and he had already lost an hour since the time they scattered. His arm throbbed, but there was no time for pain now.

"Step on it!" he shouted at the uniformed officer.

"Sir, I'm going as fast as these roads will allow. Can you tell me what in the world is going on?"

"You have no need to know at this point. Just get me to the McNichols plant quickly, or move over and let me drive!" The emotion of the evening was getting the best of Craig.

They pulled into the lot and surrounded the vehicle matching the description of their perpetrator—parked boldly in Yar's assigned place. Police vehicles were everywhere. Craig jumped out and went straight to the state policeman who appeared to be in charge.

Showing his DHS credentials, he said, "I'm Craig Reeves, and I'm in charge of this operation as of now." He had grabbed his credentials along with his service revolver and flak jacket from a secret compartment in his disabled car. He also donned a DHS hat and glasses that somewhat disguised him.

"Yes, sir. We have been directed as such. My men and the MPD force stand ready to assist."

"Spread out and guard every exit." Taking control immediately, Craig asked a couple of officers, "Come with me quickly!" As he entered the plant he headed straight for the machine shop. The factory workers were confused by the visitors and commotion. Craig led the way and motioned for the employees to get out of the way and to be quiet.

The supervisor tried to stop them. He didn't recognize Craig, as that would have confused him more. "What in the world is going on?"

"Where's Yar?"

"I told him I needed to talk with him, but he said he needed to get something out of his car."

Craig stopped the invasion. "Wait here while I go check a few things."

When he got to the machine shop, all their parts were gone, and he could tell by looking that the CNC computers had been fired up. Their screen glowed blue since they had not been shut down properly.

"We missed him. He's out of here. Set up road blocks immediately. Their pictures have already been broadcast throughout all the networks."

Craig Reeves didn't realize that, while he was driving from the convenience store, he had passed right by the inventory of parts that he had helped al-Qaeda manufacture. He had contributed to their planned attack on the United States. Their late-model generic-looking sedan was on its way to parts unknown.

"Teddy, we missed him. His car is here, but they must have switched vehicles. He has the parts and the plans. We just missed him."

"I'll get the update out through the network. Thanks for the info!"

Henry had gotten a call from his supervisor and stopped by to pick up Jason on the way to the plant. It looked like a war zone; police cars were randomly parked all over the lot and the surrounding lawn. From police scanners, the media had picked up that something was happening at McNichols, but they didn't know what. To ward off the press, the DHS public affairs officer had already drafted a made-up story about one of the McNichols employees "going postal," and it was being leaked to the press via their channels.

Jason recognized Craig in his makeshift disguise. He had assumed that something had happened with the Saudis, and Craig's flak jacket confirmed his hunch.

"What happened?"

"It's over, Boss—at least for McNichols. Jamil is dead, and Yar escaped with Jabir and the three women. We're not sure where they're headed."

A wave of relief rushed over Jason. His plant, his people, and most important, his family were all safe.

Chapter 67

Harrisburg, Pennsylvania – April 22, 2015

"All media exist to invest our lives with artificial perceptions and arbitrary values."

—Marshall McLuhan

The late news on WHPA Channel 4, Harrisburg, led with a report about a situation in the small town of Mifflintown.

"A disgruntled employee walked into the McNichols Farm Implements plant in Mifflintown brandishing a handgun. The local and state police descended on the plant, responding to the 911 call from an employee. They arrived quickly and were able to corner the young man in the plant's warehouse. During the confrontation, there were no employees hurt. Unfortunately, the employee, Jamil Khoury, turned the gun on himself and pulled the trigger." A picture of Jamil appeared over the shoulder of the news anchor. "Mr. Khoury was twenty-five years of age and had worked at McNichols for less than a year. He was apparently unhappy about the amount of hours he was working. We have a reporter on the scene; here is Charlotte Yoder with an update."

"Thanks, Christine. We have learned that Jason Lange, the McNichols plant managing director, arrived on the scene a short time ago, but he refused to comment on the situation."

Footage showed Jason and Henry as they arrived at the plant, walking past all the microphones being shoved in their faces. He was allowed to pass the police lines, which kept the reporters away.

"We have learned that the plant's mid-shift was sent home early, and the night shift has been canceled. The day shift is expected to begin on schedule in the morning. I talked with a few employees as they exited the plant, but I could not find anyone who had witnessed Mr. Khoury in the plant. They all reported hearing the gunshot that echoed through the building. I understand that Mr. Khoury worked on the night shift, and since he was new to the company, none of the employees I talked to knew him. Christine, in an interesting side story, several of the emergency and police vehicles that were here were also called to the scene of a fire at a farm several miles from the plant. I'll see what I can find out about that story. That's all I have for now, so I'll send it back to you Christine."

"Thanks for the report, Charlotte. That sure is a lot of excitement for a quiet town in the middle of Amish country. Now here's Chuck with the latest on our weather."

Chapter 68

Al-Qaeda Headquarters, Afghanistan – April 23, 2015

"It is a certain fact that not all Muslims are terrorists, but it is equally certain, and exceptionally painful, that almost all terrorists are Muslims."

—*Ayman al-Zawahiri*

Hajji treasured his alone time after his morning prayers. He liked to sit quietly in his apartment and reflect. It was a time for him to remove himself from his pressures, a time just for him to be with Allah. Dalil knew not to bother him unless he absolutely had to. Knocking, he waited for a response.

"Come in," Hajji said, knowing it could only be one person on the other side of the door.

"Hajji, I'm so sorry to bother you, but I have troubling news that I know that you would want to hear immediately."

Impatient and mildly bothered by the intrusion, Hajji asked, "What is it, man? Quickly!"

"I just heard from Esa Mann. The group in Pennsylvania has launched their escape protocol."

"What went wrong *now*?"

The blow-by-blow description made Hajji irrationally upset. He threw the book he was reading, smashing it into a nearby wall. Dalil had been with him since college and had never seen him this upset. His eyes were dark and spewed evil. His voice trembled, and veins popped on his forehead.

"How could such a thing happen? And it was their wives who had to discover the spies? This is a disgrace to all Muslims!"

"Yes, sir. I guess it's better that they uncovered their operation when they did, or it could have hurt us more."

"Hurt us more?" Hajji screamed at the top of his lungs. "How on earth could it hurt more? We have no idea what those infidels learned from those lazy, care-less, sloppy Saudis and what kind of damage we have yet to uncover."

Hajji continued. "We have operations all around the world, and none have been compromised but the one under Mann's control. First a pregnant wife and now he loses a key operation. Get him on the phone immediately and have Malcolm join us."

db

Moments later, the three of them sat across the room from the flat-panel screen showing Esa in his New York office.

With no hello or chitchat, Hajji asked, "What in the world is going on?"

"Sir, I'm still collecting information, but we underestimated the ability of our enemy," Esa barely finished before Ahsan interrupted.

"I would say we did. Do you have any other problems to jeopardize Sky Burst further? I continue to be surprised and disappointed by you!"

"Sir, I pray not."

"Did they at least exercise the escape protocol correctly and properly?"

"I have spoken to the two surviving cell members, and it appears that they have escaped cleanly, with all pertinent data. No traces have been left behind except Jamil's dead body."

"Everything?"

"Yes, sir. We have been monitoring news from the area, and it appears that our enemies are painting this as a suicide in the McNichols plant. Their compound has been destroyed by the fire."

As Hajji settled down, Esa sat, embarrassed. It seemed to Esa that Hajji was waiting for him to say something.

"I'm sorry, and I will do everything in my power to regain your confidence."

"I would say good luck with that, but I'm not sure you have enough days on earth to rebuild what was destroyed tonight. And, Mr. Mann, it is not just what happened tonight! Please keep Dalil completely plugged into the damage once you determine the extent of it."

"*Alhamdulillah!*" Hajji recited.

"*Alhamdulillah!*" Esa responded as he bowed his head.

His screen went black.

db

Turning his attention to his two lieutenants, Hajji asked, "What now, gentlemen? Can we salvage our attack?"

Malcolm had been called into the meeting before he even had his first cup of coffee, and he was befuddled by the news of the disaster in PA. Looking in Dalil's direction, he said, "Yes, sir, we can save it."

Dalil concurred. "It will take more scrambling, but we need to get the attack started with what we have."

Hajji, still angry and confused, said, "We need to annihilate them—now! Make it so!"

Dalil and Malcolm left the war room and went to work. Before the day was completed, their plan would be launched.

Trying to be encouraging to Dalil who was clearly shaken by what had happened said, "The trucks are ready to start the rotation in all five countries. Let's get them moving."

Chapter 69

Antioch, Tennessee – April 23, 2015

"Conflict is the beginning of consciousness."

—*M. Esther Harding*

B asel sat in Imam Nafi's office at the AIC, waiting for the imam to arrive. He had wanted to meet with him all week, and today was his first opening. Since his visit to Kyle's church, he was even more confused.

"Good morning, Basel. What is the issue you wish to meet with me about? Is it regarding our class?"

"I have been battling inner demons and need to talk to a man of God."

When he heard that, the imam walked from around the back of his desk and invited Basel to move to the informal seating area on the other side of his office as he closed his door and told the receptionist to hold his calls. They would need privacy. He wasn't sure what Basel had for him, but he could tell it was serious.

"What is it, Basel?"

"Sir, I'm questioning my beliefs in Islam."

"That is the worst possible thing that you could have told me. I need to know more. Talk to me, son."

"I have become close to a Christian, and we have been meeting on a regular basis. I have been teaching him about Islam, and he has been teaching me about his beliefs."

"Go on." As the imam leaned back on the sofa, his body language spoke volumes.

"We have become close friends. It all started with him helping me when I was in a bind with my car. Sir, he's not at all like the Christians who I have been taught about. He's kind and loving. We have been sharing life with each other, and our conversations go past our religions. I have been a confidant for him, as he has for me."

"There's nothing wrong with building relationships with Christians—that's what our class has been about. We hope to win all Christians over to Islam. It's our obligation to save them from hell."

"Imam, I can't really explain what's going on in me, but I sense an uncontrollable urge to seek more knowledge about their Jesus, and when I read their Bible, the words flow from the page into my head. I don't get the same feeling from my reading of own holy book. Their Bible truly speaks to me."

The imam couldn't hide his shock from Basel. He was visibly shaken and physically shaking.

"I have spoken to my friend Kyle about this, and he's convinced it's the Holy Spirit working on me."

"Basel, that's blasphemous! You do realize that they believe their God is a God in three persons, don't you? How can that be? Allah is the *only* God, and it is not possible to have three of them! What happened that prompted you to meet with me?"

"I attended church with him last Sunday, and everyone was happy, everyone was nice to me. Sir, they are nothing like the 'apes' and 'pigs' that I was told they were on the TV programs I watched as a child. I'm confused and frightened by these feelings."

"Basel, I don't know what to say. You are talking about a decision that will damn you to hell. My heart cries for your soul. What would Taj think about this conversation?"

Those words dug deep into his spirit. What *would* Taj have said? What *would* his friends in the cell say? He had been alienated from his family for many years, but he couldn't help but think about what his parents would say as well. The concept of a loving heavenly father was intriguing to him. He never had a loving earthly father and wasn't sure how that would feel.

"I'm embarrassed by these feelings, sir, but have you ever thought that they may be right and the only way to heaven is through their Jesus?"

Standing, Nafi said, "No, I haven't. I need some time to figure out what I can do to help you. See the receptionist on the way out and plan to be here at the same time tomorrow."

"Sir, I have another issue nagging me."

Almost interrupting and visibly upset, the imam responded gruffly, "We'll talk about it tomorrow."

Basel also stood and made his way to the door. The imam was no help.

$$db$$

Basel's inner battle raged. He was scheduled to work at the warehouse this afternoon, which produced more inner struggle. His hatred of the infidels had diminished significantly since joining the apologetics class. Ironically, the more he worked on the circuit boards and computer chips, the closer he was growing to Kyle's Savior.

He arrived at the warehouse and went straight to work at his soldering gun station. He was noticeably quiet, but since he had never been outgoing, it wasn't noticeable to the other guys. Evidently, word had come down to Fadi that they had to step up their production and speed up their schedule. Fadi was there when Basel arrived and was asking each of the guys if they were available to work more hours the following week.

"Basel, I need some help. There is much pressure on me. Can you work late tonight?"

"I can work until five, but I have an appointment that I can't get out of." He didn't want to cancel his time with Kyle. He needed that time. He needed to resolve his inner conflict, and he knew his friend would be comforting.

"How about this weekend? Can you give me some more time then?"

"Yes, sir. I'll see what I can do. For right now, put be down for two extra hours each day until early next week."

⚐

"Basel, are you OK?" In Kyle's mind, he looked like he had been through the ringer. His hair matted to his forehead after his sweat had dried – he looked upset and nervous.

"I have had a bad day. In fact, I've had a bad week ever since I visited your church last Sunday."

Basel opened up to his friend and shared his turmoil. Kyle was surprised by the impact that his church service had had on him, but he was pleased. He had grown close to Basel, and their weekly coffee discussions apparently had impacted him. He knew that the service was only one of many steps that Basel had taken in the direction of Christ.

"Kyle, I met with Imam Nafi this morning to talk with him about my confusion."

"Wow, you're kidding me! What did he tell you?"

"He was shocked and disappointed."

"For what it's worth, my friend, I am very pleased with you. I didn't enter into this friendship with you to convert you, but you need to know that several of my friends and I have been praying for you—praying that your heart would be opened to the Holy Spirit."

"Kyle, I'm scared."

"I understand what a bold move it would be for you to convert to Christianity, and I get the effect that your heritage and your culture has had on you." Kyle didn't know the half of it.

"Kyle, all of that is accurate, but that's not really what I'm scared about."

"Talk to me, my friend."

Basel wanted to be open and honest with his friend, but could he trust him?

"Kyle, can I share something with you, the real reason why I'm scared?"

"Of course you can."

"I need to ask that you promise me that you won't tell a soul. I hesitate to tell you, since it could put you in a precarious, awkward, and potentially dangerous situation."

"Now you're scaring me."

"Do I have your word?"

"Yes."

With that commitment, Basel revealed his desire to become a Christian, which thrilled Kyle. However, Basel then went on to share the details of his apologetics class and how, through that, he had become a member of a terrorist group that operated out of the AIC. He didn't get into all the details, because he didn't know them. He did know, though, that they were participating in a planned attack on the United States.

"My friend"—Kyle sighed and immediately regretted his pledge—"you have told me about a planned attack on my country and have asked me to remain quiet. How can I do that?"

"You gave me your word!"

"Yes, I did, and my word means something to me. But, Basel, these feelings you have toward Christianity and the desire to keep the information you have to yourself is very contradictory. I beg you to either give me the ability to tell the authorities or you let them know. I never would have given you my word if I had known the magnitude of your secret."

Now both men were deeply conflicted. They said their good-byes and went their separate ways. Both were in for restless nights.

Chapter 70

Washington, DC – April 23, 2015

"He who labors diligently need never despair; for all things are accomplished by diligence and labor."

—Menander

Teddy managed to get a couple hours of sleep in a bunkroom. HQ had become his home away from home. He kept several changes of clothing in his office and used the company's locker room for his showers. He was singularly focused on breaking this case. The dragnet had been set—so far, nothing. They knew the Saudis were running; they just don't know where.

Along every interstate highway and most state roads throughout the Northeast and into the Midwest, the images of the five surviving members of the Juniata cell were being displayed in color on digital billboards. Teddy had mobilized a system that was originally developed to alert the public about missing children as part of the AMBER Alert bulletin, but on rare occasions, it was used to track down criminal fugitives as well. Roadblocks had also been initiated, but he was certain that satellite surveillance systems were helping the terrorists. Al-Qaeda had been reported to have their own satellites back in the heyday of the nineties and the first decade of this millennium. Teddy had been studying the terrorism franchise longer and harder than anyone, and he didn't buy the image of bin Laden, Ahsan, and their followers being inefficient.

Cliff Hill had also spent the night at the headquarters building, staying by Teddy's side to lend whatever support or help he could.

There really wasn't anything else they could do regarding the Juniata cell. Back in the war room, he refocused his efforts on laying out their plan. The cell providing the brains and the electronics of the weapons was very slick. Every one of the other four cells had slipped up in one way or another, but this one hadn't. It was being run by an intelligent person—a very careful, intelligent person.

"Help me brainstorm, Boss?"

"Sure. Let's start from the top."

Teddy, for what seemed like the hundredth time, retraced the steps as to how they had gotten to today. In the five non-Muslim countries around the world, they had been able to label at least four of the five cells in each territory.

"The only cell that Ahsan knows that we know about is here in North America. The impact of that breach to his operation is unknown, but we can be certain that it has impacted his plans and, most likely, accelerated the countdown."

"I'm with you, Teddy. What do you see his options being?"

"He's an intelligent man, and the combo of him and Dalil is dangerous. I see his options as logical—continuing on his original schedule, speeding up his planned attack, or terminating it altogether."

"We both know which direction he'll take."

"The activity on his communication network escalated after Mifflintown imploded, but I still have not been able to isolate the origin of five different IP addresses. Here is what I have: The cell leader is in NYC. We have identified him and could apprehend him immediately, but that would scatter all of his minions to serve al-Qaeda later. We know he has cells in Boston, Chicago, and Los Angeles. We also know that the North American leader has a cell operating on Long Island. The mystery cell that has stumped me has the best IT of the lot working for them.

Their IP address is ping-ponged around the globe, and I can't triangulate it or track it in any way."

Cliff, trying to be encouraging, said, "Teddy, let's celebrate what you have accomplished so far. You are the quarterback of this team, and this game is more important than any Super Bowl ever. The stakes are much greater than the Lombardi Trophy, and this country will forever be indebted to you."

"Thanks, Boss. I know you're trying to lift my spirits, but we both know there won't be any more NFL games—or any other type of game, for that matter—if we lose this one."

Chapter 71

Antioch, Tennessee – April 24, 2015

"Original sin is the only rational solution of the undeniable fact of the deep, universal and early manifested sinfulness of men in all ages, of every class, and in every part of the world."

—Charles Hodges

Imam Nafi's greeting to Basel was much colder today than it had been the day before.

"How did you get to this confusion of faith? For over twenty years, you have grown up in the religion of Muhammad, and now you are questioning its tenets?"

"I'm not sure how I got here. I think, for the first time in my life, I have experienced the love of God."

Screaming to the point where his voice was audible through the walls, "That's blasphemous. How can you say that Allah does not love?"

"What I'm saying is that I have experienced the love of the people who follow Jesus, and I don't feel the same love from my own people when I attend prayer. The love of Allah is conditional; I have to follow and abide by the Five Pillars. The God of the Christians offers unconditional love; it is there for my asking. Sir, I feel that the Quran emphasizes the punishment of God more than his love."

Getting defensive, the imam asked, "Have you studied all the differences of our two beliefs?"

"Probably not all the differences, but I have been deep in study of the Christian beliefs. Are you thinking about something specific?"

"Their holy book—it was written by forty different people. Our Quran was transcribed by one. Their book is full of contradictions."

"I find their book easier to understand and read. I have learned so much in the last few months."

Feeling a bit desperate, the imam tried a different tack. "Their entire religion is based on the resurrection of their Christ from the grave. It says in the Quran that he was not dead."

"The more I read, the more I believe. His resurrection was predicted in their Old Testament Book of Isaiah, and the original scroll containing the manuscript of that book was discovered near the Dead Sea in 1947."

"You choose to believe their propaganda?"

"Yes, I do. I'm leaning more in that direction as I discover the propaganda I was taught is not true."

Silence emanated from the imam. This was a new experience for him, and he didn't know how to proceed.

Basel took advantage of the opportunity to ask the imam about something else that was bothering him. "Sir, I've been taught all of my life that we are born without sin—pure—and we learn how to sin as we grow up."

Imam Nafi, regaining his composure, said, "Yes, we are born pure."

"This has been my biggest stumbling block. The first Christian to share his faith with me was earlier this year. I didn't like him, but he made me think. He more or less lectured me from the airport to the convention center, but one of the things that stuck in my mind was the concept that we are all sinners and can't enter into heaven without a relationship with Jesus, who died on the cross for our sins. His comment about being 'born sinners' was a difficult one for me; it was the exact opposite of what I learned."

"Rightfully so. It's not correct."

"When I was a very young boy, I sinned. Imam, my parents didn't teach me to be a sinner. How did I learn that?"

"You learned it from someone. You were born free of sin."

"Sir, both of our religions cannot be the truth. Have you ever had concerns about our faith? Have you ever thought about Muhammad being wrong?"

The imam's face reddened. He hesitated a brief moment but responded with the correct response from a Muslim holy man. "Of course not—never."

Basel was skeptical of his answer. Everyone had doubts sometime.

The imam abruptly excused himself and left his office before Basel knew what had happened.

☾

The imam was depressed all day about Basel. Later that afternoon, he met with Wazir, who had some questions about the homework that had been assigned in their apologetics class on Wednesday.

Wazir tapped on his doorframe, breaking Nafi's train of thought.

"Come in, Mr. Hoda. What can I do for you?"

Trying to get his mind off the conversation with his "lost sheep" that morning, Nafi was grateful for the distraction. He was able to answer Wazir's question quickly and easily. With Basel heavy on his mind, he asked Wazir to pray for him in his daily prayers.

"Mr. Farooq is very confused, and I am concerned that he is ready to convert to Christianity."

"Are you serious?"

"He evidently has been visiting a church with a Christian friend, and they are brainwashing him."

Concerned, Wazir quickly asked, "What church?"

"All I know is that it's south of the city and it's big. Please pray for Basel during your prayer times."

db

On his way to his car, Wazir called Fadi.

Chapter 72

Somewhere between Mifflintown, Pennsylvania, and Illinois – April 24, 2015

"As long as there are religions, there are going to be people who are hiding their rottenness behind the veil of religion."

—*Juliana Hatfield*

T hey had been on the road for nearly forty-eight hours, taking the more autonomous back roads. At first, they were simply following the directions of the GPS, but they soon figured out that they were headed to northern Illinois. Logically, they suspected Chicago.

Their getaway cars were equipped with gas tanks that took up nearly the entire trunk and extended forward under the rear seats. This, along with the hybrid nature of the engine, gave them a range of nearly two thousand miles before refueling. Dried, although not very flavorful, food and bottled water was stored in every nook and cranny that the gas tank didn't occupy. They were set to travel without the inconvenience of stopping—more important, without being recognized. Their photos were everywhere along their circuitous route. It was disconcerting to see themselves on the billboards. The image quality was sharp—way too sharp to risk being around people. Yar knew that Jabir and Farah were on a similar yet different journey in a clone of the car they drove.

They had all donned simple disguises, but it was difficult to hide their dark skin. They stopped only for nature breaks in the woods adjacent to the roads; they avoided the public and kept their speed slightly below the limits. The only person they spoke to on their cell was Tamir. He had checked in with them several times during their trip and never once asked how Nyla was handling the death of her husband. The fact was, he really didn't care. He only cared that the parts were on their way.

Sounding like a child on a long, boring trip, Nyla asked, "Yar, when will we get there?"

"Several more hours. Did you have a nice rest?"

The three of them had been alternating driving and sleeping.

"How long did I sleep? It seemed like only minutes."

"It was over three hours, and Raja is still dreaming."

"For me, it is nightmares. I can't get the sound of the gunshots out of my head, the sound of my husband's murderers."

"Nyla, you know how sorry Raja and I are, but we can all celebrate Jamil's *shahada* [martyrdom]. He has gained automatic salvation and will be in the highest level of paradise."

"Thank you, Yar, but I miss him, and there is a huge hole in my heart. I feel like he was taken from me before our lives together got started."

"You knew when we signed up that it could lead to this—especially for us men. We all agreed that we have a cause worth dying for."

Their conversation was interrupted by the cell phone ringing. As expected, it was Tamir.

"As soon as you get to the safe house, there will be someone to pick up the parts. His identification will be a single phrase: مجنلا محتقا, or Star Burst in Arabic."

"What do we do after we turn the parts over to him?"

"Further instructions will be forthcoming for you and Jabir, and the women are to stay put in the house. It is stocked with enough food and water to last until after the attack. After the attack, you will be able to return to them."

Yar was hoping that Nyla could not hear Tamir and what he was saying. Looking in his mirror, he saw that, thankfully, she had fallen back to sleep.

Chapter 73

Al-Qaeda Headquarters, Afghanistan – April 24, 2015

"Things alter for the worse spontaneously, if they be not altered for the better designedly."

—*Francis Bacon*

Hajji studied the information that Malcolm and Dalil had just brought him. Two things jumped off the pages of the report: they needed to accelerate the attack, and they needed to reduce the scope somewhat, especially in the United States. He was not used to being disappointed by his people, but in the last couple of days, he had been disappointed by Mann and the fiasco in his area. He was also disappointed with his key guys—Dalil and Malcolm. The plan that he had expected by the close of business on the April 23 was not delivered until moments ago—eighteen hours late. He was an impatient man—more so recently.

"What has taken so long for you two to get me this information?"

"Sorry, sir, but it was much more complicated than we anticipated."

"The news keeps getting worse, and we need to pick a new date for the attack. We can no longer wait until Islamic Heritage Month and the start of fasting for Ramadan in mid-June. US intelligence is closing in rapidly. What is your recommendation?" Hajji asked, sifting through the information that the two guys had compiled for him. He was bored and frustrated; his personality type was not good with details and he didn't tolerate ineptitude.

The two of them paused.

"We don't have time for hesitation! What is your recommendation?"

"As we sorted through the information from our five territories, it became obvious that mid-May was as soon as we could get the parts distributed and the missiles assembled and launched. Some territories could be ready quicker, but we want the attack to be simultaneous, within minutes or even seconds of each other."

Ahsan immediately began thinking about an appropriate date. "When is Isra Mi'raj this year?"

Malcolm pulled out his tablet, then pulled up the Islamic calendar. "It's May fifteenth."

"That's our date, gentlemen. We will commemorate Muh-ammad's ascent into the Seven Heavens by sending millions of infidels to hell. I need a videoconference call with all my leaders as soon as you can pull it together."

"Hajji, it's the middle of night for New York."

"After all the trouble that Mr. Mann has caused us, it is with great pleasure that I roust him in the middle of the night. Make it happen as soon as you can."

Dalil and Malcolm rushed out of Hajji's office to arrange the conference. People flew around while Dalil got all five of the territories on the phone—all except Esa Mann. He called his cell, his home, and his office, plus sent out an urgent text and e-mail, and so far, no response. He didn't want to be the one to tell Hajji, but he knew he would. He prayed that Esa would respond soon.

The guys were required to be available twenty-four/seven, and their cell was supposed to stay close by their heads as they slept. He decided to call Esa one more time before Hajji arrived. Finally, after the fourth ring, he picked up.

"Hello? What is it?"

"You sound horrible."

"Sorry, sir, but it's two thirty in the morning, and I had trouble getting to sleep. What's going on?"

"In about two minutes, you'll be on a videoconference with Hajji and the rest of the team."

Esa headed to his home office in time to see his computer screen come alive with a countdown:

VIDEOCONFERENCE BEGINNING IN
1:46

He quickly threw some water on his face and tried to get his senses about him as the final seconds clicked off his computer screen—and there he was. The techs had just completed all the last-minute hookups and checks as Hajji entered the war room.

"Good day, everyone. Let me get right to the point. We had a major breach in our system in North America, and our plans have to be accelerated once again. Tomorrow morning, the assembly and launch protocols will be initiated at noon, Afghanistan time. Refer to the general instructions that you already have in your possession. Further detailed instructions will be delivered tomorrow to each of you and all your cell leaders. In addition, assembly instructions will arrive at your production sites. Assure that someone is there to receive the courier's packet."

Hajji and Dalil went quickly through the other events that were going to take place.

Dalil continued. "Your cell leaders will find white step vans parked outside their production sites in the morning. We will begin the transfer of components immediately. Your drivers must depart tomorrow. The interior of the step vans has been modified to make your dispatches easier. There is a coded name for each cell adjacent to a compartment. Have your drivers distribute their cell's components into each compartment. Detailed directions are in the trucks, and the optimum route is programmed into the GPS systems. Each truck has a homing device, so you'll be able to track the progress in as much detail as you like. Malcolm and I will be following their every move. Here's our revised schedule, so listen carefully: All the deliveries will be completed by May third, all of your missiles will be finished by May tenth, and the forty-eight-hour countdown will commence on May thirteenth at ten thirty p.m., Afghanistan time. It will be broadcast over our secure server so that all of our launches can be simultaneous. Once the weapons are in place, the worldwide detonation will be controlled by our computers. Our biggest enemy is the US, and the timing is such that the attack will occur during their busiest time of day for air traffic. Sky Burst will hit on May fifteenth, which also marks Isra Mi'raj."

Hajji added, "The operation had to be scaled down slightly, but Malcolm has run the calculations, and it is still going to dwarf our 9/11 victory. As people look back on this era of Islamic history, we will all go down as heroes for the cause of Muslims everywhere. *Alhamdulillah!*"

Everyone responded, "*Alhamdulillah!*"

ḋb

Esa was awake now. He was not surprised by the news, but the urgency of the situation resonated. He had a million things to do, so more sleep was not an option. He sent urgent messages to all of his lieutenants and alerted them that he would personally speak to each of them as soon as the sun came up in their cities. He advised them that the day they had been waiting for was near: the assembly and launch protocols would be initiated at noon, Afghanistan time, on Saturday.

Anxiety, excitement, and apprehension—all mixed with an element of fear—ran though Esa's body as he worked away. He was confident in the plan, but he already had two strikes against him, and as he had learned in American baseball, three strikes and you're out. He looked forward to the celebration after the successful completion of Sky Burst. Wherever that celebration took place—in New York or paradise—he was prepared and ready for either.

db

After the screens had gone blank and the IT techs had left the room, Hajji talked with Dalil and Malcolm.

"I want to put the full force of al-Qaeda on figuring out the people who are hurting us. I know Esa has screwed up, but I'm beginning to think that he has been outmatched by someone or a group of people who are figuring out our every move. Find him, find her, or find them, whoever they are, and have them taken out of the picture. We can't afford to jeopardize Sky Burst.

db

Hidden away deep in the interior of the White House, Press Secretary Ford took his planned call from Hajji.

Ahsan's assumptions were accurate—the Department of Homeland Security was hot on his trail.

"Sir, a do-gooder citizen with a friend in a DHS field office blew the lid off Mifflintown, PA, and the president is beginning to get a view of what we're up to."

"What was the name of the spoiler in Pennsylvania?"

"His name is Jason Lange."

"Thanks, Mr. Adams and keep us posted. Praise be to Allah!"

Chapter 74

Chicago, Illinois – April 25, 2015

"It is a blessing to die for a cause, because you can so easily die for nothing."

—*Andrew Young*

Yar and the two women finally arrived at the house outside of Chicago. What would have normally been a ten-hour drive took more than two days. Yar wasn't about to question their diversionary tactics, though, as they had arrived without incident. They were all stiff and sore from the car that, meant for two, had three people squeezed in among the extra fuel tanks and provisions. They grabbed some breakfast, even though it was late afternoon, and headed for the beds.

Just as they had sat down to eat, Jabir and Raja pulled into the driveway. Yar met them and motioned them to park their car in the garage. They were all grieving the loss of Jamil, but the reunion was sweet. Yar's phone vibrated—it was Tamir.

"I see from our tracking devices that both cars have arrived. Were there any incidents?"

"No, sir. We're all road weary, but we are all safe."

"I am sending a courier to your house to pick up the parts and give you instructions as to where to report tomorrow. Enjoy the time with your wife—you won't be reunited for about three weeks. The courier has something for Mrs. Khoury, so make sure she doesn't go to sleep prior to his arrival. It will be worthwhile for her."

Before saying goodbye, Tamir greeted them in Arabic, "May Allah continue to bless you and our efforts!"

Looking tired but encouraged Yar spoke to his fellow Pennsylvanian refugees, "Tamir has asked that we stay awake until his courier arrives."

⚏

A knock at the door startled them. Even if they had fallen asleep, the harsh knock would have roused them. As he opened the door, a strong gust of cold air blew into their living room. Yar was surprised to see the same man who had delivered the briefcase to Mifflintown standing in the doorway with a similar-looking case. Handing it over, Jabir and Yar shuttled the three cases of parts to his van. When they got back into the house, they saw the man hand handing an envelope to Nyla. She was surprised and opened it as they all watched expectantly.

Letter of Appreciation and Admiration

Mrs. Khoury, it gives me great pleasure to inform you that your husband Martyr Jamil has served the cause well and is reaping his eternal reward with his fellow saints. Without people in our organization like Jamil, the spread of Muslim throughout the world could not happen—I thank you from the bottom of my heart. You should be very proud of your husband's martyrdom.

With all my respect and appreciation,

Nasi Ahsan

Nyla couldn't believe that a man as important as Nasi Ahsan had taken the time to write her a personal note. She started crying, barely able to utter to the courier, "Thank you."

She started to read it aloud but couldn't get through it. Raja took over and read it the group. It released a flood of emotions. Grief had not been an option in their haste to escape. In the brief respite that they had for the rest of the day, the grieving process could begin.

The courier needed to get under way, so Yar and Jabir finished loading his van.

"Thank you, gentlemen." And as quickly as he had arrived, he was gone.

A room in their new quarters was equipped with prayer mats and a mihrab noting the direction for them to face. It was time to begin their afternoon prayers—an appropriate in remembrance of Jamil. Following their prayers, sleep was not a priority any longer. They sat around the living room sharing memories of their fallen friend.

Chapter 75

Washington, DC – April 25, 2015

"Always bear in mind that your own resolution to succeed is more important than any other."

—Abraham Lincoln

Teddy's focus on Peace Shield had damaged the few relationships he had outside of Homeland. He had no time for friends, and in reality, he was so intelligent that he had little in common with "ordinary" people. His work was his only interest, and the American public would be grateful for that. Sitting in the war room, the monitors showed lightning bolt icons when messages were detected. The color of the bolt indicated their status. The bolts went from red, to blue, to gold as they were intercepted, decrypted, and translated into useable intelligence.

Teddy had expected the screens showing maps of the five territories to be very active following the disruption in Mifflintown, but the volume overwhelmed his staff as well as those of the other four intelligence organizations. With an eye to the world but a primary focus on the United States, Teddy sorted through the volumes of decrypted messages. Some were translated, but if they weren't, Teddy could handle that task.

It was obvious that Ahsan had made a move, and the ripple effect of his announcement was making its way through the al-Qaeda franchise. Teddy knew that they couldn't bust the US operation until the unidentified cell had been located. He had a hunch that it was somewhere in Texas because of the huge population base in Houston, but the other sites had not been selected by population. Boston, for example, was way down the list of population bases. Teddy was not easily confused, but this one stumped him.

db

Cliff joined him.

"Look at those screens. It looks like a Midwest weather map during tornado season. What do we know, Mr. Brewer?"

"We know we didn't catch the fleeing Juniata cell members, and we know Ahsan is up to something."

"Do we need to pull the plug?"

"If we do it now, there's going to be remnants that escape. We know we have some time. The palladium parts that escaped with Yar Din need to be distributed. That will take time, so I want to keep plugging away to solve the last remaining piece of our puzzle. With that piece, we can bring their entire operation down and really hurt al-Qaeda."

Cliff nodded. "I agree. Let's keep after them. How is the rest of the world doing?"

"The EU, South African, and Eastern European cell networks have been completely exposed, and the agencies are ready to launch their raids. Japan is like us—they have four of the five cells identified and located."

db

Teddy excused himself, as one of his analysts was calling again.

"I was just deciphered a message that indicates that their attack is going to take place in two or three weeks and al-Qaeda is preparing for a massive PR blitz."

"Any more details?"

"No, not yet but we have many more messages to sort through."

Knowing how Ahsan liked his attacks to coincide with some historic event, Teddy decided to sift through Arabian history—real and legendary—to see if any dates aligned with mid-May.

"Teddy, according to what we are reading, like the US, Ahsan has raised the internal alert to its highest status. The word is that their planned attack is Ahsan's last big initiative. It is what he wants to be remembered by, and he doesn't want anybody or anything to get in his way."

Chapter 76

Antioch, Tennessee – April 26, 2015

"In seeking truth you have to get both sides of a story."

—*Walter Cronkite*

Without letting Kyle know, Basel attended his church again. The imam couldn't answer his questions. He went to a different service than the one he had experienced with Kyle. Would they be as kind and welcoming to him if he wasn't with "one of them"?

His yellow taxi stood out like a sore thumb amid the expensive late-model cars that were parked around him. He made his way to the sanctuary in time to see the video roll. One class offered caught his attention: "Witnessing to Muslims" was being taught by an Iranian who had converted to Christianity. His mind wandered to the class that Taj had started at the beginning of the year and the paradox of motives. Taj had been recruiting for a terrorist cell, while Basel was certain that the intent of *this* class was to spread what Christians believed as the truth and the path to eternity. Taj's class was taking his recruits on a different path to eternity.

His reception from the congregation was the same, and the pastor's message—being missionaries in their community—was particularly interesting to him. Ironically, the pastor specifically addressed the increase in the Hispanic and Middle Eastern populations. Focusing on the Muslims, he told the people how it was illegal in Muslim countries for Christians to teach the Gospel.

"What a blessing it is that they are coming to us."

Perhaps it was the pastor's message, perhaps it was the fact that he was alone, but it seemed to Basel that the members were friendlier than the week before. The pastor taught of the unconditional love of the Christian God and how he was waiting for people who didn't know him. He welcomed people to visit with him in the parlor after the service. Basel felt an urge to talk with him, but he was intimidated.

The pastor's demeanor and his soft-spoken delivery were welcoming, and there was sincerity with him that he didn't find with his own imams. His imams tended to have scowls on their faces, while Kyle's pastor displayed a perpetual smile. He wanted to go to the parlor, but his years of training, Quran school, and propaganda were holding him back.

Many people greeted him. He hung back until the parlor was nearly empty and the pastor was alone.

"Pastor Jack, can we talk somewhere privately?"

"Of course."

The two of them headed into the pastor's office, where the pastor closed the door behind them.

"I noticed you with Kyle Emerson last week. Kyle is a great young man, and I've literally watched him grow up. How long have you known him?"

"We've known each other for a little more than a month. We have been meeting regularly to learn of each other's beliefs."

"Interesting. And how has it gone?"

"Frankly, sir, I have become confused."

"May I help you?"

Basel felt much more open with him than he had with his imam, and the questions he was struggling with just spewed out. Half expecting to get the hard sell on Christianity, Basel was pleased with the kind way that the pastor dealt with his issues.

The pastor offered, "I completely understand your confusion. For twenty-one years, you have never given a second thought to any religion but Islam. What brought you to this crisis?"

"I can't point to one particular event. It was a series of things that began with one of my fares—an obnoxious Christian who made me think. Then Kyle was kind to me in a moment when I needed a friend, but after your service last week, I approached my imam with some questions about the root differences of our two faiths."

"Where do you stand now?"

"Pastor, I'm involved with a terrible thing."

"Do you wish to talk about it?"

"No, sir. I shared it with Kyle, and I'm sorry I dragged him into it."

"I understand." The pastor pulled out the Bible he had just used to preach from and began reading a series of verses from the Book of Romans that explained the steps to salvation in Christianity.

"Thank you. Kyle has directed me to read those same verses, and I have— many, many times. My heart is ready to make the commitment, but my mind keeps digging into my past and the untruths that I have learned about Christians."

"I understand, but please know that my door is always open. Here is my cell number. Call me whenever you desire to talk." Handing him a card, the pastor wrote his cell number on the back.

"Thank you for the access to you—it's more than my imam offered. Sir, I wish to become a follower of Christ. Can you pray with me?" The words flowed from Basel's mouth so naturally that it surprised him. *A follower of Christ?* he thought. *What do I do now? How do I get out of my cell?* But strangely, he was at peace.

The pastor imperceptibly wiped a tear from his eye and prayed the prayer of salvation with Basel.

As he got to his cab, he called Kyle.

"Kyle, can we meet somewhere to talk? I have something I need to talk to you about."

$$d\ddot{b}$$

Kyle rearranged his schedule, and the two of them met at a local coffee shop within minutes of their conversation.

Anxious to tell his friend, Basel blurted out almost immediately, "I'm a follower of Christ."

Kyle stood and hugged his friend. "I want to know everything. How did it happen?"

Basel backed up a few days and explained how disappointed he was by his imam's approach to his confusion and how impatient his imam had become.

"Your pastor's approach was the exact opposite of Imam Nafi."

"Basel, thanks for calling me. I am thrilled by your decision."

"I wanted you to be the first person I told." Hesitating and thinking, he added, "You are the *only* person I *can* tell."

"What does this mean for you and your cell?"

"I can't participate."

"Basel, we have to notify the authorities."

Chapter 77

New York City – April 25, 2015

"Global terrorism is extreme both in its lack of realistic goals and in its cynical exploitation of the vulnerability of complex system."

—Jürgen Habermas

T he weekend was a blur for Esa. He was weary and could have counted the hours of sleep on one hand, but somehow he kept working. Finally, the event he had worked on for years was in sight. He knew that he couldn't allow one more thing to go wrong in his territory, so his conversations with his cell leaders were intense. He reviewed their responsibilities ad nauseam and had each of them regurgitate their assignments back to him. He required certainty.

He finally stopped to take a breath as the sun set outside his Manhattan office window. He couldn't ignore the beauty of the reds and oranges reflecting off the buildings around him. On his computer monitor, he could see that all five white vans were on the road, shuttling their deadly components from cell to cell. Without checking in with his leaders this evening, he remained confident that each of them was finishing up the missile components, and if they had been completed, then they were readying their facilities for the assembly operations. He directed his leaders to give their guys a break while they awaited their white van's return; of course, he reminded them that someone had to be available at their facilities to unload the vans as they went from city to city.

As he instructed them to get some rest, he was consistent with his message to each of them. He thanked them for being part of Allah's plan to create a global Islamic state and closed each of his calls with, "There is no God but Allah, and Muhammad is Allah's messenger across the world!"

"What am I missing?" he asked out loud to himself.

Knowing what lay ahead, he decided that he too needed to take a break. He closed up his office and headed for the train to Connecticut.

Chapter 78

Chicago, Illinois – April 26, 2015

"America will disappear and Islam will remain."

—*Ahmad Bahr*

All five of them slept very well. Nyla awoke first and started a pot of the fine Arabian coffee that she'd found in their pantry. The aroma permeated every corner of the house. It was the motivation necessary for them to get going. It was time for their morning prayers, or *fajr*, and they gathered in their prayer room.

After prayers, Nyla, to keep her mind occupied, followed up the coffee with a magnificent Saudi breakfast. She prepared and served it herself as thanks for the love and kindness that she had received from her friends. The traditional breakfast included all of their favorites: olives, soft cheeses, honey, *helwa*, jams, eggs, and fresh, hot bread.

Yar was thrilled by just the scents. "Nyla, thanks so much for this special meal."

The courier provided Yar instructions as to where he and Jabir had to report—at noon. He had to figure out an appropriate time to share the bad news; then he realized there would be no good time.

"Breakfast is ready," Nyla announced.

Compliments abound as they found places around the table, Yar broke from custom and wanted them all to eat together. Nyla protested at first, but the other women helped her get the food served and they sat down together.

Yar, in an effort to exhibit the importance of what they would be doing, brought up the subject of their goal.

"Tamir shared with me that our plan for a global Islamic state is on schedule, and our upcoming activities will accelerate the schedule by years."

Smiles came from around the table.

"We all need to be diligent. The whole world *must* be under the rule of Islam."

Again, there smiles and nods as Jabir said, "We have another reason now to complete our task. We need to do it to honor my brother, Jamil."

Yar added, "Absolutely, but it isn't going to be easy, and it may be that we join Jamil in paradise if that is Allah's will." Then he continued. "The money endowed to the American universities over the years has paid huge dividends for us. This Chicago cell and our sister cells around the country are manned by our radical brothers—many of whom are Americans who developed their love of Islam from studying the Middle East at the likes of Harvard, Georgetown, and other fine institutions."

Raja spoke up. "If it were not for the Muslim Student's Association at Penn State, we may have never met."

Yar, believing that the tone was right, proceeded. "The instructions for Jabir and I were delivered by the courier yesterday." Without giving them an opportunity for comments, he said, "We need to leave today and report no later than noon."

Raja and Farah were noticeably upset.

"Why?" Farah pleaded.

"We have much work to do. Now that our operation is out in the open, our timeline had to be shortened dramatically."

"So you have to work today?"

"Raja, we have to *report* today, and we won't be back until the operation is complete."

"What are we to do?"

Yar went through the instructions that were left for them in the courier pack. Speaking to the ladies, he said, "You have to stay in the house at all times. There is ample food to last you, and we will be back in about three weeks. After the attack, we will return with more instructions. All of the electronics in this house, our cars, and our cell phones are protected from the weapon that will destroy all unprotected equipment. If you have troubles that you can't resolve, there is a number here for you to call, and someone will come to your aid."

Fear contorted their faces while tears welled in their eyes. What started as a pleasant, memorable Sunday with friends had quickly turned to a day that would be memorable, but for other reasons. It could be the last time they saw each other.

ⴆ

It was 10:00 a.m., so their time was limited. Yar pulled Jabir aside and went into detail about what they would be doing for the next three weeks—joining the rest of Tamir's team at the Chicago cell's facility.

"Be brave, Jabir. The women have to see the confidence we have. It could be their last remembrance of us."

"I'll be brave, but I am frightened. I've looked to this day all of my life, but now it is here."

"I have the utmost confidence in Tamir and everyone else, up to and including Hajji, and in addition to our fellow warriors, we have Allah."

The men regained their composure and returned to the breakfast table. No one could eat, and the remnants of food lay on their plates.

db

Yar and Jabir excused themselves and went to their rooms to gather up their belongings and the other things they had been instructed to bring. Neither had had time to unpack, so they added the miscellaneous tools, guns, and ammo that were necessary and returned with their bags ready.

"Will we be able to talk with you?"

"No, we will be in complete isolation. We almost blew Sky Burst completely by our carelessness in Pennsylvania, and we cannot risk another problem. We will be hidden in a warehouse until we move out to our launch sites."

Farah choked back tears. "Will this be our last attack?"

"Our battle will end only when we triumph universally. My hope is that this attack will do it, but if it doesn't, our battle will continue. Islam must dominate!"

With that, the two men hugged their wives and said farewell. Ball caps, dark glasses, and clean shaves changed their appearance; it would hopefully be enough to get them to the warehouse without being recognized. They stopped seeing their images on the electronic billboards about halfway through Indiana, but they knew that law enforcement and federal agents throughout the country were still looking for them.

Chapter 79

Mifflintown, Pennsylvania – April 27, 2015

"If you say city to people, people have no problem thinking of the city as rife with problematic, screwed-up people, but if you say suburbs—and I'm not the first person to say this, it's been said over and over again in literature— there's a sense of normalcy."

—Eric Bogosian

The terrorist threat status didn't impact the breakfast routine at the Lange house—it was as chaotic as ever. Anne tried to make sure that both kids had some form of nourishment before leaving for school. Hunter, like nearly all prepubescent boys, was somewhat scatterbrained and had trouble keeping track of his essentials, i.e., shoes, books, jackets, or anything else that wasn't attached to him. Ashley was maturing before their eyes and was helpful to her brother, assisting him to find his missing necessities. Everything finally together, the two of them made a mad dash to the end of the drive to catch the school bus.

Jason and Anne cherished this time in the morning, immediately after the tornado had passed through, when they could sip some coffee together.

"Honey, have things returned to normal at the plant?"

"The police have finished their investigation, and they've turned the warehouse back to us. Things are getting back to normal, but it will be a while. You know the other two Saudis who worked with Jamil took off after the suicide? Henry has his hands full."

"Yes, and the rumors are running wild around town."

"What have you heard?"

"Nothing credible—silly stuff about how deranged he was. You know he burned down all their houses as well?"

"Yes, and I never would have expected it from him. He was quiet and kept to his business." He hated being deceitful to his wife, but he couldn't be completely truthful about the situation.

"Of course, since they were Middle Easterners, there was talk of terrorism."

Jason smiled. "The people around here have never been that close to Saudi Arabians, and all they know about them was that they were involved with 9/11—it's a natural conclusion."

"I guess. Do you think there is anything to that?"

Hesitating ever so slightly, Jason replied, "No." Then he successfully changed the subject by asking if he needed to pick up Hunter from baseball practice.

They bounced around to a couple of other topics and then discussed the possibility of getting away—just the two of them.

"I love the idea. I have a ton of frequent-flyer miles, so let's start to make some plans. Do you think your parents could come down and stay with the kids?"

"I'll talk with them."

"Great. Thanks, honey. I have to get to the office, although I would love to stay here."

He leaned across the table, gave Anne a warm kiss and hug, and grabbed his briefcase on the way out the door.

Jumping into his Austin Healey, he headed to McNichols. As he drove, he thought, *It won't be long before I can lower the top and enjoy the fresh air of*

Pennsylvania springtime. He yearned for his life to get back to normal—the reason he had originally made the move from headquarters to the Mifflintown plant.

ᴄ‖ᴅ

Henry almost looked forward to Mondays now that Mary was gone. Things were too quiet for him at home. As he pulled into his parking space, he was reminded of the flashing lights and emergency vehicles strewn randomly about the plant. He would never drive into the parking lot again without having those visions. Jason arrived as he was getting out of his car.

"Morning, Boss. Did you have a good weekend?"

"Yes, I did. How about you?"

"It was OK."

"Jason, have you heard anything from Craig or your friend with Homeland?"

"No, and I haven't called them. They did a brilliant job with the cover-up, but Anne mentioned that there are rumors of Jamil being a terrorist, and the disappearance of the other two Saudis fuels that fire."

Henry stopped as they were about to enter the plant to finish the conversation without anyone eavesdropping.

"Boss, I'm happy it's behind us. I wanted to go in there with my shotgun and blow them away. I don't understand a religion that allows its followers to kill innocent people for the sake of expansion."

"Henry, I don't either, but what we have to keep reminding ourselves is the vast majority of Muslims are peace-loving people. A very small percentage are radicals bent on killing us."

"I understand that, but I also remember that in the wake of the September Eleventh attack, I didn't hear an outcry from those 'peace-loving' Muslims."

Jason opened the door for his friend as the two of them went about their responsibilities.

"Have a good day, Henry. Let's take a break together later."

"You got it. I want to hear what's happening with your family."

Chapter 80

Antioch, Tennessee – April 27, 2015

"When you turn your heart and your life over to Christ, when you accept Christ as the savior, it changes your heart."

—George W. Bush

B asel wanted to tell the authorities in person, and Kyle wanted to be there for moral support. They had to drive separately since Basel had to work his taxi until his shift at the warehouse later in the afternoon; he didn't know how this meeting would impact his warehouse work, though.

Kyle arrived ten minutes early and parked in the lot next to the Federal Building. It was a foggy morning, creating halos around the yellow bulbs in the streetlights, which looked like a scene from a horror movie. Kyle was scared for his friend and for himself. He had spoken to him first thing in the morning to make sure he was OK—also to make sure he wasn't backing out. That was nearly two hours ago. *I hope he hasn't changed his mind*, Kyle thought. It was unusual for Basel to be late for anything.

db

When Kyle walked into the marble-encased lobby, only one of the full-body scanners was operating, and two sleepy-looking federal agents stood guard.

One of them looked up. "What is your business?"

"My friend wishes to talk to someone with the Department of Homeland Security, and I'm meeting him here."

Gruffly, the agent replied, "Wait over there until he gets here."

The guard picked up his phone to call the agent on duty in DHS.

Nathan Baird picked up the phone call from the front desk on the first ring. He had arrived early; he always arrived early.

"Agent Baird."

"There's a gentleman here waiting for a friend to arrive, and they wish to speak to someone in your department."

"OK, call me when they're both here."

db

Basel raced out of his apartment. He was running late, leaving only twenty minutes for a ride that would take him at least thirty, if he were lucky. He didn't want to go, and subconsciously, he was dragging his feet. Rather than wasting more time with a call to Kyle, he drove his taxi as fast as he could—as long as his radar detector remained silent.

He was about four blocks from the Federal Building when a bullet shattered his front passenger-side window and lodged in his brain, killing him instantly. He slumped to the side, with his hand still on the wheel, and turned his taxi hard left—into the path of a minivan and a FedEx truck. All three vehicles erupted in a huge fireball.

Basel's intent on becoming an American hero ended on West End Avenue.

db

Kyle walked to the door to look for Basel, but also to check out where all the sirens and emergency vehicles were headed. He remained in the dark about both.

Chapter 81

Washington, DC – April 27, 2015

"Patience and Diligence, like faith, remove mountains."

—William Penn

Teddy studied the big board in the war room with Cliff.

"Here's what we know, Boss." With his laser pointer, Teddy pointed to the map tracking communications. "The communication has slowed to a crawl, especially when compared to the activity over the weekend. This means that they have their orders and they're all busy."

Next, Teddy pulled up four pictures of what appeared to be the same vehicle—white step vans. "These photos have come in from our contractors monitoring the four cells. The trucks all showed up Sunday." Advancing the slide, he said, "These pictures show them being loaded. Sir, they are getting ready to move. The pictures were all dated and time-stamped for Sunday morning."

"What's our next move, Mr. Quarterback?"

"We have attached a small, undetectable homing device to each truck so we'll be able to follow them. We suspect that the parts are being distributed for assembly."

"We will be able to find our fifth cell!" Cliff exclaimed.

"That's right," Teddy said, pulling up a map of the United States with four white squares moving slowly across it. "Each square indicates its city of origin, and in the tradition of Ahsan and Dalil, they are moving systematically—from LA to Chicago, to Boston, to Long Island, to our mystery cell. Some have already made their first stops, and we have one currently stopped in Tennessee."

"Where in Tennessee?"

"We've dispatched contractors to the coordinates we're picking up, and I'm expecting to hear from them momentarily."

As if on cue, there was a call for Teddy. His disappointment was hard for him to hide.

"The Long Island truck had a flat tire that was being repaired along I-40. We're no closer. It could be going anywhere west."

db

Trying to take Teddy's mind off his disappointment, Cliff asked for him to estimate how much time they had.

"We know that, with the cell in LA, the trucks' rotation will probably take to the first week of May to get the parts where they need to be. That gives us another week. Assembly will follow, and then they will be deployed to their launch sites. I'm guessing we have two weeks, at least, and possibly three or more."

"Our time is evaporating. Have you come up with a date that would be meaningful to Ahsan?"

"I have a couple of ideas, and they are both sick, perverted thinking, but we're dealing with an evil, demented man."

"Talk to me."

"One is an American holiday, and the other is Islamic. May tenth is Mother's Day."

"You're right—that is sick. But in his mind, he would be attacking the American family. His jealousy of our country and our lifestyle could be directed at motherhood. Makes sense. What is the Islamic date?"

"This year they will celebrate Isra Mi'raj on the fifteenth of May."

"I've never heard of that one. Fill me in."

"I'm not surprised, as it's not celebrated universally among Muslims, but Ahsan's Wahhabis do. They are lumped together for celebration, but it commemorates two events—the Isra and the Mi'raj. Their tradition relates that it was a miraculous journey that Muhammad took with the angel Gabriel one night in the year 620. The Isra says he traveled from Mecca on a 'winged horse' to the al-Aqsa Mosque—'the farthest mosque,' or *masjid al-aqsa* in Arabic."

Interrupting, Cliff said, "You can leave out some of the detail."

"Sorry, I get carried away. In the second part, Muhammad is said to have toured heaven and hell, and even spoken with earlier prophets, such as Abraham, Moses, and Jesus. In his visit to heaven, Muhammad reported seeing an angel with 'seventy thousand heads, each having seventy thousand mouths, each mouth having seventy thousand tongues, each tongue speaking seventy thousand languages—every one singing Allah's praises.'"

"Wow, that's a lot of praises."

There was a slight break in Teddy's intensity as he realized that he had to tone down the details for his boss—which was difficult for him. Smiling, he said, "That *is* a lot of praises—like twenty-four quintillion different languages. But seriously, I could see this being an opportunity to celebrate Isra Mi'raq for him and his followers."

"Both of those are logical. Let's get the word out to the whole team. May tenth or fifteenth is our assumed attack date."

Chapter 82

Antioch, Tennessee – April 27, 2015

"In a world without the law of God, you have chaos, oppression, tyranny, and everyone doing what is right in their own eyes."

—*Randall Terry*

I t was 8:45 a.m. and still no Basel. Kyle was upset. Basel's phone went immediately to voice mail, and he was sure that Basel had chickened out.

He went outside to check the parking lot—again. Smoke billowed from what appeared to be a fire several blocks away, and traffic was at a standstill in both directions.

Satisfying the morbid curiosity that lay deep inside each of us, Kyle walked toward the smoke.

John Paterson lurked in the back of the crowd that had gathered to view the carnage. A well-timed shot from the lane beside Basel's taxi had resulted in the horrific wreck; no one would ever know that there was a bullet in his head.

Paterson called Fadi to let him know that his mission had been accomplished as he made his way back to his car parked a block down the street.

"The money will be deposited today."

"It was a pleasure doing business with you again."

⚕

Paterson drove past Kyle as he made his way to the accident scene.

As he got closer, he started to pray for the people in the vehicles. The closer he got, the more he could make out three different objects that had once been cars or trucks—all indistinguishable by the burning masses that remained.

His heart sunk. He started gagging, as he could see the remnants of a sign on the roof of one of the cars. The distinctive yellow color was unmistakable. *Lord, please tell me it's not Basel*, he prayed and subsequently went to the curb and threw up his breakfast.

The police would not let him cross the line despite his pleas. They needed to put out the fire, and the fatality unit had already begun their investigation.

Kyle called the Yellow Cab Company.

"Yes, I'm trying to reach one of your drivers."

"Who would you like to reach?"

"Basel Farooq."

The silence on the other end was deafening as his head started to throb. He knew it wasn't good.

"Sir, are you a relative?"

"No, just a friend."

"I cannot release any information to you."

"Do you have information?"

"Sorry, sir. I can't help you." He hung up.

The dispatcher had just received word that Basel's taxi was involved in an accident, and he couldn't tell anyone until his next of kin were notified. His personnel file, however, did not list any.

Kyle sat down on the curb and bowed his head. He needed to return to Homeland Security to see if, by some miracle, Basel had shown up.

db

Walking back into the Federal Building lobby, Kyle was not surprised to see that Basel was not there.

"My friend has been delayed. I need to see the agent by myself."

Within a few moments, a slender thirty-something man arrived at the security checkpoint. Agent Nathan Baird introduced himself to Kyle, who signed in and passed through the scanners. Baird escorted him to his third-floor office.

"I was told there was going to be two of you?"

"I'm afraid something terrible has gone down. My friend was about to disclose an al-Qaeda cell operation here in Antioch, and I think they figured out what he was planning to do." Kyle proceeded to tell Baird his suspicion that his friend had been killed in the accident down the street.

Baird let Kyle know that he was recording their conversation, but he still took notes incessantly. He had run into a few shady characters since joining DHS, but Nashville was a quiet city when it came to terrorism—he always figured that Muslims didn't care for country music. The thought of an al-Qaeda cell operating out of Antioch was mind-blowing, but they had been monitoring a growing number of Muslims populating that part of the county.

"What is your friend's name?"

"Basel Farooq—he's a taxi driver, and it appeared to me that one of the vehicles was a taxi. They wouldn't give me any info. Could you get it for me?"

"Of course." He buzzed his assistant to contact the Metro Police Department for details on the crash, including the identity of the victims. "Mr. Emerson, while we are waiting, please tell me what you know about Mr. Farooq's involvement in the cell."

Kyle vividly recalled his conversation on Thursday with Basel and was able to repeat it nearly word for word. The problem was that Basel had all the details— the names, the addresses, - the project they were working on.

"Let me get this straight. You were aware of a potential attack on our country last week and didn't take it to the authorities?" Baird couldn't hide his anger. His phone buzzed. "I see. Thanks for the info."

"Mr. Emerson, I'm afraid you were correct. Your friend *was* killed in the accident."

Kyle broke down.

"Mr. Emerson, do you need some time?"

Kyle, only comprehending every other word Baird was saying, stared blankly, unable to speak.

"I'm ordering an autopsy."

dib

Picking up a secure line, Baird called Washington.

He asked for his liaison at headquarters and briefly described what was going on in the Music City.

"I'll try to find out who would be working on this and have them call you back, but it may take some time."

"Did you hear what I just said? Let me repeat a few key words: al-Qaeda, cell group, Pakistani informant. . .This is big, man. Get me someone fast!"

Chapter 83

Al-Qaeda Headquarters, Afghanistan – April 29, 2015

"Seek out your enemies relentlessly."

—*The Quran, Surah 4:102*

A hsan had learned much about the blunders in Pennsylvania, namely that a so-called "true believer" had been helping Din and the Khoury twins. Craig Reeves was not a true believer at all, but a plant from DHS, and Craig Reeves was not his real name. Dewar Jacobs had been with the CIA prior to the merger with the Department of Homeland Security and had worked in various low-level undercover positions in his brief career.

The information about Reeves/Jacobs was another oversight by Esa Mann. The agent had totally played them. They bought into his pitch, and he walked right into the cell. To make matters worse, Ahsan was informed that they hadn't even checked with his people in Afghanistan who vetted the recruits.

He was beginning to figure out where they had gone wrong. The name Jason Lange had come back several times through his channels. How did a former senior-level executive at McNichols end up in the middle of Pennsylvania? Dalil knocked and entered the room, disturbing his thoughts.

"Hajji, excuse me, but we have learned more about the failure. It appears that this Jason Lange was the person who crashed the Din cell."

"Is he a contractor?"

"He hasn't popped up in our research as a contractor, but I'm thinking that it is an extremely good cover. We think he may have been assigned to Chicago to keep his eye on Tamir Alam and somehow picked up that Din and the Khourys were going to be placed in the Mifflintown plant, so DHS sent him to the plant ahead of that move."

Leaning back in his chair and tenting his hands in the back of his head, Ahsan said, "That is an interesting theory."

"Sir, I think we need to send a couple followers to discuss some things with Mr. Lange. Homeland Security knows it was us, and we need to know what else they know."

"Make it happen."

ďb

After Dalil had left, Ahsan went back to his contemplation. He couldn't help but smile. With the exception of the problems he was having in North America, things were going according to plan. His mind wandered back over his career and the successes that al-Qaeda had amassed. Of course, the crown jewel was the Magnificent 19 of the Manhattan Raid, but there were countless others as he—and bin Laden before him—worked toward the goal of Muslim world domination.

He nearly laughed out loud as he thought about his intentionally botched attacks around the world, painting al-Qaeda as an inept threat. To him, it was funny how, in his "failures," he had still cost his enemies dearly. Following the successful Manhattan Raid and the near collapse of the US economy, they began to plan for Sky Burst, and he adjusted his strategy. They needed the intelligence community around the world, especially America, to take their eye off them. He thought about the idiot that had attempted to bring the plane down on Christmas Day in 2009; he failed, as he had known he would. He didn't kill any infidels but struck the economy with the cost of more intense airport screening and longer travel lines. He remembered his "attacks" on various children's hospitals in 2010 that had been thwarted by CIA intelligence—or so they thought. Also in 2010, they placed some "bombs" on cargo planes that were never intended to detonate. In the year 2012, they went after America's love affair with shopping by botching attacks on their famous shopping centers, including the Mall of America, on the biggest shopping day of the year—Black Friday. In 2013 was a failed attempt to simultaneously destroy the Holland Tunnel, Golden Gate Bridge, and Interstate 5 in and out of Los Angeles, which created unimaginable traffic gridlocks due to added security, making the three nightmarish commutes even worse.

Billions and billions of dollars had been spent in heightened security for airports, hospitals, cargo companies, shopping centers, and highways—money taken out of the economy, money not used to fight al-Qaeda. In addition to the money, they had successfully taken America's freedom away from her, without one of these attacks hitting their targets. They were winning by losing.

But Sky Burst would be global. *Praise Allah*, he thought.

Chapter 84

Mifflintown, Pennsylvania – April 29, 2015

"For God hath not given us the spirit of fear; but of power, and of love, and of a sound mind."

—*II Timothy 1:7 KJV*

It was two weeks ago that Jason had presented his budget and one week ago that all hell had broken loose with the Saudis. He was working on the feedback he had received on his budget and making the cuts they had requested. His years at corporate had prepared him well for this game: he padded, they trimmed, and in the end, everyone was happy.

It was nearly 6:00, so he called Anne to let her know he was wrapping things up and would be home in a half hour. After shutting down his laptop, he headed for his car. Just as he was exiting the plant, two very large men grabbed each of his arms and "escorted" him to a van, Tasering him just before they laid him in the back.

d⁞b

Still unconscious, Jason was gagged and tied to a chair at the motel on Route 322. Over an hour had passed since they made the grab, and Jason's cell phone had begun ringing off and on fifteen minutes ago, until one of the men reached in his pocket and turned it off.

ᴅb

It was unlike Jason to be late, and it was even more unlikely for him to not answer his cell on the first ring—he was good about that. Anne was concerned. She checked with Henry.

"I left work before he did. Do you want me to run over to the plant? I'm guessing that his phone ran out of juice."

"You are sweet. Would you mind?"

Arriving at the plant, Henry was concerned. Jason's Healey was in his parking spot, but his office was locked. He was nowhere to be found.

ᴅb

Slowly Jason opened his eyes. Shaking his head to clear the cobwebs, he was struck with the sudden panic that comes with waking up in an unfamiliar place.

"Mr. Lange, we wish to ask you some questions."

In some kind of accent, the other said, "We wish to know about your involvement in the situation with Mr. Din and the Khoury brothers."

Jason's head was spinning, and the burn from the Taser was painful. All that he could manage was, "What?"

The man repeated the question.

"I was their boss. Mr. Din was my night shift supervisor."

"How about Craig Reeves?"

"He was one of our employees. What is this all about?" The more his head cleared, the madder he got; fear had not yet registered with him.

"Mr. Lange, you moved here from Chicago, correct?"

"Yes."

"Why?"

"I was ready for a less stressful life. I was tired of the corporate rat race." Jason had figured out when they grabbed him what this was all about.

"We want you to tell us the truth, or we have ways to make you talk. But first, call your wife and make up a story—no funny business." Flashing his Russian-made revolver at Jason, he handed him his phone.

Anne started talking before he had a chance to speak. "Jason, where have you been? We've all been worried. You said a half hour, and it's been three times that. Why weren't you answering your phone?"

"I'm sorry, honey, but a few of the guys asked me go out drinking with them after work."

Anne was shocked. That response was wrong in so many ways she didn't know what to say. "When will you be home?"

"I'm not sure."

d̈b

Anne called Henry immediately after hanging up. "There is something wrong with him."

"Are both kids with you?"

"Yes."

"I'll be over right away."

d̈b

Henry did not want to alarm Anne, so he called a buddy at the Mifflintown Police Department and asked him to come to the plant. Thinking there had been some type of vandalism, the officer jumped in his patrol car and headed for McNichols.

"Thanks for coming, Sam." He went into the details of the past hour. "I'm not sure what's going on. He told his wife he's out drinking with some guys from the plant. Sam, Jason doesn't drink or hang out with employees. Something is up."

Sam called into the station and put out an all-points bulletin for Jason Lange, along with a photo that Henry had provided him.

Henry knew that this could be beyond the scope of the MPD and pulled out a card that Jason had given him when he first let him in on the night shift activity.

He called the number on the card.

"Hello, this is Wayne Joseph."

After Henry's introduction and a brief recap of what had happened, Wayne told him to send a couple of police officers over to the Langes' house.

"I'll call you back in a few minutes on a secure line."

Hearing that Jason had called Anne on his cell, Wayne immediately had his techs trace the call.

ᬗ

"What is your connection to Craig Reeves?"

"I told you, he was one of my employees on the night shift."

"Why did you hire him?"

"I didn't—my HR department did. I interviewed him, but that was my only involvement, and I interview all new hires."

Frustration was building with his interrogators when his face was whipped by one of their pistols, nearly knocking him unconscious. Blood flowed from the corner of his mouth. He tried to shake off the pain, but it was excruciating. He was defenseless and feared for his life.

"I still do not know any more about Reeves. I'm a businessman. I went to work at McNichols as soon as graduated and have been with them my entire career."

With that, he received another blow to the face—this time, from the fist of the other guy. Jason had been knocked out, but smelling salts quickly brought him back.

"We're going to keep going until you tell us the truth." As he said that, he brought out his Taser.

The blows continued until the smelling salts failed to revive him.

Wayne called Henry back immediately after he had gotten the tracing started.

"Henry, we should be able to see where the call was made from, and as long as they're not in transit, we should be able figure out where he is. Hold on, Henry, here is my tech."

He put Henry on hold.

"Henry, we have his coordinates, and he was stationary at least while he was on the phone. I'm on my way to Mifflintown. You keep Anne and the kids calm."

Wayne called the PA State Trooper's substation in Lewistown, and they put the call out to meet at a restaurant near the pinpointed address. Wayne was shocked by another blunder from al-Qaeda. *Could this be a trap*? he thought. Wayne dispatched a helicopter, and within minutes, a black chopper was picking him up from the roof of his office building in Harrisburg. He arrived at the rendezvous point in twenty minutes, where he was met by the local state police commander, chief of MPD, and ten other cars, each with at least two troopers.

After introducing himself, he took command. "OK, men, gather around. We have a hostage situation, and we know that the perps are extremely hostile. We need to assume they're armed and dangerous. I want them alive—they could be extremely valuable to us."

The MPD chief explained the lay of the land, and Wayne used a stick on the ground to present the strategy. They were ready with their radios and earpieces as they took their places around the room where Jason was being held. Very quietly, all the other guests were evacuated and moved to a room in the restaurant command center.

Several men went to the back of the motel while a troop of six men assembled at the front door, with two men holding "The Stinger" battering ram. With everyone in position, Wayne counted backward from five.

"Five, four, three, two, one. . .Go, go, go, go!"

The battering ram opened the door as if it weren't there, and another man subsequently dropped a tear gas canister. The perps were caught off guard, but one of them managed to get a couple shots off. Within seconds, it was over.

"Get the paramedics in here now! Officer down! Officer down! Officer down!"

Chapter 85

Washington, DC – April 29, 2015

"Most of the important things in the world have been accomplished by people who have kept on trying when there seemed to be no hope at all."

—Dale Carnegie

Yesterday afternoon, the truck that had broken down outside of Knoxville was underway again. Teddy worked his way through the flood of messages they had intercepted the week before, but he occasionally checked the route of the truck. Was it headed to LA or to the fifth cell? He noticed that it was stopped again—this time, in Nashville.

He dispatched an agent from the Nashville field office to check it out and actually expected it to be another breakdown.

"Agent John Freeze from Nashville is on the phone, Teddy."

"Put him right through."

"Sir, the coordinates you gave us led us to a warehouse on the south side of the city. When our men got there, it appeared that men were unloading things from the truck."

We found our elusive fifth cell, he thought. "We need that location placed on twenty-four/seven surveillance. Take photographs of everyone coming and going. Try to get a handle on the number of people working in there. Find out who has leased the space and who it belongs to."

Unbeknownst to Agent Freeze, Nathan Baird was three doors down the hall, collecting information from Kyle about the same cell.

ⅆ

Teddy celebrated inwardly—as excited as a person with his personality type could get. In their surveillance of the other four cells, they had identified sixty-three terrorist suspects using DHS's facial-recognition software. Teddy had dossiers on every one of them—which would hurt al-Qaeda. What shocked him about the suspects was that more than half of them had been born in the United States, converted to Muslim, and were apparently angry at the world—ready to die a martyr for Allah.

The speaker on his phone announced that another agent from Nashville was calling.

"Hello, this is Teddy Brewer."

"Agent Brewer, my name is Nathan Baird of the Nashville field office. I have information about an al-Qaeda operation in Tennessee, and my liaison in Washington pointed me in your direction."

"What do you have?"

"We have a friend of a Pakistani immigrant in our office. His friend, Basel Farooq, was on his way to our office when he was involved in a fatal car 'accident' blocks from our building. I am awaiting the results of an autopsy. The local police are ruling it an accident, but I suspect there is foul play."

"Was his friend of any assistance?"

"Fortunately, yes. His friend told him what he was doing, and it was so shocking that he recalled most of the details. He was meeting his friend at our office for moral support—Mr. Farooq planned to tell us everything. His comrades must have gotten wind of his plan."

Agent Baird proceeded to give Teddy all the details of how the Antioch cell was formed and what their plans were. Everything dovetailed nicely with the discovery of the warehouse operation.

"His friend, Kyle Emerson, didn't have any names, but he did know that there were six cell members. There were seven, but the first leader, the imam of the Antioch Islamic Center, died of a heart attack. Evidently, they are all a part of a class at the Islamic center. The new cell leader's name is Hares. He thought his first name was Fati or Fadi, or something like that."

"Agent Baird, please document everything about your conversation, and send me your report before you leave for the evening."

"Should we hold on to Mr. Emerson?"

"While we were talking, I ran him through our system—he's clean. He's never even received a traffic violation. Let him go, but make sure we can reach him easily, and ask him not to leave the city."

"Hold on, Agent Brewer, I just received the autopsy report."

"What is the COD?"

"Sir, they found a bullet lodged in Farooq's brain."

"Put some protection on Mr. Emerson."

Fifteen minutes after he had hung up with Baird, there was another call for him—this time, from Harrisburg. Jason Lange had been saved in a motel not far from the plant, and they had one Middle Eastern man in custody. They were extraditing him to DC for questioning, which meant Teddy should expect to see him in the morning.

Chapter 86

Mifflintown, Pennsylvania – April 30, 2015

"Do not think that those who are killed in the cause of GOD are dead; they are alive at their Lord, enjoying His provisions."

—The Quran, Surah 3:169

Wayne Joseph finished up the necessary paperwork to send their prisoner to Washington and waited at the Juniata County Jail for his escort, Mike Adams, to arrive. He was certain that their guest was the first Muslim extremist to spend a night in their jail. Just to make sure that there was no funny business, the MPD had him in shackles, with two officers watching him all night. He had nothing in the cell; they confiscated his clothing and provided him with an orange jumpsuit. Of course, there was no identification, and his fingerprints did not yield anything, so the mystery man remained nameless and quiet.

Seeing Mike arrive, Wayne said, "Come on in and have a seat."

"Man, what happened?" Mike asked as he pulled out a chair and waited to hear the story.

Wayne recapped the night. "The first officer through the door was shot and killed by one of the terrorists, who turned his gun on himself. When the dust settled, he was dead, along with the state trooper."

"Is Mr. Lange OK?"

"They beat him within an inch of his life, but he's alive. He's unconscious in the Lewistown Hospital. What time is your flight scheduled to leave?"

"It departs at two fifteen p.m."

"I have them getting the prisoner ready for the trip. Do you need assistance?"

"I have asked the PA State Police to escort me to the gate, and they're waiting outside. One of them is going to DC with me."

"Mike, there is no need for me to remind you of the importance of this prisoner to national security. Are you certain you have enough support?"

"I get it, and trust me, we can handle one bad guy."

db

With the prisoner in Agent Adams's custody, his business in Mifflintown was complete. Wayne headed for the hospital to see his fraternity brother. Anne was sitting next to his bed, holding his hand. She and the kids were in shock as they huddled around their husband and father.

Looking confused but happy to see their friend, "Wayne, how did you know he was here?"

"The law enforcement community is a small one, and a mutual friend gave me a call late last night. I got here as soon as I could." He had to lie to her for the sake of national security.

"Did they tell you what happened?"

Playing dumb, Wayne said, "Yes. Do you have any idea who would have wanted to hurt Jason? He has to be one of the nicest people I've ever met."

"That has been the question of the day, and no, I haven't the foggiest."

"How is he doing?"

"The doctor is concerned that his skull may be cracked, but he's not stable enough to go through more tests. He's in a drug-induced coma until the swelling goes down. We're praying that he isn't hemorrhaging. He appears to have feeling in his extremities, which is a very positive sign."

The nurses were clearly not enforcing the two visitors at a time rule, as Henry also joined the group.

Anne got up to hug him. "Thanks so much for stopping by and for last night."

He received the same update that Wayne had just gotten.

"Henry, this is an old college friend of Jason's, Wayne Joseph."

Acting like they had never heard of each other, they shook hands.

About an hour later, Mike Adams arrived at the Harrisburg International Airport. Mike carried the prisoner's personal belongings in a bag, and the two state troopers each had an arm, rushing through the airport. They went straight to the head of the security line, but they still had to go through the scanners. All of them had to remove their shoes and empty their pockets. The prisoner's shoes were the only personal belonging that they had allowed him to keep for his trip to DHS headquarters.

The three of them watched him like a hawk as he retrieved his shoes from the bin. Despite the careful scrutiny, the prisoner managed to take a small pill from a secret compartment in the heel of his shoe. As quickly as he had extricated the pill, it was in his mouth. The men were continuing down the concourse to the United gate to board their plane for Washington International when the prisoner shouted, "*Allahu Akbar!*" (Allah is the greatest!) and fell face forward. He was dead before he hit the ground.Airport emergency personnel were on the scene in minutes, but there was nothing they could do. The Middle Eastern John Doe was gone.

PART SIX

May 2015

Chapter 87

Al-Qaeda Headquarters, Afghanistan – May 2, 2015

"Make war on them until idolatry shall cease and God's religion shall reign supreme."

—*The Quran, Surah 8:36*

There was never a good time to deliver bad news to Ahsan, but the anniversary of the death of his best friend, Osama, was among the worse.

"Hajji, we have more bad news from North America." Ally reluctantly told him of the failed attempt with the McNichols managing director.

Ally could see the veins popping in Haijji's forehead. He said nothing but the disappointment was obvious. His shoulder's slumped and there was anger written all over his face.

Trying to change the subject, Dalil reminded Hajji about the conference call in an hour. "Is there anything you would like to discuss, or are we set to go?"

"Let's have Dr. Shane join us, and we'll do a quick run-through. This could be our last opportunity to rally the men before our attack, and I want it to be good."

ⅆb

The screens came alive without issue, just like Hajji had demanded. The pressure to perform flawlessly was excruciating. Legends and folklore permeated the halls of al-Qaeda headquarters—stories of public beheadings to penalize staff failures flourished. In his empire, there was no such thing as the right to a fair trial; Ahsan *was* the judge and the jury. The only thing he left to others was the execution itself, but he was present, front and center, sometimes close enough to be spattered by the blood of the victim.

Ahsan began. "Gentlemen, we are quickly coming to the day that will change the shape of Islam forever. The extended countdown has begun, and Sky Burst is within days of becoming a reality—finally. Mr. Dalil will take you through what's going to happen in the upcoming days and weeks."

Performing his normal role, Dalil explained how they would receive their third and final visit from the couriers; this time they would provide the final assembly instructions and specific coordinates on where they would set up their weapons for launch. "We know that all the vans are making their rounds with no mishaps, and all the components will be in place by tomorrow, exactly according to our plan. Well done to each of you. Allah is pleased!"

It was rare that they received any positive feedback in these meetings, and one could almost feel the relief of some pressure—some, not all.

Hajji took over, "I have asked Dr. Shane to be part of our meeting to refresh us on the devastation that's going to follow Sky Burst. Malcolm, please take over the meeting."

In his staid British accent, Malcolm said, "Good day, gentlemen."

Nods and mumblings could be heard from the five screens.

"It has been nearly a month since I first introduced the concept of nonnuclear electromagnetic pulse, or NNEMP, weapons. I know that all of you downloaded and read several of my books and papers on the subject, so what I wish to review with you today is what will happen immediately following the attack—preparation for your mind."

Everyone focused intently on his every word as he reviewed the major impact of the weapons. A digital slide replaced the headshot of Dr. Shane, and bullet points streamed down their screens:

- Our missiles are designed to detonate at 15,000 feet.
- The blast will radiate EMP blasts of 100-mile radii.
- Your locations will be strategically located to have the most civilian and military casualties.
- *All* electronic equipment will fail immediately.
- Transportation will come to a halt.
    - Airplanes will fall from the sky.
    - Cars will stop.
    - Trains and subways will stop.
- Electrical substations will stop generating. The areas around the missiles will become dark—no electrical service.
- Cash will be at a premium. Banks/ATMs will not be able to operate or even open. Credit/debit cards will not be able to be processed.
- All stock markets will shut down in New York, Chicago, and LA.
- Police and emergency vehicles will not operate, and there will be *no* communication in or around the target cities.
- Since all the infidel governments discounted the effectiveness of our weapon of choice, their military equipment has not been protected, and their armed forces will be crippled.

The screens went back to the headshot of Dr. Shane.

"Here's the great news, gentlemen. Our mosques and our followers have protection against the effects of NNEMP, and we have stores of cash. We will be in control. Sharia law will be launched, and the underground troops that have been training in your countries for years will surface and take control of all the governments. Islam will rule! Our flag will fly over the capitals of your nations."

Delivered like a motivational football coach with uncharacteristic energy from a Brit, Dr. Shane readied the coalition to leave their offices and start the attack immediately. His plan was going to work, and now they all believed it would.

Hajji followed Shane and explained that, at Sky Burst minus twenty-four hours, another package would be delivered to each of them with the strategy for worldwide domination.

Hajji closed the meeting with his rallying cry: "The victory will belong to Allah! *Alhamdulillah!*"

"Allah! *Alhamdulillah!*" his five lieutenants repeated. Their voices were still reverberating through the speakers as all the screens simultaneously went blank.

Chapter 88

Antioch, Tennessee – May 4, 2015

"Nothing but heaven itself is better than a friend who is really a friend."

—*Plautus*

It was a long weekend for Kyle, but not in a good way. In fact, it had been a long week since the "accident" that killed Basel. Agent Baird shared with him that the bullet that killed his friend had been traced to al-Qaeda ammunition that was left behind by the Russians when they were chased out of Afghanistan. The al-Qaeda connection was not surprising.

He was not able to go to Basel's memorial service at the Antioch Islamic Center for obvious reasons, but he knew where Basel's soul was, and he was comforted.

Throughout the week, a stream of interrogators questioned him, forcing him to repeat the same story over and over to people who seemed to distrust him. His life was not his own, as armed agents constantly shadowed him. He welcomed the protection, but would his life ever return to normal?

He wondered if his interest in Basel had cost him his earthly life. Would Basel still be alive if he had left him to his beliefs? As he was replaying the recent events in his mind, it was as if God Himself provided a revelation and assurance that what he had done was absolutely the right thing; it wasn't an audible voice, but a physical feeling of warmth and peace. If Basel had died without Christ, he would have been spending eternity in Hell. Kyle found peace in that.

"Mr. Emerson, we're ready for you again."

The call from the security guard brought him back to reality—time for more questioning. Kyle looked as if he had no sleep all week. His shirt was wrinkled with perspiration stains under each arm. His hair was more unkempt than it usually was. The dreary weather outside didn't help his mood. He had known that, after this break, he would have to talk to someone at Langley, but they said this would be his last.

Kyle spent the next forty-five minutes on a videoconference with Teddy Brewer. The questions were the same, and he gave the same answers, but what Kyle found interesting was that Teddy also asked new questions, which drove him deeper into the events of the week and his relationship with Basel. He also appreciated Teddy's style.

Teddy was satisfied that Kyle was a patriot and not a terrorist, as some had speculated. After Teddy had reviewed Kyle's file, he was nearly certain, but he needed to talk with him and look him in the eyes to confirm what he had read.

"Mr. Emerson, I'm concerned for your safety. These people are not nice, and if they ever figure out that you are involved in helping us break this case, you will be killed immediately."

Kyle assumed that was why he was being protected, but the way Agent Brewer stated it was much more piercing. "What am I to do?"

"We want you to spend some time with your aunt and uncle who live in Southern California."

"I haven't worked in a week. I'm going to lose my jobs."

"Mr. Emerson, you're going to lose something much more valuable than your three part-time jobs if you stay in town. We will protect you, but these people are motivated by a higher calling. They have no regard for their personal safety, and you have interfered with their jihad against the US."

The fact that they knew he had three jobs didn't completely register with him as he contemplated leaving town. "I don't want to drag my relatives into this mess."

"We have arranged for you to travel without ever going into a public airport, and we will have protection on you twenty-four/seven. Trust me, your aunt and uncle will never know."

"When do I need to leave?"

"There's a black helicopter awaiting your arrival at the Baptist Hospital heliport. A sedan is waiting at the front curb to take you there, and your bag has been packed. We will give you a secure phone to call your parents once you are safely airborne, and your aunt and uncle have already graciously invited you based on an e-mail you sent them yesterday. Your parents have also been copied on the electronic mail exchanges."

"What did I tell them?" Kyle asked with a slight smile.

"You are visiting LA in an effort to try to get your music heard, and there are a couple of executives who want to meet with you to discuss your songs. This is it, Kyle, you are getting to pursue your dream."

Kyle did not appreciate the slap about his music career. "That's funny, but I don't appreciate your humor."

"Before you were born, back in the eighties, there was major corruption in the record company promotion departments, with money and drugs being exchanged for radio airplay. The FBI and other federal agencies were involved in the investigation, and many lower-level employees helped us with our investiga-tion—they did the right thing. Many of those people are still in the business but now hold executive-level positions. They were happy to help us out. We can't guarantee what will happen, but you at least have some doors opened for you."

Chapter 89

Fairfield, Connecticut – May 4, 2015

"You have to look at the history of the Middle East in particular. It has been one of failure and frustration, of feudalism and tribalism.

—Alexander Haig

His office in NYC thought he was on a Mediterranean cruise for the first half of May, but in fact, Esa worked around the clock on Sky Burst. He couldn't sleep. Prior to taking off, he made certain that there was enough cash in their accounts to finance the last two weeks of the plan and that each of the five cells had what they needed. The end was in sight, but he wanted to assure Hajji that there would be no more miscues. He wasn't used to failures and the latest fiasco in Pennsylvania had nearly brought down the operation. Fortunately, the men were martyrs, so no more information fell into the enemy's hands. He thought the Nashville issue was nipped in the bud since Hares's operative had been exterminated—it was still a blemish. He was having doubts about himself. Was he that ineffective or had the intelligence efforts of the Unite States improved drastically?

Ahsan's courier had arrived over the weekend and delivered his final packet before the attack. In the mass of special instructions was a small flash drive. The code to open the files was kept in his home office safe, and when opened, it allowed him to run variations of Sky Burst. He ran them over and over again with different weather predictions, algorithms with missile and weapon failure rates. Even the worst of the scenarios would reap huge rewards, with countless infidels dead, wounded, or left to die; the long-term devastation would be far-reaching. He was fascinated by the technology and the exceptional graphics. From the 100 percent view on his sixty-inch flat screen, he could watch the view that mimicked a look from a low-elevation orbit over the United States. It showed the launch blasts, the contrails, the detonation, the power grids failing, and even the planes dropping from the sky based on actual airline and commercial aircraft schedules. Trains and subway disasters could also be viewed and seen as tiny puffs of smoke. It was rewarding for him to see the plan played out in three-dimensional CGI animations. He played it constantly. It was reminiscent of his adolescence in Saudi Arabia—hooked on interactive computer games. It was mesmerizing, but the stakes were so much greater now. The game would soon be real.

It was thumbs-up from all of his cell leaders when he called them this morning. They had all the components, and the assembly process was going smoothly. A few minor glitches were smoothed out locally and only shared within the group for information in anticipation of others experiencing similar problems. Excitement built among the cells. A few smaller vans were delivered to each of their facilities to join the white step vans. The fleets would be dispatched to the electronically transmitted coordinates. Esa knew the coordinates, but that info would not be downloaded until closer to the setup date—the end of the week.

In recent weeks, he had been going through antacid tablets like mints. Occasionally, he added a Pepto-Bismol chaser, but his stomach was constantly in knots. His cheeks were sunken and his skin pale—he wasn't eating properly, and his sleepless nights were turned productive by his focus on the attack. In his mind and on his desktop, the countdown had started:

T minus 10 days

22 hours

35 minutes

55 seconds. . . and counting as the numbers clicked down on a digital clock in the upper right-hand corner of his computer monitor. . .

54, 53, 52, 51. . .

Chapter 90

Lewistown, Pennsylvania – May 5, 2015

"Is anyone among you afflicted? Let him pray."

—James 5:13 KJV

Anne prayed for her husband. Her last conversation with him had been surreal. It was a comfort to have her children with her, and they seemed to comfort each other. Henry never left her side. Jason was being held in a coma by the medication that dripped into his limp body. The incessant beeping and sounds from the machine that filled his lungs had become white noise.

Interrupting one of her moments of pleading with the Lord, the doctor asked to see her in a room near the nurses' station. All of her meetings with Dr. Taylor had been in *that* room, and she was preparing for more of the same—bad news. She wanted her husband back, she wanted her life back, and she was angry with God for allowing this to happen.

Henry was at her side as they entered the room. He was comforting but she was frightened. Skipping the customary greetings, they got right down to business.

"Mrs. Lange, the swelling in and around Jason's brain is not responding to our medicine. My team is afraid that he is hemorrhaging somewhere near the concussion, and his kidneys are showing signs of distress. That's the bad news; on the good side, he has been stabilized and responding to pricks to his fingers and feet. We have to do exploratory surgery to see if we can stop the bleeding. I have scheduled a CT scan to verify our theories. He is stable enough to proceed; we just need your signature."

Anne looked to Henry. He reached out, delicately touched her hand, and nodded.

"We will prepare him for the scan. It would be a good time for you and your children to get some fresh air and stretch your legs. We will meet again prior to beginning his surgery if the scan verifies our theory."

☼

Anne had not informed Jason's family about the "accident." She didn't know how to explain what had happened. *She* didn't really know.

Anne, Henry, and the children were pacing nervously in the surgical waiting room when she heard a familiar voice.

"Anne, I called Henry to get the latest update and got here as soon as I could."

"Thanks so much, Pastor Severino. I appreciate it."

He led the group in prayer at about the exact time that Dr. Taylor started cutting. The scan had confirmed their fear, but the bleeder was very small and in a place that they should be able to get to without much difficulty. Anne wasn't informed of any of this information.

Anne was angry with God.

☼

Hours had passed—three, to be exact. The status on Jason's patient number had not changed since it first appeared on the monitor:

PATIENT 00379 SURGERY PROGRESSING

Other people had come and gone to offer their support, but Henry stayed. Groups of employees periodically made the fifteen-minute drive to Lewistown Hospital—Jason was well liked at the plant. There were no flowers allowed in the ICU, but his walls and every tabletop were covered by get-well wishes from all around the country, including his bosses at McNichols HQ in Chicago.

In and out of prayer, in and out of mindless shows on the TV that hung on the wall, in and out of conversations with Henry, visitors and the children—but the clock failed to move. Time was standing still. Where was Dr. Taylor?

Another hour dragged by before Anne heard, "Mrs. Lange, let's step into the room."

She wasn't able to read the face of his doctor—never. He seemed to exhibit zero emotion; he had probably learned that bedside manner in med school.

"Jason is resting comfortably in recovery," Dr. Taylor said, immediately taking the edge off as Anne and Henry breathed sighs of relief. "The surgery was a success, but you need to know that his heart stopped in the middle of the procedure. We almost lost him, but he's a strong young man, and we were able to shock his heart back into rhythm."

Nearly in a complete panic, Anne was unable to control her built up emotions, "What does *that* mean?"

"It happens sometimes when patients are under anesthesia for long periods of time—especially patients who have been kept in comas."

"Will there be any side effects?"

"No, it was a matter of seconds, and his heart came right back. We were able to stop the bleeding in his brain. He will be kept sedated for probably twenty-four to forty-eight hours. These next two days will be critical for him. We've done everything we can do. It's up to Jason now."

Looking around the waiting room, she couldn't help but notice the serious-looking guys with the squiggly wire coming from an earpiece watching over her and her family. They hadn't left their side since Jason's incident. *What in the world is going on, and what is Jason involved in?* she wondered. She kept praying. She wanted to talk with her husband.

♉

Within hours after receiving the call from Anne, Jason's parents were on their way from Jacksonville, Illinois, to St. Louis to catch a flight to Harrisburg. The trip would take hours—hours for them to recover from the shock that their son had just been through brain surgery.

Chapter 91

Washington, DC – May 5, 2015

"The terrible thing about terrorism is that ultimately it destroys those who practice it. Slowly but surely, as they try to extinguish life in others, the light within them dies."

—*Terry Waite*

The lightning strike icons filled the board once again. Ahsan had had another communiqué with his lieutenants, and Teddy could see the ripple effect. All week, he and his staff had been decrypting, interpreting, and analyzing. There was more urgency in the chatter. Ahsan was aggravated by the failures in the United States and wanted the head of the person causing his problems delivered to him. Teddy knew that it wasn't a figure of speech; he really did want a head—Teddy's head.

Teddy looked over a report from the hospital, and it appeared that Lange was going to survive, or as Dr. Taylor had put it, "cautiously optimistic for a full recovery."

Thank God, Teddy thought.

Teddy was confident with the intelligence that had been gathered. The picture of what al-Qaeda was trying to do was becoming clear, both here and around the world. The five-cell pattern had been identified completely in three of the territories, but there were still two that had one renegade cell each in South Africa and Eastern Europe.

Teddy ran the what-ifs should they not find the fifth cells in those two countries to determine what the casualty rates and collateral damage would be. He hated to think of things like this, but if there had to be renegades, he was happy that they were in those two countries. Based on his models, they would cause a minimal number of casualties in the scheme of things.

ḋb

Word started to come in from the surveillance teams that small white vans were delivered to the assembly points. The number varied from one to four—four in Los Angeles. Teddy ordered each to be tagged with GPS trackers as he beefed up the number of agents watching each cell to match the number of vehicles; they were going to keep visual contact with every vehicle when movement started. They could not rely on technology when the stakes were so high. They planned to keep eyes on them and physically track them all until it was time to launch their defensive.

ḋb

Teddy was going through his daily debrief with Cliff, contemplating their moves. The United States was ready to raid their operations immediately, but there were still renegades out there.

"Boss, I need to yield to your wisdom. I would prefer to wait a few more days to see if Russia's SVR and the NIA in South Africa can locate their missing cells."

"Teddy, I would too, but it will come to a point soon where we have to roll."

"Sir, all the intelligence that we have collected seems to point to the May fifteenth date for the attack, and based on our surveillance, they *are* still assembling the weapons. Can I have through the weekend?"

"My gut tells me to shut it down now. It's a risk to wait for a one hundred percent sweep."

"You're right, Cliff, but if we wait until they're on the move, we will be sure to get all the operatives, as we know they will have all hands on deck for the big day."

"You have until Monday."

Chapter 92

Antioch, Tennessee – May 6, 2015

"If you do not fight, He will punish you sternly, and replace you by other men."

—*The Quran, Surah 9:37*

After Imam Selim's class, the guys met for their usual "unwind" time at the Istanbul. The mood wasn't as upbeat as it had been; the magnitude of their mission was sinking in. They were all gung ho at the start, but things had changed. Taj died of a heart attack, and now Basel was gone. As they sat in the back room, each of them wondered who would join their martyred friends next.

They were all somber, but the most noticeable difference was the comic, Wazir. All of them were curious, but Jerome finally asked what was on all of their minds.

"What's wrong with you, Wazir?"

Wazir was trying to be low-key and blend into the group, but it was very different from his normal role. He couldn't tell them what was bothering him. He told Fadi what the imam had said to him, and hours later, Basel was dead. Wazir knew what they had signed up for. But was it a coincidence, or was it something else? He let Fadi know what he had heard so he could save Basel from his interest in Christianity. Had it gotten him killed?

"Sorry, I'm just not feeling well. I think I'm coming down with something."

"Hang in there, man. We have a busy week facing us."

Basel's absence was the elephant in the room for all of them, and finally, Darim mentioned it.

"I miss Basel. The apartment is empty without him, and we don't know what to do with his stuff."

Habib spoke up. "I never heard him mention his family, but did he ever talk about his family to you or any of the other roommates?"

"He told me one night that they were upset with him for his radical thinking— they were not supporters of jihad. When he told them he was leaving for America to join the movement here, they kicked him out of their house immediately. That was three years ago, and he hasn't talked with them since. We checked through some of his belongings but found no signs of any relatives or anything regarding Pakistan. It's like he eliminated everything from his past."

Wazir, still feeling guilty, said, "That is so sad. His parents don't even know he's dead."

"That was obvious at his funeral—since it was only us and the two guys he knew from the taxi company who showed up for the services."

Wazir didn't say it, but he was thinking how sad it was that Basel had been damned to the lake of fire for eternity. That secret was best kept between him and Fadi.

Chapter 93

Lewistown, Pennsylvania – May 6, 2015

"These things I have spoken unto you, that in me ye might have peace. In the world ye shall have tribulation: but be of good cheer; I have overcome the world."

—*John 16:33KJV*

The alarms went off loudly next to Jason's bed as mechanical-sounding computerized voice echoed, "CODE BLUE, CODE BLUE, CODE BLUE. . ." through the hospital's PA system. Nurses and doctors rushed to his bedside. Anne, awaking from a deep sleep and disoriented, was pushed aside as nurses and doctors rushed in the room. Jason's monitors were all flat lines. She didn't need the obnoxious warning buzzers to know her husband was in trouble. No one stopped to explain to Anne what was happening. She was in shock, thinking that Jason could be gone forever. She prayed over and over, *Please, God, please save him. Please, please save him.*

After what seemed like an eternity, the monitors began to beep once again as his blood pressure began to register. One nurse stayed behind as the rest went about their business. As quickly as the crisis had started, it was over. No one talked with Anne sobbed as tears streamed down her cheeks, but she was finally able to breathe again.

db

Anne had finally dozed off after a sleepless night. She was awakened by the sound of Dr. Taylor looking through Jason's chart.

"Mrs. Lange, I didn't want to disturb you, but I'm sure you have questions about what happened last night."

"Absolutely!"

"The swelling in Jason's head has gone down significantly, which is a really good sign. It appears that his head is healing. We started to wean him off the propofol drip that was keeping him in a coma. As he began to regain consciousness, we had to start morphine to manage his pain, to keep him comfortable. Unfortunately, it appears that he is allergic to morphine, and we almost lost him again. The night staff wanted me to apologize for basically ignoring you, but the protocol for Jason's condition needed to be done stat."

"One of the nurses told me what she thought happened, but I had never known Jason to have any allergies, and he had been given morphine when he had a kidney stone attack several years ago."

Not wanting to alarm her, Dr. Taylor said, "These things can develop at any point in our lives. I'm just thankful that they knew what to do."

"Will there be any aftereffects?"

"No, and all his vitals appear to be normal. I would anticipate you having a conversation with him sometime this morning. We should be able to move him into a regular room by this afternoon if he continues to improve as he has in the past two hours."

She began texting her kids before the doctor had even left the room. They had returned to school but had special permission to keep their phones with them. After she got the message to them, she called her in-laws, who had spent the night with the kids at home.

"Dad, Jason is doing much better this morning, and they are stopping the drugs that have kept him in a coma. The doc said that he expects us to be able to talk with him sometime today."

She decided not to share the near-death experience with the kids or her in-laws—it was unnecessary.

Next, she called Henry, who walked into the room before she had finished dialing.

Tears welled up in her eyes. "We almost lost him again last night. He's allergic to morphine, but they reacted quickly, and he's going to be OK. The swelling is down, and his vitals are normal. Henry, I want my Jason back. He scared me so much last night. I'm tired."

As if on cue, Jason's eyes opened, and he muttered something that caught their attention. It was inaudible, and he was incoherent. He had a frightened, confused look in his bloodshot eyes. Anne rushed to his side and grabbed his hand.

"Jason, I love you!"

She thought she saw the corners of his mouth turn upward. His confused look indicated that he had some questions to ask and so did she, but now was not the time. They would be answered later, she hoped.

db

He was still being fed through an IV, but he seemed to be getting better by the minute. Being in a regular room with the ventilator removed was a huge step in his recovery. Anne was ignoring his questions about what happened; it wouldn't help anything at this point.

Outside, the two men guarded the entrance to his room. His parents arrived with the kids, who had left school early. They were anxious to talk to their dad for the first time in a week. Jason's parents hadn't noticed the guards on their visit to the ICU, as there were so many people scurrying about, but they were more obvious now.

His dad pulled Anne aside. "What's with the guards outside?"

"Until the police have a clearer understanding of who beat him up, they are protecting him."

His confused look said it all.

Anne was thankful to have Jason's parents. Her father and mother had divorced when she was very young, and contrary to the court's wishes, her mother had not allowed Anne to see her father. He passed away several years later—alone and thinking Anne didn't love him. Her mother continued a sin that had been in her family for generations of cutting people out of her life. After severing relationships with grandparents and siblings, she eventually disowned Anne, her own daughter. She was "adopted" by Jason's parents, who loved her more than her own mother. She thanked God for that love.

Outside the room, one of the DHS agents noticed a Middle Eastern–looking young man pushing a gurney and whispered something to the other guard. Noting the name on the hospital ID badge, the agent repeated the name into his microphone as soon as he had turned the corner. A background check was started.

Chapter 94

Antioch, Tennessee – May 8, 2015

"If you should die or be slain in the cause of God, His forgiveness and His mercy would surely be better than all the riches."

—The Quran, Surah 3:156

From the beginning, they had known that this day would come, and they now understood that, for the first two weeks in May and perhaps eternity, they would be dedicating their lives to the cause of Allah. Various excuses were provided to their employers: vacations, family deaths, and so on. Some even resigned their positions, knowing that there would be something much better for them following Sky Burst. They all moved into the Twentieth Street warehouse, where Fadi had set up a makeshift dormitory with all the comforts of home. That was stretching the truth. Their bunks were bumpy, with the only amenity being a twenty-seven-inch TV set from the mid-nineties with an antiquated Sony PlayStation attached to it. None of this bothered anyone, though; as they knew the sacrifices they were making would be rewarded.

They had made great strides, and their missiles were nearly complete. The five of them living together was causing some tension, and Wazir had stopped adding levity to the situation, which had always helped the time pass more quickly. There was little talk, but much progress. The enormity of what they were preparing had set in with each one of them.

"It's time to move the vehicles into the warehouse," Fadi directed.

Jerome and Fadi opened the door as the other three moved the two vans and the step van inside the building.

ǂ

"Teddy, there's been activity at the Twentieth Street facility. The Antioch cell has moved into the facility, and there's no coming and going by any of them. Moments ago, they moved all three of their vehicles inside."

Teddy had received similar information from all five surveillance teams: all the radicals had moved in together, and all the vehicles were inside their buildings.

ǂ

Fadi pulled a device from the case that had been delivered during the most recent courier drop.

"Darim, run it over all three trucks—inside and out."

As Darim turned it on, lights flashed and a buzzer sounded. They all watched as the trucks were scanned. The buzzer and lights went off again as he approached the hood of one of the vans. The lights got brighter and the buzzer grew louder toward the front. Wazir popped the hood as the search continued. A small quarter-sized device was stuck to the inside.

"Is this what we are looking for?"

"Yes, but continue to check the rest of the van. Pop that off, but do not destroy it."

"What is it, Fadi?"

They were all shocked by his answer. "It's a GPS tracking device."

Wazir's voice reflected panic, "Did the infidels install it?"

Sarcastically, he replied, "Well, it wasn't us."

"So they know we're here?"

The thought that the enemy knew they were there was frightening. The tension in the warehouse escalated as devices were found on each vehicle.

"Leave each of the devices under the vehicle. I need to call this in."

Fadi called Connecticut on his secure satphone.

Esa calmed him down. "We knew they were getting close—that's why we had you sweep your vehicles. They don't know that we know, so don't be alarmed and assure your guys that we are in total control. We have surprises planned for them as well."

db

Tracking devices were discovered on all the vehicles throughout the country—and they all lay active but useless on the floors of the warehouses.

Chapter 95

Fairfield, Connecticut – May 8, 2015

"No nation ever had an army large enough to guarantee it against attack in time of peace, or ensure it of victory in time of war."

—*Calvin Coolidge*

The call from Dalil was startling. Launch day had been moved up by five days. Hajji had received information from his sources that his operation was beginning to fall apart. They needed to attack with what they had or run the risk of wasting years of preparation.

"I will get the word out and reset our countdowns for a launch of nine p.m., Afghanistan time. The forty-eight-hour countdown is under way."

"Esa, you and your guys need to keep praying to Allah that this attack is effective. *Allahu Akbar!*"

"*Allahu Akbar!*"

The click from Dalil's phone rang in his ears.

Taking a deep breath, Esa got on the phone with each of his cell leaders. He detected both excitement and anxiety in their voices. If they hadn't been already, they were now in hyper speed. The missiles needed to get into position, and the trucks needed to roll tonight.

He adjusted the countdown clock on his computer, reducing it by the five days that had just gotten snatched away:

T minus 1 day
23 hours
18 minutes
43 seconds...42, 41, 40, 39

Happy Mother's Day, infidels!

Chapter 96

Washington, DC – May 8, 2015

"Let's roll."

—*Todd Beamer*

here go the lightning bolts populating his US map once again.

Pushing the intercom button on the conference table, he said, "Cliff, you better get in here. We've got another flurry of activity."

Teddy then notified all the surveillance teams to be on high alert. He also added additional agents and an extra vehicle to each cell location, as word had started to come from the analysts decrypting and translating their intercepts.

Secretary Knowles was with Cliff when they arrived. Knowles was obviously shaken. Her tidy, pressed professional appearance was long gone, replaced with wrinkled clothing—her faded make-up added to her very uncommon look. She took charge, with no hellos or other pleasantries. "Fill me in, Mr. Brewer." She knew what was at stake, and she was strictly business.

Everyone huddled around Teddy, their pulses quickened. The details indicated that al-Qaeda's attack was imminent. Suddenly, the room temperature seemed to elevate as beads of sweat formed instantaneously on everyone's foreheads.

"Grab your things. We need to get to the White House."

The secretary's assistant had the black SUVs waiting outside. Three of them were lined up, with their blue-and-red strobe lights flashing.

Secretary Knowles called President Wheeler's chief of staff from the caravan. "We have an urgent matter. Please ask the president and his cabinet to meet us in his Situation Room, and we'll be there in moments. There is nothing more important on any of their agendas than what we have to brief them on."

The caravan sped through the city; traffic lights changed to green before they reached them. Only inches separated each SUV, thanks to their specially designed coordinated breaking systems. Secret Service agents filled the seats not occupied in the middle truck and also filled the lead and trailing trucks. Teddy had the NSA detail at the White House patch into the other intelligence groups in the other countries so they could track the developments worldwide. The SUVs screeched to a halt at the West Wing entrance. Teddy, Cliff, and Secretary Knowles were rushed into the Situation Room, where the president waited.

Wheeler nodded to each as they entered, but quickly took charge of the meeting. He wanted answers. "In my PDB this morning, I was told that the planned attack was taking place on the fifteenth and you had everything under control. What in God's name has happened?"

Secretary Knowles began but quickly turned it over to Cliff and Teddy.

"Sir, it appears that Ahsan has been spooked," Cliff said.

"What do you mean?"

Cliff looked to Teddy for the details.

"Let me show you what happened about two hours ago." Screens came alive around the room. "The images you are looking at come to us from a combination of National Reconnaissance Office low-orbit satellite images and photos taken by our surveillance teams at the assembly facilities. In these photos, you see their trunks are parked outside, and as we jump ahead fifteen minutes, you see the trucks are gone. They moved them inside their buildings."

President Wheeler asked, "Is this movement of the trucks the reason for the emergency meeting?"

"No, sir." Teddy pulled up the map with the lightning bolts and explained what they were looking at. "The actionable intelligence that we learned from this activity is that they accelerated their launch date. We now expect it to be within the next forty-eight hours."

"We need to raid all their sites now?"

"No, sir. I called in the first wave of reinforcements and have an extra vehicle to chase them when they depart for their launch sites. We also have groups of black helicopters ready in each city."

"Why not send the SWAT guys into their warehouses immediately?"

"Sir, we're afraid that they're rigged with explosives. We want them alive, and we don't want our guys massacred. These people do not value life, and we can't give them an opportunity to kill our people or themselves. They are very adept at both."

"Are we in control?"

"Yes. Each vehicle is tagged with a GPS device. We will be able to track them easily. We're ready and have been preparing for this day for months. The information we get from these operatives will be invaluable in our quest to bring Ahsan and his al-Qaeda down. Trust me, sir, we're ready."

Press Secretary Ford rolled up his prayer mat and headed to the Sit Room to observe what was unfolding.

Chapter 97

Antioch, Tennessee, and Washington, DC – May 8, 2015

"Do not look down upon any Muslim, for even the most inferior believer is great in the eyes of God."

—*Abu Bakr*

T he men moved with greater intensity; the countdown had started. The trucks were loaded, one missile per van or step van. Each missile was self-contained with individual computerization and launch stand. The countdown had been initiated in each weapon from Afghanistan, and the LED readouts allowed them to see how much time was left before detonation. They *would* detonate wherever they were, so they *had* to get them in place.

⚕

The leadership of the US government was watching the screens as Teddy continued his briefing when the low-orbit satellite views suddenly showed the overhead garage doors of each facility open.

The surveillance teams jumped into their chase vehicles as they phoned into headquarters what they were seeing.

Teddy tried to sound calm and in control but his voice cracked slightly, "Not sure what's happening, but the doors are open in Nashville!"

No sooner had he delivered the message than the first van rolled out of the building. Having practiced and choreographed their moves for weeks, each agent was assigned to follow a truck in the order they exited the building. They were set. First the step van rolled out, followed closely by a van, and then a second van. There was something wrong. The GPS indicated that they were still in the building, but there was something worse. Three *additional* vans rolled out.

Teddy nearly lost it, "Where in the world did they come from?"

The extra team stationed at the Twentieth Street warehouse was able to take one, but there were two uncovered renegades.

Teddy was perplexed by the satellite images of additional vans in Chicago, Los Angeles, Long Island, Boston, and Nashville.

Teddy had caught the discrepancy immediately, but the president was the first to verbalize it.

"Mr. Brewer, what is going on? You said there was a truck and two vans at each facility except LA. There are more—many more!"

Teddy was shocked. Once the dominoes started to fall, it had been easy for him to figure out what al-Qaeda was up to.

"We have contingencies. Our helicopters are standing by. We will dispatch them immediately."

His outward appearance was calm, but his insides were in turmoil, as months of his efforts were falling apart before his eyes. It was frightening that this had happened at all, but to see his plan fall apart in front of every important person in his life was unimaginable. But worse, what did this mean to the American public? It was all happening at once; he couldn't watch all five screens. But reports were coming in on his PDA from his agents. All total the five cells had sixteen additional vans hidden inside and out of sight—evidently moved into the warehouses prior to their twenty-four/seven watch.

"Scramble the helicopters and report back to me on how many vehicles are unaccounted for!"

db

Reports were coming in as some of the vans reached their locations. So far, they were all higher elevation remote sites close to the cities. It appeared that one of the Long Island vans was traveling south on I-95, headed for the nation's capital, with a black helicopter keeping close tabs from above.

Some "good" news finally hit the White House Sit Room: they were able to determine the exact time of the attack. Several agents reported the red LED readouts indicating the countdown was positioned and visible for the terrorists' benefit. The times reported from around the country were synchronized. They had images of the LEDs from their long-range cameras:

42:12:43

Similar images came in from everywhere, with different numbers in the seconds field. They had forty-two hours, twelve minutes.

db

In addition to assembling their missiles, the cells had practiced the setup and launch of the NNEMP devices. Once they reached their location, as directed by their vehicles' GPS systems, they knew exactly what to do. When the weapon was pointed in the correct direction and angle, the red LED numbers would turn to green.

Text messages were coming in to Fadi, who relayed the information to Esa, who continued to adjust his computer model with the new information.

Chapter 98

Washington, DC – May 8, 2015

> "Terrorism has become the systematic weapon of a war that knows no borders or seldom has a face."

—*Jacques Chirac*

Teddy was flushed. He was never surprised. He excused himself from the Sit Room, as he needed to be able to speak to his agents and foreign counterparts without the most powerful people in the free world listening. He was flustered but not defeated. When Operation Peace Shield had begun, he started compiling information; his brain had worked through every possible outcome. The ingenuity of al-Qaeda was surprising in light of their recent history; they were smarter than he had given them credit for.

Once he had determined the enormity of what al-Qaeda was planning, DHS was given free reign the US government's resources, including detachments of the military. Teddy's plan from the start was to allow them to get set up and then take them down. For this final step, there were special squads from the 82nd Airborne Division from Fort Bragg TDY (temporary duty) in each of the cell cities. Over five hundred (roughly one hundred assigned to each city) explosive ordnance disposal (EOD) troops had been drilling and prepping for the past month to disarm al-Qaeda's missiles, and based on their intel, they were ready for the task.

Teddy's big problem at this point was that he had sixteen vehicles unaccounted for and unsupervised—throughout the country. Similar stories came to him from intelligence agencies around the world. They all needed to be found.

He had a few more tricks up his sleeve, and they had just taken off from Langley AFB to remote airports near each of the five cities. His last-ditch effort was untested; Teddy had never dreamed he would have to use it. He had trouble keeping his hands from shaking as he reentered the Sit Room.

⚉
db

The entire group was mesmerized as they observed al-Qaeda's plan unfolding around the globe. President Wheeler was just completing a call from the European Union president, Chancellor Detrick Amster, who had just been briefed by his EUIA chief. Amster was not able to hide his anxiety as well as President Wheeler could. During Teddy's time out of the room, he had talked with his counterparts; the EU had more renegade missiles than the US. Teddy was sharing his strategy with the world, but he had to focus on saving the United States.

All eyes turned to him when he entered the room.

"Other agents have experienced a similar ploy. Extra vehicles were hidden in all the facilities, and they're all freaking out."

The president chimed in, "Freaking out, Mr. Brewer?"

"Sorry for the colloquialism, but yes, they are all scrambling."

"This group needs to focus on our country and then help others. We are about to see vast sections of our country thrown into the nineteenth century. Give us an update—now!"

Teddy's voice sounded unstable as he mustered up all the courage he had to explain the situation—the sixteen renegade trucks.

The president ordered, "Shut it down now—the hell with the missing trucks."

"Sir, with all due respect, we still have over forty hours left until launch. Please give us some more time. I want our raids to be decisive and complete, and I want to get all of the intelligence we can. I'm convinced that the Americans who they recruited for this operation will fold under pressure; their beliefs about death have not been driven into their heads from childhood like the Middle Easterners. I want to stop this attack, but the bigger prize would be to stop Ahsan and his al-Qaeda for a long time, if not forever."

Teddy saw a few heads nodding around the table.

Looking extremely skeptical the president asked, "How much time, Mr. Brewer?"

"Give me twenty more hours."

The president thought about it, and eventually, gradually, he nodded his approval.

"Thank you, sir. I will not leave the compound, and we need to keep this group assembled for quick decisions if we need them."

"None of us are going anywhere until this is over except Vice President Long. For obvious reasons, she will be relocated outside of Washington. "Looking toward his press secretary, he asked, "Where do we stand with the press? Has any of this activity leaked out?"

Press Secretary Ford was certain there were no leaks in the States, but he was personally making sure that Ahsan knew everything. "No, sir. The closest we came was in the Pennsylvania factory, but it was covered up nicely by diverting attention and calling it a suicide. There have been no questions at any of our recent briefings, so I think the lid has been kept on."

"Great, we need to keep it like that. News of this would cause widespread panic. Mr. Brewer, we have an office area for you down the hall. We will continue monitoring the situation from here. You have twenty hours before I pull the plug."

Chapter 99

Antioch, Tennessee, and Washington, DC – May 8, 2015

"Let it be understood that operations carried out by Muslims will come with a price. Regardless of what that price is, they will continue."

—*Ayman al-Zawahiri*

F adi was pleased to see the LED readout on his missile turn to green. He was set. Text messages were coming in on his satphone from his guys—all was well. Their instructions were to stay in their vans, guarding their sites, and at T minus 25 minutes, they were to depart and meet at their warehouses.

The waiting game had begun. It was time for afternoon prayers. Fadi unrolled his mat and went through his normal prayer ritual. From his vantage point, he had a beautiful view of downtown Nashville. It was quite impressive, especially with the beautiful sunset. *Praise be to Allah.*

Sweat was running down Wazir's back. It was a beautiful spring day and about ten degrees above normal spring temperatures for Nashville. Carrying his extra weight and lugging his missile into place on a mound overlooking the exclusive

Belle Meade community had totally exhausted the normally jolly Wazir. The death of Basel weighed on him. The wealth of Belle Meade exhibited in the size of the estates just fueled the fire of his hatred for the infidels. He had been looking forward to this attack for months. Finally, Allah would be praised—praised by all who wished to survive.

He worked with his missile and finally had it in position. His red LED numbers turned to green. He was set. *Allah Akbar.*

dɓ

A pair of agents was watching and dispatched the exact coordinates to the EOD troops. In their camouflaged fatigues, they were nearly invisible. Their count-down was aligned with the missiles' clocks. Anticipation was building. Their training helped them remain calm, but the pregame butterflies were flying. They all had experienced several tours in Iraq and Afghanistan, where they disarmed countless land mines and bombs, some strapped to would-be suicide bombers—suicide bombers who chickened out on their assignment. This task seemed less stressful, but this time, they were on US soil. They knew there were bad guys involved, but they didn't know how evil. In their wildest dreams, they couldn't imagine the devastation that these weapons were destined to deliver.

dɓ

Four F-15 Eagle fighter jets touched down nearly simultaneously in Boston, Chicago, Nashville, and Long Island, with a fifth scheduled to land in Los Angeles within the next hour. After landing, they immediately taxied to remote corners of each airport, where Teddy's precious cargo was transferred and installed on the bellies of black helicopters. The wireless-control consoles were placed within reach, but out of the pilots' way. CIA observers were watching every step of what was happening from touchdown through taxi.

Once installed, test strips were passed under the sensors. Teddy received word from each pilot that the wands were installed and operational. They took to the skies.

In speaking to each pilot, he was confident that they knew the importance of their missions. They were looking for late-model white Ford vans, most likely parked near wooded or isolated areas in higher elevations.

Two hours of Teddy's twenty had evaporated.

Chapter 100

Fairfield, Connecticut – May 9, 2015

"Seek out your enemies relentlessly."

—*The Quran, Surah 4:103*

For the first time in months, Esa felt confident. He reported into Dalil every hour. With their vehicles stripped of their GPS discs, along with the extra vehicles, he finally had the upper hand on the infidels. With the exception of a couple locations in Los Angeles, all the missiles were in place and set to launch.

His phone rang.

"Mann," he answered.

Dalil was to the point. "What is your status?"

"We are good. Within the next thirty minutes, all will be armed and ready to launch."

"Call me back when all your missiles are green."

Chapter 101

Washington, DC – May 9, 2015

"Fear of man bringeth a snare: but whoso putteth his trust in the Lord shall be safe."

—Proverbs 29:25 KJV

Teddy was down to twelve hours. His time was evaporating. He was thankful for the distinctive isotope signature of palladium, which allowed his detectors on the helicopters to be effective. They found twelve of the sixteen renegades. With four launch sites still left to find and the president and his Cabinet were in a state of panick.

In an uncharacteristic volume, President Wheeler ordered, "Get Brewer in here. We need an update. It's been over eight hours!"

Before his chief of staff could get to him, Teddy had heard the president's order bellowing down the hall and was on his way to the Sit Room.

Teddy was also uncharacteristic, with sweat on his forehead, under his arms, and dripping down his back. He felt every eye in the room burning holes through him; they looked to him for answers. Just as he was ready to begin his briefing, a text vibrated his satphone.

"Please excuse me as I see what this is."

"Mr. Brewer, now!"

The text was from his LA helicopter pilot. They had located another van high in the Hollywood Hills. There were still three to find.

"We have three renegade vans at large. I suspect that we'll have them located within hours. Our devices on the helicopters are working. There are missiles still unaccounted for in Nashville, Chicago, and Boston. As soon as we nail down their locations, we're ready to start the raids. I need to get back to it. Are there any questions?"

The president had to demonstrate his power. "Mr. Brewer, I'm nervous."

Time ticked away, both on the LED missile displays and on Teddy's grace time:

33:47:31

Teddy was becoming visibly frantic: his hair was wet from perspiration, and he was certain his blood pressure and pulse were off the charts. He had several hours left, but the weight of the world—literally—was on his shoulders. A text message hit his satphone. Another renegade had been located. He ran back to the Sit Room with the news.

"Good news, Mr. Brewer. Now find the other two."

33:27:17

Teddy knew the president was right. They needed to get rolling to defuse the launch sites they had located, but he wanted to get them all.

Time was running out, and even though they all hadn't been located, Teddy realized what he had to do. He raced back to his West Wing office and broadcast the codename Peace Shield out to all of his agents and the EOD troops—the signal for them to move in. They knew what to do. Once the order had been given, he went back to the Sit Room to watch the operation unfold.

The still images stopped as the agents made their move, but satellite surveillance continued. There weren't enough screens to monitor thirty-one launch sites, but Teddy was able to bounce from one to another, as the CIA had fixed locations over each of the five cities, with all of the coordinates programmed into the system. Teddy was in control and, in a typical male fashion, was jumping from location to location looking for action. He also had access to remote-controlled drones that were armed with cameras, along with missiles, waiting as a last-ditch defense.

Muzzle blasts caught the attention of the group. There was gunfire outside of Chicago. In his headset, Teddy had the gunfire reported back to him; it was enemy fire. There were troops down. Teddy wasn't prepared for the sight of soldiers lying lifeless on the ground near the missiles. It appeared that the surviving troops had taken out the bad guy, but they had to leave their injured comrades while they disengaged the weapons.

32:58:29

Teddy's attention was drawn to more gunfire—this time, from the hills of Nashville.

Wazir was taken by surprise at first. Everything was going flawlessly when, out of the woods, camouflaged men seemed to appear from nowhere. Their M16s were on automatic, and Wazir was knocked back several feet from his missile. He was hit—several times. He felt the warm liquid dripping down his leg. He quickly pulled his revolver and fired away as the pool of blood grew around him. The last words out of his mouth as he prepared to meet his virgins were, "*Allah Akbar!*"

db

The operatives were not going down without a fight. Reports from all of the cities indicated that the casualties on both sides were high. Teddy was hearing similar reports from his counterparts around the globe.

While they were frantically working to defuse the missiles, the numbers on the green LEDs suddenly changed:

1:59:59

In his headset, Teddy heard the first report from one of the Central Park locations, and then his ears rang with the same reports from all twenty-nine EOD teams. And he still had two missiles unaccounted for.

"We just lost thirty-plus hours of buffer."

President Wheeler's eyes pierced Teddy as he asked, "Do we have time, Mr. Brewer?"

Teddy pounded away on his computer, trying to determine how long the EOD guys had put into the deactivation, but he didn't have a good handle on that number. He had to say what he had hoped he would never have to say to the commander in chief. "Sir, I'm not sure. It's going to be close."

"Close? There is no margin for error here."

"I understand, Mr. President, but they just stole thirty hours of our time." Teddy relayed the casualty reports. "There are sixteen terrorists in restraints being taken to DHS offices, two committed suicide, ten were killed by the Eighty-Second Airborne troops, and one ran and is still at large. Unfortunately, we have thirteen soldiers dead, nine injured, and an injured agent."

"Well done, Mr. Brewer, but it's all for naught if those missiles fire."

The countdown clock in the Sit Room was adjusted again to align with Ahsan's timetable, and it seemed to Teddy as though the minutes were moving like seconds. An hour had flown by.

With forty-five minutes left on the countdown, the first report came in from an EOD group that they had neutralized their missile. One after another, reports of neutralization came in. All the missiles were neutralized except the final two, which had just been located by the copters, one in Nashville and one in Chicago. Extra EOD specialists were called in—the best in each vicinity. They had twelve minutes left, but time was flying. The EOD specialist in Nashville was nervous, and a more experienced sergeant took over.

The wiring on this bomb was a bit different—possibly by design. As he prodded and probed, he was praying that he didn't accidently start the launch sequence. All the wires were the same color and very close to each other. He was sweating profusely, both hands trembled, and his brain failed to function. Everything was moved in slow motion as the seconds ticked away. He took a deep breath to steady his nerves. As he was testing the wires, word came into his earpiece that the Chicago missile had been disabled and this was the final one.

He was nearly certain he had figured out which wire to cut as he took his snipes. "Hold on, guys. . .Here we go!"

With all that fanfare, nothing happened. The lights on the LED screen went blank.

The last missile was neutered, with the clock showing twenty-three seconds on it.

Cheers went up in the Sit Room as President Wheeler high-fived and fist bumped his cabinet members. "Mr. Press Secretary, please arrange for me to address the nation this evening. We have a story to share with the American people."

Conversely, the press secretary had a disappointing message to deliver to Hajji and did not know his own fate after this failure. The promise of a high position in the Islamic nation of the United States was gone. He needed to get out of the country as fast as he could, but he had no idea where to go.

Looking to Teddy, President Wheeler said, "Mr. Brewer, I want you to be present. Obviously, we won't show your face or mention your name, but you are a hero today, and I want you to be near me for this victorious announcement."

Looking to everyone, he added, "We have made a statement today, and the information we will get from our captives will send Mr. Ahsan deeper into his cave—hopefully forever. Thank you all for your support. I'll see you all in the Oval Office at seven p.m."

Truthfully, the last thing that Teddy wanted to do was to attend a White House press conference, but he smiled and nodded. He was drained. Every last ounce of everything he had was just laid on the line. Peace Shield was a success.

Chapter 102

Lewistown, Pennsylvania – May 9, 2015

"Be strong and of a good courage, fear not, nor be afraid of them: for the Lord thy God, He it is that doth go with thee; He will not fail thee, nor forsake thee."

—*Deuteronomy 31:6 KJV*

Anne helped Jason gather his belongings, get-well cards, and flowers. Dr. Taylor would be coming by after his evening rounds to release him. Sleeping in his bed at home never sounded as good, and for Anne, she couldn't ask for a better Mother's Day gift.

Jason and the kids were lounging around watching the early edition of Fox News when Henry walked in.

"It's about time you get out of those pajamas. We need you back at the plant."

"Trust me, Henry, I need to get back to the plant for my mental health."

Henry didn't say anything, but he noticed as he walked into Jason's room that the guards were gone. Looking to Anne, he said, "I wanted to stop by and see if you needed any help getting him home."

"Thanks, you are so sweet. I couldn't have made it through this ordeal without you. I still have many unanswered questions."

Suddenly, the TV screen showed, *WE ARE INTERRUPTING OUR BROADCAST TO BRING YOU A SPECIAL REPORT*—the announcement that usually heralded something horrible. All eyes went to the screen and conversations stopped.

The announcer said, "We now take you to a special report from the Oval Office of the White House."

The screen showed President Wheeler flanked by his Cabinet.

"Good evening, my fellow Americans, my distinguished Cabinet, and members of the White House press core. I am pleased to announce to you this evening that America stood tall today. Today, and over the past month, our intelligence and military forces have been working round the clock to thwart an attack from al-Qaeda—an attack targeting our homeland. Their attack was stymied, and we have apprehended sixteen enemy combatants and eliminated another twenty-five—all with plans to bring our country to its knees. In addition, I'm happy to report that four of our world allies have also withstood Ahsan's planned attacks in their countries. We had a worldwide effort of intelligence communities, and I am particularly proud of the efforts of one of our own who directed the operation." With that comment, he made casual eye contact with Teddy who was just off camera, beaming from ear to ear.

"We can all rest easier tonight as a result of the heads-up detection of citizens who first called some suspicious activity to our attention. In small towns across the country to large cities to the nation's capital, people joined forces to combat our enemy intent on bringing us down. This attack was the most intricate plan out of al-Qaeda to date. It was comprehensive, global, and was years in the making. We estimate that their plans began before their attack on the US in 2001. This attack was a priority for bin Laden prior to his death and carried forward by Nasi Ahsan.

"Their plan was spoiled by the joint efforts of the British MI6, the newly amalgamated EU intelligence agency, Russia's SVR, Japan's Naicho, and Africa's NIA. It was a team effort of the free world against the Islamic extremists."

The president was uncharacteristically relieved and calm as he comforted the American people. Fortunately, they were spared the gruesome details and how close al-Qaeda had come to being successful.

"Our victory tonight is not without a cost. We lost thirteen of our military's finest, with nine others injured. We also had some casualties along the way within our Department of Homeland Security."

The president honored the deceased by reading their names as their photos appeared on the screen—a meager tribute to people who had made the ultimate sacrifice for the sake of freedom.

"My heartfelt thanks to everyone who assisted, and may God continue to bless America. Good night!"

As the political analysts took over with their commentary, Jason had a smile similar to Teddy's. He knew he had just been recognized by the president of the United States. Then the phone rang.

"Hello, this is Anne."

"This is Randall Kent, the president's chief of staff. I have President Wheeler for Jason Lange."

Anne handed the phone to Jason, convinced it was one of his college buddies playing a trick on him. "He says it's the president."

"This is Jason Lange."

"Jason, this is President Wheeler. I wanted to call you personally to thank you for your part in bringing this al-Qaeda operation to light. I have Teddy Brewer with me here in the Oval Office, and I am presenting you both with the highest honor that a president can bestow on a civilian. It is with great honor and appreciation that I present you both with the Presidential Medal of Freedom on this, the ninth day of May 2015."

Anne was still skeptical after he had hung up, especially when he told her why the president wanted to speak to him.

No congratulations came from his wife as he looked in Henry's direction. The two of them exchanged a knowing glance.

"Jason, after we get home, you have some explaining to do."

THE SEQUEL – Deadly borders

The protagonist and hero of *Deadly Beliefs*, Teddy Brewer, continues his quest to rid the world of radical Islamic terrorists. This time he's focused on the US-Mexican border where Hezbollah has joined forces with the ruthless Mexican drug cartels to infiltrate the United States. Radical Islam meets ruthless drug lords to utilize their well established distribution channels. Terrorists, firearms and other deadly weapons are funneled easily through the tunnels that run the length of the border. The Muslim religion flourishes in Mexico. The Department of Homeland Security's failed SBInet is a blemish on the Wheeler administration so the president calls on his ace Middle Eastern expert, Brewer, to battle the radical terrorists partnered with the drug Lords.

About the author

Rod Huff is a successful business executive with thirty five years of experience in various C-level positions. ***Deadly Beliefs*** is rooted in Mr. Huff's interest of the differences between Christianity and Islam. His idea for the book came out of today's headlines.

An avid reader, this will be his second book. His first work is a non-fiction book, ***Coaching Made Easier, How to Successfully Manage Your Youth Baseball Team*** which was published by Coaches Choice of Monterrey, CA in 2009. This book was birthed from his love of youth baseball and his coaching experiences. When he started coaching he looked for a book that would teach him how to be a good coach. He found countless drills and skills books but none directed exclusively at the volunteer coach. Consequently, he developed his own system and after he stopped coaching he put it into a book to assist other coaches. His system worked— in his nine-year record as a head coach he landed five league championships and four runner-up titles.

Academically, the author holds a Bachelor of Arts degree in Economics from Shippensburg University in Pennsylvania and a Master of Business Administration from James Madison University in Harrisonburg, Virginia. He resides in Brentwood, Tennessee with his wife of forty-one years, Lisa, a well-known Interior Designer that has worked in Los Angeles, Nashville and the Gulf Coast. They have two adult children—daughter, Whitney Huff Phelps, is married to Dylan Phelps. Both are graduates of the University of Kentucky in Lexington, Kentucky and son Austin who is a recent graduate of the University of Missouri with a Journalism degree and works in sports-talk radio in Nashville. He married his college sweetheart, Meredith Roberts. The author has had the joy of seeing both of his children run onto Division 1 football fields—his daughter as a cheerleader at Kentucky and his son as a Mizzou football player. Rod values his family life, serves on several for profit and non-profit boards, and is a Deacon in his local church in Tennessee.

CPSIA information can be obtained at www.ICGtesting.com
Printed in the USA
LVOW120705190513

334374LV00002B/3/P